More praise for
Christopher Fowler and
RUNE

"[A] tale of international deviltry and horror . . . Taut and well paced, acutely observed, written in refreshingly sophisticated prose."

Publishers Weekly

"*RUNE* brings black magic into the video age with excitement and suspense."

Library Journal

"Wonderful characters, snappy lines, dead-on atmosphere, *Spy*-class social commentary—the last things one expects to find this close to fantasy. And it all works."

The Kirkus Reviews

Also by Christopher Fowler
Published by Ballantine Books:

ROOFWORLD
THE BUREAU OF LOST SOULS

RUNE

Christopher Fowler

BALLANTINE BOOKS · NEW YORK

Copyright © 1990 by Christopher Fowler

All rights reserved under International and Pan-American Copyright Conventions. Published in the United States of America by Ballantine Books, a division of Random House, Inc., New York, and simultaneously in Canada by Random House of Canada Limited, Toronto.

Library of Congress Catalog Card Number: 90-42440

ISBN 0-345-37768-0

Manufactured in the United States of America

First Hardcover Edition: January 1991
First Mass Market Edition: July 1992

CONTENTS

1. Willie   1
2. Harry   4
3. Dorothy   9
4. Grace   13
5. Bryant and May   19
6. Whispered Secret   24
7. Devils in Pursuit   31
8. Cause of Death   34
9. Mourners   40
10. Womb   47
11. Blinded by Reason   53
12. Angels of Death   59
13. Instant Image   68
14. Blaze   73
15. Conundrum   79
16. Slattery   84
17. The Arrival of Evil   92
18. Problems with Blood   104
19. The Nature of Accidents   108
20. Underground   116
21. Sarcophagus   124
22. Carmody   130
23. The Fatality File   135
24. The Code of Hatred   144
25. Documentation of Evil   148
26. Criminal Minds   154
27. Harry and Grace   165
28. Pride Before a Fall   171
29. A Surfeit of Information   176

30. Prayerdevils   180
31. Break-in   185
32. Invitation   193
33. Cracking the Ice   202
34. The Glass Halo   207
35. The Camden Town Coven   213
36. The Empty Man   222
37. Enemy Territory   228
38. Celestial Flight   233
39. White Noise   244
40. Rufus   253
41. Celia   256
42. Vision   261
43. Disinfo   268
44. Barricades   276
45. Infection   291
46. Tape   299
47. Gridlock   306
48. Beat the Devil   313
49. Empire   317
50. Remembrance   331

"All through this hour Lord be my guide,
And by Thy power no foot shall slide."
—*Lines used by Denison to set
the chimes of Big Ben.*

1.

Willie

O N THE STREETS of London, nobody notices a running man.

This one, however, was different. He was old, in his late sixties at least, and he was frightened. He had run across the width of Soho, and now stood panting against the construction-site scaffolding which bristled over the buildings above Carnaby Street. The filthy drizzle filtered onto the shoulders of his suit jacket, blackening them. Searching left and right, he launched himself across the road once more, running by the side of the stalled traffic, his steps falling back into a rhythmic beat. He knew he was too old to be running, but he was much too scared to slow down.

Back at the turn of the century, London's traffic had clattered across the capital at an average speed of eleven miles per hour. Ninety years later, that speed had fallen to around six miles in sixty minutes. And in Regent Street on a wet April day at one in the afternoon, it had ground to a complete standstill. Rain drummed heavily on the pulsing roofs of black cabs as they attempted to maneuver their way across the blocked intersections ahead of him. Finding themselves locked in seas of steaming steel, disgruntled pedestrians clambered between the glistening chrome fenders as they struggled to reach the safety of far sidewalks.

In Great Marlborough Street the deluge had darkened the timber facade of Liberty's, causing the great Tudor rooms which had been furnished from the wreckage of HMS *Impregnable* to cast a saffron light over the vehicles jammed in the roadway below. A typical lousy spring day in London. It looked like night.

At the corner of Kingly Street the searing pain in his side grew so great that he surprised himself by doubling over and sinking to the sidewalk, the flooded flagstones soaking the knees of his trousers.

He became aware of his body's growing inner heat as it contrasted with the icy slickness of his skin. Absurdly it crossed his mind that if he did not suffer a heart attack, he would probably catch a cold. He stayed crouching over for a minute, allowing the pain in his side to lessen. An elderly woman passed by, hesitated, then returned to ask if he was all right. He had meant to reply that thank you, yes, he was fine, but instead found himself crying out the most terrible things until the woman looked aghast and backed away from him in alarm, just as the Indian lady in Frith Street had done a few minutes earlier.

He wondered if he should try calling Harry again, then remembered how the telephone change had spilled from his shaking hands. Besides, how would his son ever believe what he had seen? He knew that he had remained crouching for too long when his legs streaked lines of fire as he tried to stand. The signals glared RED as he broke into a hobbling run again, reaching the opposite curb as his vision blurred with hot tears of pain. He could feel the muscles in his chest burning and tightening, constricting the flow of blood to his heart. His breath now came in ragged gasps. Dimly he recalled that there was only a little farther to go before he reached—what? Safety? It was a possibility he had not dared to consider until now.

As he neared the lower end of the street he glimpsed a startled face behind a windshield, car brakes screaming as the driver sought to avoid a collision with this strange hurtling figure. They must all see how I am possessed by devils, thought the old man, it must show! I must seem like some kind of escaped lunatic. Perhaps if he stopped to look back he would find a trail of imps sent to torment him, descending from the clouds in a black rain. Slowing as he ran across the sodden litter which spilled from the tourist traps in nearby Carnaby Street, he tugged on his sopping jacket belt in an attempt to tighten it, but the wet material bit together and refused to draw in. At the corner of Beak Street, water was boiling over drains blocked with McDonald's wrappers, flooding the gutters. Here too the road was filled with immobile cars and vans, their drivers resigned to a long wait.

He took the corner so fast that he overshot the sidewalk, running wide into the drowned road. His strength was ebbing fast as he swung into the narrow alleyway that led to the multistory car park in Brewer Street. He realized that in his panic he had run much farther than he needed to, but it no longer mattered. Here in the alley were a few parked cars, a rack of courier cycles, and a single large truck wedged between the walls with two vast tires parked on the sidewalk.

Through the descending gray mist he could just make out the car park at the base of the alley. His hand flew to the jacket pocket which held the keys to the little Renault. Their weight, combined with the nearness of safety, brought a warm flood of relief. Chest pounding, he wiped the sodden flap of hair from his eyes and slowed to a walk.

As he approached the vehicle parked ahead, he found himself taking the inner path formed between the side of the truck and the building wall. Passing beside the raised cab, he failed to notice the truck's sidelights flick on, failed to see the driver turn the ignition key, failed to hear the cough of the engine as it chugged into life.

Halfway along the side of the truck, moving more slowly in the dank canyon it formed with the side of the building, he became aware that the steel wall to the left of him was gradually pulling away. The driver checked the rearview mirror and eased the truck forward, the immense wheels trundling along the curb as they sought to regain contact with the road.

The old man stopped and peered ahead, alarmed. Steel struts jutted several inches out from the side of the vehicle. Ordinarily, they were used for tethering ropes. Now they took on a lethal appearance. They had begun moving toward him with frightening celerity.

It seemed that he had almost cleared the truck, running so close to the wall that the rough brickwork was pulling and tearing at his jacket, when he realized that the shadow of death was upon him. The whole thing was over in an instant. One of the struts snagged the broad belt loop on his jacket. The force lifted him off his feet, upward and backward, swinging him in to face the patterned brickwork. His throat-rending scream was lost in the roar of the truck's powerful diesel engine as he was pressed face-first against the wall and dragged a distance of twenty feet. The screaming had long ended by the time the horrified driver had jumped down from the cab and reached its source. In the gloom of the vehicle's near side, all that could be made out was a crumpled hanging figure, torn and dripping, its anterior consisting of little more than shredded skin and gleaming rain-washed knobs of bone.

2.

Harry

DARREN SHARPE WAS a heavy sour-faced man with a square head, vast square shoulders and hands like wet meat puddings which he was in the habit of continually wiping down the sides of his trousers. Standing in front of the window which overlooked the verdant southeasterly corner of St. James's Square he all but eclipsed the sickly afternoon sunlight. For the past three-quarters of an hour the group assembled before him had patiently listened to a recital of statistical analysis, market research tables, dietary reports and random testing data, a welter of percentages and estimates designed to provide absolute proof that what the world needed now, more than anything else in this final decade of the twentieth century, was a new carbonated fruit drink.

"Harry, you've been unusually quiet through all of this. Do you have anything valuable to add before we wrap up?" Sharpe sucked hard on an enormous Cuban cigar, then removed it from the corner of his mouth and examined the end. As usual, it had gone out.

Harry Buckingham looked up from his notes with a twinge of alarm. It appeared that he had been caught out by teacher for not paying attention. The atmosphere in the room had become dry and overheated, and he had just been sliding into a soft-edged state of coma when Sharpe's voice snapped him back to attention. The problem, of course, was that his familiarity with the campaign bordered on contempt. He could not imagine why the client was taking so long to be convinced about the viability of the product. His hesitancy had wrecked the pacing of the presentation.

Harry pushed the note folder aside and turned his chair to face the client, studying him carefully. There was a time when guys like this were a pushover, he thought. You baffled them with advertising bullshit and they forked over the account. Look at him, a tired CEO with thinning hair and a mass-market suit. Some challenge.

"Thank you, Darren," he began, flexing his arms in a body-language display of relaxation and confidence. "Leaving aside the negative findings on the random product tests, I think we all have to agree that there's a natural window in the C2 preteen market. The NRG report suggests that kids are sick to death of being sold the idea of health. But I'm sure our client would prefer guesstimates on a two-month consumption rate following ad-shells and regional TV spots, say thirties with back-up tens."

Advertising doublespeak was second nature to Harry. Smooth talk had always come easy to him. At the drop of a hat he could interpolate obscure sentences Henry James would have been proud to have written, had he been in the marketing business. This ability had brought him a long way. He had no doubts that it would take him much farther. He smiled at the client encouragingly. It was a smile that said "I'm on your side. Trust me." In the ad game, *trust me* is another way of saying *fuck you*.

Sharpe seemed more interested in relighting his cigar than in formulating a response. The client just sat there, an inert vegetable. While he waited for something to happen, Harry studied the corporate art which dominated the room. Enormous blocks of pastel gouache swept around them in tasteful rolling curves. The pictures were not designed to be looked at directly. They were supposed to be registered in the corner of the eye, to provide background harmony, like elevator music. The client finally opened his mouth to comment when there was a knock at the door and Eden entered. The silence in the room suddenly deepened as the account men stared at her cantilevered breasts. Only a death could interrupt a client presentation.

"There's somebody to see Mr. Buckingham," she said in the hushed tone of someone standing in a cathedral. Harry turned in his seat, puzzled. To his knowledge there were no outstanding appointments double-booked for this afternoon. If anything, he had been hoping to creep off after the presentation and get in a round of golf. "Who is it?" he mouthed in a corresponding whisper, even though it was obvious that everyone in the room was listening.

"The police," replied the secretary, embarrassed.

The police turned out to be a single policewoman, and an extraordinary one at that. Tall and pale-skinned, heavy but not fat, she reminded him of a postwar pinup. Her auburn hair was swept up in a glamorous style last seen in the late nineteen fifties. Even her lipstick appeared to be of a shade found only on weathered Technicolor film stock. She introduced herself as Sergeant Janice Longbright of Bow Street police.

"Mr. Buckingham." She shook his hand with a firm dry grip. Her voice was low and delectably husky, Joan Greenwood in *Kind Hearts and Coronets*. "Is there a place where we can talk quietly?"

"I'm afraid the offices are open-plan," said Harry. "Here is as good as anywhere. What's the problem?" God, he thought, surely the parking tickets haven't mounted high enough to warrant an arrest? Sergeant Longbright caught his eye and held it with the look of someone who was used to imparting bad news on a professional basis. In fact she would normally have given the job to one of her constables, but, in view of the unusual circumstances in this case, had decided to personally inform the deceased's next of kin.

"It's about your father. He's met with an accident."

"What kind of accident? Is he hurt?"

"Please sit down." The sergeant pulled out a secretarial chair and ushered Harry onto it. "It's more serious than that. I'm afraid he's dead."

A brief silence. Harry gave a look of disbelief. "What happened?" he asked quietly.

"He was knocked down while crossing the road just after one o'clock this afternoon. It took us a little while to trace you." Longbright turned to one of the nearby secretaries. "Could you make us some strong tea, please?" The secretary hurried off.

"Can I . . . see him?"

"Mr. Buckingham was very badly injured, and we would ordinarily advise you not to view the body. Of course, if you feel strongly about the matter, I'm sure it can be arranged."

"Whose fault was it? The driver's? My father's an old man, his eyesight isn't what it should be." He became aware of speaking in the wrong tense, but could not bring himself to correct it. "He can't see far," he concluded.

"There were a number of witnesses," said Longbright softly. "Three or four people saw the accident occur."

"Why didn't they do anything to stop it?"

"They were looking from the windows of the offices nearby. There was nothing that anyone could have done in time to save him." She glanced across at Harry, who was sucking his top lip, head down, lost in thought. "If it's any comfort at all, I'm assured that there was very little pain involved. He died instantaneously."

Longbright studied the figure before her, trying to decide whether to tell him anything further. He seemed to be taking the news very well. The accident had a bizarre quality which would probably warrant a brief column in the later editions of the *Evening Standard*. For his part, Harry was sure that he would find out the details from someone around the office soon enough. People seemed to revel in the minutiae of misfortune.

"I imagine you'd like to be left alone for a while," said Longbright finally. "We can talk at a later time."

"When?" Harry raised his head and regarded her with tired eyes. "I've already left the presentation. I can't go back in there now. Where can I find the driver of the vehicle?"

"Down at the station, although I don't recommend a meeting unless you feel it's absolutely necessary."

"I'm not going to lose my temper, if that's what you're worried about. I just want to get this over with as quickly as possible. I'll come back with you."

"Very well. I have a car waiting outside. I can give you a lift."

"Let me use the washroom first."

In the mirror above the tiled sink he studied his face as if searching for some visible sign of loss, but found that nothing had changed. The shadows beneath his eyes had deepened of late. His slick black hair had retreated a little higher, too. A few lines were etching themselves around the slate gray eyes which Hilary supposedly found so fascinating. A light patina of stubble was starting to shade his broad chin. But there had been no sudden transformation, nothing in his reflection to point up the fact that now, for the first time in his life, at the age of thirty-two, he was suddenly free of all filial obligation.

Harry bowed guiltily beneath his reflection and splashed some cold water on his face. Then he reknotted his tie and returned to the waiting police sergeant. A minute later they headed down the steps of the agency together and climbed into the waiting squad car.

3.
Dorothy

IT WAS A cruel joke to have played on a public building. The library had been erected in the year of Oscar Wilde's arraignment, and its present situation ironically reflected that esthetic fall from grace, for the high-Gothic Victorian edifice now found itself in perpetual twilight, tucked beneath the vast concrete wing of a modern overpass. The lead-saturated airwaves which shuddered over its redbrick facade served to keep customers from its portals, but still the library remained open to serve the area's few remaining residents.

Within its corridors the uneven parquet flooring continued to smell of lavender polish, and the passageways between the shelves remained agreeably underlit, but much of the reference section was now incomplete. Too many of the remaining books had brittle, chalky spines and damp-stained pages, and creaked as their covers were raised, like doors into empty houses.

To Dorothy Huxley it was a library that eschewed modern gimmickry and still reflected a serious respect for books. Here there were no gaudy displays designed to entice the disinterested young into reading. This was a place planned not for pleasure but for hard eye-straining study. And as the council could find no spare cash to spend on redecoration, it was just as well she liked it this way. Lately the library had only been able to stave off the persistent threat of closure with the help of local support groups, something for which Dorothy was eternally grateful. After all, she had been employed here as head librarian for over twenty years. Now, as she watched the shelves deplete and the membership dwindle, she found herself wondering what she would do when the ax finally fell.

A sharp sound made her look up. Two young West Indian boys were running between the bookcases in the children's section, the soles of their sneakers squealing on the waxed floors. Catching the eye of the older child, she released a laser beam of disapproval which cowed them both into silence. It had taken her years to cultivate this Evil Eye stare, but it seemed to have a minimal effect on today's children. Most of them looked upon a trip to her library (she thought of it as hers—hadn't she earned the right?) as a grim penance. It was only natural for them to prefer playing games in the street to being cooped up here in the cheerless half-light. The sweeping curve of the overpass blocked all sun from the halls, sealing the main reading room in a perpetual damp gloom. Today's children knew the names of all the characters from the TV soaps, but couldn't tell you who Robinson Crusoe was, or what could be found on Treasure Island, nor had they much desire to find out. Passive learning was such a dangerous thing . . .

Dorothy glanced at her watch. Another three hours to go. Hardly anyone had been in all day. It was tough finding something to do that would make the time go faster.

"Here's another one for you." Frank Drake passed the newspaper clipping across the desk. Dorothy peered at it over the top of her spectacles. *Evening Standard* second edition, she noted, today's date. PEDESTRIAN CRUSHED TO DEATH IN LONDON STREET ran the headline, and underneath, "MP demands heavier fines for pavement parkers."

"Squashed flat," said Drake with relish. "The best one so far this week. Of course, it's only Monday." There was no reply from Dorothy. "Well," conceded the assistant librarian, "at least it belongs in the folder. That's six since the middle of last week."

"Show me the others." Dorothy gestured at the pile of clippings which lay spread out on the other side of the desk. Drake slid them across.

" 'Man electrocuted with floor polisher.' Not really an uncommon occurrence."

"It is for a man."

" 'Prisoner stabbed through heart with fountain pen.' I thought murders didn't count."

"It wasn't murder. He slipped and fell on it."

"That's what they always say in prisons." She turned over the next news item. " 'British tourist in death fall from Statue of Liberty.' Oh, *really* Frank. That can't possibly count. A fall is just a fall, no matter where it's from."

"You're wrong." Drake moved forward, speaking in the habitual half-whisper all library staff quickly learned to adopt. "Read the circumstances of death. This woman was incredibly overweight. It's because of the Statue of Liberty that she died. A railing support gave way as she leaned over it trying to take a photograph."

"So you're allowing it to go in the file? You're changing the rules. She's dead because of her weight problem and her own stupidity. Just like the woman who came out of the roller coaster in Blackpool. *She* was so obese that the attendants couldn't get a safety belt to fit around her. If I remember correctly, the clipping said that she shot out at the top of the first arch like a champagne cork leaving a bottle."

"And I kept that clipping?"

"No, you said it didn't count."

"Okay, I concede." Drake tore the paper in half. "But if you keep criticizing, I'm never going to get the damned thing written."

"Yes, you will, Frank." Dorothy patted his hand reassuringly. "You bring something more than dedication to your task. You're an obsessive, and for a project like this, that's good."

Drake pointed a finger at her. "You must understand that all natural and man-made disasters are linked by the laws of probability, and that those laws are created by basic political decisions. I can prove the government's complicity in all kinds of . . ."

"I know, Frank," said Dorothy with a weary sigh, "you've explained the big conspiracy to me before."

"It's just a matter of gathering enough evidence and pinpointing coordinates to prove *any* theory." Drake was determined to plow on, regardless of Dorothy's attention. "A friend of mine knows a Labour MP who is prepared to testify under oath that the government is financing scientific experiments on the laws of probability. Think how politically useful it would be if you could predict disasters. The channel tunnel is passing through Tory heartland. They'll have to cover up any accidents so that the voters don't know . . ."

"Frank, sometimes I don't think you and I inhabit the same world."

Drake exhausted her. His enthusiasm was boundless and mostly misapplied. As she returned a pile of books to their rightful places in the fiction section, she glanced back between the stacks. Her assistant sat hunched across his desk like a Victorian ledger clerk, scribbling furiously into a notebook. Still, she felt an occasional stab of sympathy for him. Some people lacked the necessary equipment to face the rigors and responsibilities of modern life. Frank Drake was one of them. Academically bright but physically useless, he was doomed to be a perpetual student, full of ideas about how to change the world, but incapable of changing a plug.

Dorothy regarded the depleted reference section sadly. Kids were forever stealing the books. Working in a small branch library was hardly the most demanding of jobs, yet she knew she had every reason to fire Drake. He possessed an aptitude for a startling array of skills, but his ever-shifting attention destroyed his prospects in any single career. His mind was a jumble of good intentions, a confusion of half-baked plans that constantly intruded into his work. Twenty-eight years old, slightly built and prematurely balding, he seemed destined to pass into middle age ten years ahead of other people. She knew she could never turn him out on the street. Where could he go? The system wasn't structured to accommodate such people.

His latest plan was to use his scientific prowess to produce a book entitled *Politics, Paradox and Probability*, a study of the mathematical chances linking everyday events. He regularly explained his theory to Dorothy, with varying degrees of success, and had also encouraged her to help him collect information, cutting reports of bizarre deaths from voucher copies of the daily newspapers. She knew he would never finish the project. His investigations would take off at a sudden tangent as he sniffed out fresh conspiracies, and the file would wind up with all the others in the battered cardboard box behind his desk.

She took a deep breath and climbed back up the stepladder with an armful of frayed Stephen Kings, chiding herself for thinking bad thoughts about her fellow worker. After all, it was obvious to most people that *she* was the crazy one. She supposed she gave them good reason to think such a thing, what with the business of the basement and the witches . . .

Well, they would both have to stay on here, she and Frank, batty old woman and student misanthrope, until the first of the bulldozers succeeded in dispelling the ghosts and splintering shafts of sunlight through the dark, deserted corridors.

4.

Grace

SERGEANT LONGBRIGHT TOOK the steps into Bow Street police station in a couple of healthy strides, leaving Harry to catch up. She negotiated a path through the overcrowded waiting area and had just raised the flap of the duty desk when one of the officers called her back.

"Your driver left about ten minutes ago, Sarge." He indicated one of the interview rooms along the corridor. "Didn't want to hang around any longer than was necessary. It wasn't an official detention, so we couldn't . . ."

"That's all right," said Longbright, "as long as you've

left me the statement on file.'' She turned back to Harry. ''I'm afraid you've had a wasted trip, Mr. Buckingham. Come to my office. I'll give you the number of the physician who attended your father. The rest can wait until a more appropriate time.''

As the sergeant led the way along the corridor, Harry found himself becoming more and more annoyed. How could a man who had just caused a fatal accident be allowed to saunter from the building as free as a bird?

''I don't see how you could let the driver leave so easily,'' he complained as they entered the office. ''We're not talking about some minor traffic accident. There could be a lawsuit. Surely he can't get away with this?''

''Mr. Buckingham, nobody is getting away with anything. We've already taken a full statement, and we have a number of additional statements from eyewitnesses corroborating the details of the accident. I'll be very happy to furnish you with a copy of the full report as soon as it's completed.''

''I want the address of the driver before I leave.'' Harry sat back in his chair. There was no tone to his voice, no flicker of emotion in his face.

Sergeant Longbright seated herself behind her desk and rooted around for a clean sheet of paper. ''I'd prefer it if you conducted any interviews with involved parties here at the station. We find it keeps tempers on a more even keel.''

''I want to hear exactly what happened before the details are forgotten. For my own piece of mind.'' Longbright studied the disgruntled executive seated before her, his fingers tugging at his watchstrap in a habitual gesture of anxiety. He was the type who would make a fuss if he didn't get what he wanted. She unclipped an old marbled fountain pen from her top pocket and began to write.

''Can I trust you, Mr. Buckingham?''

''I simply want to understand,'' said Harry, ''nothing more.''

''Don't make me regret this.'' She wrote out an address and handed it to him. He folded the sheet and rose to his feet with a grunt of impatience. She stopped him at the door. "If you have any problems, I want you to ring me immediately. Are you married?"

"No, and I fail to see what . . ."

"It's useful to have someone to talk to at a time like this. There are a number of support groups who can help you come to terms with the situation. If you like, I can put you in touch with them."

The glare he threw her as he left the office suggested that coming to terms was the last thing he had on his mind.

Harry supposed he should have called first. He had been determined not to without knowing why, as if he thought that there was something to be gained by catching Mr.—Crispin, was it?—unawares. He studied Sergeant Longbright's neatly rounded handwriting once more. Flat 3, 27 Inkerman Road, NW5. North London. No more than a twenty-minute drive.

The street in question proved to be a small cul-de-sac leading from Kentish Town Road. The squat brick terraces had originally been built in the late 1860s to house workers constructing North London's maze of railway lines. Most of the streets were named after the major battles of the Crimean War. The recent boom years for the city's upwardly mobile professionals had seen the area gentrified, but now the boom had crested, and the houses were being converted back into apartments.

Harry rang the doorbell and stepped back from the porch. Nobody seemed to be home. He checked his watch and realized that he would have to call his office within the next few minutes. The fact that his absence from the agency was due to a personal misfortune would cut no ice with Sharpe. Above him came the sound of a window sliding up.

"You looking for me, mate?" A young woman was calling down to him. Her dark hair was cut in a neat, broad strip down the middle of her head. The sides were completely shaved. She seemed to be wearing fifteen feathered earrings in each ear. She looked angry, or at least appeared to be upset about something.

"Is there a Mr. G. Crispin living here?" Harry resented having to shout up at her.

"Crispian. Grace Crispian. That's me."

Oh my God, he thought. It couldn't be this . . . apparition.

"Who are you, then?" This in a Cockney accent loud enough to make the people on the other side of the street stop and look over.

"My name is Buckingham. You just ran over my father."

"Oh shit. Hang on." The strange head vanished, and the window slammed down. Moments later Grace appeared at the front door. She was short, no more than five feet three inches, somewhere in her middle twenties Harry guessed, dressed in a black roll-neck sweater and jeans. She would have been attractive too, he thought, if it weren't for the earrings and the seriously startling haircut.

"You better come in. I'll put the kettle on." She said *better* and *kettle* without the *t*s. "I don't know what to say. The whole thing's been so terrible. I don't know how I'll sleep." She ushered him through the hallway and up a steep flight of stairs. Noticing a strong smell of wet paint, he kept his Simpsons overcoat clear of the walls.

"I suppose the police gave you my number."

"I came to the station but you'd already left."

"Sorry about that. I came over faint, had to get some air. I've never been involved in an accident before, let alone watched someone deff out right in front of me. Had to go and have a drink." She pointed into the lounge. "In there. I'll bring in the tea."

Harry gingerly lowered himself onto a cheap sofa smothered in dog hairs. The small front room was filled with movie posters of every size, color, and description. Reprinted quads advertising *This Island Earth* and *Eraserhead* were pinned over the fireplace. Above the dining table, *Attack of the Fifty Foot Woman* was billed with *The Incredible Shrinking Man*. *Barbarella* and *Witchfinder General* were tacked over the sofa. Sleeping virtually on top of an electric radiator's glowing bars was an incredibly ancient, moth-eaten dog of indeterminate breed. Its fur was surely scorching, but the animal did not seem to have noticed. The only proof he had that it was actually alive came when it began to emit random noises from alternate ends of its body. He decided to keep the interview as brief as possible and get the hell out.

"Oh God, I'm sorry about the dog." Grace lowered the tea tray onto a stack of magazines and passed him a mug of seething brown liquid. "He's very old." She pushed the creature away from the fire with the toe of her boot. "You saw the sergeant? The big woman, Longbright?"

"She came to my office."

"Then she must have told you that it wasn't my fault."

"Yes, but I'd like to hear what happened in your own words." Harry drank some tea and was surprised to find that it was actually very good. Grace looked down at her bootlaces, suddenly awkward.

"See, I work for this art studio, mostly doing odd jobs," she explained. "I wouldn't mind being employed as one of their paste-up artists, but my portfolio isn't good enough yet. So I fill in, and sometimes I have to drive the supply truck. It's pretty big. It was built to carry theatrical equipment." She took a sip of her tea and looked over to the radiator, unable to catch his eye. "This afternoon I made my delivery and climbed back in the cabin. I checked the rearview mirror first, then the side one, and saw that there was nothing coming toward me in either. I even leaned my head out of the window and checked behind. But I swear it was clear. I started up the engine and slowly began to pull out. There was the most terrible sound, like . . ." She lowered her head once more. "The old man had run between the wall and the truck. The people working in the offices opposite said that they saw him dash in after I'd checked the mirrors. He just appeared out of nowhere. It was all so fast, they didn't have time to open their windows and warn him."

"I don't understand," said Harry. "Why was he running?"

"I don't know. Perhaps he was late for an appointment. He must have seen me preparing to move off, but he didn't stop.''

''It makes no sense.'' The tea mug was burning his hands, but he took no notice. ''My father never ran anywhere in his life. Everything he did was slow and methodical. It used to drive my mother crazy. He never took a chance, never broke a routine, never missed a bus or a train. He'd cancel an appointment rather than be late for it.''

''I know it was an awful way to die, but at least . . .''

''Please don't say it was over quickly.'' He turned to face her. ''Look—Grace—to tell the truth, we weren't exactly close. I just hate to think of him being killed in such a stupid, avoidable way.'' He set down the mug and rose to leave. The girl was obviously upset. There was nothing to be gained in continuing the conversation. It could only make matters worse. He brushed the dog hairs from his coat distractedly.

''Thank you for sparing me the time, Miss Crispian. I want you to know that I don't hold you to blame for what happened.''

''I appreciate you saying that.''

Harry had opened the front door and was about to step out into the street when Grace touched him lightly on the arm.

''I feel so terrible. If you need to talk to me . . .''

''I have your address.'' He studied her face for a moment, then turned to go.

''I almost forgot, did the police tell you he spoke to someone?''

''What?''

''Your father, just before he died . . .''

Harry paused on the step and stared up at her. ''You mean, right after the accident occurred?''

''No, I think it was a few minutes before. I heard one of the constables mention it. Apparently your father stopped someone in the street.''

''Do you know what he said?''

''I have no idea. Still, you might want to find out. I suppose they were his final words, after all.''

Harry walked away from the house with a feeling of

unease steadily growing in the pit of his stomach. As he unlocked the door of his car, he looked back and found that Grace was still standing on her doorstep, quietly watching his departure.

5.

Bryant and May

"**Y**OU CAN'T POSSIBLY be serious about retiring, Arthur. Can you honestly see yourself pottering about the garden building trellises for the roses? Why, you'd be dead within a year."

"Don't be so offensive, John. I'm quite capable of enjoying retirement without turning into a vegetable. Millions of ordinary people do it."

"Ordinary people? Pah!" John May pulled his coat a little tighter against the chill mist drifting across the water. "Ordinary people queue up in post offices with their pension books. They sit on park benches feeding the pigeons. They relive their memories of the Blitz. They don't get up at half past six in the morning to watch a body being fished out of a canal." He pulled a handkerchief from his pocket and blew hard into it. "I know you too well. Your idea of a pleasurable evening is making dinner for a beautiful woman and describing the Brighton trunk murder to her while she eats it. You may as well face facts. You couldn't let go if you wanted to."

John knew that despite all protestations to the contrary, his colleague was at least two years past the force's statutory retirement age, but as always he was careful not to raise the point. Arthur was forever threatening to retire. Nobody in the department took any notice of his complaints. Just lately, however, a new note of seriousness had begun to creep into his voice.

"My work has always come first, John, you know that. I've never had time to do anything for myself." Arthur Bryant stepped across a flooded section of the towpath and stood beside his old friend. "The long hours come with the job, it's something we all accept. There's never been the chance for a proper home life. Why, I even had to cancel my wedding day."

"That was because war broke out, Arthur. You can't blame the force for that."

At their feet, three young officers were standing up to their waists in the icy canal water trying to unsnag a corpse from the bottom of the channel. All that could be seen of the body was a section of dirty brown camel-hair coat and part of a trouserleg. A handful of onlookers silently studied the proceedings from a nearby bridge. May unscrewed the lid of his thermos flask and poured a coffee for his partner.

"There's something else, John. I'm not getting any younger. I'd hate to feel that I was losing my touch." Bryant was facing straight ahead, staring into the sluggish black water. May turned to him in surprise. "Whoever said you were losing your touch, you silly old fool? How long have we been working together as a team?"

"Seventeen years."

"Exactly. Another ten and we'll be in line for promotion." May grinned at him, but his partner continued to stare at the misty water without replying.

"Anyway, you've got a good six months left in you yet. Now have a coffee and cheer up. You're still doing better than this poor devil." He gestured at the corpse in the canal, then walked forward to the edge of the pathway and shouted at one of the constables. "Pace it up a bit, lad. My colleague here is concerned that he may die of hypothermia before you manage to pull the body out."

"It's stuck, sir," the boy called back. His face was the color of frozen pastry. The dirty water had seeped halfway up his chest, discoloring his shirt.

"You might try cutting his coat off," May suggested. "Go and get a knife from the van." Eager to be out of the freezing muck, one of the constables sloshed off, his teeth chattering.

May had been sifting through stolen-vehicle files on the early shift when the call had come through. An office cleaner had spotted what she thought was a body, floating facedown in the canal near the main bridge at Camden Lock. Unable to resist a visit to a crime scene so close by, he had immediately called his partner, and twenty minutes later they had simultaneously arrived on the tow-path.

Now they stood inhaling the cold April air, side by side, waiting for their first glimpse of a fresh victim to homicide. May was just a little taller, and at sixty-four nearly three years younger than Bryant, but to all intents and purposes they were the same man, so close had their minds grown over the years. For one to work without the other was as unthinkable as it was impractical. They had remained in the field long after they should have right-fully taken their places behind desks. This was one of the reasons why they were so widely respected by the younger members of North London's detective squad. The other was that their success rate in the location and ap-prehension of murderers continued to be phenomenal. Nobody quite understood how they managed this; their working methods seemed erratic at the best of times. But as long as the area's Serious Crime statistics reflected their zeal, nobody complained, either.

When the time had finally come for Bryant and May to confine themselves to offices they chose not to go to Scotland Yard, but instead set themselves up in Kentish Town, at the heart of a notorious trouble spot. Here they divided their time between teaching, and stealing all the interesting case files.

The men in the water now cut the restraining coat away from the corpse and threw it to the canal bank. They waded backward as the body rose slowly to the surface, limbs lifting like a puppet coming to life, hair blossom-ing in a gray corona above the still-submerged skull. One of the constables grabbed a foot and began hauling it in the direction of the bank.

"I suppose suicide's out of the question," said Bryant, starting to take an interest now that the body was fully revealed. "You'd have to be very determined to drown in such shallow water."

"Unless he jumped from the bridge and hit his head on the bottom. It looks a lot deeper than it is."

"Hmm. I'll have them check out the skull and the base of the neck first." Bryant tilted his head around to study the face of the corpse. "Not a young man. Certainly not a drunk or a derelict. That's a Turnbull and Asser shirt, by the look of it. Cufflinks. And the hands are far too manicured."

The officers were now attempting to hide their find from public gaze by wrapping it in an orange plastic tarpaulin. May knelt beside the body. "There's a wallet in his jacket." He carefully withdrew the waterlogged calfskin wallet and prized it open. "The name on the Visa card is Henry Dell. There's forty-five pounds here. Hang on a sec."

He felt in the jacket pocket again, and removed a dripping British passport. "Looks like he's been doing some traveling. Nasty photo. Nothing like him. Mind you, they never are, are they? He's obviously been in the water overnight. Hello, that's interesting." He leaned over the half-closed tarpaulin. "Take a look at this, Arthur. He's holding something in his left hand." The men moved back to let the other detective through.

"We won't be able to get his fingers open here," said Bryant. "The cold water's advanced the rigor." He turned to one of the officers. "Make sure you keep the towpath closed until the rest of my men arrive. I want casts taken from the mud surrounding the pathway and prints lifted from both entry gates by the lock."

"Have Anderson dust the upright bars of the gates as well as the catches," added May. "He might have climbed over the top. And get your boys to cut two-inch sections of grass and hedge the length of the path from the gates to where the body was first sighted."

"What's that for?" asked the officer, eyeing the corpse which lay in shadow within the plastic bag.

"Take a look at the lapels of his jacket. They're made from some kind of rough tweed. There are burrs attached to them, and what look like pieces of straw. If they came from around here we'll at least know where he died, and we can probably assume that there was some kind of a struggle which knocked him into the bushes.''

"What about his overcoat?''

"Unbuttoned.''

"You assume.''

"I checked.''

"No visible punctures or slashes to the clothing. The face is pretty banged up, though.'' Bryant gestured for the officers to turn over the body, then stooped to examine the blackened striations running over its swollen left cheek and neck. "Multiple contusions at the back of the head, although I should imagine they occurred after he went into the water.''

"The knees of his trousers seem to be damaged, too.'' May rose and stretched, his own knees cracking audibly as he did so. "We'll let Finch and his chaps do the rest of the work.''

"What do you say, John? Concussed and drowned? Or drowned first? There don't seem to be any stab wounds.''

"Yes, it's odd, isn't it? Assuming he died in the late hours of yesterday evening I'd have happily put him down for a punctured lung.''

"Why's that, sir?'' asked one of the young constables. It was generally considered to be a good idea to remain within earshot when the two detectives were thinking aloud.

"The victim is well dressed and in his mid to late fifties. It's safe to imagine that he wasn't involved in a drunken brawl. More likely to have been a robbery. The most common form of mugging involves a knife or sharpened instrument of some kind. Yet no money or credit cards were taken, and there seem to be no entry wounds from a blade. All in all, a bit of a puzzlement.''

Bryant and May watched as the body was sealed up and made ready for transportation. A fair-sized crowd had now gathered along the walkway of the bridge behind them.

"Look at the disgusting state of this canal.'' Bryant pointed at the polystyrene boxes and Coke cans that bobbed in the oily water and gathered at the corners of the lock gates in a brown tidemark of detritus. "It used to be beautiful here when I was a nipper. We'd sit and have a picnic, and watch the painted barges passing by."

"Of course, Queen Victoria was still on the throne then, Arthur." May took his arm and led the way back to the towpath gate. "Let's hope Finch comes up with something interesting on this one," he said. "It's been a while since either of us had a case we could really sink our teeth into."

Arthur turned to watch the officers struggling along the towpath with their grisly burden. "God knows we could both do with the exercise," he said.

6.

Whispered Secret

THAT EVENING HARRY had dinner with Hilary in a precious expense-account restaurant behind Kensington Church Street. At dusk it had begun to rain heavily, and as Harry stood rattling the water from his overcoat in the foyer of the eatery he attracted glances of disapproval from the waiters. He hated their hauteur and the fussy flourishes with which they presented the nouvelle dishes, but it was Hilary's favorite place to dine. She had suggested keeping the date as a way of helping him feel better. Instead it merely reminded Harry of his last meeting with his father. They had fought, as they did every time they met, and Harry had stormed from the table before the arrival of the main course. As usual, both sides had spoken without listening. He wondered how the conversation might have gone had they known that that was the last time they would ever see each other . . .

Hilary was already seated at the table waiting for him. Her customary Badoit stood unsipped. He bent and kissed her cheek, less the fulfillment of romantic desire than the liturgical gesture of one visiting a sacred relic. It was true that he worshiped her. Hilary was the perfect ad-man's companion, immaculate and glacial. Her face was a mask of untroubled beauty. She bore the same light, distant smile whether she was watching an opera or being propositioned by a tramp. As he approached, she raised a slender hand to her glass and caught his eye, an ex-pression of concern briefly crossing but not actually creasing her face.

"I'm so sorry about your father, Harry. You know, we could have canceled tonight if you'd felt too wretched." She took a tiny swallow of water and set down the glass. Harry was enveloped in an aura of citrus.

"No, I wanted to see you. I thought it would help." Even in a Savile Row suit he felt scruffy sitting next to her. It was the effect she always had on him. Hilary sat upright, her sleek blond hair braided tightly at the back of her neck, the single rope of pearls arcing down toward the crest of her pale bosom. He turned to look for a waiter but they were all beetling about with silver trays on the other side of the restaurant, noisily serving some-one of higher social standing.

"Fancy being run over by a lorry." She sounded em-barrassed by the circumstances of his father's demise, as if this particular method of dispatch had failed to appear on her list of socially correct ways to die.

"He spoke to someone shortly before it happened, ap-parently."

"To whom?"

"Some woman. Grabbed her in the street. I rang the police and they gave me her number."

"Whatever did he say to her?" She was interested now. This came under the heading of gossip.

"I don't know yet. I'll find out tomorrow."

"Have you decided when the funeral is to be?"

"Thursday morning. I don't suppose there'll be too many mourners in attendance. Will you be able to make it?"

"You'll have to pencil me in for now. I think I have a meeting."

"I got a message to call the Cleveland woman."

"You hardly ever mention her, or your father for that matter," she said suspiciously. "I take it you didn't approve of them living together."

"They deserved each other." Harry gave a snort. "He was an awkward old bugger. We never spoke much after my mother died. She was all we had in common. Once she'd gone he was free to do as he liked." He looked across at her and realized that he had said enough. She had asked out of politeness, and was now idly perusing the menu.

"I just want a main course." She waged war against obesity with the precision of a military campaign. "The turbot is served in a nectarine sauce. I can't have it."

Summoned by the menu closing against her fragrant decolletage, a waiter soared in from nowhere and took Hilary's order before poising his pencil and raising an insolent eyebrow at her dinner companion.

"Hilary, how would you feel about getting out of town for the weekend?" Harry's plan to reach forward and take her hand was thwarted by her sudden movement away from him. The waiter waited.

"You know I can't, darling. We've got the trade fair starting next week and Saturday's crucial for me. Display stands. The Japanese are hopeless." She turned to the waiter. "He'll have the turbot."

There was always some reason why they couldn't be by themselves.

"Wouldn't you like us to be alone together?" he asked, exasperated. "Away from telephones and faxes and beepers, just for once? I don't want the turbot."

"Really, Harry, this isn't like you. I thought we'd discussed the career thing." She leaned forward, confidential. "I know this is a tragic occasion and everything, but please don't get into one of your moods. Have the turbot, then I can have a piece of yours." She unfolded her napkin and smoothed it into her lap, blankly waiting for the conversational topic to change.

"I don't want the fucking turbot," said Harry through clenched teeth.

The food arrived. He found himself staring at a triangular cutlet of fish lying in a puddle of vermilion sauce. The portion was just large enough to be carried in the beak of a passing seagull. "Just a taste." Hilary reached across and speared a flake of fish with her fork. She popped it between shining coral lips.

"For a couple building their careers in social communication," he said, watching her, "we don't seem to talk to each other much."

"You are silly, Harry. Of course we talk. We discuss things all the time."

"But never anything important." He was familiar with this particular conversational dead end, but was unable to prevent himself from blundering into it.

"That's because we know where we stand on the important issues. I know you love me. I also know that I'm only ready to commit myself emotionally at this stage." She chewed her fish pensively. "That's good. We have the security of knowing that we're committed to one another, without having to worry about the sex thing. Besides, we have jobs to perform."

"Why must you be so damned reasonable all the time?" Harry tore into his sliver of turbot and wrecked the design of the sauce. "Don't you ever feel passionate? Consumed with lust?"

Hilary considered the question for a moment. Incredibly, she still seemed to be chewing the same tiny piece of fish. "Not really, no," she decided. "Women are able to control their feelings more than men. They don't get the same urges. Your problem is that you still think with your penis." She gave him a kindly look. It was the look of a veterinary surgeon about to put down a sick old dog. "You're such a sixties throwback. Romance is different these days. There's more to take into consideration."

"Like the fact that you won't sleep with me because you're worried about AIDS," he said suddenly, pushing the plate to one side.

"Condoms tear. It's a medical fact. HIV tests aren't reliable. I don't know where you've been. I'm no prude, but some doctors think even kissing may be risky. You wouldn't believe some of the germs you find in a single fluid ounce of saliva." Hilary sounded as if she were speaking from experience. She gave him a quick smile, a dispensing chemist administering advice, all starch and sense.

"It works both ways," said Harry. "I know nothing of your sex life."

"Don't be silly, I'm virtually a virgin. We shouldn't be talking like this. Your father has just died."

"Hilary, he's not going to be there watching us fuck."

And that was that. Once again he'd trashed his chances. She refused her usual black espresso with a minuscule shake of her head and chilled the table into arctic silence until they were ready to leave. The dinner bill was numerological pornography. He tossed the waiters his gold card and they responded like seals to a bucket of fish.

On the pavement outside she relented a little and gave him a short but tender kiss before insinuating herself into a taxicab. He knew he would have to be more patient with her. After all, as she was quick to point out, they had only been dating for three months, and compared with the longevity of sexually transmitted germs that was hardly any time at all.

Harry tracked the door number along the seemingly infinite gray corridor of the apartment building, one of the redundant and repetitive slabs which comprised this particular South London estate. The place was a shrine to the errors of council planning. He looked back over his shoulder. There was no one to be seen in either direction. Stopping before number 47 he raised his fist over the door, then let it fall to his side. There was no logical reason for his hesitation. The matter was virtually closed. This was just a single loose end to be tied up and forgotten. Why did he feel so unwilling to involve himself? He drew a breath and gave two hard raps. There was a shuffling sound within the flat, then light, hurrying footsteps. A burglar chain was slipped into place, and the door was opened by a tiny Asian woman in her early fifties. She nervously eyed him through the crack, ready to back off and shut the door at the first sign of trouble.

"Mrs. Nahree?" He held out his hand, a tentative offer of friendship, but was unable to insert it beyond the stile of the door. "I rang you earlier about my father."

"Oh yes. Mr. Buckingham. Please come in." She unlatched the chain and led the way through a low dark hall, turning back to check that he was following. She moved with the wincing, staccato movements of a mistreated bird.

"I have to be careful. My son is at work and I am alone. My health is poor. It is not safe here, but where else to go? I can get you some tea, perhaps?" She opened the door to a smart lounge filled with polished brass ornaments, obviously a room designated for guests.

"No, thank you. I can't stay very long." He allowed himself to be guided into a seat. "I must get back to my office. I just wanted to hear what my father said to you."

Mrs. Nahree stood before him with her hands knotted, anxious to please. "I will tell you how I met your father," she began. "You see, I am returning from a visit with my son—he works for a jeweler in Regent Street— when I see an elderly gentleman running toward me. He is running not on the pavement but in the gutter. It is raining hard, and his clothes" —she indicated the front of her saree— "are very wet through indeed. At first I think nothing because, you know, everywhere in London there are people running. But the look on his face is, oh, as if the devil himself is chasing after him! Then, as I start to cross the road he turns the corner and is running straight at me!" Her eyes widened as she told the tale. "But he is not looking where he goes, he is always looking behind, and suddenly crash wallop I am on the floor in the rain. Well."

Mrs. Nahree pulled a chair to her and sat, as if reliving the collision had exhausted her. She plucked at the front of her saree, a theatrical indication of her fluttering pulse. "I am not hurt, just a wind in my heart. He helps me to my feet, but in a rush, and still he does not look at me. It is as if he is expecting wild beasts to leap from nowhere and attack us both." Her eyes remained fixed as she paused, an eidetic trapped within the memory of the event. "Then he stares at me like a crazy man, his hand reaches for my hand, he clutches at my coat. At first he says something I cannot catch. After all, I am thinking who is this man and is he after my handbag, it is only natural. But then I hear what he is saying.''

''And what exactly was he saying?'' Harry moved forward on his chair.

'' 'The Devil's prayers,' he tells me. 'Soon the Devil's prayers will be all around us.' I think this man is mad and I am very scared, but he lets go of me and runs on again, across the road into the traffic. The wind in my heart is strong and I walk fast to get away. Two streets, three streets and I am feeling better in my constitution. But as I turn the next corner here is a tremendous commotion going on and your father is lying dead as if he has been torn apart by wild animals.''

''This is what you told the police?''

''Just as I have told you now.'' Her tale recounted, she folded her hands together once more. Harry sat back, puzzled.

''What do you think he could have been referring to?''

''I don't know, don't know.'' She shook her tiny head vigorously. ''Perhaps nothing. He was very frightened, talking very fast. I tell this to the sergeant.''

''Well, thank you for sparing me the time.'' He rose to leave, no wiser than when he had arrived. ''If you think of anything else, perhaps you could call me.'' He handed her his agency card. ''My home number is on the back.''

Returning to the office, he tried to equate Mrs. Nahree's description of a babbling, rainsoaked madman with the dapper little figure which had presented itself at the restaurant table two weeks ago. They had met for lunch at the older man's instigation, to discuss a business matter that he was apparently concerned about. Before the arrival of the starter Willie had rearranged his cutlery, folded the corners of the heavy linen napkin, frowned at his son's consumption of wine, tutted and fretted and fussed, complaining that he felt uncomfortable without Beth Cleveland by his side. Exasperated beyond measure, Harry had failed to see that there was something seriously troubling his father. He knew now that he should have paid much more attention to their final conversation.

7.

Devils in Pursuit

"**F**IRST INTERVIEW?" ASKED the receptionist. The girl on the far side of the desk nodded and smiled shyly.

"Well, you've no cause to be nervous. You'll *love* Mr. Meadows." She pronounced each word in an exaggerated fashion, in case others were listening. "Everyone does. He's a sweetie, he really is. A charmer of the old school, you might say. He has these cute little half-moon glasses. And I've never seen him without a collar and tie. Always has a cheery word for his staff." She checked the clock behind her. "Shouldn't be long now. He's on a long-distance call."

The girl crossed the outer office and took a seat. She waited with her handbag clasped on her knees. The receptionist, a friendly middle-aged woman, returned to her paperwork. Five minutes later, she glanced up at the clock again.

"He does seem to be a long time. His light's still on." She tapped the telephone console with a manicured fingernail. "Overseas buyers. They talk for ages. Mr. Meadows is the senior partner, but he still likes to take the calls himself. Dedicated." She pursed her lips again. "The hours he puts in. I'm sure the pope gets more time off than he does."

Silence fell once more. The girl shifted her position on the couch and studied the opposite wall. She cleared her throat. There was a dull thud from within Mr. Meadows's office.

"Ah ha." The receptionist checked her switchboard. "He's off the phone at last. He knows you're here. He won't keep you." They both stared at the door. From behind it came the sound of breaking china.

"He does Santa Claus for the orphans every Christmas," said the receptionist. From inside came a muffled bellow of rage. "A living saint," she added lamely.

Suddenly the door was thrown wide open to reveal the company's senior partner of thirty-five years' standing. His eyes were wild, his suit was torn, and he was smothered in gobbets of blood. The office behind him was virtually demolished. Thick arcs of blood smeared the white walls. Mr. Meadows threw back his head and screamed through tattered scarlet lips. The girl and the receptionist screamed too. Then Mr. Meadows hurled himself past them and out into the corridor. Secretaries scattered. A young clerk carrying a sheaf of papers was slammed against a wall.

"Mr. Meadows has gone mad!" screamed the receptionist. "Somebody stop him!"

The senior partner trailed destruction as he ran. He brandished a paper knife in one hand and appeared to have stabbed himself several times with it. He roared and threatened anyone who approached. As staff members advanced on him with their arms outstretched, his eyes narrowed with insane cunning and he darted between them into the stairwell.

"Call security," shouted someone. "Stop him from leaving the building before he kills someone!"

In the car park beneath the office block, the noise of the revving V-8 engine made Walter look up from his crossword puzzle. The elderly attendant knew the sound of that car anywhere. He rose and peered from his sentry booth, but could see nothing in the neon-lit gloom ahead. He was just returning to his seat when a piercing squeal of tires echoed through the vast concrete bunker. That can't be Mr. Meadows driving, he thought. He'd never take a corner like that.

He was still pondering this puzzle when the sleek green Jaguar burst upon the frail box, smashing through the walls in an explosion of vitreous shards. Walter barely had time to register Meadows's demented face behind the wheel of the car before being hurled aside in a spray of glass and metal fragments.

The Jaguar slammed onto the street with a steely bang and surprised the hell out of the city's homebound drivers. Then, with horn blaring, it screamed across two lanes of traffic and made off along Cannon Street, heading away from Ludgate Circus on the wrong side of the road.

The first report came into West End Central after a double-decker bus which found itself in the Jaguar's path was forced to mount the sidewalk and plow through the window of a crowded public house. By the time any patrol cars had managed to converge on the area, Meadows's car was sliding across the wet tarmac at the main intersection in front of the Tower of London. Vehicles and pedestrians scattered in every direction as the Jaguar hurtled through one set of red lights, then another. The vehicle's bottom grounded against the curb in a shower of sparks as it thundered through a chaos of braking traffic toward Tower Bridge. One patrol car skidded across the road in an attempt to seal off the bridge's entrance.

With an insane scream, Meadows revved the powerful engine to a little over seventy miles per hour. The speed limit on the bridge is twenty miles per hour. One of the tower patrol officers watched in amazement as the automobile raced past. His mouth fell open when he realized that it was not aiming for the bridge at all. As he snatched up his radio mike the ensuing cacophony drowned his voice.

The Jaguar shot over the crest of the slip road at the side of the bridge, routing tourists from the Tower Hotel and clearing the low railings at the end of the street to slam furiously into the swirling river beyond.

Scant seconds later no trace of Meadows and his car remained, save for the swirling signature of bubbles which glistened on the marbled surface of the Thames.

8.

Cause of Death

Daily Mail   Thursday 17th April

BERSERK BUSINESSMAN
"WAS CHRONICALLY DEPRESSED"

The senior management executive of a successful mail-order company who yesterday afternoon went on a murderous rampage through the city was remembered by his colleagues as being a "cheerful, happy-go-lucky" man. But beneath his carefree exterior deadly, destructive impulses were waiting to surface.

For Arthur Meadows, 57, was concerned that he would have no place in the company when it began a "restructuring process" in the summer. Recently his business had been successfully taken over by part of Britain's expanding ODEL Corporation. Insiders warned that Meadows and other senior executives might find their departments "streamlined" in the near future. A company doctor revealed that he had recently treated the man staff members referred to as their "friendly uncle" for a bout of chronic depression.

Meadows's homicidal spree left three dead and seventeen injured before his car mounted embankment railings and plunged into the Thames, instantly killing its driver.

Police divers are expected to recover Meadows's body from the river later today.

MP calls for riverside crash barriers. See page 7.

Arthur Bryant liked to sit in the incident room at the start of his working day, watching the activities of the previous night being logged and the consequences dealt with. As usual, he installed himself at one of the vacant desks with a mug of bitter mahogany-colored tea and monitored the calls with his head lowered, his fingers running absently over his bald head as he listened. It was one of the rituals he would miss most when he left the force.

This morning everyone was talking about the Meadows suicide. The newspapers were full of it. *The Times* featured a map of Meadows's disastrous route through the City, and *The Sun* had a center spread of the deceased's wife's sister modeling underwear.

Bryant was captivated by the ingenuity of the various reports. At the basis of every article was a single simple question. Namely, why should anyone do such a thing?

John May unbuttoned his jacket and threw it across a spare chair. He glanced down at his partner, who seemed to be shrinking within the coils of a huge woolen scarf and the voluminous folds of his ratty brown overcoat. Bryant raised his head, displeased at the interruption. The creases around his eyes and his small, flat nose gave him the appearance of a tortoise that had been woken in mid-hibernation. He studied May briefly, taking in the dapper gray suit with the modern cut, and noted the heavy fleece of white hair which had now grown to touch his colleague's collar.

"You know, Arthur, I think you're shrinking," said May breezily. "You're definitely smaller than you were last summer. Or have you started buying your clothes in bigger sizes?"

"I'm attempting to grow old gracefully. This is a classic suit," said Bryant, groping around in the folds to produce a tweedy lapel. "Hand-finished, not like that off-the-peg Oxford Street tat you wear. Has your barber passed away? What is it you want?"

"I'm sorry to disturb you." May sat down beside his colleague. "I know this is your half hour of quiet time . . ."

"Oh, that's all right." Bryant pushed the newspapers away from him. "I've just been reading about this chap Meadows. Extraordinary business. More to it than meets the eye. Pity he didn't bash his car up over here." Unfortunately, the case was out of their jurisdiction.

"Don't worry, you're going to be busy enough. We've

had confirmation on our canal man, Henry Dell. His ex-wife just identified his body.''

''When did she last see him?''

''Three weeks ago. She has custody of their kids and he was visiting. The background's all rather predictable. He was living alone, running a small business . . .''

''Successfully?''

''He hadn't filed for bankruptcy. Wife seems to think that he wasn't the type to commit suicide. Video dealer with a couple of nicely located stores. I'd like you to come with me to his apartment if you can spare the time.''

''Why, are you expecting anything out of the ordinary?''

''You could say that. The lab report on his clothing is in.''

''I assume you've already had a sneak through it.'' Bryant looked across at his colleague and noted an unusual glitter of interest in his eyes.

''You remember the pieces of straw we found stuck to his jacket? Forensics couldn't get a match with any of the hedge cuttings taken from the canal site, but they were able to identify several of the microbes found within the straw by running a computer match.'' He leaned over with a crooked smile. ''This is the part you'll like, Arthur. Tell me, what do you know about the impala?''

''It's a car made by Chevrolet.''

''The *animal*, you silly sod.''

''Nothing. Why?''

''According to this''—he tapped the report—''the impala is a member of the family *Bovidae*, 'a fast-running antelope found on the savannas of central and southern Africa.' ''

''How fascinating. What on earth could this possibly have to do with our client?''

''It would seem that Mr. Dell has visited just such a place in the last forty-eight hours. Give us a sip.'' He leaned over and took the mug from Bryant's hands. ''There's some kind of microscopic parasite found exclusively on the impala that humans can catch, apparently quite harmless. Dell was smothered in them.'' May drained his partner's tea and rose to leave. Bryant tried to join him but had trouble climbing out of his chair, and was left struggling like a baby wrapped in too many blankets until May gave him a pull.

"Where are we going?"

"To see Finch."

Oswald Finch had the same effect on everyone who met him. He depressed the life out of them. He was an excellent pathologist, a man not given to delegation, who preferred to trust the judgment of his own mind and the experience of his own hands. It was a pity that he smelled so terrible. Cheap after-shave, at least a gallon of it, Bryant decided as he watched Finch rinsing up at the biopsy sink. He wore it to mask the powerful smell of the chemicals which stained his lab coat. Instead, the cloying sweet odor of dying violets saturated his person with an emetic intensity. Tall and thin, with a long nose and unkempt receding hair, he reminded Bryant of a stretched Stan Laurel.

The two detectives had hoped to catch Finch in his office. Neither of them much relished the thought of conversing with him across a freshly opened cadaver. The forensic staff could generally be relied upon to exercise discretion when visitors were present. Finch never seemed to be hampered by this particular concern.

"Arthur, John." Finch turned to acknowledge them as he finished drying his hands. "You're in luck. I've just closed up your man. To be honest, I was just wondering how on earth to fill in the report without sounding daft. I think you'll be rather surprised at what we've turned up.'' He led them from the silent green-and-white morgue, with its waiting steel tables, into a small glass-partitioned office. His legs creaked in protest as he sat back on the edge of his desk.

"You were right about him not drowning. As I'm sure you know, drowning is simply suffocation, cutting off oxygen to the brain. It's possible to die from a laryngeal spasm just by the act of falling into water, what we call a 'dry' drowning. When a ship sinks, the passengers sometimes die from cardiac arrest as they hit the sea. Incidentally, you drown faster in fresh water, did you know that? Salt water has a higher osmotic pressure than blood so it doesn't get drawn through the breathing membrane, though of course the chloride concentration . . .''

"I'm sure you enjoy your work, Oswald, but is this detail really necessary? We know he drowned in fresh water, if you can call the canal that."

"Sorry, just thought you'd be interested. Okay, on to our man. Normally, very little water gets into the lungs because the mucus formed in the air passages is churned into a thick foam by the victim's attempts to breathe. If water does enter the lungs it distends them like balloons, but in this case neither the distension of the lungs nor the constitution of the heart blood was particularly consistent with drowning. On the outside of the body, you'll normally see a fine froth of bubbles at the mouth and nostrils. However, Dell had been in the water overnight and any frothing which had occurred had long been washed away. We can pin an accurate time of immersion on him by measuring the wrinkling on the hands and feet. I'd say he went into the river at about nine P.M. the night before. Next, we carried out diatom tests . . .''

John raised his index finger. "That's to determine whether Dell was dead or alive when he fell into the canal, I take it?"

"Right. Diatoms are microscopic algae with tough silicon shells. There are over fifteen thousand different species and they turn up in all kinds of different areas. If a body is in the throes of drowning, diatoms enter the lungs and bloodstream, and are pumped around the body to the heart. If Dell had already been dead when he entered the water, we would only have found diatoms existing as far as his air passages. So here's the odd thing. He *wasn't* dead when he entered the water. But I'm pretty certain that he didn't drown. He'd swallowed a small quantity of algae, and it was consistent with the type found growing in various parts of the canal."

"You mean to say that we know the identity of the victim, the time, place, and manner of his death," said Bryant, "but we don't have a cause?"

"Actually, Arthur, that's not quite true." Finch picked up a pencil and studied the end of it intensely, as if he was embarrassed about something.

"You mean you *do* have a cause?"

"Well yes, but it doesn't seem to make any sense. It was because of his hands, you see."

"His hands?" May sat forward. "What about them?"

"It was hard to see anything at first because of the wrinkling. Both the palms and the backs were covered in tiny puncture marks."

"Perhaps he grabbed at the undergrowth as he fell," said Bryant, "in a—what's it called . . . ?"

"A cadaveric spasm," declared Finch. "I think not. They looked like stings to me. There was a fair amount of localized tissue damage, necrotic lesions consistent with insect bites. I ran a poison match and finally came up with this." Finch reached behind the desk and unfolded a sheet of computer paper. *"Latrodectus mactans."*

"What the hell is that?"

"Black widow spider. There are only a handful of poisonous arachnids. Most of them are found in the tropics, and their venom isn't usually fatal to humans. The brown spiders and the widows will give you severe abdominal pains, but that's about all. However, our unfortunate victim must have been attacked by a very large number of them indeed. The poison went to work on his nervous system straight away, paralyzing him."

"It cramped up his stomach, and he blundered into the canal. Then, when he couldn't catch his breath, the water filled his windpipe."

"I think that's the most likely explanation, Arthur."

"Do they have black widows in central and southern Africa?"

"I'm not sure about that," said Finch. "I think you'll find them more common to America, in the warmer states. Why?"

"Because we've got a dead video-rental store manager who seems to have done a lot of globe-trotting in the hours immediately preceding his death," said Bryant, voicing his partner's unspoken thoughts.

9.

Mourners

THE FUNERAL OF Willie Buckingham was held on Thursday morning. It was a dismal affair, not least because it took place in dazzling sunshine. Harry had always felt that a decent funeral commenced to the accompaniment of distant thunder, and that the first raindrops should fall from a dark and injured sky just as the vicar launched into a low, woeful litany. It appeared, however, that there were to be no such atmospherics. The clergyman in charge of this morning's interment could not have been more than twenty-five years old. He had sparse blond hair and a ruddy fat face which looked as if it had been repeatedly scrubbed with steel wool. Perhaps in keeping with some newly provided set of guidelines, he was adopting a cheerful no-nonsense attitude about the proceedings.

Watching from his vantage point in the front row of the pews, Harry studied the vicar with distaste. Of course it's a sad occasion, he seemed to be saying, but come on chaps, it happens to us all, so let's just enjoy this chance to chat in God's front parlor.

He looked across at the walls. There were finger

paintings of Easter eggs everywhere. No tortured saints glared down from the shadows with dire warnings of repentance here. The place looked as if it had been built in the late sixties: from the outside it could have been mistaken for a hamburger joint. That was the worst part about being christened Church of England, he decided. It was so user-friendly. In the table of world religious worship it was the rough equivalent of being agnostic. Few sacrifices were demanded of its followers beyond an occasional hour of inattention on a Sunday morning.

The vicar was telling a story about a mean old miser who beat his donkeys. Apparently God let him into heaven anyway. Listening to him spreading sound advice and good cheer like the plague, Harry suddenly wished he was Jewish. They knew how to mourn their dead with dignity and reverence, he thought to himself. True, he had never enjoyed much of a relationship with his father, but he had still expected something more than a brisk canter through a couple of truncated, modernized hymns and a perky three-minute synopsis of the old man's life.

As the thin congregation trudged out into the irreverent glare of a blazing spring sun, he examined the other mourners. At one end of the graveside stood two wizened old ladies in matching fox furs, seasoned professionals in grief. He vaguely recalled them as cousins of his father, last seen at his mother's funeral seven years ago. He was surprised to find them both still alive. There was a younger woman near them, a girl from Willie Buckingham's office, very overweight. She saw him looking at her and gave a watery smile of acknowledgment before casting her eyes down at the Astroturf which surrounded the edge of the burial pit. Farther along stood Beth Cleveland, the fearsome battle-ax who supposedly had been having an affair with his father for a number of years. It was rumored that her romantic involvement with the old man predated his mother's death. She loomed at the graveside like a stone sentinel, her shadow plunging the few floral wreaths which lay nearby into chill twilight, robbing them of color. She had met with Harry on a single previous occasion, when she had made it abundantly clear that she did not intend to justify her existence to him. He didn't suppose she approved of his life-style much either. He wondered why the couple had lived together without marrying. She was physically bigger than his father. He couldn't imagine them having breakfast together, much less making love.

Behind her was a smartly dressed man in his mid-fifties, cashmere coat, navy suit with a tightly knotted black tie, glistening polished brogues. One of Willie's business colleagues, perhaps? He returned his attention to the vicar, who had come to an abrupt end and was now glancing impatiently at his watch as if he expected the gathering to troop past him in single file with their tips at the ready. There was to be no wake. Beth had insisted on taking care of all the arrangements. He imagined that she would now adopt the role of faithful old dog that would never leave its master's graveside.

As the little band slowly dispersed—there appearing to be no alternative instruction issuing from the vicar—Harry saw the smartly dressed gentleman moving quickly toward him.

"If I could have a word with you," he begged, tentatively reaching out his hand to Harry's shoulder. "Such a terrible, awful tragedy. You must be the son."

"That's right. I'm afraid you have the advantage of me."

"So sorry, Brian Lack." They shook hands. "You came to our office once but I didn't get to meet you. I had the pleasure of working with your dear father. I'm one of the partners, actually." Brian had the self-effacing attitude of that vanishing breed, the British Home Counties Apologetic, the sort of person who, if offered a cup of tea, would say "Only if you're making one for yourself."

"A pretty poor turnout from the rest of his company, don't you think?" asked Harry, looking about. "I thought there were quite a few of you."

"It all happened so suddenly," said Brian, his voice dripping contrition. "Some of the staff had prior appointments this morning. Business must go on, after all. Of course, we'll all miss your father terribly."

"Willie wasn't working at the company on a full-time basis anymore, was he?"

"No, that's true, but he still acted in a supervisory capacity, he was still on the board, a very active man, a model to others."

The wind had risen during the service, and was starting to lift the straggling hair which Brian had carefully combed across his bald patch. The effect was distressing for both of them. Harry decided to keep the interview as short as possible.

"I believe Mrs. Cleveland is taking care of my father's personal effects. I'll make sure that she contacts you about emptying out his office. Can I ask you something?"

"Certainly," agreed Brian, anxious to be of help.

"Did you see my father recently?"

"He came to the office only last Friday. He was training some of our lads, you know, showing them how to use the equipment."

"And you spoke to him?"

"Indeed. We had lunch together."

"How did he seem to you?"

"Oh, right as rain, very cheerful. Unusually so, I thought."

Harry's forehead wrinkled into a frown. He extended his hand. "It was a pleasure to meet you, Mr. . . . ."

"I'm afraid there'll be some papers to sign," added Brian hurriedly. "There's his share of the company to be sorted out."

"I'll make sure my solicitor gets in touch with you. Here." Harry fished a card from his pocket and handed it over. "Call me if you have any problems."

Brian turned to leave, then stopped. "I'd never have recognized you from your photo, you know."

"What photo?"

"There's a framed picture of you on your father's desk. And one of your mother."

The walk back to the car was passed in puzzlement. The old man had put their pictures on his desk. He was amazed, and just a little touched.

"Hi again."

She was leaning on the hood of his car as he approached. The blue-black mohawk stood up from her scalp like the plumage of an exotic bird. She was wearing a man's gabardine raincoat, white stockings, and heavy black Doc Martens with broad toecaps. Harry found himself checking to see if anyone else had spotted her. He was thankful she hadn't come over to attend the service.

"I figured I wouldn't be too welcome at the funeral, so I watched it from over here. Didn't last long, did it?"

"They've probably got another one lined up immediately afterward. I don't wish to appear rude, Miss Crispian, but I have to get back to my office . . ."

Grace moved away from the gleaming BMW and rebuttoned her overcoat. "I wanted to talk to you. Could you give me a lift?"

Key half in the lock, Harry swung around to face her. "Look, I really don't think we can get acquainted after what's happened."

"You know it wasn't my fault. The police said . . ."

"I know what the police said. I believe you, and I believe them. It's just not right, don't you see that?"

"I suppose so. It's just that—if I don't talk to someone about this . . ." She trailed off the sentence. "I dread having to get back into the truck. The thought makes me sick. But I must or I'll lose my job. I keep seeing the accident over and over again."

"The memory will fade in time, I'm sure." He opened the car door, then looked up and saw a pale hand rising to her eyes. "You'd better get in," he said finally.

He called Darren Sharpe at the agency and left a message saying that the funeral had caused him a further delay. As they approached Waterloo Station and the sunlit bridge beyond, he turned the car into a side street, parked, and led Grace to a small, crowded tapas bar. They managed to locate a table in a far corner, seated themselves, and ordered red wine and meatballs.

On a television screen above the bar, grainy video footage shot by a tourist showed Meadows's Jaguar clearing the embankment railings.

"It's not the best place to eat but there's very little choice around here," he said, raising his voice above the recorded flamenco music.

"I don't care," said Grace. Her eyes were dark, as if she had not been sleeping well. "I've never got enough money to eat out anyhow."

"I have the opposite trouble. Too many client lunches." He patted his stomach and smiled uneasily, aware of the financial gulf which separated them. She looked terrible. The hand-me-down clothes, the hair, the slouching pose. Lack of capital was only part of her problem. He supposed she was making a statement, out to shock in order to prove that she had retained her individuality in the face of the system.

"You shouldn't keep thinking about what happened," he said. "It's over. We both have to forget about it."

"It's not that simple. I killed him. The police know how I felt. They didn't even give me trouble for parking on the sidewalk. They realize there's no other way when you're delivering something in those backstreets. If I hadn't started the engine up just then . . ."

"It was a million-to-one chance, a freak occurrence. You can't hold yourself responsible for that." Harry poured a glass of wine, pushed it across and watched her drink. "You know, my father and a couple of other guys had a small company. It handles some kind of photographic duplication process. I went there one time to pick him up. The place was making a tidy profit, the last I heard. It just doesn't make sense." He sipped his wine thoughtfully. "There had to be something wrong with him to make him act the way he did. I called his doctor to find out if he had been taking any medication. Apart from a touch of arthritis he was completely healthy. It's almost as if he was hallucinating when he died. Maybe he found Jesus.''

"Why do you say that?"

"The Devil's prayers." Grace gave him a quizzical look. He described his visit to Mrs. Nahree, and what the old lady had told him.

"Could he have taken something that causes delusions? Could someone have given him poison?"

"It sounds a bit unlikely, don't you think?" Harry refilled their glasses. "Too Agatha Christie. It's more likely that he had something on his mind, something he couldn't discuss with anyone."

"Like him," said Grace, pointing up at the newsreel footage on the TV screen. Police had cordoned the route of Meadows's careening vehicle with flashing markers and orange plastic tape, a bizarre commemorative ritual which recorded the executive's final journey for posterity.

"Wasn't this guy about to lose his job?"

"His company was being taken over. According to the papers he couldn't handle the idea. Maybe you should go and see the people your father worked with. Perhaps he had a similar problem." Grace was leaning forward across the table, waiting for a response. Harry was suddenly aware that he was being asked to share a family problem with a virtual stranger.

"What difference does it make to you?"

"I'd like to know if he deliberately chose to kill himself," she replied. "It changes my role. I can't go back to work until this is sorted out. I'm off my food . . ." Harry looked skeptically at her empty plate. "I don't even feel like seeing a movie, and I *always* feel like doing that. Don't you see? You want to know where you stand. Well, so do I."

10.
Womb

ARTHUR BRYANT'S OFFICE reflected the state of his mind. It was an orderly, symmetrical room, a softly lit area which remained defiantly out of step with the glass partitions, strip lighting, and desktop computers on the rest of the third floor. The furniture was of an unfashionable prewar design. Murky prints by the more generally disliked Victorian artists cluttered the walls. The books which filled an entire wall of shelves veered alarmingly in subject matter, so that *Toxicology Data Review* and *Advanced Courses in Cryptanalysis* found themselves sandwiched between *The Annotated Gilbert and Sullivan* and *Hancock's Half Hour: The Collected Scripts*.

In the corner a primitive Dansette gramophone played a copy of Mendelssohn's *Elias Elijah* which was so worn that it was starting to sound like the scratch dub remix.

"Does the music have to be quite so loud?" asked John May as he seated himself on the green leather couch beside his partner's battered desk. "You can't hear yourself think in here."

"On the contrary, John, that's the one thing I am able to do perfectly well. You recall that our man was holding something in his hand when he was pulled from the water? A piece of paper?"

"I'm afraid it went off to forensics before I had a chance to examine it."

"But not before I did. Rather interesting. I asked one of the lads to make a trace of it for me." Bryant had the result on a sheet of foolscap in front of him, but he had turned it facedown, like a magician witholding a card. His eyes twinkled as he slowly revealed the page.

"What is it, some kind of foreign language?"

"I'm not sure." He peeped around the corner of the paper and studied the strange hieroglyphic scrawl which ran across it. "It was printed on a scrap of thin card about three inches long. Some of the characters have been destroyed by the immersion."

"Give it to me, Arthur. I'll run it through the computer and get you a language match."

"No," said Bryant, suddenly animated. "Damn your confounded computer, I'm quite capable of working out where it's from without having to consult some electronic oracle." He rattled the paper irritably. "If it *is* a language, it's not one that's in use today. It's more like Sanskrit. Or Urdu."

"Urdu's not dead," said May with a smile. It wasn't easy catching Arthur out, so he enjoyed the opportunity when it arose. "It's the official literary language of Pakistan. Do you know what Sanskrit looks like?"

"No. This is what I *imagine* it looks like."

"I see." He sat back, amused. "And if I told you that my desktop PC could pinpoint the origin language and translate it in a matter of seconds, I suppose you'd still regard technology as the Devil's curse on mankind?"

"Absolutely."

"That's one of the things I like about you, Arthur. Your consistency." May laughed. Several months earlier, Bryant had set down a bag of fingerprinted property pertaining to a murder inquiry on top of May's assistant's computer console. The bag contained a window cleaner's magnetic wiper. The force field it set up erased the entire case from the files. Bryant had never trusted computers. Now he was careful to stay away from them altogether.

"Anyway, while you're still fooling with your floppy disks I'll finish working out how Henry Dell died."

"Finish? You mean you have an idea?"

"I have more than that. I know where he was in the hours immediately preceding his death, and how he came to be in the canal." Bryant reached behind his chair and removed the needle from the record. He rose, scissored his hat between two fingers and pulled it down on his head, then moved toward the door.

"Wait, where are you going?" asked May, trying to head him off.

"To have a nose around Henry Dell's apartment. Coming?"

"Only if we take a tube or a taxi. You know how I feel about your driving."

"Nonsense," called Bryant over his shoulder. "I need the practice. Come and ride with me."

With a shrug of resignation, May followed his partner.

The traffic behind the rusty blue Mini Minor had built up considerably as it crawled along Marylebone Road at just under fifteen miles per hour, straddled between the lanes. Bryant had been trying to pass his driving test for the last seven years, without any success. He found traffic signals boring and repetitive. The whole system seemed to him to be designed without any allowance for creativity or imagination. This was a situation that he set out to rectify on every journey. He interpreted the road signs in interesting but not entirely legal ways, and he liked to drive at a leisurely speed which would allow him to appreciate the architecture of each passing area. He abhorred printed instructions of every kind, and constantly slowed down to criticize the huge advertising hoardings which obliterated so many of the fine buildings that stood hidden in their shadows. Oblivious to the hooting and gesturing of the motorists around him, he pottered along the carriageway discoursing on art, history and modern society's lack of direction. He was well qualified to discuss this last point, having turned the wrong way into two separate one-way streets in the last ten minutes.

May found it difficult to pay full attention while there were truck drivers leaning from their cabs loudly vocalizing their doubts about his driver's parentage. He was glad that they weren't in a hurry to reach their destination.

"Did you get a chance to study a map of the surrounding area?" Bryant asked as a brace of buses overtook them on either side, briefly plunging the interior of the car into darkness.

"You mean where the canals are situated?" asked May, making sure that his window was firmly wound to the top. "No, why?"

"It became obvious to me as soon as I looked. Dell hadn't been out of the country at all. The fact that he had his passport with him when he died merely meant that he was about to take his leave. But there were no appropriate stamps or visas in it, and his name wasn't found on any airport passenger lists, so we can assume that this was very much a last-minute decision."

He failed to take notice of the red lights at Baker Street's intersection and drifted into the cross-traffic amid a barrage of horn blowing. May shut his eyes.

"It's obvious when you think about it," said Bryant, nosing the car ahead as if rafting across a river. "I noticed from the Ordnance Survey map of the area that the northerly section of the London Zoo is divided in half by the Regent's Canal. I trotted along and took a look for myself. The insect house stands above it, and the impala enclosure is built on the sloping bank of the canal itself. A helpful zookeeper informed me that they have an entire tankful of black widow spiders in the insect house—or at least, they *had*, because someone broke in and shattered the case on Monday night. Somehow Dell managed to get himself bitten. He staggered from the building, fell over the low wall enclosing the impalas and rolled down the slope, collecting pieces of straw on his jacket as he fell. How he scaled the fence at the bottom of the enclosure is a mystery, but scale it he did. Presumably this increase in physical activity would have caused the poison to enter his bloodstream more quickly, and he fell into the canal."

"But the zoo must be about a mile from the murder site, and there's no direct current to tow him. So how did he wind up at Camden Lock?"

"Ask yourself this," said Bryant. "What moves regularly from the zoo to the lock and back again?"

"Of course." May's eyes widened as his colleague made a right hand signal and performed a very slow left turn. "The tourist barge—what's the thing called—the *Jenny Wren*."

"Exactly. Corpses usually float facedown. Dell's body was probably just below the surface of the water when the barge snagged the back of his jacket. It towed him to the other end of the canal, which explains the tears in his trousers, then disentangled the carcass when it began the journey back again. End of mystery."

"Or the start of a fresh one," May muttered. "What on earth was he doing in the insect house after closing time?"

Henry Dell's apartment was situated on the third floor of a purpose-built apartment building in St. John's Wood. At the rear of the gilt-and-marble foyer sat a uniformed doorman, who greeted the detectives and provided them with a set of passkeys.

"Who else has been up here so far?" asked Bryant as they rode the elevator. May leaned back against gold-flecked walls of marbled plastic.

"I'm not sure that anyone has. His ex-wife didn't have the keys. No one else could gain entrance without a written pass from Sergeant Longbright."

"Janice Longbright from Bow Street? Lovely woman, I always imagine her modeling for posters, 'Come to Brightsea,' big white smile, holding a beach ball. I hear she's coming up to Kentish Town to coordinate the material on this case."

"I asked her."

Dell's apartment was directly opposite the elevator bank. May inserted his key and pushed the front door wide.

"Good God."

The door swung shut behind them. Neither one could believe the evidence of his eyes. They found themselves standing in a narrow hallway which had been radically altered from its original design. Vast banks of plaster curved from the carpet to the corridor walls, and again from the walls to the ceiling, so that the hall appeared to them as a dark oval tunnel. Carefully passing through to the lounge, they found that there the floor, walls and ceiling had been plastered into smooth white parabolas that transformed the room roughly into the shape of an egg. On the far side, the windows had lost their corners beneath pounds of plaster. Even the struts which separated the panes had been smothered. This obliteration of all formality within the lounge lent the room an organic feel, as if they were standing beneath the roots of an exotic plant. There was no furniture of any kind to be seen.

"How extraordinary. It's rather like being inside the womb. Are all the rooms like this?" Bryant passed through a doorway of curving plaster into the bedroom and found that, here too, the same effect had been achieved.

"This is still fresh." He dug his nails into the landscaped cement. "Certainly not more than a week old."

"How do you know?" May entered the room and gazed around. A narrow mattress and blankets lay on the floor.

"Can't you feel it?" asked Bryant. "The place is wringing wet. Look at the condensation on the windows. The moisture hasn't managed to fully evaporate from all this plaster."

"There are no doors. There's no furniture. What about cupboards?" May crossed to the back wall of the bedroom and examined the built-in wardrobes. Their edges had been planed and hacked so that they no longer closed properly, but hung like props on a surrealist film set.

"This is madness," said Bryant quietly. "It's as if he was rebuilding his home according to some secret set of rules. There's a single suit of clothes and one pair of shoes in here, nothing else. We know that Dell was in fine spirits just three weeks ago. He must have transformed the place since then."

They checked the kitchen. All of the fitted units had been ripped out and removed from the premises. An electric kettle, a milk bottle and a single coffee mug stood in the middle of the floor.

"Come and look at this, Arthur." May was standing on the far side of the room pointing at the wallpaper, a bright design of circles and squares. "Now why would he have gone to all the trouble of doing this?"

Someone had meticulously drawn on the walls with a black Magic Marker, numbering every shape to be found in the pattern from floor to ceiling. All four walls had been carefully annotated with neat, tiny figures.

"It must have taken him ages." Bryant shook his head sadly. "This is the work of a psychotic."

"There were plaster bags coming into the building," said May. "There was a ton of debris going out. Somebody must have seen him doing it. They *must* have asked him what was going on."

"The concierge."

Bryant was already on his way to the door.

11.

Blinded by Reason

MRS. NAHREE WAS a devout woman, but her religious beliefs were tempered by practical demands. The building in which she was incarcerated stood far from any accessible place of worship, and like the majority of her fellow tenants she was not inclined to risk walking alone through the steel-shuttered, shit-smeared concrete maze which surrounded her. Instead she chose to pray at home, kneeling daily before the small candle-lit shrine that stood in one of the kitchen cupboards.

Apart from her son, Rasheed, Harry Buckingham had been the first person to call at the flat in almost a month, and trouble had followed in the wake of his visit.

She had been emptying the pocket of her overcoat when the slip of paper fluttered from it to the carpet. Picking it up, she studied the strangely printed letters carefully.

Clearly, this did not belong to her. Where could it have come from?

Then she remembered that she had been wearing the coat on the afternoon of her collision with Harry's father. Could the crazy old man have shoved it into her pocket as he helped her from the ground?

She studied the paper more closely, and now a great darkness seemed to grow within her. Without consciously comprehending the symbols on the slip she at once became aware of their precise meaning, and she grew deathly afraid. Mrs. Nahree was a resourceful woman. She pushed the fear aside and forced herself to think. Making herself a glass of tea, she returned to the lounge and sat there with the curtains drawn, waiting for her hands to stop shaking. Finally, she decided on an appropriate course of action.

It took her most of the afternoon to properly secure the apartment. Rasheed had left a hammer and nails beneath the kitchen sink after building her some shelves. These she now used to batten the windows with crossbars. The front door was easier to take care of. Carefully splitting several wedges of wood from a leftover section of shelving with the aid of a bread knife, she jammed them beneath the door with her foot and drove them firmly into place with the hammer.

She unplugged the telephone first, then the television—it was a shame to do so, for she enjoyed her afternoon shows—and, as an afterthought, returned to the hall and emptied a full tube of superglue across the mouth of the letterbox.

The larder was well stocked with canned food, but there was hardly any bread, and worse still, no milk. No matter, she told herself. She could do without. Rasheed would come to call on her eventually. He would understand that something was wrong. She would not be able to admit him to the apartment, of course, but surely it would be all right to talk to him through the door. She would explain her predicament. He would be able to help, she felt sure. If he didn't, she would surely die.

Placing the slip of paper in a saucer, she struck a match and carefully lit one end. It ignited quickly, burning with a small blue flame. In moments, only a gray curl of ash remained. This she tipped into the sink and washed away, running both taps at once.

The night passed slowly, but at least the rooms were warm, even if she did not dare to use the electric lights. Her supply of candles would see her through two nights at most, but by that time Rasheed would surely be here.

Suddenly a terrible new thought struck her. Suppose the invocation had already begun its work, and was using the gloom to gather its resources? Raising a bony brown hand to her mouth, she climbed from her bed and hurried into the darkened lounge, crouching down behind the sofa. It was too late. Wasn't there something already forming in the room? A penumbral blur, a black cloud that was stealing energy from the night, a living evil that now lay gathering its strength in the corner? At head height, a pair of yellow eyes glittered in the congealing mist. The temperature of the lounge began to drop as the presence grew in size and strength.

She rose and walked unsteadily into the corridor. Would it follow her, or merely reassemble itself somewhere else in the apartment? As long as she could see it, she knew it could kill her. Suddenly she released a bitter cry of laughter. The answer was obvious. The shrine, her shrine, surely it would offer protection. She ran to the kitchen and wrenched open the door of the cupboard. The matches still lay beside the sink. She grabbed them and hastily lit the candles, one by one, until a flickering pyramid of light issued from the cupboard.

Falling to her knees she began to pray, then watched in mounting horror as, one by one, the candles were snuffed by an unseen hand. Before her terrified eyes, the image of Christ mounted at the top of the shrine diffused and broke, to be replaced by something even older and far less comforting.

Harry wearily turned his briefcase out on the bed and began to sort through the piles of paperwork he had collected during the week. His flat comprised the lower half of a terraced Victorian house in a fashionable part of Highgate. The bedroom windows looked out across the city in a broad, spectacular view which explained to visiting dinner guests why the four-room apartment had been so outrageously expensive. The place had been decorated in fin de siècle advertising-executive rag-roll gray, complete with angular plaster sconces and matt black freestanding halogen lamps. It was a look which would require updating in a year or so, before the fashion faded. The bleak monochrome bathroom with its black wood shutters seemed to exist solely for use in razor-blade commercials. The bedroom, where Harry now sat in his underwear, suffered from a similar design malaise, the transitory triumph of style over comfort.

Harry studied the new research reports on his carbonated fruit-drink project without enthusiasm. His attention drifted away from the computer sheets of tabulated consumer reactions to memories of his father. The redoubtable Beth Cleveland had called by to deliver a few letters and photographs that Willie had apparently wanted his son to have. She would not be drawn across the threshold of the apartment, and had sought the first available excuse to take her leave. Still, thought Harry, it was good of her to bother at all.

Most of the photographs he had not seen for years. There were several that he had never seen before. These pictures were taken in the late nineteen-fifties and showed happier times for the Buckingham family, rides through Kent in a motorbike and sidecar, his grandmother on a hop-picking holiday, his father and mother seated outside a country pub with their arms around each other, closer than he could ever remember seeing them as a child. He recalled only the later violent times, the bitter recriminations and the mealtime fights that occurred in the year before his mother died. He slipped the photographs into an envelope and locked it in his desk.

The letters explained very little. What they said revealed less than how they looked in his hands. The handwriting was small and sharp, the pages meticulously folded to fit each envelope exactly. They reflected Willie's infuriating attention to the smallest detail. These he also locked away.

It was no use. Something had to be done. Harry decided that he would definitely pay a call on his father's colleague at the weekend, just to see if Brian Lack could shed any light on the old man's behavior. Grace had asked if she could accompany him. Should he call her? After a moment's consideration he decided against the idea. The last thing he needed right now was to become involved with a—strange person. It would be far better to make amends with Hilary by asking her to dinner tomorrow night, despite his growing conviction that the strain of spending several hours in her company would soon prove too much for his genitals.

Hilary defined safe sex by always having a return taxi booked for 11 P.M. Her reference to the sexual act in biological terms forced him to think of her in the same distant way that he considered female newscasters. The allure of her perfume was slowly being doused by the bitter tang of disinfectant.

He shoved his briefcase from the bed, promising to start work on the reports early the next morning. As he extinguished the lamp and lay back against the pillow, his father's face stubbornly reappeared.

You're supposed to be an intelligent man, it said. Discover me, before it's too late.

Mrs. Nahree was beset by devils.

She couldn't see them yet, but she knew they were all around her. The shrine lay smashed on the kitchen floor, the last guttering candle about to admit the darkness. With her eyes shut tight she rose to her feet and felt for the jamb of the kitchen doorway. She had to ignore the noise and try to think. If she had not studied Mr. Buckingham's note she would not now be cursed. By the same token, if she could not see the devils, they would leave her in peace. She would have to prevent her eyes from seeing. The devils would demand a sacrifice in return for their departure.

Her son Rasheed worked for a jeweler. In his spare time, he earned a little extra money by repairing gold chains and brooches, fixing pins, and resetting stones. He kept his equipment on top of the cupboard in the spare room. It was the only way. She would have to find it without uncovering her eyes.

Plugging in the soldering iron was the hardest part. She found the outlet by crawling on the floor and striking at the skirting board. Around her rose the deafening wind of a thousand malignant voices, virus-borne creatures moving through the feverish air. They tried to pluck her eyelids wide, to make her stare into their vile features, but she resisted them. She would defeat them yet.

The only way she could discover whether the soldering iron was hot enough was by testing it on the back of her hand. She cried out when the flesh hissed, but her voice was lost in the susurrant chattering of imps. Two moments of agony, that was all. The wounds would cauterize. It was the only way.

She raised the soldering iron and pressed the glowing tip through her eyelid and into the cornea of her right eye. After the initial shocking sensation of pain she felt nothing at all. Removing the sizzling, sticky iron from the socket, she repeated the operation on her left eye. This time the pain blossomed like a poisoned flower. Her frail hands sought their grip on the handle of the iron, forcing the shaft against the socket until it seemed as if her brain would explode.

Only now did she become aware of the fact that she was screaming, and very loudly. As consciousness fled and she fell to the floor, the iron skipped from her hand and fell against the bedroom curtain, dissolving the factory-made fibers as quickly as it had destroyed the encumbrance of her vision.

12.

Angels of Death

O<small>N</small> F<small>RIDAY</small> <small>MORNING</small> Grace rose early. Once out of bed, she unpinned the garish poster advertising Russ Meyer's *Faster Pussycat, Kill Kill!* and replaced it with a quad copy of Dan O'Bannon's *Dead and Buried*, once more obscuring the damp spots which continually bloomed through the wallpaper above her bed. The flat was in lousy condition, but there was no chance of persuading the landlord to pay for repairs—at least, not until she had paid her rent arrears. Grace climbed down from her chair and pushed it back in the corner. She sniffed the air suspiciously, then shooed the dog out into the hallway.

With the weekend approaching she found herself with no plans, and, worse still, not even enough money to go to the movies. Perhaps I could call Harry and tap him for a few quid, she thought, even though he didn't seem too thrilled to see me after the funeral. She had to admit that she found him quite attractive, in a smarmy sort of way. Obviously he wasn't short of a bob or two. He didn't look as if he'd ever been on a bus or had to do his own ironing.

Grace rolled up the discarded poster and threw it under the bed. He hadn't been wearing a wedding ring. She wondered if he had a girlfriend. She imagined him as the type of man who liked to be seen dating an emaciated blond with a Kensington drawl and a mouthful of tax-deductible bridgework. How could a man who earned a living from exaggerating product claims ever be trusted with a woman? His life was spent reinforcing role models and stereotypes. Did he ever tell the truth, even to himself? What the hell, she thought as she turned back the bedspread, perhaps I should try to save his soul. For all he knows, I could be his last chance. Perhaps our meeting was predestined to occur. A familiar gleam grew in her eye. Seating herself on the bed, she obtained Harry's telephone number from Information, then quickly punched it out.

He answered on the third ring. No, he replied with incredulity creeping into his voice, he could not make dinner tonight. Was she aware that it was seven-thirty in the morning? Harry acknowledged her distress over the unfortunate circumstance they shared, but did not see any reason why they should have any further dealings with each other.

"Call me Grace," said Grace.

"All right, Grace. But I can't have dinner with you. Apart from anything else, I have a girlfriend."

"That's better than being married."

"For you, maybe. Goodbye, Miss . . ."

"Grace. You can't escape fate, you know."

"What?"

"Maybe we were meant to meet."

"And my father had to die for it? It's a hell of a way to get a date, Grace. Good-bye."

This is going to be tougher than I realized, thought Grace. Replacing the receiver, she sat back on her bed and worried a fingernail between her teeth. It would be a challenge finding a way through to him.

But that would be half the fun.

As she did every morning, Dorothy Huxley took the bus to work and sat staring from the window lost in thought. Like the proverbial Beatles lyric, she wondered if she was still needed at sixty-four. Physically, she was fit and strong. Spiritually, she felt herself growing frail. Her mind was an inquiring one—too much so for her own good—but the more she learned about the world in which she lived, the more she read in the newspapers and saw on TV, the less she wanted to be a part of it. The library remained her real home, far more so than the apartment her daughter had encouraged her to take. Her flat was too modern, too light and airy. Its aluminum-framed windows swallowed the sunlight and threw it in searing panels across the carpets, splashing it against the walls as if trying to fool her that the building had been erected on the coast of Spain instead of in South London. Books withered and died in the glare of so much glass. Instead, she retreated to the mildewed depths of the library to study. Here the hardbacks grew old with dignity, just as she did.

Her daughter had once asked her if she believed in God. Not God, she had replied, no single deity has the right to monopolize belief, but gods, and gods in plenty. Baffled, her daughter had patted her hand reassuringly and returned to Australia with her new family, to subject them to the desiccating sunlight. There were no shadows of doubt in her life. And Dorothy lived on alone, searching for something that would convince her of a pattern to her existence.

At night, as her bedside light kept the shadows at bay, she would settle back in the pillows and study the Eleusinian and Orphic mysteries, the Rosicrucians, the Temple of Solomon. But the only things she ever found were mere tantalizing scraps of clues, buried in the rituals of forgotten religions, hidden beneath the embellishments of supernatural experience. Her search ran between pinpoints of enlightenment, flashes of clarity which formed the same contours as those on Frank Drake's map of paradox and probability. The ballpoint crosses on his graph-paper plans revealed the same inadequacies in his own search; as yet, there were not enough coordinates for either of them to draw any solid conclusions. One day perhaps, within the pages of her beloved books she would come to understand the nature and need for true belief.

"Good morning, Frank." She passed his cluttered desk, dropping a copy of *The Independent* on it. "You're early." The library was not due to open for another twenty minutes.

"I've been updating the file." He lowered his glasses at her. "Is it raining?"

"Just started. There's one on page four for you. Coffee?"

"Please." Frank thumbed open the newspaper and located the inch-long article.

"Just the identification of a drowned body," he said, disappointed. "Nothing we get this week is going to beat the guy who drove his jag into the Thames. This is too ordinary."

"Not really," replied Dorothy. "It says he drowned in the canal at Camden. It's very shallow there, not a place where you'd try to commit suicide."

"You can drown in an inch of water."

"Yes, but this feels like murder." She returned with coffees, watching as Frank carefully cut around the item, glued it onto a piece of card and added it to the others, like a child filling a scrapbook with memories. "Have you started writing anything down yet?" she asked.

"Any day now. As soon as I've finished collecting. The trouble is, there seem to be more cases every time I open a newspaper. It's a deluge. Look at this." He unfolded a section of graph paper and held it up for her to see. "Scotland Yard just released some figures." Dorothy adjusted her reading glasses and studied the multicolored chart. "The majority of homicides in England and Wales last year—over a third of them—were the result of stabbings. Strangulation or asphyxiation account for a quarter of all further deaths. This is followed in descending order by blunt instruments, kicking and hitting, shooting, burning, then way down the scale, drowning, and finally poisoning."

"So much for Agatha Christie."

"Huh?"

"She always favored poisoning. I guess it's too detectable these days. None of her murderers would ever get away with it now."

Frank failed to hear her. He was warming to his subject. "Seven hundred murders in Great Britain last year. Ninety from Scotland. Over a hundred of them in London, but by far the largest number occurring in the West Midlands. So far this year the figures are almost double those of the previous similar period. Why should that be?"

"I don't know. That's a lot of dead angels."

"What do you mean?"

Dorothy smiled at him. "They say every time a life is wasted, an angel dies. The violent-death rate is bound to be higher in areas of high-density population because of low incomes, unemployment, and so on. Did you know there are seven distinct levels of violence?"

Frank looked up from his chart.

"They're brought about by changes in social and financial circumstance. There's violence which occurs because of a basic deprivation, the need to breathe, to eat, to go on living. At the other end of the scale there's cruelty of great subtlety and sophistication, the kind developed and practiced by certain religions. There are many documented examples."

Frank studied her in surprise. "I worry about the information you carry about in your head," he said.

"It stores up over the years." She smiled thinly, tapping the side of her skull. "My mind is a repository of redundant information, just like this place. None of it will ever be of much use. Perhaps the books in the basement will come in useful, though."

"Ah yes, the basement. When will we be seeing your friends from the Camden Town Coven again?" There was gentle mockery in his voice. Dorothy shrugged off the question.

That morning, opening the doors of the library to an apathetic public, she felt the vaguest glimmer of alarm, and wondered if she would ever be called upon to employ the esoterica that was stored away in the library of her mind.

Dave Coltis had received more than a few death threats in his twenty-six-year-old life, but never one like this. He turned it over between tattooed hands, studying it carefully as he tried to decipher the lettering.

Who were his enemies at the moment? He thought of the people he had most upset recently. There was the hostess at the Mayfair club whom he had suddenly decided to stop seeing after she'd lent him money. There was the old queen he'd been blackmailing from the St. Martin's Lane sauna, who was now refusing to pay up.

And there was his ex-partner in crime, whom he'd been avoiding ever since the failure of the computer-programming swindle the two of them had devoted so much time to.

But no, this couldn't have been from any of them. His partner was still being detained at Her Majesty's pleasure in Parkhurst, and the handwriting on the envelope was too sophisticated to be from either of the other two. He hadn't given his new address to anyone, yet the sender had even included the correct postcode—something Dave himself had yet to figure out.

He screwed the envelope into a ball and tossed it into the gutter. Then he slipped the page containing the strange hieroglyphics inside his jacket for study at a later date. There was work to be done.

For the last half hour he had been looking for a car to steal. He was holding out for a convertible, preferably one of the new BMWs. He figured that if he couldn't find one in Hampstead he might as well renounce his profession.

On a Friday morning the streets of Hampstead were filled with well-heeled women shopping for skirts. Once the shops had sold quail and fennel and kiwifruit. Now they sold clothes. The men who had not yet made their way to their offices were buying hair gel and shoes and the morning papers. Dave picked at his dirty nails as he leaned against a tree watching them pass. He looked up at the darkening sky. It was just starting to rain.

A frizzy-haired woman in a green quilted jacket called her offspring into the doorway of a shop by suddenly shouting "Jonquil! Tarquin! Pippa is *most* cross!" Dave turned and stared at her. Stupid bitches like that knew nothing of the real world. Did she have anything worth stealing? They were all the same, this lot. All of a type. Their money was always "tied up." Farther down the hill he could see them all queuing at the cashpoint, wallets out, plastic at the ready. His mouth twisted into a bitter smirk. They put on airs and graces but most of them were penniless. The strain of covering the mortgage on the Norfolk bolt-hole barely left enough to cover the cost of bunging little Jocasta through private school. They were lucky he was flush for cash today.

At that moment a brand-new racing green BMW pulled up behind him, its hubcaps rasping horribly against the curb. He recognized the sound of the engine immediately and pushed away from the tree to take a look.

He was in luck. The driver looked like a stupid rich git. As soon as he had hauled his spivvy designer suit from the vehicle and trotted into a nearby newsagent, Dave made his move.

Lifting the keys from his victim as he browsed through racks of interior design magazines was like taking candy from a baby. After that it was simply a matter of swaggering toward the motor as if he really owned it, swinging the door wide, and hopping in. As he pulled smoothly into the flowing traffic he saw that the only person to notice his departure was the jerk in the Merc who was waiting to leap into his parking space.

The glistening BMW descended through an avenue of tall budding elms toward Belsize Park as Dave searched the glove compartment for some decent music and found nothing but Andrew Lloyd-Webber tapes and new-age jazz. That was the trouble with people today, he decided. They had no class. It would have to be the radio instead. He tuned the stereo and located a piece of classical music, Vivaldi by the sound of it.

Stacked with enormous logs cut from the nearby heath, a mud-spattered council truck moved ahead with a grinding of gears. A red flag fluttered from the longest of the protruding trunks like a flickering flame of warning. He eased the car back warily. The traffic lights ahead showed green as the truck accelerated to take its place in front of him.

The radio signal blurred and was replaced by a sound that was presumably produced by hammering nails into an electric guitar. Seconds later this was replaced by howling static. He reached forward and tapped the deck's touch-sensitive panels, but the interference merely grew in range. He's tampered with it, thought Dave. He doesn't deserve to own such precision equipment.

Ahead, the rear lights of the council truck flicked on.

Reacting automatically, he applied gentle pressure to his own brakes, then attempted to retune the radio.

Belsize Park tube station passed him on the left side of the car. As he drove, he withdrew the symbol-covered note from his jacket and reexamined it. What was it supposed to mean? It was now that he noticed the oddly spaced symbols on the other side. Holding the paper against the windshield, backlighting revealed that the cabalistic signs, while making no separate sense, suddenly became clear when combined together.

The young thief's brow furrowed as he slowly absorbed the message. He shook his head, as if to clear the alien thoughts from his mind, then hastily corrected the steering wheel when he saw that the BMW was straying from its course.

As a confusion of voices began to fill his brain, for the first time in his life he knew exactly what he had to do.

On Friday evening, Grace sat curled on the sofa watching Channel Four's seven o'clock news. A reporter was sheltering beneath an umbrella near Belsize Park tube station, speaking directly to the camera.

"It was here that the car thief made his stop." The reporter pointed behind at a hardware store.

"He came in here and asked to buy a length of strong nylon rope. Like this." The hardware store owner held up a prepared sample. "He was sort of staggering, and holding his head."

"Then what happened?" coaxed the reporter.

"He bought the rope, and a pocketknife. I packed it up for him and he left."

The camera followed the reporter outside to a new location. "The thief was next spotted by passersby in the high street." He turned the microphone in the direction of a young Chinese girl.

"I saw him get out of his car, over there," explained the girl, pointing to a section of rainswept road. "At first I couldn't see what he was doing. Then I saw that he'd tied this heavy white rope around a lamppost. He made sure the knot was secure, then ran back to his car with the line. He was shouting all the time."

The camera switched to an elderly man with a dog in his arms. "I saw him get into the driver's side of the car. It was parked about fifteen feet from the lamppost."

"Then what happened?"

"He slipped the other end of the rope over his head."

"How did he do that?"

The old man looked at the reporter as if he were stupid. "He'd tied it into a noose. Then he turned on the ignition and revved the engine up high. I didn't think he would pull away. I mean, the rope was round his neck."

The Chinese girl appeared close to tears. "He roared away from the curb, very fast."

"Did you see what happened next?"

"I will never forget," said the Chinese girl. "The rope was only so long. It pulled tight, and his head was torn from his shoulders."

"You should have seen the mess," added the old man unnecessarily.

The television cameras had not arrived in time to reveal the horrified pedestrians coming upon the accident scene, watching as a fountain of blood spurted like a burst water main from the stump of the young thief's neck. Nor had their microphones been able to record the Vivaldi orchestra suddenly resuming their piece on the car radio, providing an inappropriate background accompaniment to the pattering sound of blood on steel.

Back on the screen, the TV reporter made his way to another location and pointed at the shattered remains of the green BMW. As the camera moved unsteadily in, Grace's hand flew to her mouth.

"Oh my God," she cried aloud. "That's Harry's car."

13.

Instant Image

"**Y**OU HEARD ME, I had my bloody car stolen."

"But darling, that's awful." Hilary sounded genuinely concerned. "Where on earth did you leave it?"

"In Hampstead High Street, of all places. I was on my way to work and stopped for the papers. This was in broad daylight!" Harry withdrew a cigarette, remembered that he was trying to quit, then lit it anyway.

"I thought the car was alarmed."

"You don't bother setting it for a newspaper, for God's sake. Anyway, he picked my pocket and took the keys."

"Oh honestly, Harry . . ." He recognized the tone at once. She was blaming him, implying that he was standing idly by while the thief drove off. "Well, what did the police have to say?"

"Quite a lot, as it happens. The chap who stole it made a fairly spectacular job of killing himself just a mile farther down the road."

"What, you mean he actually killed himself *in* the car?"

"Yes. Then it hit a brick wall at about fifty miles an hour."

"Oh my God." There was a brief silence. "I hope it was insured."

"To the hilt."

"Could you get blamed for it?"

Harry was rendered speechless for a few moments. "What—what are you *talking* about, Hilary? How the *hell* could it have been my fault?"

"Perhaps there was something wrong with your brakes."

68

"I don't believe this. Some stupid thief steals my car and kills himself, and you try to tell me that it's *my* fault he's dead?"

"There's no need to be so unpleasant." The temperature of her voice fell. "I don't like your tone, Harry. I don't think it's such a good idea that I meet you tonight."

"Jesus, Hilary, give me a break." Harry ran a hand through his hair, exasperated. "As it is, I've lost another day in the office when I'm supposed to be working on the Schweppes pitch."

"Why, where have you been?"

"I just spent the afternoon in Kentish Town police station, where do you think? This has been the most bizarre week of my life! Even Janice had to agree that I've had a rough time."

"Who is Janice?" The voice prickled icicles.

"She's the police sergeant I met when I was dealing with Willie's accident. Luckily for me she'd just been transferred to the station from Bow Street. She saw me coming in."

"How very convenient that she did. Well Harry, you're obviously very busy. I won't keep you."

"No, Hilary, wait, about tonight . . ."

He found himself holding a dead line.

"I don't know why I'm taking you with me," said Harry as they entered the empty slip road which led from the overpass.

"You're not. I'm taking you. You have no car anymore, remember? You're lucky I even bothered to call you again."

Grace changed gear as the truck approached the monochrome wasteland of the Shepherd's Bush shopping center. Behind them the sky had cleared. A low sun threw amber spears across the broad tarmac, causing shreds of embedded glass to glitter past the rear windshield.

"Have you wondered why he chose your car to kill himself?" She removed her eyes from the road long enough to look at him. He had not noticed the color of her eyes before. They were deep green, like the coldest part of the sea. "Maybe it was more than just a coincidence."

"I don't see how." Harry did not hold with conspiracy theory. He watched as Grace smoothly switched traffic lanes and turned the truck toward the river. There was a loose-limbed elegance in the way she moved that he found appealing. She quickly noticed his attention.

"Why do we have to see this man on a Friday evening?" she asked.

"Why, do you have something better to do?"

"Yup. Go to the pictures. I go every Friday. Most Saturdays and Sundays, too."

"And what do you see?"

"Anything. Everything. Thrillers, sci-fi, art movies, horror. I never buy a ticket."

"Then how do you get in?"

"I walk in as everyone else is walking out. It works. You should try it sometime."

"I don't have to."

"All the more reason. I collect the posters."

"Which I suppose you steal from the foyer as you leave."

"Exactly. I am attracted to the lurid and the sensational, to areas of questionable taste. That's probably why I like you. This must be the place."

Despite the narrowness of the suburban side street, Grace adroitly maneuvered the vehicle into a tight space. They checked the address as they climbed down from the cab. Harry doubted that Brian Lack would be able to shed any light on the circumstances of his father's death. As he unlocked the neatly painted garden gate, he turned to Grace. "Try not to say or do anything. We don't want to cause any trouble."

She threw a furious look at him as she rang the doorbell. Chimes sounded in the hall.

"You made jolly good time for a Friday evening," said Brian as he opened the door. He was wearing a plastic apron with SHE'S THE BOSS! written across it. "The rush-hour traffic on the Westway would test the patience of a saint." He unsnapped a rubber glove and shook Harry's hand. "Sorry, I was just doing the washing-up."

"This is Miss Crispian." Harry introduced his companion.

"Charmed, I'm sure," said Brian uncertainly. He directed them to a pair of grotesque floral armchairs in the lounge. "The wife's out at her batik class," he said, "but I'm sure I can muster up a pot of tea." He waddled off to the kitchen, leaving the pair seated beneath an array of homemade shelving units.

"He must spend his weekends cruising do-it-yourself superstores," whispered Grace. "Harry, you have to get me out of here." She mimed choking. "Somebody call the Decor Police and tell them it's an emergency."

"Try to behave yourself for half an hour and we might find out something," said Harry, looking around. "I know what you mean, though."

Tea was served and consumed. "Your father will be greatly missed," said Brian cheerfully.

"You saw him not long before he died, didn't you? You said he was in excellent spirits."

"Oh, top-hole, first class, absolutely."

"Yet on the day of his accident, he acted in a way which suggests that he was disturbed about something. I can only imagine there was some kind of problem preying on his mind. Have you any idea what this could have been?"

"Willie had no reason to be upset." Brian shook his head slowly in a parody of puzzlement. "Quite the opposite, in fact."

"What do you mean?"

"Someone had just put in a very generous offer to buy the company, and we had more or less decided to accept it. The other remaining director is due back at the office on Monday, and she has already indicated to me that the takeover should go ahead."

"What exactly does your company do?" asked Grace, eyeing the hand-crocheted tray cloth beneath her cup with distaste.

"Instant Image is a video duplication service. We handle transfers. For example, we can take a one-inch master tape and make a hundred simultaneous copies from it."

"How many of you are employed there?"

Brian counted on his fingers. "Secretary, booking clerk, loggers, and three duplicators, plus the three directors, two of them—your father and Mrs. Cleveland—part-time."

"You're not talking about Beth Cleveland, the one who attended my father's funeral?"

"Indeed. Willie brought her into the business last year. She's an extremely efficient administrator. I assumed you knew about her."

"I only knew that she was shacking up with the old man."

"I believe they were living together, yes." He balked at Harry's turn of phrase.

Grace looked up. "You said she was away."

"Beth took a few days off . . . you understand. This has been very inconvenient. The company is going through an extremely busy period. Actually, we have part-ownership in a number of video-related facility houses in the Soho area."

"So selling off this particular company would pose no problem?"

"Quite the reverse. There's a lot of money to be made, so it's no problem at all. That is, except for the question of your father's share. As you know, in the event of his death you are nominated to handle the dispersal of his business affairs."

"No," said Harry, "I had no idea. It's not something we ever discussed."

"Technically speaking, we'll need your signature before the proposed takeover can go ahead. It's merely a formality, of course."

Brian's eyes shone bright with the thought of so much profit to be made. Grace gave Harry a grimace of disapproval. She was obviously anxious to leave. He thanked Brian for the tea and led her from the cluttered lounge.

"I don't get it," said Harry as they drove back into town. "He was about to make a fortune by selling his share of the company. Willie had every reason to be happy."

"Unless he had a reason for not wanting to sell."

"You never knew my father. If a mugger had held a gun to his head and said 'Your money or your life' he'd have tried to do a deal with the guy."

"Maybe that's it. Something threatened his life."

Harry dismissed the idea with a wave of his hand. But the possibility rose in his mind and refused to go away for the rest of the journey home.

14.

Blaze

"YOUR LANDLADY WAS sure that I'd find you here."
A tall figure dressed in a smart navy blazer and cream slacks was approaching on the concourse which ran between the litter-filled basins of the fountains. John May had managed to track him down, and on a Sunday, too.

"Mrs. Sorrowbridge?" Arthur Bryant awoke from the torpor induced by the watery afternoon sunlight and reluctantly surrendered part of the park bench to his partner. "Alma always seems to know where I am. Interfering old hag. I'm beginning to wonder if news of my whereabouts isn't posted somewhere." He sat upright on the bench and shoved the ancient trilby back above his eyes, entirely unembarrassed at being caught in his old gardening clothes. Behind them, dark water slapped against stone as the Thames rose on a high spring tide. In front lay a large area of derelict concrete. Rusty fountains thrust up through the paving stones like huge metallic weeds. Few people bothered to visit this part of Battersea Park anymore. Most preferred the playing fields and floral walkways farther to the west.

Bryant lived nearby in a small but elegantly furnished flat. He was one of the few original inhabitants remaining in an area now usurped by disinterested young professionals.

"They held the Festival of Britain here," he said, gesturing at the wasteland ahead of them. "Nineteen fifty-one. I visited it several times. Pavilions, exhibitions, inventions. There was a walkway through the tops of the trees, filled with great paper dragons. In front of us was a lake of fountains spraying misty blue water. Look at it now." He thrust his hands back into his pockets.

May knew that it was better to let him remember the past before interrupting with news of the present. "We were still in Whitechapel then," he said. "We never came to the festival. I can't think why. It must have been great fun."

"Good God, not at all!" exclaimed Bryant, suddenly animated. "It was absolutely bloody ghastly. There were slogans everywhere, 'Power and Light,' 'Forward with Britain,' 'Look to the Future.' You never saw anything so ugly in all your life. Great swirls of wrought iron painted in Union Jack colors. Giant molecules, italic lettering, and spiky concrete pots. It was supposed to show the shape of things to come. Instead, it looked like the Russians had flicked through a few old sci-fi comics and designed the future on a limited budget." Bryant rose and beckoned his partner to join him beside the empty concrete lake. "They meant well, of course. They wanted to cheer us up after the war. The new Elizabethan age approached. A grotesque tin phoenix, rising from the ashes. Was there ever an era quite so impoverished and depressing as Britain in the fifties?"

"Come along, Arthur, things weren't that bad."

"No? There was a ridiculous thing over there," Bryant pointed at the side of the park, "a space needle, the 'Skylon,' three hundred feet high and held in place with wires. You could see it for miles. Cynics used to say that it was like Britain after the war, staying up without visible means of support."

"But surely it was intended as a symbol of our indomitable spirit, countered May. A representation of the nation's indestructibility. What happened to the treewalk?"

"It fell down."

"Oh. What about the rest of the buildings?"

"They kept the bits which didn't fall down and used them for a funfair. Then that fell down and now it's just somewhere to sit and get molested."

May decided that it was time to bring the conversation into the present. He tried to sound as casual as possible. "I was doing some thinking about our case," he said. "Our drowned man. Trying to understand two things."

"What he was doing in the insect house at night."

"That's one."

"Why he had barricaded himself into his apartment and rebuilt it."

"That's the other."

"I was wondering about that before you arrived." Bryant also seemed happy to change the subject. "The concierge wasn't much help, was he?"

"As he said, Dell was perfectly within his rights to remodel his apartment. His lease allowed him that. Nobody on the outside could have known just how drastic his plans were. He certainly wasn't expecting any visitors."

"You're wrong. I think he was trying to keep someone or something out. Nobody destroys their own home unless they're crazy or scared. I drew a blank at the zoo, by the way. Nobody saw Dell enter the insect house. There are footprints on the outer wall, and the keeper agrees that he must have climbed over. The lock on the main door had been forced. The spider case was smashed, and several glass segments bear Dell's prints. But if he was going to kill himself, why pick such a grotesque method?"

"You're telling me that no crime has been committed beyond a simple B and E, and an act of vandalism?"

"It looks that way."

As they walked, May withdrew some papers from his pocket. "The piece of card in Dell's hand, the one with the symbols on. I ran it through the computer, without much luck."

"Ah *ha*!" Bryant laughed, his theory about the uselessness of technology proven.

"It just means that the lettering doesn't come from a

language in common use. I'm trying to match it with archaic alphabets, but we need to find an expert.''

"You mean you need to have someone do it the old-fashioned way, by looking in a book. Ha.'' Bryant walked on ahead. May narrowed his eyes at the detective's retreating back.

"There's something else. Since I had already encoded the symbols onto a disk, I decided to input all data concerning the crime into a special LAN program, access the past month's crime files for Central London, and run a match.''

"You're talking gibberish, John. I'm hearing nonsense.''

May sighed. "I asked the computer to see if anyone had filed a case with any similarities. It came up with this.'' He passed a single typed sheet to Bryant.

"David Coltis, twenty-six, criminal record as long as your arm, kills himself by arranging to have his head torn off. Arthur Meadows, fifty-seven, no criminal record—not even a parking violation—kills himself and three others on a reckless-driving spree. Both of them had pieces of paper in their pockets bearing symbols that match the ones found on Henry Dell.''

"But you're talking about freak accidents, John, *suicides*. Not murders.''

"I know. That's the puzzle. If you've an hour to spare, I'd like you to come with me to Dell's video store.''

"I thought we already sent some lads there. The place was clean. I saw the report.''

"Dell's note, the one with the symbols, was printed on a particular kind of high-gloss paper. Two-fifty GSM laminated stock. They use it to make the advertising jackets for video boxes. Dell had over six hundred video titles in his store. I want to go through his inventory.''

Bryant perked up. "I'll drive.''

May eyed him steadily. "We'll go by tube,'' he said.

Emerging from the station into a deserted Finchley Road, the store proved easy enough to locate. They could hardly have missed it. A nest of writhing hosepipes covered the flooded pavement in front of the shop. The building had been gutted by fire. Smoke still billowed from the smashed windows, filling the air with the acrid smell of smoldering plastic. May pushed his way to the front of the crowd and identified himself to one of the firemen. "What happened here?" he shouted. "When was the alarm raised?"

"About an hour ago. The whole structure is damaged, but we think it started on the ground floor or in the basement. That's where the flames were first spotted."

"In the video store, you mean?"

"That's right."

May knew that the shop had been locked up since its owner died. The smell of plastic hanging in the air suggested that it had not yet been cleared of stock. "Have you any idea what the cause could have been?" he asked.

"Electrical, possibly," replied the fireman. "It's too early to tell. We haven't been down to the basement yet. Two of my men are in there at the moment checking to see if it's safe to use the stairs."

May pushed back toward the diminutive figure in the battered trilby. "It looks like we're too late. Our boys found nothing suspicious when they went over the place? No illegal merchandise? Dell wasn't dealing in porno, video nasties, anything like that?"

"Not that they could see. I asked them to log the names of all the video distribution companies featured on the boxes so that we could double-check."

"At least that gives us a start point tomorrow."

"We should take a look inside." Bryant approached one of the firemen emerging from the store and spoke to him for a few minutes. Finally he beckoned his partner. "They say it will be all right if one of their men accompanies us."

"Don't touch the walls," warned their guide. "They're still hot."

The interior of the store was crusted with ebony ash, and appeared almost as formless as Dell's apartment. None of the shelves or counters had survived the blaze. Water dripped eerily from the ceiling, as if they had entered a subterranean cavern.

"We're not going to find anything in here," said May

uneasily. The floor was shifting beneath his feet in black miasmic pools. The fireman shone his torch doubtfully onto the stairway ahead.

"Can we go down?" asked Bryant.

"The treads are steel," he pointed out. "They're solid. But I wouldn't if I were you. The ceiling doesn't look too strong." The fireman's words came too late. Bryant was already on his way. Below ground level the air was more acrid and burned their eyes. Their torches picked out walls of melted black plastic hanging in ductile stalactites.

"This is where the bulk of the stock was kept," said Bryant. "There's not much left of it. Lend me your torch, would you?" He shone the beam across the flooded floor, then crunched off between the steel shelving stacks.

"You should stay close to us, Mr. Bryant," called the fireman. "These ceiling panels could come down at any time."

"I'll just be a minute."

He crouched at the base of a shattered storage unit and tugged at the white square illuminated in his torch beam. Raising the sodden scrap of paper to the light, he found himself staring at a familiar set of hierogrammatic markings.

"Over here, John. More symbols, just like the ones found on Dell, Meadows, and Coltis." He had turned back to study the paper further when a blackened arm dropped heavily onto his shoulder. Shouting with fright, he overbalanced and sat back in the water as the burned body rolled out from between the shelves.

"Jesus, where did he come from?" asked the fireman, arriving at his side. May followed and knelt down. The melted plastic boxes of the videocassettes had dripped in the heat and coagulated on the boy's skin. His hair was completely burnt away. They tore open the scorched fabric of his shirt and checked for a heartbeat.

"I don't believe this," said the fireman. "He's still alive. Barely."

"Why didn't he suffocate?" asked Bryant.

"He'd crawled between the shelves." May pointed to

the spot where the boy had lain. ''There's an extractor fan in the wall. It kept him alive.''

''Let's just hope we can do the same,'' said Bryant.

15.

Conundrum

JANICE LONGBRIGHT SEATED herself on the far side of the desk, crossed her seamed nylons, and watched as John May tacked through the busy open-plan office, stopping briefly to greet his colleagues and to collect a large envelope from the young Asian programmer who sat hunched in front of her console. The cheerful yellow tie he wore was a thoughtful gesture. Longbright had presented the dapper detective with it on the last occasion that they had worked together.

''I don't usually make tea for men,'' she pointed out as he entered, ''but I'll make an exception for you today.''

''It's my charm, isn't it?'' said May with a smile.

''No, the teaboy's off with varicose eczema. Isn't Arthur joining us?''

''My colleague is determined to carry out part of the Dell investigation by himself,'' he said, tearing open the envelope. He had decided to let Bryant have his way, if only to keep his mind on the job and away from thoughts of retirement. Besides, he had worked with Sergeant Longbright on several major investigations in the past, and found her refusal to accept easy solutions immensely refreshing. Longbright was well liked by her colleagues, who nevertheless avoided her socially because of her long-standing affair with one of the toughest senior officers at the station. Everyone speculated about her torrid nights with Detective Inspector Ian Hargreave. The affair was the force's most poorly kept secret, yet the two of them crept furtively into the building from different directions each morning and seemed genuinely unaware that everyone knew they had spent the night together.

"I've read the case file," said Longbright, "just tell me what I can do."

May laid the contents of his envelope on the desk before him. "I need to make some connections. We have to find the line between a small-time thief and a couple of respectable, prosperous businessmen. Check and see if Coltis or Meadows ever bought or rented videotapes from Henry Dell's store. Go through their backgrounds and see if their paths could have crossed anywhere. I also want you to check all the companies who regularly supplied Dell with rental tapes. See if any of them are involved in anything shady. Bryant is contacting an expert in esoteric languages, ancient handwriting, a—what do you call them?"

"A paleographer."

"That's the ticket. He's going to show him the hieroglyphics we found in Dell's basement. It looks pretty much the same as the pieces we found on the bodies, but those are both out with forensics. We need to establish a time and date of origin for all three notes—and, of course, it would be nice to know what they say. You'd better keep in touch with Arthur to see how he's doing, although I warn you he has an irritating habit of working from home and leaving his phone off the hook."

"I'll see if I can get him to wear a beeper."

"Forget it, I've already tried that. He dropped the last one down the toilet before he had a chance to use it. Assured me that it was an accident."

Janice laughed. "I'll find a way to keep tabs on him, don't worry. What are these?" She pointed to the data sheets laid out on the desk.

"Something else that's been bothering me. I extended the data match on deaths in the Central London area to cover the past two months and left the computer on search. I reasoned that if our suicides were somehow linked, we might gather more evidence from a study of other so-called 'marginal' cases. The program has revealed a whole stack of accidental deaths, not one of which has yet been confirmed as a homicide.''

''You think some of them might be related?''

''It looks that way. If we were dealing with three clear-cut murder cases here—and we're not, because the Meadows case is beyond our jurisdiction—we wouldn't be surprised to find corroborative evidence linking them. But each victim died by his own hand! I mean, Dell was poisoned because he appears to have broken into a zoo and thrust his mitts into a display case filled with poisonous spiders, for God's sake—unless someone else forced him to do it at gunpoint, which seems unlikely. Yet there *has* to be an outside party involved. Why would he brick himself into his apartment if he wasn't trying to keep someone out?''

''You're right, it makes no sense,'' agreed Longbright. ''How many other possible related deaths did the computer turn up?''

In reply, May held the data sheets aloft and released one end. To her amazement, the perforated sheets flipped open until they touched the floor.

Arthur Bryant pulled his scarf a little tighter over his nose and knocked again. He knew there was someone at home. He could hear the doctor clumping about inside. It was freezing out here. Why Kirkpatrick was refusing to let him in was a mystery. He hammered on the basement door for the third time. Suddenly a gaunt gray face appeared beneath the net curtains at a nearby window, then vanished. A moment later bolts were drawn back and the door swung wide.

''My dear fellow, I am so terribly sorry! Contrite! Repentant!'' The doctor clasped Bryant's arm with both hands. ''What a surprise!'' He led the way indoors.

''I was standing on your step for ages,'' grumbled Bryant. ''It's below zero this morning, or perhaps you hadn't noticed.''

''I couldn't hear a thing. Had the Walkman on.'' He gestured at the headphones fixed around his scrawny neck. The gloomy interior of the basement was a literary Aladdin's cave which acted as an extension of his mind.

Books of every size, color, and description lay in stacks across the room like Colorado rock formations. All four walls were lined with overflowing shelves which seemed to absorb the light and render the room intensely claustrophobic.

The doctor threw a stack of *Scientific Review* back issues from a seat and gestured to Bryant. "You should get one of these things," he said, switching off his personal stereo. "I always listen to it while I'm researching."

Bryant eyed the device suspiciously. "I suppose a nice piece of Mendelssohn could help to focus the mind," he conceded.

"Mendelssohn? Good Lord, no! Heavy metal. I find it gets the blood circulating. Meat Loaf was always my favorite, *Bat Out of Hell* and all that. Now I've grown quite fond of Def Leppard."

Dr. Raymond Kirkpatrick gave a broad grin, and in doing so looked not a little mad. Tall, gray, and stooped, dressed in a ragged old sweater, he actually seemed to be covered in dust, although on closer inspection this proved to be merely an apposite illusion. The doctor rarely left his cluttered basement these days. He was a kindly soul who lived for the study of semantics, a recognized expert whose papers on the changing role of the modern English language were renowned throughout the world. The police often sought him out when they were unable to decipher the latest street slang.

"What can I do for you?" he asked. "I'm always ready to help you chaps, although of course I disapprove of such a totalitarian concept as policing *per se*. Where's the other one?" He waved a bony gray hand at a space two feet to the left of Bryant.

"The other what?" asked Arthur, mystified.

"You are usually binary. Duplex. You always travel in a pair. Like bookends. Castor and Pollux."

"Oh, you mean John, my partner. He's following his own leads on this." Bryant pulled the page of hieroglyphics from his overcoat pocket. "I need your opinion on this. All I know is that it's not from any alphabet in common usage." He passed the note to Kirkpatrick, who donned a pair of thick spectacles and studied it with his long nose almost touching the paper.

"An enigma! A cryptographic conundrum! Totally wicked, as recent street parlance would have it." He crossed to a wall of books and ran his fingers lightly over their spines, as if reading the titles by braille. "I think I have something here which may help."

With great difficulty he pulled free a heavy volume and set it on the table with a thump. "These configurations are very old, very old indeed." He riffled through the pages of the book with practiced ease and stopped at a particular chapter. Bryant sat forward, alert, as Kirkpatrick carefully traced over the photocopied lines with the tip of his Biro.

"This has many of the characteristics of an ancient language. The alphabet looks Etruscan, first or second century B.C. I should imagine, although the sentence structure—if that's what it is—doesn't appear at all familiar."

"What area are we talking about, geographically?"

"The Etruscans lived in northern Italy." He examined the lettering again, comparing the page against the book. "No, the characters are Etruscan but the language is something else, possibly Gothic. The Goths lived nearby, of course, so it's quite likely. I don't know, though. It doesn't look like an actual *language* to me. Even without translating the individual characters, the word groupings look wrong, out of balance. And it's very angular. That's extremely unusual. It's been written from right to left, you'll notice." Bryant had not noticed. "One only finds that in the most ancient alphabets, like Hebrew. It certainly predates Christianity."

Kirkpatrick looked up from the page and removed his spectacles. "Can you leave this with me?" he asked. "I doubt I'll be able to get a translation much beyond a general gist of things, a tenor, a pith as it were, but I'd like to give it a try. Where did you discover it?"

"Not *it*, *them*. They're turning up on corpses."

"All the same?"

"The lettering looks similar in each case, but the messages are of different lengths," said Bryant, rising from his armchair and accidentally dislodging a pile of paperbacks with his arm. "Presumably they're threats, and they cause their victims to panic after receiving them. They aren't identical, so they must mean different things to each recipient, none of whom have anything in common, by the way."

"Are you sure about this?" Kirkpatrick seemed doubtful. "How odd."

"Odd indeed. A car thief, a video dealer, and a businessman, none of them with university educations, killing themselves after translating a bit of Etruscan-Gothic. Whatever happened to good old easy-to-solve trunk murders?"

"If anyone knew, Arthur, I'm sure it would be you. I'll call you as soon as I have something. And don't be such a stranger. I hardly ever see you or John these days."

"That's because you hardly ever see anyone, you miserable old hermit." Kirkpatrick stood at the bottom of the narrow basement steps and watched as the elderly detective climbed slowly to the top. Then, as if this brief glimpse of daylight had proven too much for him, he hurried back into the penumbral comfort of his study.

16.
Slattery

EDEN WAS THE embodiment of late-sixties style. She looked, walked, and talked like the kind of Technicolor starlet who featured in romantic Riviera comedies, theme music by Matt Monroe. Her lipstick and nails were of palest coral, her breasts ebullient beneath her polka-dot bolero blouse. She scoured suburban dress shops for old stock, filling her wardrobe with fetishistic fragments of the past.

At her desk she posed in toreador tights and pedal pushers, elasticized peek-a-boo ribbon-knits, and rayon acetate empire-waisted traffic stoppers trimmed in marabou. She typed slowly and could not read shorthand. She had trouble making coffee. Her hair was a starched honey blond, Jane Fonda in *Barbarella*. She was seventeen, and not as dumb as she looked.

Eden had wanted to work for a fashion house, but found herself employed in a similar position where looks counted more than ability, as a secretary in an ad agency typing reports for Harry and his colleagues. Many of the account men who passed her desk, men whose moral senses were tilted by the nature of their profession, assumed her to be sexually available. Eden was smart enough to realize that their assumption freed her to do whatever she wanted. And all she wanted to do at the moment was read her magazine.

"Come on, Edie, you have to cover for me. Telling lies is practically part of your job description." Harry looked at his watch, then checked the hall to see if Sharpe was in sight. Eden had attended an extremely loud rock concert the night before, and was having great difficulty deciphering Harry's speech through the tintinnabulation of her recovering eardrums. He appeared to be desperate. It was a look she saw regularly on the faces of older men. Eden knew about older men. She was seeing one at the moment. He was twenty.

"He'll be here any second. Listen carefully. When Sharpe finds out that I've gone missing, he'll go red in the face. He'll want to know where I am. Tell him I'm under doctor's orders."

"What shall I say is wrong with you?"

He thought for a second. "Stomach cramps."

"He's going to shout. I hate it when he shouts because it's all swearing."

"I'll make it up to you, Edie. I'll take you to dinner."

"I don't eat, Harry. Waistline."

He had a brainwave. "I'll buy you shoes." Her eyes lit up. He knew no woman could resist new shoes.

"I have my eye on a pair of satin-quilted cossack loungers."

"Fine. Now get out there and lie through those perfect teeth."

"You've got it."

In the taxi, he examined the paperwork once again. He was sure they could not proceed without his vote, but the fact that the directors of Instant Image had called an emergency meeting suggested that they had an ace up their collective sleeve. Unfortunately, the meeting coincided with Sharpe's soft-drink presentation.

The more Harry thought about Grace's parting remark, the more he was sure that Willie had discovered a reason for not surrendering his share. It was a discovery that had affected his behavior, and had ultimately caused his death. There could be no other explanation. Until some kind of solution presented itself he was determined to stand against the merger.

Brian Lack was furious. His amiable manner had tightened up like hardening ice, but as he did not know any other way to behave, he continued to be polite. Harry declined the only spare chair in the cluttered Greek Street office as he explained the reason for withholding his vote.

"I don't want to screw up your deal," he explained, "but I'd like to be sure that I'm carrying out my father's wishes. Obviously, I'm anxious to sort out the situation as quickly as possible."

Brian Lack clearly thought him mad. This man had shown no interest in his father's affairs before—why should he start now? He decided that he was probably acting under the influence of that crazy-looking girl.

On the other side of the room, Beth Cleveland studied them dispassionately and made copious notes in an office diary.

"I consider your decision to be somewhat premature, Mr. Buckingham," Brian complained. "You haven't yet been made aware of the terms of the offer. The representative of the interested party is due here any minute, and I know he'll be extremely upset when I inform him of the delay. He made us a very generous offer, and there is a time restriction upon us to complete the deal."

"How long have they given you?"

"Until tomorrow night." The voice came from the doorway of the office. Harry turned to find himself facing a balding, gingery man in his late forties. Even his eyes appeared ginger, as if someone had shaken pepper into them. He carried a large black attaché case at one side, like a saddlebag.

"At midnight tomorrow I am instructed to withdraw the offer. It will not be re-presented, that I can assure you."

The arrogance in his voice made Harry bristle. "Who are you?" he asked.

"This is Mr. Slattery," said Brian, hastily interposing. "He's the lawyer representing the ODEL Corporation."

"ODEL is behind the bid? The communications company?" Across the table, Beth Cleveland nodded. "Why would such a huge multinational be interested in a tiny firm like this?"

Slattery walked into the room and drew out a chair. He seemed familiar with his surroundings. As he sat, he turned to give Harry a careful examination. This was obviously the first time someone had questioned any aspect of the offer. "And your name is . . . ?" he asked.

"Harry Buckingham. My father was a partner of the company."

"Ah yes." Slattery's manner implied that he had heard of Harry, and the report had not been favorable. "Well, Instant Image is a solid, profitable concern with an attractive client list. If you know anything at all about us, you'll realize that this is exactly the sort of company the ODEL Corporation likes to build up."

"That's bullshit," said Harry. "I've looked at the figures on this place. With respect to the other partners, it's a small-time operation. Its turnover is low, and most of its equipment appears to be obsolete." He was glad that the Cleveland woman had delivered his father's papers. At least he was familiar with the company's production figures. "There are a dozen places like this in Soho. How much are you offering?"

Slattery gave Brian Lack a measured look as he replied. "Two-point-five million pounds to merge the company and take it public."

Harry released a guffaw of disbelief. "Are you insane? Who could possibly have authorized you to go to such a figure?"

"The managing director himself," replied Slattery. "Daniel Carmody."

Curiouser still, thought Harry. Carmody's photograph constantly appeared in *Campaign, Broadcast* and other industry magazines. The man was a *Fortune* 100 heavyweight, a designer-suited captain of the communications industry. He walked through life shedding lawsuits. Not someone to tangle with lightly, thought Harry. He needed time to think.

"Tell me, Mr. Slattery, is it normal business practice to offer such large amounts of money as inducements to sell?"

"I hardly think that concerns you," answered the lawyer. "I understand that you possess your voting share by default. You know nothing about this company. And you have no right to deprive the other directors of their chance to make a healthy profit."

"I have the right to conform to my father's wishes."

"Then it's up to the other partners to make you change your mind."

"What do you suggest they do, beat me up?"

Brian appeared to be in great discomfort. Clearly this conversation had passed beyond the boundaries of what he considered to be good taste. "I'm sure we can prevail upon Mr. Buckingham to reconsider his verdict in a civilized way," he offered lamely.

"I hope so," said the lawyer, clearly ruffled. "Mr. Carmody is on the boards of over sixty corporations and nearly forty registered charities. He is an extremely busy man, but he has taken a personal interest in this transaction, and is anxious to proceed in the swiftest possible manner."

"Why is he prepared to offer us a sum way beyond our market price? What's he up to? Is there some kind of under-the-counter deal here that I don't know about?"

The lawyer's eyes reddened further as his composure

flickered. "Daniel Carmody's integrity as a businessman is beyond reproach. He is not used to having his generosity questioned, and is prepared to safeguard his reputation in court if necessary. ODEL is a highly respected corporation that will not be treated in a cavalier fashion. I came here today to represent Mr. Carmody's interests at the directors' meeting in good faith. You still have until tomorrow night to confirm your decision."

"I'll tell you one thing, Mr. Slattery. I'm beginning to understand my father's reservations about your client. Clearly you can see that we need more time before reaching a unanimous decision. I want you to request an extension to the deadline."

After the meeting, Brian Lack refused to talk to him and Mrs. Cleveland stayed behind in the boardroom making notes.

Harry realized he was an obstacle that nobody wanted, but the situation gave him a bad feeling. He hoped he'd be able to explain his objection to the others, though the luminous greed which shone in Brian Lack's eyes whenever money was mentioned suggested that he would meet with little success.

He decided to cut his losses and head home rather than risk walking in on the aftermath of Sharpe's client presentation. He rang Eden from the reception desk.

"Sharpe's going completely crazy," she warned. "He had to do the presentation by himself and it went really badly. Also, he saw what was left of your company car on the news. I told him you'd been taken ill."

"How did he handle it?"

"He's talking about replacing you on the account."

"Maybe I should call him and explain. Where is he now?"

"Locked in his office with a bottle of Scotch listening to old Neil Diamond tapes."

"Sounds bad."

"He seems to like them."

"Cute. He only does that when he's about to fire someone. I owe you one, Edie. Don't forget to give me your shoe size."

He replaced the receiver and was about to leave the building when he was called back.

"I'm glad I caught you," said Beth Cleveland. Her voice had a surprisingly gentle lilt. "You can understand that Brian is very upset with this development. All the same, I can't help thinking that you're right to ask for extra time."

Harry smiled and held out his hand. "Perhaps we should get to know one another a little better," he said. It would prove useful to have an ally within the company. "I'll stand you a drink if you have time."

Surprised and pleased, she accepted.

They walked to a small, comfortably furnished club situated in an alleyway behind the Coliseum in St. Martin's Lane.

Beth excused herself and returned a few minutes later with her hair loosened from its customary tight bun. The effect softened the contours of her face and humanized her. Perhaps the forbidding demeanor she adopted on formal occasions was a matter of protective camouflage. As their drinks arrived they moved to a brace of leather armchairs and sat beside the small coal fire.

"Your father wasn't an easy man. I'm sure I don't need to tell you that." She watched the flames flicker in the grate. "But he was good to me. And I stood by him. He was happy to include me in his business affairs. No man had ever let me do that before. He saw that I enjoyed it, and he wanted to please me. When he offered me a part-time directorship of the company, I jumped at the chance."

"How did the ODEL group first get in touch with you?" asked Harry.

"Brian Lack had done some business with them in the past."

"What kind of business?"

"I'm not sure. He was reluctant to talk to me about it. I have a feeling it might have been something vaguely illegal."

"So you think Brian might be returning the favor by taking ODEL's side in the buyout?"

Beth shrugged and sipped her whiskey. "It's a fantastic opportunity. He'd be crazy not to."

"So how come you have reservations?"

Beth's face suddenly grew animated. "The whole thing stinks, Harry. Brian made some deal with these people and got his fingers burned. Willie knew more about it than he told me. ODEL went through Brian to approach us with the bid. It seemed like the opportunity of a lifetime. Slattery pitched to each of us in turn."

"What did that involve?"

"He went through the figures, promised us the earth if we agreed to cooperate. It was almost evangelical, like getting a presentation from the Moonies. He made us watch some awful short film called *ODEL—The Way to the Future*. I know it sounds irrational, but he gave me the creeps. Willie didn't buy the deal and neither did I. Then . . . Slattery doubled the offer."

"Let me get this straight. You considered the deal, turned them down, and then they came back to you?"

"No. They doubled the money purely because we hesitated for a moment. And you know what? I had the feeling that they would have doubled it again if we'd asked them."

Harry watched the fire shimmer in his glass. "Maybe we shouldn't look a gift horse in the mouth."

"Your father did." Beth stared down at the flames. "He was quite proud of you, in his own way. He talked about you a lot. Now I can understand why." She pointed to Harry's hands. "That habit you have of tugging at your watchstrap, he used to do that. You remind me of him so much."

Harry studied his hands. "I must have picked it up from him."

They sat in silence for a moment and watched the fire.

"I think they killed Willie," said Beth quietly. "I don't understand how, but they did. I want people to know. I want him back."

"Nobody can bring him back," replied Harry. "But we can prevent ODEL from getting what they want." He caught her eyes and held them. "You want to give his death some kind of meaning?"

"Tell me what to do," said Beth.

They bade each other farewell in the doorway of the club as a light rain began to darken the side of the building. Beth had agreed to search Brian Lack's desk for confidential documents relating to the ODEL offer. Maybe they would find something damning enough to reveal to the relevant authorities.

"There's one thing I regret," he said as they took their leave. "That's not getting to know you earlier."

"At least we can be friends now," said Beth. "Willie would have been pleased with that." Harry smiled. Perhaps the old man would have more to feel pleased about by the time they had finished. As Beth Cleveland strode off through the drizzle in the direction of Charing Cross Station, the black Mercedes which had been waiting for her to emerge flicked on its sidelights and pulled away from the curb, following her at a safe distance.

17.

The Arrival of Evil

"SOMEONE ELSE MUST have noticed this." Dorothy studied the graph-paper chart. With her gray hair tied in a bun and a woolen cardigan draped over her narrow shoulders, she appeared more like a pensioner checking for the latest romance novel.

Frank sat up from his clippings and rubbed his eyes. "I don't know," he said. "The odds are way out. It's exactly the kind of thing I was looking for, and yet . . ." He trailed the sentence off, perplexed by his own discovery.

Rain slashed against the skylight windows far above them. Ten-thirty on a dark Tuesday morning. No customers had yet braved the elements. Dorothy had been forced to switch the lights on in the main hall of the library.

"Frank, you've got fifty-seven suicides and self-mutilations listed here." She examined the network of colored lines, attempting to interpret Frank's spidery annotations. The cluster of red ink dots which dominated the center of the graph represented a shift away from any rational set of statistics. "What time scale is this over?"

"Six weeks. If I could hack into hospital files or one of the police nets I'd be able to fill the data gaps."

"Could you break these numbers down into social categories, the way advertising companies do?"

"Difficult. According to various newspaper reports, quite a few were professional males, city types. An equal number were in communications."

"High-stress jobs. Have you started writing this up for your book?"

"I've made stacks of notes. There were more oddities this weekend. The *Telegraph* carried a report of a computer engineer who committed suicide by sealing his nostrils and lips together with superglue. There often seems to be a confusion about the circumstances of death in these stories. The verdicts are left open due to lack of evidence. I need to break into a decent databank to find out more."

"You realize that the apocalypse is something we're supposed to bring on ourselves, a kind of mass suicide," said Dorothy, pulling her cardigan more tightly around her. It was cold in the hall. The rain pattered endlessly around them.

"This has nothing to do with religious prophecy. It's a social phenomenon."

"I was thinking more of the occult. Something like voodoo. You can make someone have an accident quite easily, so long as you let the victim know he's cursed. It's well documented. Mother had all kinds of books on the subject."

She rose and headed for the darkened stairs at the back of the hall. Although most of the general library sections were depleted, the building's greatest strength lay in the volumes on ancient history and the supernatural which

Dorothy's mother had collected together. A red rope separated the entrance from the public section of the library. The stairs led down to the occult reference collection, housed in the basement.

"Dorothy, there's no need to go down there." Frank shrugged and began to clear his clippings away. Dorothy ignored him. She suffered from selective deafness, an affliction which only appeared when people made suggestions contrary to her wishes.

The overhead light panel flickered on. As the smell of decay filled her nostrils, she took stock of the room. The far wall of the basement had a severe case of rising damp, and most of the stacks nearest to it—TEMPLARS, TETRAGRAMS, THOUGHT READING, TRANSMUTATION—were steeped in mildew. Many of them were arcane oddities published in the forties and fifties, rare enough to be of interest to a handful of collectors, but not, in the eyes of the council authorities, of sufficient value to be rescued from decomposition. Three years ago Dorothy had dried out some of the more unusual volumes, but their pages had become brittle, the prose indecipherable. Now she only ventured between the stacks when a specialist organization ("Your witches are here," Frank would announce) required a particular book. It was sad to see the collection slowly falling apart before her eyes.

Still, who could believe in spirit rappings and second sight in this enlightened technological age? Such shadowy superstitious nonsense had long been subjected to the merciless glare of scientific examination. Evidence from the "other side" had been exposed as simple Victorian parlor trickery. Secret societies had been revealed as mere Masonic cartels, shabby clubs designed to prevent the undesirable classes from trading as equals.

She looked around at the redundant volumes. There wasn't much left to believe in. These days the supernatural was suffering from post-Watergate syndrome. How could the secrets of forgotten religions compare with corporations that were prepared to practice genocide if it meant opening up new markets?

Here, on one whole shelf, were nearly thirty books covering the myths and religions of Haiti and the islands of the Caribbean. Trashy potboilers were sandwiched between serious works of study. The paperback she required had been repaired with tape, which now disintegrated in her hands as she tugged the tome free. Its pages were mottled with damp, but she soon found the passage she sought.

With the moist, cool volume in her hands she walked back to the foot of the stairs. Frank could not be persuaded to venture down here. He said there were rats—he'd seen them dart by at the corners of his vision. There were certainly some very large spiders. But for Dorothy, who remembered many of the books from the days when they occupied the shelves in her mother's study, the reference basement was still a magical place.

"You can curse someone and cause them to have an accident, but both parties have to believe in the power of magic. There's a picture." She held the book aloft and pointed to an engraving of a terrified Negro impaled in a pit of knives.

"That's hardly possible in the city, is it?" said Frank. "Curse someone to fall into a hole full of spears."

"Here's another one." She turned to a plate which depicted a wart-faced crone tumbling into a flaming hearth. "It's not really magic. All you do is make someone so nervous that they eventually do harm to themselves. In some occult systems you invoke a demon to cause the injury, but you must be very careful."

"Why?"

"Because demons are generally regarded as being very stupid, and you have to make sure that your plans don't backfire. There are some *grimoires* downstairs which show you how to do it. I think we still have a copy of the *Pope Honorius*, but it's rather obscure and unreadable."

"Do you actually believe in all this?" asked Frank.

"It's best to keep an open mind. I believe in . . . certain forces."

"The concept of evil hasn't stood the test of time very well."

"I agree. The image of Lucifer astride a pale horse, with the head of a leopard and the wings of a griffin, offers little more than baroque charm. But people still die because they believe in a supreme being. And where there is goodness, you'll find evil.''

"Well, Madame Arcati, what do you think we should do? Go to the police and report a sinister conspiracy at work?''

Dorothy looked perplexed. "I suppose it's just a ridiculous imagining on our part. We could go and see Mrs. Wagstaff. She knows about these things.''

"Is she a statistician?''

"No, a medium.''

"And I suppose she practices the black arts in a remote woodland cottage beset by elves.''

"No, she lives in a council flat on the Isle of Dogs. She's not at all like you'd imagine. Do you believe in alternative medicine?''

"Some of it.''

"Well, think of her as an alternative theologian. Come with me if you want. I'll see if she's free.'' Frank did not respond, but as she reached for the telephone, Dorothy noticed a gleam of interest in his eyes.

Beth Cleveland pushed the cardboard box aside and checked the mantelpiece clock. Nearly six-thirty. She had left the office early in order to finish sorting Willie's belongings. It was an extremely depressing task that she was anxious to complete. She removed his remaining shirts from the wardrobe and had just finished packing them into bundles for the local charity shop when she discovered the heavy sealed envelope lying at the back of the shoe cupboard.

Kneeling forward, she brought it into the light and immediately recognized Willie's handwriting on the front. It read: "Shipment Contact: David Coltis.'' The reverse side was blank. Intrigued, she unstuck the flap and slid the contents of the envelope into her hand.

At seven o'clock that evening, Dorothy and Frank closed the library doors and passed through the rubbish-strewn archway formed by the struts of the adjacent overpass. The rain had eased to a light, fine mist. As they waited for the bus, Dorothy studied her companion. She rarely saw him away from his desk. He looked slight and sad, a pale unremembered face in the crowd. She supposed few people noticed her, either. The old are an invisible rank, she thought. They encourage themselves to be so. The world sidesteps them and moves on. But not me, she thought, stepping onto the bus. Not yet. I still have discoveries to make for myself.

The Isle of Dogs is a peninsula created by a bend in the Thames. In the Middle Ages it had been known as Stepney Marsh. Nobody knew when or why the new name appeared, although it seemed that royal kennels were once kept there. Perhaps, thought Dorothy, the nomenclature was simply a corruption. At the start of the nineteenth century the West India Docks had opened, and a canal had transformed the area into a true island. The Isle of Docks. It seemed a more likely origin for this gloomy, run-down maze of silted canals and humpbacked bridges. In the last few years, the graffiti-spattered tenements had been demolished to make way for the postmodern townhouses of the new city elite. These security-controlled luxury estates had forced their owners into reluctant civil war with the island's original inhabitants. Dorothy and Frank were heading for a neighborhood that clearly fell into the poorer of these two categories.

Edna Wagstaff lived in one of the grimmest remaining council properties. Vandalism had necessitated the boarding-up of the ground floor apartments, yet it was here, incredibly, that the occultist lived.

Dorothy gingerly skirted a pair of feuding feral dogs and stopped before a panel of unmarked chipboard, rapping her knuckles hard on the wood.

"Try not to be too alarmed," she told her companion. "Some people are blessed with a power they can barely control. Edna is a good woman. She's buried two husbands and never missed a day's work, but she's growing old and living alone with her spirits. That's not healthy." She drew Frank closer. "You may find her a little . . . unusual."

There was a protesting groan as the door before them was pulled inward. "Evening Echo told me you'd be late," said Edna, ushering them into a darkened hallway which reeked of incense. The medium was tall and dry and thin, a collection of sticks in a frock and a strangely shaped wig. Introductions were swiftly completed.

"Evening Echo?" asked Frank.

"She's my spirit guide."

"Sounds more like a newspaper," he muttered to Dorothy.

"Oh dear, you've brought me another unbeliever. That could make things difficult." She led the way into the boarded lounge and switched on a heavily shaded lamp.

The room was filled with stuffed cats. Some were standing on their hind legs, glued to wooden squares in awkward human poses. Others were swaggering, leaning on each other in frozen jigs and waltzes. Four tortoise-shell kittens had been arranged in a tableau on the nearby upright piano. They were seated with their paws out-stretched on a little table, playing cards. Far from being comfortably at ease in the pursuit of these feline leisure activities, their screaming mouths and asymmetrically squinting eyes suggested to Frank that they had been sealed for eternity during moments of extreme pain. He wondered if they could give him fleas. He glanced across at Mrs. Wagstaff. Her wig appeared to be on backward. She looked a little like one of her stuffed cats.

"Frank has promised to keep an open mind, Edna." Dorothy stepped back and pressed Frank's toes with the heel of her shoe. "How is Evening Echo keeping?"

"She's not been well," said Edna, pouring three cups of crimson herbal tea. "She's still trying to locate her tribal elders on the astral plane, and her legs are playing her up. I'm not using her much at the moment. I'm going through an RAF pilot called Smethwick, a very obliging chap, although his patriotism is a little trying at times."

"Oh, was he shot down?"

"No, he fell out of a Ferris wheel on Wimbledon Common."

Frank barely managed to stifle a laugh. Edna glared at him.

"Now," she said, "what did you want to know?"

"We're not entirely sure," began Dorothy. She explained the reason for their visit, feeling a little foolish as she did so. The surreal, stifling atmosphere of the room actually lent their tale a kind of twisted plausibility. Edna seemed very interested. She sat forward with her hands clasped together in her lap, giving little nods and squeaks of agreement from time to time.

"I knew it would start soon, I *knew* it," she interrupted, unable to contain herself any longer. "You have just described the first symptom of an event which has long been predicted by reputable occultists the world over."

"Don't tell me Armageddon is approaching," said Frank, his voice reeking of skepticism.

"Nothing so vulgar," said Edna. "No, a slower, subtler change is overtaking us. I can probably coax one of my children to tell you about it." She pointed to the cats which surrounded them. "These are my familiars, my conduits to a world beyond this one. A place where past, present, and future meet in a single fleeting moment of time. Perhaps Kelly here would like to explain what's happening." She sounded like a newscaster handing her viewers over to Westminster for an economic report. The room fell suddenly quiet.

Beyond the boarded windows, Frank could hear the dogs tearing at each other. Edna had closed her eyes and slumped back in her chair. She seemed to have fallen asleep. He tried to attract Dorothy's attention, but could not catch her eye. A full five minutes passed in silence.

The high, strangulated voice, when it came, made Frank jump out of his skin. He turned around and stared at a particularly nasty example of the taxidermist's art, a squashed-looking ginger tom mounted on a wrought-iron bicycle.

"It has long been suggested by the major occult authorities that the Lord of Darkness will return in the latter half of the twentieth century," said the voice. "He will first make known His presence in the Scandinavian countries. In Finland. In Germany. And in Great Britain. He will appear in mortal guise. He will appear not as one, but as many. His name will be Legion." The voice grew more piercing. Frank rubbed his arms. The temperature in the room had begun to fall.

"He will perform the following tasks: The Deception of Fools. The Corruption of the Innocent. The Destruction of the Pure. The Veneration of Evil."

"That's a wide brief, even for Lucifer. He'll find the people of today a lot less ready to believe," said Dorothy. She didn't seem to find it odd that she was discussing occultism with a voice that emanated from a stuffed cat. Quite the reverse—she was clearly familiar with the system. "Tell us, how will He achieve these goals?"

"Through the blind obedience of His disciples."

"What is His new name on earth?"

There was a pause. "It cannot be found in the alphabet of today."

"How will He carry out His will?"

"Through the power of prayer."

Dorothy looked across at Frank, puzzled. Their breath hung in the air as the temperature continued to fall. "You mean through the prayers of His worshipers, or Christian prayer?"

"The Devil's prayers."

"What form do these prayers take?"

"A secret form, both ancient and modern. An evil that will deceive fools, corrupt the innocent—"

"And destroy the pure," continued Frank. "How will it destroy them?"

"Make them die." The voice was starting to fade.

"But how? Can He make it look like an accident?" He stared at the cat but there came no reply. Its marble eyes faced different directions. Needle-toothed, its mouth held the insane rictus of a frozen grin.

"We'll not be getting any more out of him, I fancy," said Dorothy. She rubbed her forearms briskly as chill air continued to circulate through the room. Edna still seemed to be asleep. She rested her head on her bony chest, panting faintly.

"When the Angel of Death has been summoned," said the cat with a startling burst of renewed vigor, "it cannot leave until it has been appeased." The room fell silent again. As the medium came slowly to her senses, Frank eyed the cat warily. He half-expected it to recommence its oratory.

"I hope Kelly was of some use," said Edna, now fully recovered. "He's a very old, reliable familiar. He's not normally wrong." Her arms and legs creaked audibly as she stretched.

"Personally I found him a bit vague," said Dorothy, pouring her friend a fresh cup of tea. Slowly the room was regaining its normal temperature. "If what he says is to be believed, the hordes of Lucifer are heading back to earth, to claim us through the power of their master's prayers."

"You could read anything you like into that." Frank reached down and lifted the cat, checking beneath it for hidden microphones. "It was like the Delphic oracle, all ambiguity and no solid facts."

"I suggest you read your books, Mr. Drake. You'll find all the corroborative facts you need in there." Edna rose unsteadily from the table. She was clearly offended.

"Don't get me wrong," said Frank hastily. "It was very interesting. It just doesn't help us."

"The spirits can't be expected to solve all your problems," snapped Edna. "They're astral entities who occasionally agree to remove the barriers between the living and the dead. It's not a phone-in."

"I'm sure she had that cat wired up to the stereo," said Frank as they left the housing estate. "Maybe she implanted a microchip in its head and turned it to the TV remote."

"Edna's integrity as a spiritualist was renowned throughout South London during the war," said Dorothy. "She located children in the rubble of bombed houses. She reunited families. I should never have brought you with me."

Frank shook his head. "The old girl was right, I'm not a believer. Satan heading back to earth! I dare say she means well. She simply gave you what you wanted to hear."

Dorothy was annoyed. This trip had been largely for Frank's benefit. "Last week you wondered if your suicides had found some way of attracting the angel of death,'' she said.

''Yes, but I didn't mean it literally . . .''

''And now here's a third party . . .''

''Hardly a disinterested one . . .''

''Who tells us that this is *exactly* what is happening.''

''Come on, Dorothy, it's in her interests to promote these . . . forces, it's good for business.''

''She doesn't take money for her services, you saw that.''

''I bet clients bring her gifts. I bet they bring her cats, so she can practice stuffing them. 'Vocal projection through taxidermy.' She could write a book on it.''

They continued to argue until the bus arrived.

She was supposed to destroy the box in the envelope. The instruction was burned on her brain. Beth Cleveland pulled open the neck of her blouse and mopped at the sweat with a handkerchief. She had called Harry at home, but there was no reply. There was no one else she could risk telling. If only she hadn't run the damned thing, but no, her curiosity would not allow her to leave it alone.

She stood in the center of her apartment wondering what the hell to do next. It was dark outside. The wind threw squalls of rain against the windows. She understood now why Willie had died. And why so many others had to die. Harry was in terrible danger. His office said he had left for the night. He had gone out somewhere, but where? She rubbed the heel of her hand across her throbbing forehead. She couldn't risk leaving messages for him. No one could be trusted. Besides, she now had her own instructions to follow.

Beth Cleveland possessed a strong, logical mind. At first she tried to resist the orders, but everything became much easier as soon as she realized that it was useless to fight back. The most important thing now was to destroy the envelope and its contents. But how? There was nothing in the flat that would do the job . . . Then it came to her. Pulling a raincoat over her shoulders, she tucked the package beneath her arm and headed for the street.

* * *

The rain had slickened the grassy slope and made it difficult to maintain a foothold. She tried to dig in her heels as she ascended, but several times she fell hard onto the bank. The rain was battering her back, but she could now see that there was only a short distance left to climb.

Minutes later, smothered in mud, she reached the summit. Now, she wondered, where would be the best place? Picking her way over the concrete sleepers, she arrived at the junction of several lines. Behind lay the lights of King's Cross Station. Ahead, the railway tracks ran off into darkness, parallel lines which met.

Beth knelt down on the wet gravel and listened to the rumbling rails. The night train was accelerating as it left the station, heading along this track, probably bound for Scotland. She prepared to remove the package from her coat pocket and place it on one of the rails. The thing was presumably made of plastic; it would shatter easily. But would this be enough to ensure that the contents were eradicated forever? Suppose the vibrations caused the envelope to slide from the rail seconds before the great steel wheels thundered over it? There was only one solution: she would have to hold it in place. Falling to her knees on the sharp crystals of granite which lay between the sleepers, she paid no heed as her shins began to tear and bleed. She had to ensure that the packet would be crushed. The pinging of the rails told her that the train was approaching. It was less than a quarter of a mile away from her and advancing at great speed. Carriage windows snaked around a bend in the track. Her attention returned to the business at hand.

But now she felt inside her coat and found that there was no packet.

Where was it? When had it last been in her possession? Could she have dropped it somewhere? At the fence? On the embankment? She tried to rise as she realized that the train was bearing down on her with terrifying speed. The very air itself was being forced aside, tearing the breath from her contracting throat as the leviathan's immense bulk shoved its way through the night toward her, blotting out the stars.

The night train roared across the points, a spectral serpent bearing down on its prey, and Beth Cleveland hit the front carriage with a clap that was lost beneath the sound of the racing wheels. She was sliced into three separate parts, the upper half of her body sailing over three hundred yards from the track while the passengers on board dozed over their newspapers, unwitting participants in a mechanized execution.

The envelope lay hidden in the tall grass to the side of the track, where it had fallen some minutes earlier. The videocassette within had slipped out, and as the rain renewed its vigor, the hand-inked lettering on the plastic label was washed away into the sodden earth.

18.

Problems with Blood

H ARRY CHECKED THE clock above the EXIT sign. Eight-fifteen. He twisted around in his seat and studied the smiling stoned skinheads balancing empty lager cans on the armrest behind him.

"Where on earth do they find these people?" he asked. "You can hardly breathe in here for the smell of dope. I have more important things to do tonight than sit through—what was it?"

"*Cannibal Holocaust* and *I Spit on Your Grave*. As an advertising man I'm sure you'll find them interesting from a sociological viewpoint."

"In other words they're terrible movies."

"If it was standard entertainment you were after we could have gone to a mainstream cinema in the West End."

"Grace, I haven't been to a cinema, mainstream or otherwise, since I could afford to dine out instead." Min-

utes after Hilary had canceled their dinner engagement,
Grace had called to suggest that they meet. His accep-
tance had delivered them to a run-down repertory cinema
in King's Cross which Grace frequented during the week.

"This 'girlfriend' of yours is obviously avoiding you,"
she said, reading his mind. "It sounds to me like she's
found someone else. Forget her. She wasn't worth it."
She slipped her hand beneath his arm as the lights in the
peeling roof began to fade.

"You don't understand. Hilary and I have something
very special. If we don't nurture it, do you know what
will happen?"

"Sure. She'll spend it all."

He sighed and settled back in the springless seat as the
curtains opened. The titles for *Cannibal Holocaust* appeared on the screen.

"Anyway, you're obviously not sleeping together,"
whispered Grace.

"That's none of your—why do you say that?"

"A woman knows."

He gave her a skeptical look. "Somehow, I don't think
of you as a woman," he confided. "Take a look at yourself."

"What's wrong with the way I look?"

"It's so . . ." he searched for the word, ". . . severe.
Wacked out. People give you strange looks in the street."

"You mean I don't conform to your idea of feminin-
ity," she said angrily. "I don't squeeze myself into
clothes designed to give the average male a hard-on. It's
always the same. As soon as women starting thinking
independently, men accuse them of being castrating
bitches."

"I'm not accusing . . ."

She tore open a chocolate bar and munched it discon-
solately, studying the screen. "It may surprise you to
know," she hissed suddenly, "that some of us are capable of choosing our own life-styles without being force-
fed the latest fads. I have better things to do than worry
about the efficiency of my soap powder."

A man seated in front turned around and hushed them.

"Stop overreacting," said Harry with a smile. "I like your company. And I don't disagree with you. Now that you've discovered the world's a rotten place, perhaps you can start enjoying it."

He turned his attention to the film, and for the next fifteen minutes sat in mesmerized silence. Grace quickly began to wonder whether she had chosen the right double bill for someone who was obviously a horror-film novice. On the screen, a tribal native was pulling a crocodile's head off. He ran his blade across the belly of the creature, exposing heavy red flesh, then wrenched out a handful of intestines. Even in the dark she could see that the blood had drained from her companion's cheeks.

"Harry, are you okay?"

The native was chewing the crocodile's intestines. Other members of the tribe appeared and began wedging their hands into the bloody cauldron of internal organs. Harry's face took on the slickness of waxed paper. By the time a luckless explorer was torn apart and eaten by the cannibals, he was on his feet and moving toward the EXIT sign.

Outside, a chill mist hung in the streets. Harry thrust his hands in his pockets and drew a deep breath. "I need to eat something," he said as they began walking. A fire engine and two squad cars barred the entrance to the King's Cross terminus, their rotating lights glancing beams through the hazy air.

"I had no idea you'd react like that," said Grace. "Look, there's something going on at the station." She pointed across the road. Police were cordoning off the approach to one of the platforms.

"I have problems with blood."

"Really? You should have told me."

"I usually pass out. It's a psychological thing, no big deal."

"You're lucky we didn't stick around for the castration scene. That's pretty heavy."

In the neon arcades around them, runaways gambled their last coins. Grace led the way to a dingy snack bar fronted in yellow plastic.

"You mean you've seen it before? Why do you watch these things? What's wrong with you?"

"It's extreme, I'll admit, but it's more provocative viewing than an average night's TV." Grace ordered coffee and baklavas for two. The owner of the Cypriana snack bar registered his disapproval as he served them, assuming from Harry's complexion that he was an addict undergoing withdrawal symptoms.

"Television's good enough for most people," said Harry defensively. "Why should everything be a provocation?" He wiped his brow with a balled-up Kleenex. A pale young man seated himself at the next table, probably thinking that he could score.

"To remind us that we're alive," said Grace. "Too many people need prodding awake." She bit into her baklava and allowed the sugary juice to run down her chin. "Now, what are we going to do about your father?"

Harry was unprepared for her question. "Slattery's takeover offer runs out tonight, and I've failed to come up with a single solid reason for turning it down. Maybe it was a false lead after all."

"I don't blame you for being suspicious. There's something creepy about big corporations taking over small companies. They don't do it for the right reasons."

"That's being naive." Harry drained his coffee. "Multinationals are here to stay. It's all about distribution. More outlets, that's what everyone wants. You think business is too big now? We've seen nothing yet. Did you know that last year GEC turned over about forty-five billion U.S. dollars? They've got defense contracts worth at least nine billion. They own the most successful television network in the USA, and they're moving into international communications. Does that sound sinister to you? If you thought the future was about having a bigger choice, then explain to me why there are only two major retail chains distributing books in America." He shook his head wearily. "Everyone bitches about the McDonald's ethic, but they still queue up at the counter for a cheeseburger and a Coke."

"That's because there's no other choice."

"Wrong. There are more choices than ever, but you know what? They're all the same. We're simplifying the way we behave, the way we think. It makes life easier, and that's what people want. Who needs anything different? A cheeseburger and a Coke, it's a meal that never lets you down."

Grace reached across the table and took his hand. "You know Harry, sometimes you sound just like me. Maybe we have more in common than you think." She shrugged. "So what's our next move?"

"I suppose I could call the Indian woman again. Mrs. Nahree. She might have remembered something more."

"At least it's a start." They rose from the table and headed for the nearest telephone booth.

19.

The Nature of Accidents

O N WEDNESDAY MORNING, Harry arrived at the agency to find his colleagues already locked in the conference room with Darren Sharpe. He was beginning to feel that he was being excluded from some major change in company structure. His department head had failed to confide any details of the meeting, so there was nothing for it but to sit in his office and wait for the assembly to disperse. In the outer room only Eden remained at her desk, half-heartedly typing up contract reports.

Unable to gain an answer from Mrs. Nahree's telephone the night before, he had hopped a cab at the tube station, leaving Grace—and the sexual tension that had come to exist between them—in a convenient state of unresolve. He thought about his next move while he thumbed idly through the tabloid newspapers.

WOMAN DECAPITATED BY NIGHT TRAIN

Passengers traveling north on the 7:35 P.M. from King's Cross looked on in horror as the eight-carriage-long express smashed into a figure standing in the center of the track last night. The victim, a well-dressed woman in her early fifties, was torn in half as the driver attempted to bring the speeding train to a halt. The body has been identified as that of Mrs. Elizabeth Cleveland of Hackney, East London.

Last night the driver denied suggestions that the express was exceeding the regulation speed limit as it left the terminus.

Cleveland apparently committed suicide by scaling the embankment at the side of the tracks and waiting for the nonstop train to pass by. Friends say that a recent bereavement had left her in an extremely depressed and emotional state of mind.

Foul play is not suspected.

MP calls for tougher safety measures on BR property. See page 12.

Harry was staggered. Unable to frame his thoughts with any clarity, he read the brief article through a second time. What could have made such a rational woman behave like this? He admitted that he barely knew her, but could he have seen so little? "Extremely depressed and emotional," friends had commented. Who were these people? Could she have been taking some kind of medication?

He seemed to be passing into some kind of alternative universe, where everyday occurrences took on grotesque new aspects. He was certain of one thing. Beth Cleveland's death was connected with his father's, and they were both somehow tied to the Instant Image buyout. Perhaps even the mental case who'd stolen his car was involved.

He felt sure the conspiracy would soon be revealed. After all, Carmody's deadline had been passed at midnight.

The balcony of Arthur Bryant's Battersea apartment looked out over the olivine grasslands of the park and the river beyond. It was here that John May and Janice Longbright found their colleague basking in the pale afternoon sun. Surrounded by potted plants of every description, he was stretched out across an ancient striped deck chair, fast asleep.

Walking lightly across the lounge, Longbright reached through the French windows and gently tapped him on the shoulder. Bryant blinked like a tortoise emerging into light, then looked grumpily around at his colleagues.

"What time is it? Who let you in? Am I to get *no* peace?" He pulled himself up in his chair, annoyed at the intrusion.

"It's half past three, your landlady gave us the key, and no, you are to get no peace so long as the British taxpayer is footing the bill," said May.

"Alma would hand out the key to this flat if she opened the door to armed terrorists," he muttered. "It's because I'm behind with the rent." Irritation gave way to a plea for sympathy. "It's not fair. I'm old. Old people turn back into babies. They need a nap during the day. Be a good fellow and bugger off for a while. Take a walk in the park for an hour."

"We need to talk to you, Arthur," said Longbright. "There's been a development in the Dell case. I'll make us some tea."

"That's better," said Bryant, suddenly brightening up. "You could learn some manners from her, John. Janice knows how to care for someone in the twilight of his years."

"Can we drop the senile routine, do you think?" snapped May. "You're not fooling anyone." He examined one of the plants on the balcony. "I suppose you know you have a marijuana plant growing here."

"No!" exclaimed Bryant, genuinely shocked. "Which one?"

May narrowed his eyes to suspicious slits and pointed at a tall plant with a number of missing stems. "It looks to me like it's been recently harvested," he remarked. "You should be ashamed of yourself."

"It's medicinal. For my arthritis. I understand that doctors prescribe it these days. It's terribly easy to grow, you know."

"I thought you said you were turning back into a baby,

Arthur, not a teenager." May seated himself in an empty deck chair. "It's been over a week since we began the Dell investigation. That wouldn't matter if it hadn't been for the fire. We've an ID on the burn victim."

"How is he doing?"

"I'll get to that in due course. Hargreave is taking flak from upstairs about our lack of progress. I don't suppose you've come up with anything new on the case yourself?"

"I rather thought I'd see how you two managed first." He rose from the chair and stepped inside, so that May was forced to follow. "How's the tea coming along?"

Bryant's lounge was like his office, an eclectic mixture of the old and the ancient. Oval portraits of forgotten colonial relatives shared wall space with framed song-sheets from Gilbert and Sullivan operas. A crumbling fretwork statue of Buddha stood in an art nouveau fire-place, while nearby, a stylish art deco sideboard of fumed ash sported an African pot so amorphous and unsightly that it could only have been displayed because the donor was a regular visitor.

Bryant drew a chair from the dining table and sat down as Longbright placed tea before him. May and the sergeant were exasperated by Bryant's erratic appearance at police headquarters, but both knew better than to complain. They had long been aware of his unusual working methods, and of his ability to achieve results in the unlikeliest manner possible. May seated himself opposite his partner and opened his brief-case.

"By the way," said Longbright, "what's happened to your beeper? We tried calling you several times."

"Oh. Er." Bryant screwed up his eyes and studied the ceiling in a passable imitation of genuine puzzlement. "I must have left it in my other suit."

"You haven't got another suit," said May. "You're a lousy liar, Arthur. Let's get down to business." He opened the folder on the table before him. "The boy in the store. His name is Ashdown, Mark. Sixteen years old. He came in at the weekends to update the stock and help out behind the counter. He turned up because no one had remembered to contact him. He's still alive.''

''Where is he?''

''In the Serious Burns Unit at Hammersmith Hospital. He's sustained a terrible amount of tissue rupture. Over half of his body will be covered with scar tissue.''

''And his face?'' Like May, Bryant knew that if more than nine percent of his head and neck was burned, he would be unlikely to live.

''Not too bad. But his lips are extremely split, so obviously he's unable to talk.''

''The psychological damage must be phenomenal,'' said Longbright.

''What are his chances of survival?''

''Better than fifty percent, but I'm waiting for the doctor's report. We know that he was conscious and unharmed when the fire started. The presence of inhaled carbon particles in his lungs proves that.''

''Could he have started the blaze himself?'' asked Bryant.

''Unlikely. They found petrol residues at the back of the basement, where the heat was most intense. Dell's stock was totally destroyed, but the contents of his safe survived. We found nothing remotely illegal inside.''

Longbright opened the folder and spread its contents. ''First—our suicidal car thief, Coltis. As far as we can tell he never visited Dell's store, never rented tapes from him. The same goes for Meadows. None of the companies supplying Dell with tapes are involved in particularly dubious practices. We did get one piece of corroborative evidence, though. Cross sections of the papers found on Dell, Meadows, and Coltis showed identical fiber structure. They originated from the same source. Video sleeves.''

''As we suspected. Do we know whose?''

''Afraid not,'' said Longbright. ''Most major distribution companies print on the same paper, but the thickness varies. We're running a check on the inks used.''

"Now," said May, "this business of suicides and accident-related deaths." He produced the sheets which the computer had printed out. "The figures for London seem to have quadrupled overnight. Statistically it's impossible, unless some of these 'accidents' have been engineered by a person or persons unknown."

"You're suggesting that they're disguised murders?"

May cleared his throat. "Yes. I know it sounds insane, but that's exactly how it seems."

"Remember one thing, John. No statistic is impossible—only improbable. In the statistician's world there's no such word as *never*. If this month's figures are high, it doesn't mean a thing."

"I don't understand," said May.

"Let me try to explain. Imagine a tube station. It's designed to handle a flexible number of travelers, but there's an upper limit to the amount of people it can contain. The system works because of the law of averages. Not everyone who travels by tube arrives on the platform at precisely the same moment. But they could. And then many of them would be crushed to death. Statistically it's feasible, but it's unlikely because of something called the Chance Barrier, which limits the possibility of these disasters occurring."

"So you're saying it's not possible."

"Not in any rational sense. How would it be possible to engineer such a system of mass murder? You would have to be able to influence the law of averages, a natural law. Why, it would be like defying gravity."

He's making too big a deal of this, thought May. He's discovered something and he's excited about it. "We asked the computer to register each fatality as a type," he pointed out, "home, auto, factory, and so on—but there was no common pattern."

"Actually, there *is* a link between two of the accidents," said Longbright, consulting her notes. "The car Coltis stole belonged to someone named Buckingham. Quite a coincidence, because I met Mr. Buckingham the previous week in connection with the death of his father."

"You'd better go and see this chap," said Bryant.

"Find out if the father had a similar scrap of paper on him." He reached down into a battered leather bag. "Now, perhaps you'd like to hear my report from the paleographer. If I can just find Kirkpatrick's disgusting jottings. Ah." He withdrew a single grubby sheet of foolscap filled with crabbed, inky handwriting, then adjusted his spectacles carefully on the bridge of his nose. "They're curses. Runic curses."

"You can't be serious." May gave an uncertain laugh.

"I am, or rather, Kirkpatrick is. They're written in an amalgam of runic alphabets stemming from Germany, Scandinavia, and Britain. Pre-Christian, of course." Bryant always enjoyed himself when he had information to impart. "What gave the game away was the angular shape of the letters. There's no other alphabet like it in the world." He laid the photocopied runic scraps side by side for the others to study.

"You see, the earliest runes were drawn with sticks. There are all kinds of theories about when they first appeared, but the general consensus is that they came into being a couple of centuries before Christ. The funny thing is, they seem to have turned up in several different parts of the world at the same time. So the theory is that they possess magical powers." He tapped the papers with his forefinger. "There are those who believe that these absurd scribbles can be used to create great riches. And to destroy enemies. Remember M. R. James's story 'Casting the Runes'? Supposedly, if you drew runes on a piece of paper and slipped them to your opponent, he would die within a given period of time unless he found a way to pass them back."

The soft evening light was slowly fading in the room. Outside, the gray sun ebbed below a band of deep blue cloud. The old detective drew his chair in closer as he imparted his information.

"There are three basic alphabets. The one thing they have in common is a lack of curves." Bryant had a familiar twinkle in his eye. "Does that fact mean anything to you?"

"Dell's apartment," said May. "He'd obliterated every straight line and angle in the entire flat. He'd hacked at the edges of his cupboard doors. He'd even numbered the designs on the kitchen wallpaper.''

''So that he could check to see if they'd been tampered with. He was a very frightened man. He thought someone was going to try to hide one of these curses in his apartment.''

''And by removing all of the straight edges, he stopped them from drawing on the walls or disguising it in the furniture. Ingenious.''

''I can't imagine anyone believing in the power of such things,'' said Longbright. ''This man rebuilt his entire apartment to keep out an ancient curse? I don't buy it. Nobody would.''

''Unless you had a very good reason for believing it to be true,'' said Bryant. ''Imagine, Dell is convinced he's about to receive one of these things at home. Instead, it arrives at his office. He reads—and more importantly, *understands*—it, then kills himself. But not in any of the usual ways. He goes to the London Zoo, breaks into the insect house and gets poisoned! Coltis receives his, and stages an elaborate public death. Meadows just goes berserk. What are we to infer?''

''That each curse affects its victim in a different way,'' said May. ''I think you'd better talk to your cryptologist again. We need to know more about what we're dealing with. If there's someone out there posting death threats, it's less likely to be a supernatural agency than a religious freak taking revenge on sinners.''

''But if that's the case,'' said Bryant quietly, ''how the hell is he making people die?''

20.
Underground

EDEN HAD FOUND the dress, black taffeta with a hand-painted cocktail motif, in a second-hand shop in Camden, and had planned to return home and change into it before meeting the others. Unfortunately, the backlog of work Harry handed her that Tuesday morning had put paid to the idea. Her typing speed did not allow her to finish the research reports until nearly seven o'clock. As soon as she was through she freshened up in the sixth-floor ladies' washroom, which was smarter than the one on her own floor, then headed for the Mexican restaurant in Argyll Street where she was due to meet Dexter.

Upon her arrival she found him already seated at the bar, morosely squeezing lime into a bottle of dark beer. His clothes, mostly made of tight black leather, accentuated his thin body. Perched on the stool he had the folded-up look of an insect.

"You're late," he said, swiveling around to appraise her. "I thought you were gonna go home and change."

"I couldn't," she replied, clambering up beside him. "Everyone was out with the research group today. I got stuck with their work as well as Harry's." She called to the barman and ordered herself a beer—it was quicker than waiting for her boyfriend to do it. "Harry's in terrible trouble with the account director. They're talking of firing him." She watched Dexter's fingers drumming on the bar in time to the music. "Aren't you interested in hearing about my day?"

"Sure," answered her boyfriend unenthusiastically. She knew that talking about her job bored him, particu-

116

larly since he was currently between videos, waiting for free-lance work as an assistant director.

"Something strange happened this afternoon. A courier came in with a package for Harry . . ."

"So?"

"He'd already left. I said I'd take delivery, but the guy insisted it was really urgent."

"Wait, I forgot. Who's Harry?"

"You're not listening! I've told you loads of times. Mr. Buckingham, my boss. The package had one of those red warning labels on the side, USELESS IF DELAYED, so I thought I'd better open it myself." Dexter drank his beer and stared into the mirror on the far side of the bar. She could not tell if he was listening to her.

"Well, there was a videocassette inside the package, a Sony U-matic. I assumed it was a transfer of a commercial. They're always labeled like that for station transmission. Anyway, I ran it, and it wasn't a commercial at all."

"Tell me later, eh? In bed." Dexter drained the beer bottle and set it down. "We're gonna miss the support band if we don't get a move on." His leather trousers creaked as he heaved himself off the stool. He paid the bill and leaned against the bar, impatiently waiting for her to finish her drink.

The evening was not a success. They walked to the Astoria Club in Charing Cross Road and met their friends, a young couple who were arguing with each other even before the performance began. Their ill-humor quickly rubbed off on Eden. The support band was little more than adequate, and the sound quality of the main attraction was deafening and distorted. At eleven-fifteen Eden pleaded a headache and left. Outside, Dexter grew annoyed at being forced to leave before the encores at the end of the performance. Half-drunk, he sulkily suggested that they should find a place to eat.

"I'd like to," said Eden, "but I've still got to get rid of this." She opened her shoulder bag and withdrew the package that had been delivered to Harry at the agency.

"What are you going to do with it at this time of

night?'' Dexter stamped back on the pavement. ''Couldn't you have left it on his desk?''

''He's supposed to take delivery today. The instructions were very specific. I can leave it at his girlfriend's flat.''

''Forget it. If you're gonna start running errands on the money they pay you, just forget it.''

''She's only a few streets away. I'll post it through the letterbox. I've done it loads of times before. Then we can eat.''

''I'm not hungry anymore.''

Mention of her job in the face of his unemployment was infuriating to Dexter. He suddenly announced that he was going home by himself, pecked her on the cheek, and jumped on a passing bus in Oxford Street, leaving Eden to angrily handle the chore alone.

It took her nearly half an hour to drop the package off in Wigmore Street. Harry would have to keep his promise about the shoes now. With her stomach rumbling, she headed back toward the tube station.

Eden's black stiletto heels ticked across the sidewalk and paused before the brilliantly illuminated window of a department store. She studied the clothes on display with distaste. A pair of white plastic androgynes faced each other, their backs arched, their arms raised in threatening gestures. One wore a conical rubber hat, red cycle shorts, and a blue leather jacket with beerbottle labels stapled across the back. The other wore a T-shirt with the words SAFE SEX printed over the chest in raised plastic bubbles. Everything was so ugly these days, she thought. What had happened to the elegance she saw in her mother's old magazines? She looked along the south side of the street, toward the Centrepoint building, and was surprised to find it completely deserted. A faint mist hung across the road like a veil of gray chiffon.

According to the clock on the wall of the Athena poster shop it was nearly midnight. She could not be sure of the times of the last trains, so she moved quickly on toward the station. An empty bus drove past, its interior lights casting yellow squares on the sidewalk around her. There was no other traffic at all. As she crossed one of the small roads leading down into Soho, a chill side wind lifted her skirt, blowing a sticky ice cream wrapper against her right thigh. For a second it felt like the fingers of a thin hand. She brushed at the litter until it spiraled away from her.

An image from Harry's videotape blossomed in her mind, and for a moment she was seized with an irrational sense of panic. Pushing the half-formed thought aside, she continued along the deserted sidewalk.

The mannequins in the passing shops looked out on her with dead eyes. Perhaps they came alive after midnight, and were merely waiting for her to pass by before they roused themselves. Certainly she had never felt so out of place in the city before. The shops in Oxford Street were cheaper and their clientele less fashionable than in other parts of the West End, but she had always found the atmosphere of the area cheerful. Tonight was different.

As the blue canopy of Tottenham Court Road tube station approached, she saw that even this normally busy corner was devoid of activity. A single cab sped over the intersection with its FOR HIRE light off. On either side of the station, the newsagent stalls stood barred and bolted in ankle-deep litter. A steel trellis had been half-pulled across the station entrance, but lights still shone within.

Slipping inside, she ran lightly down the steps to the main hall. With the exception of the elderly black woman sitting in her booth half asleep, the ticket area was deserted. Eden scooped her change from the vending machine and approached the escalator.

"Damn." She studied the handwritten signboard. Both escalators had been switched off.

ESSENTIAL REPAIRS BEING CARRIED OUT
PASSENGERS PLEASE USE THE EMERGENCY STAIRS

She hated the spiral stairwell which descended to the damp, narrow emergency tunnel below, but she was used to using it. The escalators were forever being repaired. As she turned into the stairwell, the emptiness of the station struck her again. She often made the journey northward late at night, but had never seen the place this empty. Below she would surely find the usual mixture of confused post-theater tourists in Burberry raincoats and drunken suburbanites projectile vomiting at the platform edge. Here on the staircase, though, it seemed that she was alone. Her stilettos rang out on the heavy steel steps as she hurried downward.

But she was not alone, because there suddenly came the sound of another set of shoes hurrying down behind her. She looked back, but the curve of the stairs prevented her from seeing anyone approach. She glanced down as she ran, careful not to slip on the narrow wedges which passed beneath her feet. The air in the shaft was warm and used, and smelled of stale urine. It was probably laden with germs, she thought. No wonder so many commuters caught colds, traveling back and forth within the network of century-old tunnels.

The footsteps behind her were closer now. She turned around once more, but could see nothing. It was irrational, she knew, but she increased the pace of her flight into the shaft in order to widen the distance between herself and her fellow traveler. The tightness of her skirt prevented her from moving much faster. Ahead, the tiled stairwell snaked down in an endless vertiginous spiral. A newspaper lay strewn across the steps below. She looked behind again, then turned her head in time to watch her foot slip on the sheets and vanish beneath her. Suddenly weightless, she felt her body pitching forward. The footsteps continued behind as she fell headlong. Her last conscious thought was that perhaps her follower would, with a heroic burst of speed, catch up and overtake her plummeting form, breaking the fall with his own body . . .

The tiny calcified stalactites hung from rivets which covered the ceiling. Occasionally one of them released a drip of sooty water. They were the first things she saw when she awoke. A fiery pain burned in one of her legs. Without looking, it was hard to tell which one. The right side of her temple throbbed with a steady dull pain. She raised her hand and gingerly touched her face. The skin of her forehead felt stretched. There was a gash—not large—but blood had dripped into her eyebrows, tightening as it dried. Her arms and chest seemed to be lying lower than her legs. She was still on the stairs, pointing downward. Carefully she turned her head.

She lay at the base of the stairwell, near the entrance to the corridor leading to the platforms. She managed to sit up without too much pain. Her hands and knees were badly scraped. There seemed to be no major bones broken, although she had certainly wrenched the muscles of her right leg. Why had the other occupant of the stairwell not come to her aid? Could she have translated the echo of her own shoes into the presence of a pursuer?

She rose unsteadily to her feet. The light fabric of her skirt had torn along one side. How long had she been unconscious? The face of her watch was broken, the hands having stopped at a little past midnight. As she brushed herself down, she realized that her hands were shaking. Speckles of dried blood covered her blouse. With one arm reaching out to balance herself against the wall, she staggered from the stairwell into the cramped corridor beyond. The lights were still ablaze. Perhaps the last train had yet to pass through the station. Or did they leave the passageways lit all night?

Both of the Northern Line platforms were deserted. The electronic timetable which hung from the roof appeared lifeless. She fell back against a film poster advertising a new Steven Spielberg picture, and tried to gather her thoughts. Could they have possibly locked up the station with her inside? Perhaps she would have to pass the night alone save for the dust-colored rats that scavenged between the rails. The thought terrified her.

A flicker of movement appeared in the corner of her eye. She looked up at the information board as it burst into life. The red LEDs fed the message across:

HIGH BARNET   3 min

Thankfully, she collapsed down onto an uncomfortable metal bench and began to breathe slowly, calmly. Her hands were sore. The cut on her knee had begun to bleed again. She looked back at the board.

HIGH BARNET   2 min

She closed her eyes and pressed her head back against the cool tiles of the wall behind her. If Dexter had taken her home with him, this would never have happened. This was the end, she thought. They were through. When he wasn't thinking of sex, he ignored her. His videos were boring, anyway. Eden tried to ignore the smarting of her palms as she waited for the train. She opened her eyes and looked up once more.

HIGH BARNET   1 min

Her skirt was ruined. She would sue London Transport for negligence, or at least for the price of a new outfit. She could have been killed! How the elderly managed to cope with such treacherous stairways she had no idea. As soon as she got home she would call Dex and tell him what happened. Or perhaps she should run a bath first, a really hot one. She hoped the cut on her head was not serious. It might need a stitch. She felt in her bag for a compact as the air in the tunnel began to vibrate with the approach of the train. She studied the board again.

HIGH BARNET TRAIN NOW APPROACHING

Suddenly the lettering wiped away and was replaced with flashing red capitals:

CORRECTION

They were probably going to announce that this train was bound for the other branch line, Edgware. It made no difference to her. She alighted at the last stop before the lines separated. The sound of the approaching train augmented and changed to a deep, reverberating rumble. There was no contact of metal in the noise, as if the carriages were being rushed forward on a blast of wind.

She watched the sign as it changed once more. New capitals rolled on.

EDEN

She stared at the sign, uncomprehending. It couldn't be printing out her name. How could such a thing be possible? The letters quickly rolled off, and new ones were transmitted in their place.

BURN IN HELL BITCH

Her breath caught in her throat. There was no train approaching. Something big and dark and unstoppable, a ferocious evil, but no train to bear her to safety, and she needed safety now. She rose from her seat as the roaring wind burst from the tunnel like a living thing. As she ran for the exit, clouds of filth-laden air flooded over her in a swelling tide of heat, snatching her breath away, slamming her into the wall of the platform. A geyser of litter exploded from the wastebin beside her. She pushed away from the wall and stumbled on toward the escalator bank, the tunnel thunder billowing against her eardrums in wave after wave of painful pressure. As she turned into the hallway she felt her heart plunge. The stairs at the bottom had been removed for repair work. Oiled machinery shone darkly from the pit beneath the escalator. She shoved the red metal guardrail aside as the poisoned maelstrom hammered against her back. The bottom four steps had been taken away, creating a gap of about eight feet. If she could climb across the hole, she could run to the top and awaken the sleeping ticket collector.

She gripped the rubber handrail as she clambered to one side of the gap. The howling gale was doing its best to tear her free. She swung one leg across, then the other, and suddenly she was on the stairs above the pit. She knelt down, releasing a burst of desperate laughter in the abrupt realization that she was safe on the far side of the escalator. The wind around her abated as quickly as it had arisen. In the total silence which descended, Eden rose to her feet and began the steep climb back to the street.

And instantly, the treads beneath her shoes were thundering downward as the stairway shifted with her weight. Unbalanced, she fell backward into the machinery pit beneath the escalator, and the rolling stairs closed over her head with a deafening, final slam.

21.

Sarcophagus

S HE AWOKE IN darkness. Oily heat pressed down on her slick skin. Her body was wedged within structures of steel. Twisting her bruised head, she saw sharp yellow light glittering through the slats of the stairs overhead. She felt as if she were suffering from a heavy hangover, knew that she would probably be sick if she tried to sit up. Muffled sounds filtered through the machinery: men's voices, talking casually. A piercing sound rang out, metal on metal, a staccato rhythm which reverberated through the cogs and columns which comprised her prison. She would have to find her voice, let them know she was here, below, inside. But first she listened.

It was her last mistake.

The young laborer climbed through the steel safety trellis and called to his workmate at the foot of the escalator. "Oy, 'ave you got the spanner bag down there, Ray?"

The older man looked up. "Someone's been playin' silly buggers," he said, "shiftin' things around. I left this open last night." He gestured at the staircase which had closed over the escalator mechanism.

"You wanna hand openin' it?" asked the younger man, preparing to climb down to his partner. The station had been operational for little more than half an hour, and as yet only a handful of commuters had arrived at their destination to begin work in the West End.

"No," called Ray, reaching behind to the control panel on the escalator post. "Step back and I'll bring it around again." He inserted his key, turned it, and punched the red start button. There was a tearing sound as the stairway juddered into life, and an unearthly, horrified scream rose from the bowels of the machinery.

"Turn it off! Turn the fucking thing off!" The men clawed at the gap in the stairway, trying to prize it open with a claw hammer and a crowbar.

As they fought to widen the hole, the cry died away, subsumed by the sound of bubbling liquid. Ray snatched a torch from his pocket and shone it down into the mechanism. The sight which met his eyes would live with him to the end of his days. The body of the girl lay where it had fallen the night before. But now it was barely recognizable as human, torn diagonally in half by the powerful chain links which drove the escalator stairs.

Ray sat back against the rail, his face turning to chalk. "I didn't know," he tried to explain. "How could I know? It was an accident."

"How can I know?" asked Sharpe. "You have to tell me what's going on, Harry. If you're not happy here, tell me and we'll come to some arrangement." He paused to let the threat sink in. "You've hardly been in the office during the past week. You let me down badly on the soft-drink presentation." He rose from behind his desk and walked in front of it, leaning back against the edge in what Harry took to be his fatherly pose. "There are plenty of people waiting in the wings for a position like yours. Leaner, hungrier, *younger* people with nothing to lose. I know your father's death was a shock, but corporate life goes on. Talk to me, Harry." Satisfied that he had stated his side of the case succinctly, Sharpe sat back and sucked wetly at his dying cigar.

Harry wondered just how much he should tell the account director. He generally treated conversation with Sharpe in much the same way that his public-speaking course had told him to handle the tabloid press: by keeping his mouth shut. This was hardly the right time to discuss his growing disillusionment with the job. "There are a couple of things going on at the moment that I have to sort out," he said finally. "I'm going through a rough patch, but it's okay."

"Maybe for you, Harry, but not for me. I need to know that every member of my group is out there pitching for our clients." His voice softened. "Harry, Harry . . ." For a brief horrible moment he thought Sharpe was going to throw a paternal arm around his shoulder. He was fond of the gesture, although he was scarcely older than Harry. "You used to be the toughest man on the team. What's happened? You don't seem to care like you used to. Maybe you just need a challenge. Well, you're in luck." He removed the cigar and studied its dead end as he pulled a piece of leaf from his lips. "Our agency has won a new account."

"I didn't think we were pitching for anything at the moment."

"We weren't. This is an acquisition made through a long-standing connection with our chairman. I propose to commission a report from you. Our client wants to know about the cost-effectiveness of peak-time national television campaigns. I told him that you were the man for the job."

He lifted a plastic-covered folder from the desk and handed it over. "The details are all in there. He needs the figures a week from today."

Harry looked down at the embossed silver logo on the folder. It read:

THE ODEL CORPORATION
COMMUNICATING THE FUTURE TODAY

"I told the ODEL people all about your past successes," said Sharpe. "They're looking forward to meeting you."

Wednesday afternoon passed in a haze of confusion and misinformation. First, one of the typists was seen crying in the ladies' washroom. Next, a call from Eden's family brought news of her death. No details concerning the exact circumstances of the accident were imparted, so, like whispers in wartime, word spread quickly through the building as the basic fact of her demise became embellished with grisly detail. Finally the full story was revealed, splashed across the later editions of the *London Standard*. Filled with foreboding, Harry picked up a copy of the newspaper and gingerly unfolded it.

London Standard   Thursday 23rd April

GIRL DIES TRAPPED IN TUBE ESCALATOR

Consumer report of stairway dangers went unheeded, says official.

In the early hours of this morning, workmen discovered the body of a young woman wedged inside the escalator mechanism at Tottenham Court Road tube station. She is believed to have been returning home late when she stumbled into the open working site. Her identity is being withheld pending notification of relatives.

No "Undue Hazard" to Commuters

Repair work has rendered two out of three escalators intermittently inoperative at the busy station for the past six weeks, and although the worksite is always left open and unattended at night, station officials were quick to point out that the danger area was cordoned off with guardrails and warnings posted in accordance with standard safety procedures.

"Works such as these continue throughout the tube system without undue hazard to the commuting public," said an LRT spokesperson this afternoon.

Report "Warned of Stair Danger"

Police are at a loss to explain how the victim scaled the safety barrier, or why she failed to spot the highly visible warning signs posted at the foot of the escalator.

Although the possibility of murder has yet to be ruled out, police investigators suggest that early indications show the possibility as "highly unlikely."

Six months ago an *ES*-commissioned report warned of the danger to the public posed by building works within the tube system.

Full story, page 4.

MP slams "deathtrap stations." Page 13.

Harry tucked the newspaper into his ODEL folder and returned to his office. How could Eden be dead? He tried to erase the thought of the girl trapped within a sarcophagus of steel, slipping and clawing as she sank into darkness. Ridiculously, he wished he had taken the time to buy her the shoes she had wanted. Now it was too late. As he entered his cubicle area, he was surprised to find Grace seated on the couch waiting to see him.

"I had to come here," she said, standing as he entered. "It couldn't wait."

"Apparently not." He poured scalding coffee into a pair of plastic beakers. "I'm sorry my secretary didn't announce you, but she's just been found dead inside an escalator."

"What?" Her shock registered more visibly than his own. "How is that possible?"

"I think she was mistaken for me. The press have already gotten hold of it." He threw the newspaper across to her. "I'm living some kind of nightmare. Is that what you wanted to talk about?"

Grace slowly raised her eyes from the headline and looked at him. "I rang your Mrs. Nahree again," she said. "She wasn't there. I spoke to her son."

"Where is she?"

"In the hospital, Harry." Grace's voice was low and measured. "She's gone blind."

"It was self-inflicted, I'm afraid," said Doctor Clarke, guiltily taking a final drag on his cigarette before flicking the stub into the littered quadrangle below. "With a soldering iron. Her son found her barricaded inside her apartment, crying. She'd been like that for several hours, but her neighbors had ignored the noise." The three of them stood on the concrete terrace which enclosed the rear part of the hospital. It seemed to be the only place where they could talk quietly. "I examined her on Saturday morning, after she'd spent a day under sedation. We performed two operations, one to remove the damaged tissue and another to try and save her retinas. We were hoping to return partial sight to one eye. We did not meet with success.''

Grace stood back from the railing and stared across the doctor's shoulder at Harry. She looked exhausted.

"There have been other instances of this in the past—it's hardly a common occurrence, but it's not unknown. We've had people lose their sight by simply staring at the sun. It takes about six hours to do the job. In previous recorded cases, the patient has partially recovered his eyesight for a day or so, but only for a short period of time. Permanent blindness quickly follows.''

"Why would anyone do such a thing?" asked Harry.

"It's sometimes associated with religious fanaticism, although I don't know that this is the case here.''

"When do you think she'll be able to talk?''

"She's awake right now, but I can only permit visits by next of kin at the moment. She's talking, but making little sense. We've administered large doses of antibiotics to minimize infection—her eyes are crusting up as the ducts try to repair the damage. She'll be undergoing psychiatric therapy once the condition has completely stabilized.''

"Have you spoken to her yourself?" asked Harry. "Has she given you any idea of what was going through her mind?''

"Oh, she seems quite happy about the whole thing, that's what's so disturbing. It was a deliberate, conscious act on her part.''

"But why?''

"She told her son that it was some sort of insurance,'' said Clarke, absently removing another cigarette from the battered pack in his top pocket. "She says she did it so that she'd be protected from the Devil.''

"This is getting too weird for me," said Grace as they headed back across the hospital car park. "What the hell is going on around here?''

"I thought you'd be able to shed some light on that,'' said Harry.

"What is that supposed to mean?''

"Well, you seem to have started the whole thing.'' His

frustration needed somewhere to go. It found its outlet in an irrational bitterness aimed at Grace.

"I started it? Jesus, that's a good one." She climbed up into the cab and slammed the door. "This is all your father's fault. What was he running away from?" She angrily gunned the engine. "If you're such a hotshot, why can't you figure that out?"

"Wait! Listen, I'm sorry." Harry waved his arms in front of the truck as she backed it from the space. "I need your help."

This, at least, was what Grace had wanted to hear. "Keep talking."

"I have to get access to Instant Image."

"How are you going to do that? Right now, Brian Lack would be happy to see you dead. I suppose we could break into the building at night and go through his desk."

"Let's try a legal way first," said Harry. "I'm about to begin work on the ODEL account. I'll request a meeting with Daniel Carmody and ask him about my father's company." He explained what had happened with Sharpe earlier.

"Fair enough," said Grace, beckoning him into the cab. "If we're going to get into serious trouble, we may as well start at the top."

22.

Carmody

THEY MET IN the boardroom on the seventeenth floor, after the offices had closed for the evening. The project directors of ODEL had been told to attend without fail. None of them could imagine why the meeting had to take place at such a late hour. Even Old Man Harwood had grudgingly agreed to sit in at the far end of the table for a while. One empty chair remained. The directors lit cigarettes, fiddled with their notepads, talked among themselves—anything to disguise the fact that they were being kept there by one whose authority exceeded their own. All heads turned as the double doors folded inward and Daniel Carmody appeared.

The new managing director was an exceptionally tall, thin man, with gray-black hair tied in a small, smart pigtail at his back. His left eye was a brilliant, piercing blue, but although his right eye roughly matched that hue, it possessed a flat lifelessness that revealed it as colored glass.

Daniel Carmody took his place at the head of the table, set down his briefcase, and withdrew a black leather pocketbook from it. He acknowledged Harwood with a curt nod, then turned to address the others who were seated about him.

"This won't take much of your time, gentlemen, I assure you. As you know, our proposed expansion into new areas of technological growth is due to begin its next phase at the beginning of July, in just under three months time. After careful consideration, however, I have decided to bring this date forward to next month." His voice had an unplaceable mid-Atlantic accent.

There was a murmur of astonishment around the table. "You can't make this kind of decision by yourself, Carmody," said one of the directors. "We're nowhere near ready. It'll have to go to a vote before the committee."

Carmody turned his gaze upon the speaker, one eye swiveling around, the other staying still. "That is precisely why I have asked you here tonight," he said slowly. "I need your agreement and support before I can proceed with the launch."

"Why do we need to go any earlier?" asked a small, balding man on the left-hand side of the table.

"There is a problem." Carmody held his pocketbook aloft. For a moment he looked like a hellfire preacher about to lecture on the evils of drink. "Our competitors have just unveiled plans which, if implemented, will put them into the New York and Hong Kong markets ahead of schedule—and at least a month ahead of us.''

"Really? I find that very hard to believe. I've heard no reports to that effect from our representatives in the field.'' The gruff crackle of a voice came from the far end of the table. Sam Harwood had been the chairman of the company for many years, and had seen it through name changes, mergers, and incorporations without mishap. At the age of seventy-one he still commanded the respect and loyalty of his employees. Furthermore, he was the only person around the table who was prepared to contradict the new managing director to his face.

"Perhaps your representatives aren't quite as in touch with the market as you think they are, Mr. Harwood. This afternoon our rival's share index has jumped several points following their announcement concerning the planned use of new fiber-optic technology.''

Daniel Carmody had an unsettling effect on most of the executives. He seemed able to turn aside their criticisms with curt truths. Although he had been in power for only three months his aloofness, his condescending attitude to his employees, and his seeming lack of heart had already made him a considerable number of enemies. But no one could deny the profitability of his unconventional business ideas or his farsightedness in creating long-term company policy that would ultimately benefit every one of ODEL's employees.

"I will undertake to provide each director here with documentary proof that unless we move our commencement dates forward, we will lose the lead we have recently created with so much success.'' Carmody rose and leaned forward, his palms planted flat on the table before him. "Gearing up to meet the new demand is a difficult, but not insurmountable task. Our biggest problem is fear. It's an emotion I can feel emanating from every one of you. Fear of expanding too quickly, fear of failure. That is why I am here. To remove your fears and replace them with something I know you will all appreciate. A corporate aggressiveness that results in increased profitability.''

He seated himself once more and looked at Harwood. ''The old ways aren't always the best,'' he said pointedly. ''We can't sit here and wait to see how the market responds. We have to hit hard and fast, and we have to act *now*.''

By the time the directors filed from the room, Carmody knew that he had their votes in his pocket. He was the new order, disliked by them, but not distrusted. He had the confidence and the ability to pull together this ragtag group of companies and present them to the world as a unified whole. Soon they would be involved in every area of communications, from owning the studios manufacturing TV product for sale to the satellite networks, through to printing the listings magazines which lay on the viewers' laps. A complete system, from start to finish. A dream within touching distance.

As the last man passed through the double doors, Sam Harwood pulled them shut.

''I want a word with you in private, Carmody.'' He eased the weight on his arthritic legs by leaning against the back of a chair. ''None of the networks are planning to shift their expansion schedules forward and you know it. I want you to give me a concrete reason for suddenly altering the dates.''

''I think you already know why, Sam.'' Carmody took a step toward the old man, towering over him. ''You agreed in principle nearly two weeks ago.''

''What choice did I have? You said it was essential that this . . .'' he searched for the correct euphemism, afraid that someone might be listening beyond the doors, ''this *mishap* . . . was properly taken care of.''

''And it has been, I assure you.'' He placed a bony hand on Harwood's shoulder in an unnerving gesture of reassurance. ''By midnight tomorrow the last of the culprits will have been removed from circulation. But there's a new problem, Sam. There's an outlet we must purchase, and we have to do it quickly.'' Carmody walked back to his seat and consulted his pocketbook. ''A video business called Instant Image. God knows we don't need it, but it has to be done.''

''What if they won't accept an offer?''

''Way ahead of you, Sam. Two of their directors have recently died. The remaining one favors a buyout.''

''You mean we . . . ?''

''We did nothing. They brought tragedy into their own destinies. The point is, I can't just keep purchasing companies without reason. By moving the official launch date forward I can minimize undue interest in our smaller acquisitions.''

''But why this company?''

''They received part of the shipment.''

''Oh God, not another one.'' Harwood sat down heavily in his chair. ''How many more?''

''There can't be many others, Sam. Not by my calculations. You see now why this has to be done?''

''Very well, but there must be no bloodshed, do you understand?''

''I can't promise you that. No blame can be traced back to ODEL, you know that.''

''Don't you see how wrong all this is?'' Harwood shouted at him, no longer caring who listened. ''For years this business has been run with a sense of propriety. We wanted to make a profit, of course, but we had morals. Was that all for nothing?''

''Spare me the holier-than-thou bullshit,'' snapped Carmody, suddenly fierce. ''You mean to say that nobody ever got hurt by you? That nobody ever got a raw deal? Running a business is like waging a territorial war. You don't go into battle if you're not prepared for limited destruction. Let me remind you of something, Sam.'' He brought his face close to the old man's. ''This company was on the verge of complete collapse when I presented my solution. I explained what was involved and you agreed. You saw what I would have to do to make it work. You liked the plans for vertical expansion, for moving into international markets. How did you think we'd do that? This is just the tip of the iceberg, Sam. If you think I've been ruthless so far, you've seen *nothing* yet. Haven't you heard the Prime Minister? It's a free market now. Every man for himself. Think of it as a race. The one with the unfair advantage wins, and cripples get trampled on.''

He regarded Harwood's appalled face with amusement. ''Cheer up, Sam. There are no cripples in our organization. We don't hire the handicapped, we let the winners have their parking spaces. There are vast fortunes to be made. The ODEL Corporation is about to go global.''

Harwood sat back in his chair to remove himself from the proximity of Carmody's staring eye. His heart was pounding beneath his ribs. He had never expected to experience real fear this late in his life. Carmody snapped his case shut with a bang.

''Now, this little company. There'll be some papers to sign. You'd better have someone draw up the appropriate forms.'' He smiled back at Harwood from the doorway. ''After this is over, why don't you take a holiday? Somewhere nice and quiet, where you can forget about running the show for a while.''

Alone in the boardroom, the old man looked down at his hands and found them shaking. If only he had not allowed Carmody's organization to buy into the company . . . but it was too late for regrets. Something would have to be done. He would have to be stopped before he took them all to blazes. He grimaced at the thought. Hell was exactly where they were heading.

23.

The Fatality File

''**I** CANNOT AFFORD to entertain the idea that people are dying because they've been cursed,'' said John May, slamming the file drawer shut. He was beginning to dread the thought of reporting their findings to anyone. "I'm embarrassed to even discuss the theory aloud. Hargreave would probably have us thrown out of the building if he knew." He had momentarily forgotten that he was referring to the sergeant's lover.

"I don't see why," said Longbright. "He's been involved in some pretty strange cases himself. There was that business with the Leicester Square vampire. The Telecom Tower massacre. The Savoy murders. Of all people, he should keep an open mind."

"His previous involvement with the lunatic fringe is precisely why he won't countenance the risk of public ridicule again," said May. "Now we've got this man—what's his name . . ." He clicked his fingers at the air.

"Buckingham, Harry Buckingham."

". . . who's connected with four separate unnatural accidents. His father gets carried off by a truck, his secretary disappears into an escalator, the fellow who steals his car commits suicide, and his old man's girlfriend is hit by a train. Yet only one of these four—Coltis—has the magical piece of paper which is supposed to bear a curse. It's a pity we can't connect Buckingham with either Dell or Meadows. What did he tell you when he came in?"

"Nothing, although I think he knows more than he's prepared to say." Longbright consulted her notes. May and the sergeant had prepared a Crime Identification Database for the section's Local Area Network system. Each accident had been logged with a short description of the victim and the circumstances surrounding the death. Fresh cases which conformed to the parameters set in the database were then siphoned off onto the newly dubbed "Fatality File." Longbright and May planned to monitor it throughout the investigation. Any relevant new information could then be sifted for leads.

Longbright reached up and closed the small window behind her. Raindrops had spattered the notes spread across the tabletop. The operations room was surprisingly quiet for a Friday morning. "Where's Arthur? I thought you asked him to come in."

"He's gone to meet Dr. Kirkpatrick, to get some further information on the curse notes. He'll meet us later."

"Fair enough. There's no point in trying to explain the file system to him anyway. He took a word processing course a couple of years ago—very much against his will—and managed to erase several important files before we banned him from the room."

"You and Mr. Bryant have been working together a long time, haven't you?" Longbright watched as May typed another information capsule into the file.

"Oh, yes, we're old friends."

"I've heard that some people in the department find him difficult to manage," she ventured. "He seems to take more notice of you than anyone else."

"Well, we have a lot in common. At least, we used to." A cloud passed over May's face, as if he had recalled a sad memory. His hands paused above the keyboard for a moment. "These days Arthur's only really happy when he's working hard." He resumed typing. "You can always tell when that is, because he moans all the time. If he starts being pleasant, that's when you have to watch out." He looked across at Longbright's notes. "The girl in the escalator. Dig out the statement from the workman who turned the machinery back on."

"It's already loaded." Longbright leaned over, called up the file and scrolled through the reports. "According to both men, the gap in the staircase was left open by about eight feet."

"Would it have been possible for the stairs to have closed over her after she had fallen in?"

Longbright checked her notes. "They say no."

"So either someone shut her inside, or she did it herself. She had just had a row with her boyfriend . . ."

"He didn't accompany her as far as the station."

"And Buckingham was nowhere near the area either. Pity."

"Want to run a forensic match on all the cases going into the file? Prints, contact traces, spectrum tests?"

"I can't say I *want* to," said May with a sigh. "It's

too labor intensive and it's too late. The biggest technical limitation in forensic science is in the selecting of vital evidence during the initial search. I should imagine we've had a pretty motley band of investigating officers on the crime scenes, bearing in mind that the first calls would have reported accidents rather than homicides, which means ambulance men, constables . . . bootprints and handprints everywhere.'' He sat up and stretched his aching arms. ''I need to find a common strain, no matter how oblique. I don't care how unlikely it seems, if it's remotely out of the ordinary I want it here in the file.'' He thought for a second. ''And get Harry Buckingham back in for questioning. Today if you can. Keep him hanging around for a while.''

Longbright smiled. ''It'll be a pleasure,'' she said.

''Tell me, Mr. Buckingham, is your life always like this, or are you just having a particularly bad week?'' The sergeant's voice had taken on a cool edge that it had not possessed at their previous meeting.

''Please, call me Harry,'' sighed Harry. ''We may as well get to know one another.'' He studied the high windows of the interview room, at the rain speckling the sooty glass. Longbright was out of uniform, but her manner retained the starched formality of her hours spent on duty. She had changed her clothes, but not her attitude. The room, small, cool, and green, offered no visual stimulus to its guests. A bare wooden table, two chairs, and a neon striplight. Harry had been brought to the station against his will, where he had been kept waiting for over two and a half hours. He glanced at his watch and saw that it was nearly six o'clock. Much to his account director's fury, Harry had been yanked from another client meeting to attend to police business.

In addition to losing time at the office, he was supposed to be facing Hilary in the confessional of the restaurant at seven that evening, in order to explain his recent erratic behavior and to beg absolution for his sins.

''I must admit that I don't know where to start,

Harry.'' Longbright leaned back on a chair that had done nothing to deserve such treatment and carefully studied him. ''You seem to be the calm center in a tornado of misfortune. There's death and disaster whirling all around you.'' Her immaculately penciled eyebrows folded into a frown as she set the chair back on four legs. ''If circumstantial evidence was enough to build a case, I'd be booking you right now on at least four individual charges of murder. They'd be taking your shoelaces away as we spoke.''

Harry decided that it was best to say nothing. He felt that if he tried to talk now, he would only make a fool of himself. He knew that Longbright had not finished with him.

The sergeant leaned forward and laid a manicured hand on his arm. ''Harry, let me ask you a question. You're an advertising man. What do you know about statistics?''

Harry thought carefully before he replied. ''I can tell you how often married women under twenty-five change their detergent brands, things like that.''

''What about the statistical odds of you being in contact with so many victims of misfortune?'' She removed the hand and sat back in her chair, watching him.

''Was Eden's death an accident?''

''We know she was alive when the workmen turned the escalator back on. We don't know how or why she happened to be inside it. I need your help, Harry. We've got beat cops armed with questionnaires doing door-to-door interviews, we've got forensics working on blood types and fiber matches, we've got lab techs searching sites for latent prints, we've got a string of complex autopsies in progress, and you know what we've really got? Nothing. Now, whether you like it or not, you seem to be heavily involved in this. It would be a good idea if you could tell me why. If you've seen anything unusual in the past two weeks, I hope you feel duty-bound to share the information. Because all we've got is a murder investigation that isn't, and a hundred leads that go nowhere.''

Harry looked into the sergeant's earnest hazel eyes and wondered if he should tell her about the Devil's prayers. No, he decided firmly. Not until he'd had a chance to check it further for himself. "I'm sorry," he said, shaking his head. "Nothing out of the ordinary springs to mind."

"Nothing out of the ordinary." She threw him a look of disbelief. "You'd better think of something, because right now you're the nearest thing we've got to a prime suspect."

"What if you find proof that any of these people have been murdered?" he asked.

"Go Directly to Jail, Harry. We'll figure out the motive after you're behind bars."

"What about now? Am I free to go now?" He rose from his chair.

"I suppose so." She motioned for a constable to open the door. "But, as they say in the movies, don't leave town for a while."

"Sergeant, you have my word."

Harry's ordered world was coming apart at the seams. As he attempted to hail a cab outside the station he felt a strange disorientation from his surroundings, as if his life had been given a shove that had jarred it out of reality. Longbright was right—everyone with whom he came in contact seemed to suffer for it. It was as if he possessed a deadly, twisted version of the Midas touch.

It occurred to him that the police knew his father had spoken to Mrs. Nahree on the afternoon of his death. But Longbright had not mentioned the old lady's act of self-mutilation. Perhaps she had not yet been informed of it. Good. That gave him time to get to her son before the police did. He resolved to visit the jewelry shop where the boy worked first thing in the morning. Now, though, it was time to meet Hilary.

He could see her seated at the table, staring lugubriously into her Badoit as she waited for him to appear. Her honey blond hair had been tied up into some kind of Grecian knot, presumably the latest fashion. As he walked past the bar toward the dining area, there was a sound like steam escaping and someone grabbed his arm.

"She looks like one of Hitchcock's leading ladies, Harry. Grace Kelly or—no, Tippi Hedren in *Marnie*, that's it." Grace tilted her head admiringly and sat back on her stool.

"What the bloody hell are you doing here?" he whispered. "Why are you following me?"

"Don't flatter yourself. I'm having drinks with an old friend. This is just a lucky coincidence." She hoped he had forgotten his passing remark about Hilary's dining habits. Grace had dyed her hair a rich chestnut and had arranged it to appear less conspicuous than usual. She had also donned a midnight blue dress which accentuated her slender figure, and had forsaken her Doc Martens for a pair of low-heeled evening shoes. The effect was nothing less than startling. Harry glanced nervously across the restaurant at Hilary, mistiming the moment so that she looked up and caught him looking through the ferns at her like a Peeping Tom.

"Oh God, she saw me. I have to go."

"Don't let me stop you."

Harry stopped. "Who are you having dinner with, anyway?" he asked, suddenly suspicious. "This is an expensive joint. What are you up to?"

"Me?" she asked innocently, her hand rising to her throat. "Whatever makes you think that there's an ulterior motive?"

"I know your type. There always is."

"What's the matter, Harry, does the thought of me eating in your swanky rendezvous bother you? Perhaps you think it should be reserved for exclusive use by the expense-account crowd? As I said, I'm just here for drinks. I may be a lowly serf, but I can still scrape together enough for a gin and tonic."

"You are a very antagonistic young woman," said Harry through clenched teeth, "and you are jeopardizing my relationship with my fiancée."

"It's *me* who's jeopardizing it? You'd better take your hand off my arm, then." She plucked his fingers away as if removing a spider from the bath. "Try the crepe de langouste," she called after him. "I read in a magazine that it's delicious."

"Who was that strange young woman?" asked Hilary, inclining a cool cheek to be kissed.

"Oh, er, she's at the agency. One of the typists." He concentrated on disentangling his napkin from the elaborate swan into which it had been folded.

"You appear to be on very intense terms with her, considering she's just a typist."

"Ah, everyone's like that at the moment. After the tragedy, you can imagine." He made a show of studying his menu.

"The escalator girl. Yes, I suppose it must have been awful." He could tell she was about to change the subject. Unusual circumstances of death seemed to be a recurring conversational theme for them over dinner. "I hope you haven't forgotten that we're having lunch with Mummy on Sunday."

"How could I forget?" said Harry, who had completely forgotten. He surreptitiously watched Grace around the side of his menu. A tall, pale man in spectacles had just seated himself by her side at the bar. He reached across and whispered in her ear, making her laugh about something. He looked very young. Harry frowned.

"Harry, you're not listening to me. I asked if they'd given you another car yet."

"Um, no, they haven't." He closed the menu.

"But they *are* going to?" Urgency crept into her voice. Hilary did not drive. She failed to see the point of learning while there were people available to chauffeur her around.

"I suppose so. I haven't talked to anyone about it yet."

"Well for heaven's sake you *must*, Harry. You could end up with anything. I'd rather die than be seen in a hatchback. It's not like you to leave something so important. You're behaving very oddly at the moment."

Across the restaurant, Grace had excused herself from her companion and was heading toward the ladies' washroom. Harry rose from his seat. "Order for me, Hilary. I'll be back in a minute. Call of nature."

"But I don't know what you *want*," cried Hilary helplessly.

"Harry, you'll get thrown out if they find you in here," said Grace, laughing. "What do you want?"

"I didn't mean to be rude earlier." He looked around at the pink marble washbasins, checking that they were alone. "I've been at the police station all afternoon. They want to charge me with four murders but they don't have any proof. They think I'm part of some conspiracy. No wonder I'm on edge. And seeing Hilary tonight was the wrong thing to do. She's just so . . ." he searched the air for the right word.

"You don't have to explain," said Grace. "I've met her type before. Too interested in balls."

"Balls?"

"Society functions. You're probably wondering who I'm with, not that you're the jealous type. I'll tell you the next time I see you." She did not want him to know that she had arranged tonight's meeting as part of their investigation. "I'm sorry you were detained by the cops. Still, you can't blame them. You're not a safe person to be hanging around with. What are you going to do?"

"Wait, wait, what am *I* going to do? I thought you were helping me."

"It's okay, the Ice Princess can take over from me now."

"I don't want her to help."

"Why not?"

"I want you."

Grace leaned back against the pink-tiled wall. "Well, Harry," she said, her smile slowly broadening, "this is a surprise."

As he reached forward and kissed her, the hand drier at her back clicked on and enveloped them in scorching, radiant heat.

"You must think I'm a complete fool," said Hilary when he returned to the table. The menu lay untouched where he had left it.

"I don't know what you mean." He resumed his seat, casually flicking the napkin across his knees.

"I saw you follow that little tart into the bathroom. Is this where your desperation for sex is leading you? Into public toilets? Are you perhaps becoming some kind of heterosexual Joe Orton?"

"Don't be stupid, Hilary, I just—"

"I'm not in the mood for excuses, Harry. In fact, I'm not in the mood for dinner." This made it serious. She rose from the table. "God knows I was warned. This is what always happens when they start letting working-class people into smart places. Get my coat, please."

Grace's eyes widened at Harry as he passed the bar. He shrugged helplessly as he eased Hilary into her fur. As she swiveled back to her companion on the next stool, Grace's smile broadened into a grin of triumph.

24.

The Code of Hatred

BENEATH THE HUGE copper dome of the British Museum Reading Room, where Shaw and Lenin and Marx had sat working before him, Arthur Bryant seated himself at one of the curved mahogany tables and waited for Dr. Kirkpatrick to reappear. Shafts of afternoon sunlight illuminated the circular floor as carts laden with books wheeled silently past. Here were over ten million volumes of literature both ancient and modern, treasured and studied by students and scholars from all over the world.

"Ah, you're here!" called Kirkpatrick in a loud stage whisper. "Thought I'd nip along and give the trolley girl a hand with my request. When it comes to finding your books they're so dreadfully Fabian. Quiescent;

blockish. Still, I think I may have something of interest for you.'' He seated himself beside the elderly detective and lowered half a dozen thick volumes onto the table.

''I need you to tell me everything you can about the curses on these pieces of paper,'' said Bryant. ''I'm not so much interested in their direct meaning as their background.'' Bryant hoped that a talk with the paleographer would enable him to determine the character of the person behind the notes.

''Where shall we begin? Runic symbology is steeped in superstition and myth,'' explained Kirkpatrick, cracking his dry, gray knuckles before opening the first book. ''Traditionally those who have studied the language have come to be greatly feared. If you're looking for a murderer who needs something to make his victims feel scared, it's a good place to start.'' He riffled through the pages before him. Arthur discreetly blew his nose as fine paper dust filled the air.

''You said there were different alphabets.''

''That's right. It's a single root with three systems, English, German, and Scandinavian. There's a variety of different meanings proscribed to the word 'rune.' It originally meant 'to roar' but later came to mean 'secret writing' or 'whispered secret.' The system we're dealing with here is the Germanic *futhark*. There are twenty-four letters, in three groups of eight, according to three deities. Each group is called an *aettir*. It just means 'family.' ''

''So there are gods involved?''

''Indeed, yes. Runes are generally most associated with Odin, or Woden. He's the god of inspiration, and of battle. Also of wisdom—and death. He gives us the word 'Wednesday,' of course, or 'Woden's Day.' ''

''Can the runes be translated?''

''Not easily, and not by me. The problem is not so much in translation as interpretation. Only a handful of runic manuscripts have survived, and as these originate from the four corners of the world it's hard to ascribe a single meaning to each symbol.''

"But I thought you said the notes stemmed from a particular German alphabet."

"Exactly so, but the Germanic race traveled the world, you see. They originated in India and Iran, and went on to found tribes in Austria, Iceland, all over the place. And as the runes were drawn on tree bark, is it any wonder so few survived?"

"Then how did they come to be used as curses?" asked Bryant tetchily.

"Well, to understand that you must appreciate what was happening to people's beliefs. Initially, Christianity replaced paganism only in the upper classes. The common folk hung on to their gods. It was a system which governed the lives of working people. In pagan life, wrongdoing and sickness were seen as cause and effect. Evil could be warded off with the use of talismans, and talismans were merely runes used back again. They provided safety for travelers and could even be used for raising the dead. In fact, the Jewish tefillin . . ."

Bryant brought him up short with a tap on the shoulder. "You're wandering off again, Kirkpatrick. What happened to the runic writings?"

"Well, they went underground. The Christian church forbade their use, and even refused to let the Germans use the word 'Wednesday,' but they survived. People kept the more practical bits of the system alive right through medieval times. But runic lore slowly died."

"Because of Christianity."

"Only partly. Actually, there's a simpler reason. The industrial revolution arrived. Runic lore demands an immense amount of study. Nobody in the major cities had the time anymore."

"What about in the country?"

"Runes are symbols of nature, so naturally they took longer to die out in rural areas. Things stayed quiet until the Victorians decided to revive them and attach occult meanings. Occultism was having a heyday in the second half of the nineteenth century. Transcendental theories connected the runes to Atlantis, the spirit world, and every other crackpot belief. What a time of darkness and imagination! But now began a real and most sinister change.'' Bryant's attention perked up. ''Would you like a cup of tea?'' asked Kirkpatrick, producing a thermos from his briefcase and filling a pair of beakers.

''The German *Volkisch* movement adopted the runes. The word 'volk' means 'folk,' but it's a racist term used by the Aryans, the very men who created Hitler. Their organization, the Thule Gesellschaft, financed right-wing groups and encouraged them to hate Jews. Runic symbols adopted the concept of purification. I don't need to tell you where that led. Take a look at this.''

He pulled a pair of white cotton gloves from his pocket and slipped them on. Carefully withdrawing an opaque plastic folder from his book pile, he unsealed it and removed a small volume stitched in wrinkled brown leather. A sour smell filled Bryant's nostrils.

''What is it?'' he asked as Kirkpatrick raised the cover and examined the flyleaf.

''Human skin, I'm afraid. Badly cured. I'm allowed to handle it because it was I who donated the album to the library in nineteen forty-nine. This book provides a virtual code of hatred, a blueprint of evil.'' Bryant studied the volume with unease. Kirkpatrick found the chapter he was looking for.

''Most people know about Hitler's involvement with the occult, but the roll call listed here also includes Ernst Röhm, the leader of the storm troopers, Rudolf Hess, the deputy Führer, and Heinrich Himmler, the head of the SS. Hitler's interest in runes resulted in his use of the swastika and the lightning-bolt SS symbol. But he turned the swastika over, so that it faced away from the sun. Big mistake.''

''This means that we could be looking for a member of an extreme right-wing organization.''

''Very likely. And still the runes survive as an underground current in our society. Look at urban graffiti: pure tribal identification. The kids who have adopted the present-day style of 'bombing' walls with complex symbols use no curves. It's all angles. The runes live on.

Throughout the ages, they'll always find a way to surface.''

"I'm going to require you to make some further notes for me on this," said Bryant. "Transcribe everything you've told me today. I want to develop a psychological profile of the person—or people—we're looking for."

"Happy to be of use," said Kirkpatrick, slipping the grotesque manual back in its bag. "I don't envy your task."

"Collating material isn't difficult so long as you work to a system," said Bryant, reassembling his notes.

"I wasn't thinking of that. I meant it's going to be hard convincing anyone to take you seriously. You're no longer just dealing with an ancient language—you're messing about with the occult."

"Frankly, my dear chap, I'd rather do that than interview members of the National Front, which is my next task. Thanks for your help."

As Kirkpatrick watched the detective making his way across the great room, he realized that he had forgotten to tell Bryant how the runes had been passed down from one generation to the next. Considering it unimportant, he filed the information at the back of his mind and immured himself once more in the literature of the world.

25.

Documentation of Evil

HARRY HAD PLANNED to rise early on Saturday morning and take a therapeutic stroll across the damp green pastures of Hampstead Heath. He had promised to weigh up the various courses of action available to him; to somehow replace his derailed life on a normal track.

But when he awoke to the sound of rain teeming across his bedroom windows, his resolve weakened. The events of the past fortnight had drained his energy reserves. Until recently he had always felt secure, even complacent about the trajectory of his life. Now it was as if some malevolent outside agency had taken control and was removing the safety barriers, section by section. He was considering this when the telephone rang and there was Grace, full of vitality, speaking too fast as usual.

"Harry, I know my voice is the last thing you want to hear first thing on a Saturday . . ."

First thing? He looked at his alarm clock and groaned. 7:30 A.M.

"But if we don't do something . . . I mean you keep *saying* let's do something, but we don't."

"Good morning, Grace."

"Have you spoken to the ODEL people yet? What about breaking into Brian Lack's office? That was your idea, not mine . . ."

"I'm putting the phone down now."

"Don't you dare hang up!"

Harry was about to replace the receiver, then thought better of it. She would only ring again. "Listen to me," he said. "Right now I don't know what the hell I'm doing. I'm not even sure that I'm still sane. I've become some kind of death magnet."

"That's why I called, to help."

"Okay, try to figure out what Beth Cleveland could have found out about my father before she died."

"You think she killed herself because of something she uncovered?"

"Can you think of any other reason why a sane woman would stand in front of a speeding train?"

"Yes. Maybe Willie's death affected her more than anyone realized."

"It's a possibility. Listen, I'll call you later."

"Wait, where are you going? Back to sleep?"

"No, to the jewelers."

The small Regent Street shop was just opening for business when Harry arrived. It was the kind of store that was featured in in-flight magazines, its windows filled with expensive, tasteless trinkets. Pekinese puppies carved in silver rolled playfully on their backs, golden galleons weathered tiny seas of mirrored brass, and diamond-crusted ballerinas aped Degas poses with American Express symbols hung around their necks. The main door was sealed; a buzzer permitted entry.

There was no mistaking Mr. Nahree. The fastidious motion of his hands as he arranged a pair of imitation Georgian teapots in a display case echoed the movements of his mother. As his gaunt face turned, Harry could see the sleepless nights in his eyes. He felt that his presence here was an impertinence, but there were questions that had to be asked.

"Mr. Nahree, my name is Harry Buckingham. I heard about your mother's tragic accident. I wish to send her my condolences. How is she?" The length of the counter between them forced him to raise his voice. He held out a hand, doubting that it would be accepted. To his surprise, it was.

"Mr. Buckingham, yes. My mother spoke of your visit. She is as well as you may expect." The young man looked away, unsure of himself. Clearly he knew of Harry's involvement with his mother, but his attitude did not suggest a mind disposed toward prejudgment. "The doctor holds little hope that she will recover her sight. But I suppose he told you that."

"Can you tell me what happened?" asked Harry. "Dr. Clarke was very vague."

"I found the front door barred. I managed to break open a window into the apartment. She was barely conscious. I raised her head and saw her eyes . . . the memory of that moment will always remain. Even now I cannot bear to look at her face. Yesterday I asked her why she should have done such a terrible thing. She tells me it was because of the paper your father gave her."

"Wait, what paper is this?"

"She said it contained one of the Devil's prayers."

Seeing Harry's alarm, Mr. Nahree raised a placating hand. "My mother has always possessed a powerful imagination. She is of the old world. Her life is the province of spirits and demons. English customs hold little rationality for her."

Harry was beginning to know how she felt. He drew a breath. "Do you still have the piece of paper?"

"Unfortunately, no. She burned it just as she burned her eyes."

"Did you mention this to the police?"

"It does not concern them."

"You must forgive me for asking, but why do you think she inflicted such terrible damage on herself?"

"She was frightened of seeing," said Mr. Nahree calmly.

"Seeing what? Her spirits and demons?"

"I was hoping that you could tell me." The conversation was obviously painful to Mr. Nahree, whose polite tone was wearing thin. He lowered his voice as a customer passed within earshot. "Mr. Buckingham, I do not believe that your father was to blame for this tragedy. Nevertheless, he placed something in my mother's coat pocket that terrified her when she read it. So much so that she acted to prevent further harm from coming to her."

"She thought she would see something that would make her die."

"It seems that way. I have no wish to be rude, but I don't think we have anything more to say to one another." He turned back to the display shelf and began to rearrange the silver teapots.

"Don't you think we should find out why your mother behaved in this fashion?" asked Harry, annoyed by the young man's placidity.

"The psychologists will ask her that when she is recovered. They will understand nothing. She was in an appropriate frame of mind for such a violence," said Mr. Nahree, his back still turned. "It simply took something to trigger it off."

"You mean she recognized whatever it was she saw?"

"Mr. Buckingham, she is an old lady who sees omens

and portents in everything about her. This time she was unlucky enough to see one which made some kind of terrible sense.'' He closed the display case harder than he meant to. ''Now, I wish you—please—to go away.''

''She's been downstairs for an hour now. I'm sure she's starting to lose her marbles.'' Frank Drake wedged the receiver under his chin as he tore another patch from his newspaper. ''She stands guard over her precious collection while I spend my time clearing up after incontinent old sods in the reading room and trying to stop students from walking out with the entire reference library stuck up their jumpers.'' There was a queue building up at the checkout point. Their Saturday girl had failed to show. ''I have to go. I don't know what she does down there.''

Dorothy stood in the basement of the library and felt the frightening weight of the words which surrounded her. It was as if the sheer volume of thought held here had created an artificial gravity within the room. She felt the bloating damp which mottled the pages of each ancient tome pressing against her skin, but still she could not leave. Here were thoughts fit for burning, ideas so dangerous that their mere transcription had caused untold suffering. Lives had been lost building this collection. Theories with their seeds in one volume had been nurtured in another decades later; and later still had borne their poisoned fruit in detailed manuscripts. The collection, completed by her mother as she neared her final breath, now lay in waste and decay, its secrets undiscovered.

But this was how it had been intended.

For although the collection represented itself as harmless esoterica to the casual browser, it revealed to the dedicated scholar a universe of cruelty, for the simple reason that it was perfectly complete. No further study was needed than careful perusal of the books within these walls. Their knowledge, once it had been truly comprehended and applied, would yield a harvest of such darkness that no light would ever penetrate the void again. The library could kill. Of this much, Dorothy was sure.

She had read many of the works which packed the mildewed shelves, but not all. Access to certain categories of the literature stored here had been denied by her mother.

And there were those volumes whose covers she was glad to shun. Too well she remembered the guilty childhood visits to the library to gaze upon the documents expressly forbidden her. She particularly recalled one volume which paralleled the practices of an ancient alchemical sect with certain excesses that took place within the Nazi concentration camps. The memory of those pages could still raise sour bile in her throat.

Evil was the subject of the collection, its genealogy, its dissemination, and its remedy. The books were not evil in themselves; they merely provided the subject with documentation. In this respect, Dorothy was far more than a librarian. She was a guardian. Loath to destroy the painstakingly assembled repository, she remained the only barrier between the unspeakable energy of its knowledge and the fools of the world.

But now she sensed a change in the people who surrounded her in everyday life. The minute transformations which had long been predicted by the collection were slowly occurring. As the century neared its end, she could sense the alignment of certain conditions, from the nervous predictions of the press, from the warning signs on the evening news. The time was approaching when the library would be needed to turn evil back against itself.

The familiar sinking in her stomach was always there when she approached the forbidden library. On certain nights the room seemed to be alive. This time, the step which completed her descent into the cellar had brought a rolling wave of sickness with it. She stared into the darkened aisles, wondering if she would be strong enough to summon the power within them, knowing that there would come a time when she would have no other choice.

Perhaps she would be able to enlist the help of others.

Frank was too weak, too much of an unbeliever. He would only hinder her and endanger himself. A figure of authority was needed. Someone who could make people understand, who would help prevent the approaching cataclysm. Such a thing had been done before, although not in her lifetime.

As Dorothy extinguished the bare bulb and hastily ascended the stairs, she decided to embark upon a recruitment drive. Corruption was blossoming like the damp which stained the cellar walls. It would take a sounder mind and more able body than hers to rout the poison at its source.

26.

Criminal Minds

Daily Telegraph   Saturday 25th April

CAPITAL'S SUICIDE RATE SOARS TO ALL-TIME HIGH

The number of successful suicide attempts occurring in London is on the increase, according to a new report commissioned by psychology experts at the Central London Medical Analysis Bureau—and the figure is set to rise further.

"An augmentation between the months of January and March is common," says Dr. Marwan Al-Kaffadji. "During the darker, colder months more people are treated for depression, but the figures usually reduce with the arrival of spring. This year, however, we have seen an alarming rise in the death toll, especially in the professional business sector."

This fact is surprising in the light of positive economic factors, i.e., a strong pound and healthy export levels. Traditionally, white-collar workers suffer more symptoms of stress than manual labourers.

**"HAMBURGERS CAN
MAKE YOU LOSE
WILL TO LIVE"—MP**

While doctors are at a loss to justify the change, the Conservative
MP for Richmond, Mr. Michael
McFee, suggests that poor diet is
at fault, particularly blood-sugar
levels affected by working-class
meal patterns which include a
high percentage of junk food. He
suggested that fast-food outlets
could help combat depression by
inserting "messages of good
cheer" in their hamburger con-
tainers. (Cont'd page 17.)

Brian Lack was avoiding his calls.

Harry left one further message on the machine, requesting that they meet, before setting off to attend Eden's
funeral service. It was, he reflected grimly, the second
cemetery he had entered that month, and there was still
Beth's cremation to follow.

Owing to the bizarre circumstances of the death and
the general public's voracious appetite for such matters,
several members of the press were mingling with the sensation seekers behind the church, waiting to pick up an
unguarded remark from one of the mourners. Harry
looked above their heads and watched as thick coils of
cloud rolled low in the sky, preparing to provide the at-
mospheric rainfall which his father's funeral had so sorely
lacked.

Standing at the head of the graveside gathering, Harry
was able to identify Eden's parents, small and dark, Italian perhaps, the mother's face almost concealed by a vast
white handkerchief. The young man who had been dating
Eden stood a little apart from the family, weathering their
cold stares with defiance. His dark leather jacket and tight
black jeans offered minor concessions to current fashion
even here, and in doing so, gave offense. The father's
pained countenance somehow implied that Dexter's association with his daughter was responsible for her death.
Harry turned away, upset that the burial should be taking
place in such an atmosphere of acrimony.

In an abrupt sermon consisting of little more than ab-
stract vagaries, the vicar had made no reference to Eden's
sartorial passions. He had clearly failed to read the brief.
Even now, the fund for the construction of a modern
coffee-morning annex was receiving another mention.

Harry left in disgust, passing the unobtrusive figure of John May, who duly recorded the early departure in his notebook.

The agency had finally arranged another car for him. By the look of it, the dust gray Ford Granada with the dented passenger door had been chosen as a punishment for his recent poor attendance record at the office. As he fought to keep the misfiring engine turning over in the heavy high-street traffic, he decided to head into the West End and drive past the offices of Instant Image, on the off-chance that Brian Lack had gone there.

Greek Street was misted in drizzle and clogged with vehicles. The video company's reception lights were on, so he parked the car, squeezing into the only available space and cursing as he scraped the side of the Ford against a concrete litter bin. He tried to think of a plausible excuse for his visit. The reception area was deserted. He was searching for an internal telephone directory when Brian Lack suddenly rushed out from the foot of the stairs leading to the rest of the building. Harry caught him as he shoved open the glass doors to the street. Brian spun around and stared at his assailant, guilty and fearful.

The transformation in his appearance was considerable. His features seemed to have lost their sharpness, the flesh appearing sallow and loose. Violet smudges of sleeplessness shadowed his eyes. He had even ceased to bother with the elaborate macrame which normally camouflaged his bald patch. Extrusions of paperwork thrust from the carelessly packed briefcase he had wedged under one arm.

"Ah, Brian! The very person I was looking for," Harry began with what he hoped was a disarming smile. "Has there been any news about the merger?"

Brian pulled his arm free and prepared to move away. "What do you mean, any news?" He moved off along the sidewalk, but Harry caught him and shoved the pair of them into the darkness of a shop doorway.

"Is there something wrong?" he asked with casual menace. "What's been happening to the deal?"

"It went ahead without you, what did you expect?"

Brian tried to free himself, but Harry's grip on the sleeve of his suit tightened.

"How could they do that? My father's share—"

"Your father's share meant as much as Beth Cleveland's."

"What do you mean?"

"The terms stated that a merger could take place where the majority of the directors were in agreement."

"That meant you and Beth. But she told you she'd changed her mind about the deal. She went against you and your buddies at ODEL, and now she's dead. Do you realize how that sounds?" Harry grabbed Brian by the lapel of his jacket and pressed him against the wall. "We were never talking about a merger, it was a buyout with a sweetener thrown in, wasn't it? A takeover bid that was a lot more hostile than anyone realizes."

"Call it what you like," said Brian, frightened now. "ODEL are bulldozing the deal through at less than a quarter of the original offer."

"Bulldozing, Brian? There was only you left to persuade, and you were begging for it."

"Not like this. You don't understand. I have to go now, Buckingham. This doesn't concern you anymore." The man was a trapped animal, exuding fear from every pore.

"I want to know why you let them do it. Was it just the money? Or are they putting pressure on you? There are laws against intimidation."

"You really have no idea." Brian was close to tears. He tilted his head up at the distended clouds, ashamed. Part of his hair flap had slipped into his eyes. "If they see you and me together, I'm finished."

"They killed Willie and Beth," Harry shouted in his face, "and whoever else gets in their way dies. But you already know that, don't you?"

"No, it's not possible. The police said Beth wandered onto the track . . ."

"Forget what the police said. Someone at ODEL had them killed, and you can bet that if there's any comeback they'll pin the blame on you."

"I have to go." Brian struggled to free himself, but Harry held tight.

"Then meet me somewhere later. Help me and I'll find a way to help you."

Brian seemed to consider the proposition for a moment, then shook his head violently. "They'll know about it if I do."

"My father is dead, Brian."

"You think I don't know that?" His face mottled with sudden fury as the words burst from him. "I was his friend, probably a damned sight closer to him than you ever were. You were his son and you never even saw him! I know all about you."

"Then talk to me," begged Harry. "We can go anywhere you like. Nobody will ever know that we met."

"I'll have to think about it."

"All right, but if you haven't contacted me by this time tomorrow, I'll take matters into my own hands." He relinquished his grip on the jacket, and the little man fell away from him.

"I'll do what I can, but things are different now," Brian said, pushing his hair back in place. "This is big business, bigger than you can imagine. I'm part of them. I've seen what they can do."

Harry watched as he shoved out of the doorway and walked quickly away. He wondered whether Brian's loyalty to his father would prove stronger than his loyalty to the new owners of Instant Image. As he walked back to the car, he tried to piece together the train of events. He had no idea why ODEL wanted the company so badly, but they had been prepared to do anything to get it. They had blackmailed Brian Lack into complicity, and with him on their side they had offered the directors a fortune to sell out. Willie and Beth had agreed to the deal in principle. The lawyers had drawn up contracts. Everything was proceeding smoothly until . . .

What? What had happened to make them change their minds, even though they had placed their own lives in jeopardy by doing so? Harry knew that if he didn't uncover the answer soon, there might be no one left alive to tell him.

* * *

One look at the ward sister's hard, pale features told John May that she would brook no nonsense from the police. The grim set of her jaw suggested that she would grant him no more time than she would to any other outsider attempting to enter her ward. The unit had been forewarned of May's visit, but she had refused to commit herself to an interview.

"It's not just a matter of Mark's physical condition," she told May. "Burns are extremely traumatic. The patient's mental state can be profoundly affected. At the moment he's handling it fairly well, but I don't want that balance to be upset in any way. Besides, right now he is still unable to speak. The fumes he inhaled have caused severe edema of the mucous membrane lining his respiratory tract. His air passages are secreting pus."

"What is the condition of his skin?" May knew that if the burns were third degree, the resulting fluid loss could cause fatal circulatory shock.

"We took a decision to debride the more serious blistering, and later on we'll have to perform autografts, but we've been able to minimize the risk of infection. Without anesthetizing drugs he'd be experiencing a tremendous amount of pain."

"Would it be possible just to see him for a minute?" May indicated the folder in his hand. "His testimony is essential to the progress of this investigation."

"I'm afraid that's out of the question. Mark is currently undergoing exposure therapy. We're treating him with Neosporin." This would allow the burns to form a crust and fall off, but opened the patient to the risk of bacterial infection. It meant that May would not be able to carry out any form of questioning until all danger of reinfection had passed.

"Obviously I am not prepared to compromise your patient's recovery in any way, Sister." May held out a card. "Perhaps you'd call me as soon as he's fit enough, in your judgment, to respond to a short interview."

Like a bird defending its nest, the nurse became friendlier with the realization that she had successfully protected her patient. As she saw him to the head of the corridor, she promised to call as soon as the boy's situation improved. May turned to her as he pushed against the swing doors of the exit.

"I want to leave you with this thought, Sister," he said. "There is every chance that young Mark recognized his assailant. He was found in the basement of the store, where the fire started. He must have witnessed the entire event at close quarters. A word from him could bring this arsonist—a person who was prepared to let him perish in flames—into the courtroom." He paused, allowing the effect of his words to take full force. "Now, in my experience, the pain of recalling a traumatic event can sometimes be offset by the satisfaction gained from seeing a criminal brought to justice. In this case, I believe that's a risk worth taking with the patient. Please, call me."

In the foyer of the burns unit he rejoined Sergeant Longbright, who had been taking an official statement from one of the doctors. She was still holding the wrapped package May had given her to hold before entering the ward.

"No dice," he said. "We'll have to bide our time for a witness. You can give me that back now." He took the brightly colored box from her.

As they left the hospital, the rain renewed its strength. The Hammersmith roundabout was unsurprisingly choked with traffic.

"Look at this weather," complained May. "It's like living underwater. If this is global warming, I'm very disappointed. How did you get on with the video-sleeve printers?"

"Most of the replies are in," said Longbright. "None of them recall a specific order from Dell. Anyway, the sleeves aren't commissioned by the outlets. They come from the video departments of the film distribution companies, who in turn farm the work out to small studios."

"So the paper Dell was holding came from a film company," said May as they squeezed between the stalled vehicles in King Street on their way to the Metropolitan Line tube station. "We'll pursue that line of enquiry after the weekend. Right now we've less than half an hour to get to Gog and Magog.''

''What's that?''

''Special delivery.'' May held up the box and tapped it. ''We've an appointment with Arthur.''

Fitzrovia is the name that was given near the start of World War II to the area running between Oxford Street and Euston Road, and is bordered by the blackened Georgian facades of Gower Street to the east and the broad thoroughfare of Great Portland Street to the west. It houses the glass spindle of the Telecom Tower, a pleasant pedestrianized piazza named Fitzroy Square after the son of Charles the Second, and—as it has done for decades—a number of penniless writers and artists. Just a few doors along from a house once occupied by George Bernard Shaw stands the curious English restaurant, Gog and Magog. It derives its name from the statues of warrior giants which had adorned the City's Guildhall until the Blitz, and was filled with reproductions of ancient prints depicting its namesakes in battle. The menu offered an eclectic and bewildering display of early English dishes. The air in the restaurant was redolent with herbs and spices rarely used since the Edwardian era, all of which was very much to Bryant's taste, if not May's. They had agreed to meet here on this sopping Saturday lunchtime not because it fulfilled some integral function of the investigation, but because it was Bryant's birthday.

''I might have known you'd be late.'' Bryant looked up from his newspaper as May and Longbright came through the door. He was wearing a voluminous brown jacket which looked as if it had last received an airing in the reign of George V. ''You're like a pair of drowned rats. I'm defying the weather with a large malt whiskey. I suggest you do the same.'' He beckoned to a waiter as they seated themselves.

''Your very good health,'' said May as he raised his glass a few minutes later, ''in this, your sixty-sev—''

''That's enough about age,'' snapped Bryant. ''It's a

vastly overrated subject. What have you brought me?''
He indicated the box beside Longbright's chair.

"You'd better pass him the present, Janice. It might
make him a little more amenable.'' May watched as his
partner snicked the wrapping paper open with a steak
knife and removed the framed print as carefully as an
archaeologist unpacking a burial relic.

"Why, my dear fellow,'' said Bryant, genuinely
touched, "this is magnificent. Wherever did you find it?''
He turned the frame to Janice, who made sounds of approval. The picture, a watercolor entitled *Over the Moon*,
depicted a parade of characters from the Gilbert and Sullivan operas.

"If I told you, you'd only go there and spend a fortune.''

"Better to do it now than wait until next year, when
I'll be on a police pension.''

"Rubbish, Arthur. You'll still be on the force in five
years' time and you know it.'' There was an uncomfortable pause in the conversation. May gave Longbright an
uneasy smile and studied the menu, unable to raise his
eyes to his colleague.

"I'm afraid I've already put in for it, John.''

"What?'' The smile faded from May's face. "When?''

"Today. I promised myself that I would formally apply
for retirement on my birthday.''

"But we're in the middle of a case!'' May's voice rose.
"You can't walk out on me now, just like that.''

"Calm down, nobody's talking about walking out.
I'll see the investigation through before I go. Don't
spoil my birthday. Order a decent bottle of wine and
loosen your collar. Your face has gone red.'' He directed Longbright's attention to the menu. "You must
try the game pudding, and for dessert they do marvelous things with figs, it's all coronary-inducing and quite
delicious.''

During the course of the meal, May attempted to dis-
suade his friend from his chosen path of action. In this
argument he was assisted by the sergeant, who felt that
without Bryant and May in the department her advancement to the status of inspector would be considerably less

likely. While colleagues harbored no doubt about her abilities, their resentment over her long-standing affair with the chief would surely count against her. Bryant, however, was not to be moved in his decision.

"You reach a point where all felonies start to look the same," he explained, "and you no longer care about crime as passionately as you once did." He gently swirled his brandy in its bowl. "The criminal mind has lost its originality, but none of its viciousness. There's a depressing uniformity to the modern-day lawbreaker. So much casual cruelty, and so much of it exactly the same. The kids think that by committing acts of violence and vandalism they're attacking the status quo, but all they're doing is becoming a part of it. There are no crimes of passion any more, only acts of spite and ignorance. It's time for me to go."

"Arthur, as long as I've known you, you have always had the greatest admiration for individuality. You've always had us assigned to the quirky cases, the bizarre problems that no one else has wanted to bother with. Remember the extraordinary way you and Hargreave reached a solution in the Savoy history murders? How it nearly got you killed?"

"Ah, the Savoy," said Bryant, savoring the brandy at his lips. "My favorite hotel. They still let me stay there for free, you know, as a gesture of gratitude. A unique establishment."

"So are you, Arthur."

"I'm not sure I like that." He withdrew his pocket watch and studied it. "It's later than I thought. I have an appointment in South London in an hour. Some further research on the Dell investigation, just in case you thought I'd already thrown in the towel." He picked up the picture and folded it into his overcoat. "A charming gift, and a most agreeable luncheon. I'd better walk it off before my arteries start to harden."

"I suppose there's no chance of you wearing your beeper this weekend," suggested May.

"Not much, no," agreed Bryant cheerfully. "I put it somewhere sensible and now I can't find it. I suppose it might be in the washing machine. Can I offer anyone a lift?"

"No, thank you." May shuddered at the thought. "I can catch a bus to the station."

"You're going back there tonight?" asked Longbright, surprised. May never discussed his home life. The reason for this, she suspected, was that, like many dedicated detectives, he didn't have one.

"Cheerio, then," said Bryant. "If anyone needs me, I'll be at the library finding how to summon up devils." The warped trilby he had plonked on his head almost covered his ears.

The sergeant gave May a look of puzzlement. "How are you going to do that?" she asked Bryant, pulling the restaurant door toward her and preparing to step back into the steadily falling rain.

"By availing myself of the resources of a remarkable woman," he replied, a dark twinkle returning to his eyes. "While your computer logs investigative minutiae, I shall be entering the realm of the supernatural."

"Really, Arthur," said May with a sigh, "there's no need to be so theatrical. We've got enough problems on our hands without dragging in the spirit world."

"Forensic science isn't going to help us much this time, John." Bryant stepped away from the restaurant canopy and pulled down the brim of his hat. "On Monday morning, I have arranged to consult a professional from a far less respected field."

"Whom do you have in mind?"

"One of the country's leading experts in paranormal psychology, although whether she realizes it is another matter. You may remember her. A woman named Dorothy Huxley. Toodle-oo for now."

"Don't you think he's heading a little too far out with this?" asked Longbright as they watched Bryant pass beneath the dripping boughs of the oaks on the far side of the square.

May scratched his chin thoughtfully. "I don't know. We've always operated this way, with me sifting through endless piles of paperwork and him following the wild hunches."

"And that's how it works?"

"It's always done so in the past. The best discoveries are made in teams where the partners provide cover for each others' deficits. I'm the realist," he said a little sadly. "He's the dreamer."

27.

Harry and Grace

SATURDAY EVENING BEGAN with Grace unsuccessfully attempting to gain access to Harry Buckingham's apartment via his entryphone. When the account executive finally realized that Grace, true to her word, was prepared to pass the night on the doorstep, he had admitted her on the condition that she would be prepared to leave in exactly ten minutes. His hostility toward her was born of fear. Hilary had agreed to attend a reconciliatory meeting, and was due to arrive at the flat at precisely 7:30 P.M. It was now a minute past seven. Harry figured that it would take twenty minutes after Grace's departure for him to rid the rooms of her fragrant but stubbornly persistent perfume, which left ten minutes, or rather nine, in which to conduct the interview. Grace all but fell through the door as he opened it. She quickly moved from room to room, casting her enormous eyes about with a look of mounting horror on her face.

"Is this your own place?" she asked, "or are you minding the furniture for a TV quiz show?"

"You can't stay," said Harry briskly. "Hilary's on her way here and it's my last chance to patch things up with her."

"What about the other night in the restaurant, you and I, snogging in a romantic corner of the ladies' lavatory, doesn't that count for anything?" Grace threw him a defiant look and headed in the direction of the kitchen. "I might have known you'd have a Gaggia."

"Of course it does," said Harry, hastily moving after her, "but we have this long-standing thing going. Her family knows my family . . ."

"Cozy." Grace made a face and closed the refrigerator door. "Your milk's off. I don't suppose *she* takes milk unless it's skimmed. Watching her figure. Women like that inflate to the size of hippos minutes after you marry them; it's something in their metabolism."

"Grace, I let you in because you said you had some news for me. Tell me and I'll catch up with you tomorrow."

"Okay." She shook salt onto a stick of celery and bit into it. "The guy I was having drinks with at the restaurant, I said I'd tell you who he was. His name is Frank Drake. We attended art school together, only he dropped out after a year. He's a bit weird, but we used to get along quite well."

"He's weird and you became friends?" said Harry with heavy sarcasm. "I would never have believed it." He glanced at his watch. Seven-fifteen.

"Listen to me, Harry. I told him about the problems you were having . . ."

"Perhaps you mentioned that I'm now under suspicion in a fascinating variety of murder cases? Sorry, verdicts of accidental death are being returned on each of them, but that fact apparently counts for nothing with the police."

"That's where you're wrong." She fished into the refrigerator for another celery stick. "Frank's been investigating a similar phenomenon. He thinks the police know all about it. According to him there's a pattern forming to these mishaps, and it's not just us who are involved, there are loads of people across London who have all recently—"

"What is this guy, a private detective?"

"He's an assistant librarian, but he's very bright and he makes connections, things that other people overlook . . ."

"Then why is he only an assistant librarian, why isn't

he the junior health minister?'' Hilary was due to arrive in eight minutes. She was never late. He attempted to steer Grace toward the front door, wondering if he could remove the smell of perfume by using an air freshener. ''Grace, I have to sort this out, surely you can see that? I'll call you in the morning and we'll discuss it.''

Grace held on to her position in the doorway. ''You say that now,'' she said, ''but you won't call, because you don't trust me.''

''I *trust* you,'' Harry insisted as the downstairs entryphone buzzer suddenly sounded. ''You just come on too strong, too . . .''

''Marlene Dietrich in *The Blue Angel*? Or Katharine Hepburn in *Bringing Up Baby*? Face it, Harry, I scare the pants off you. That's the front door.'' She moved across to the intercom. ''Want me to get it?''

''No!'' Harry threw himself across the room and pressed the intercom button on the wall. ''Who is it?''

''Harry, who else could it possibly be?'' Shorn of its bass modulation, Hilary's voice emerged from the metal speaker with an edge one could sharpen pencils on. ''It's absolutely pouring. Let me in.''

''Uh, hold on just a minute . . .'' He turned back to Grace, desperate. ''There's a back way out of here,'' he pleaded. ''Please take it.''

''Oh, I see, more like Celia Johnson in *Brief Encounter*. I might have known.'' Behind them, the door buzzer sounded furiously. Harry gingerly depressed the intercom button, as if he was in danger of receiving an electric shock.

''Harry, what on earth are you doing? I'm getting soaked. Open the door!''

''I'm trying to, Hilary, I think there's a fault with the mechanism. Have you tried pushing?'' He snapped his finger from the intercom before she could reply.

''Look at it this way,'' said Grace logically. ''At the moment Hilary is a very attractive woman, I'll grant you that. But I know her type. That blond girly look soon grows hard, bitterness sets in, and after a handful of semi-successful lifts, tucks, and collagen implants you'll find yourself stuck with a hysterical, manic-depressive, over-dressed vegetable.''

"I am not a violent man," said Harry through clench-ing teeth, "but if you don't head for the fire escape in the next ten seconds I am going to throw you down it."

Grace backed up against the crazily buzzing intercom as Harry advanced on her. "Wait, let me just ask you one question: has she ever spent ten minutes enthusias-tically telling you about a book she just read, yes or no?"

Harry was thrown for a moment. He thought fast. "No. She's far too busy to read, she's on committees, she's captain of the tennis—"

"How about a play she just saw? A newspaper arti-cle?"

"Okay," he shouted, "she's no great intellect but that doesn't make her a bad person!"

"Just as I thought. Bimbos do wonders for a man's self-esteem. What's she like below the surface?"

"I haven't found out yet."

"I wasn't talking about sex, Harry."

"She wasn't talking about sex, Harry!" screamed the intercom. Grace guiltily slipped her finger from the in-tercom button as he pushed her out of the way.

"Hilary," he shouted at the microphone, "you don't understand."

"I don't, do I? Tell me, is this your new company car outside, Harry?"

There was a tinkle of glass at the other end of the intercom. He dashed to the window in time to see Hilary breaking a milk bottle against the windshield of the Gra-nada as if launching a ship, before storming off into the rain on unsteady high heels.

Harry walked slowly to the couch and sat down with his head in his hands. "I think you had better leave now," he said, his voice muffled through latticed fingers. "Un-less perhaps you'd like to set fire to the place before you go."

"I have a better idea." She pulled her sweater over her head and knelt beside him, sliding her hands between his arms. "We're responsible, adult people. Let's discuss your inability to handle mature relationships in the bedroom.''

Harry found it hard to believe that her lightning moods could incorporate such a sudden change. But he found it even harder to believe the ease with which he accepted the proposal. Thinking about it afterward, he wondered aloud if she had somehow planned the entire encounter. She assured him she had not, and the matter ended there. Meanwhile, the evening passed in gentle caresses and darkened smiles, as she removed her asexual tomboy image and replaced it with that of a responsive woman. Harry's sexual technique seemed to consist of little more than surprised acquiescence, but perhaps this was due to the circumstances surrounding the encounter.

Grace lay in the crook of his arm as she stared at the ceiling, her breathing matching the rhythm of his heart, and hoped that despite their differences they would continue to seek out each other's company.

She slowly became aware that the telephone, a high-tack job of chrome and perspex, was making a constipated bleeping noise. She lifted herself from Harry's body, noted that he was still asleep, and answered the call herself.

"Harry, wake up. He wants to speak to you." She shook him until he raised an eyelid.

"Who is it?"

"Brian Lack. It sounds urgent."

He sat to attention and pulled the receiver from her hand. The voice at the other end began to speak before he could bring his ear to it.

". . . to talk to someone and it has to be you. What time is it now? Half past ten, can we meet at eleven? Can you do that? It has to be tonight, you see, and the sooner the better . . ." The voice ran on, bewildered and nervous.

Harry tried to cut in. "Brian, what's the matter? Are you at home?"

"No, no, can't go there, that would be the worst place to go, I'm in the West End, at the office, home's too risky, couldn't get across the city, too far to travel now . . ." Harry had no doubt that he was listening to a man in fear of his life, or deranged to the point of believing that he was.

"For God's sake, Brian, slow down, I can't understand you. Look, I can be there in half an hour."

"No, don't come here, I'll meet you in the light, somewhere open, bright, and safe, although there's nowhere really safe. I should have confided in someone before this, but who would have understood? No one would believe me. That's what makes it so perfect. Daniel Carmody has the ear of the government and the respect of the nation. The legislature is all on his side. You know what they say about him, don't you? They say he's living proof that capitalism can care. Of course we trusted him. How was I to know?"

"Know what, Brian? What do you know?"

"There's no such thing as corporate accountability. They can do anything they want and nothing will happen to them. A fuss in the press, a temporary drop in the share index, but nothing will really happen. They can't die like we can. They can kill, but they can't die. Having power is like being immortal."

"Brian, tell me when I get there. I'll meet you . . . hold on." He cupped his hand over the receiver and turned to Grace. "Well-lit place near Soho, open area, somewhere he can see people coming."

"Trafalgar Square."

"Brian, I'll meet you in the center of Trafalgar Square and we'll work this out together. Is that busy enough for you?"

There was a sigh of relief at the other end of the line. "Okay, Harry, but when? How soon? I'm marked now. Every step I take is dangerous."

"I'll see if I can get there in twenty minutes."

"Will you believe me?"

"I'll try, Brian, I'll try."

In spite of Grace's protestations, three minutes later he left the apartment alone, punched out the remaining glass shards which clung to the frame of the Granada's windshield, and drove toward the West End with the rain flooding over his face and the dashboard.

28.

Pride Before a Fall

BRIAN LACK PAUSED beneath the rustling plane trees on the west side of the square and took stock of his situation. The area surrounding the vast silent fountains was almost deserted, as were the walkways and staircases which led down to them from the National Gallery. As he skirted the square, keeping close to the trunks of the trees, he kept watch for signs of untoward activity. Even the perpetual picket outside South Africa House was depleted in numbers tonight. A handful of students and a single police constable kept lonely vigil here, where once the stuccoed elegance of Morley's Hotel had faced out across the granite fountains.

A sudden night breeze pressed cool fingers against the back of the accountant's jacket as he moved through the shadows. Starting, he turned to stare nervously behind him, but found nothing. Along the southern side of the square, double-decker buses queued behind each other as patiently as elephants, waiting to pass into Whitehall. The quietness of the square itself was unusual but not unwelcome, for it lessened the danger of a surprise attack. A dozen or so bedraggled pigeons scurried by his feet on their way to a wastebin filled with hamburger cartons and popcorn bags. Brian's scalp prickled beneath his intricately woven strands of hair. He checked his watch once more. Surely Harry should have been here by now? Perhaps he had already arrived and was standing on the upper terrace, looking out upon the empty square. But wouldn't he call out, and raise a hand in recognition?

Brian donned the spectacles he sometimes wore for

driving, and the horizon jumped into focus. The magnificent fluted Corinthian column from which Lord Nelson surveyed the city stood no more than a hundred yards ahead of him. He found himself facing one of the bronze bas-reliefs which adorned the base of the column, a scene depicting the Battle of the Nile. There was a warbling noise by his foot, and a grotesque one-eyed pigeon hobbled past.

Brian raised his face to the sky, his forehead glistening in the light of a nearby streetlamp. There was no one here. But they could be watching him from the buildings nearby, couldn't they? Any one of those darkened windows could conceal a figure hunched over a rifle. What an easy target he'd make walking into the center of the square! What he knew now was enough to have him killed. Could these thoughts of snipers be merely insane imaginings, or could the last moments of his life be quietly draining away even as he stood and considered his fate? His fingers traced lines of pain across his forehead, like tightening bands of wire. He had to force himself to think, to clear his mind and remember the events of the evening.

Unable to settle himself at home, he had gone into the office. There he had found himself guiltily sitting in Willie Buckingham's old chair, facing his desk. The old man's few remaining belongings had been collected after the funeral by poor Beth.

Brian remembered the night of the confrontation, when Willie had stood before him demanding an explanation. At first he had tried to feign ignorance, but it quickly became apparent that Willie had grasped the truth. He had spotted something extruding from the bottom drawer of Brian's desk, he said, a corner of white. He would normally have minded his own business. The concertina of paper which had opened in his hands was only a memo, a note detailing a mistake in the stock, nothing important, and yet . . .

Willie Buckingham had admitted that he had the mind of a bureaucrat. It was a blessing and a failing. Some considered him to be petty-minded, but he knew the importance of attention to detail. That was why he could remember all the shipment numbers—and the one referred to in the memo did not exist.

He had gone to the storage bay. Searched through the cases. Located the impossible shipment. Matched the serial number on the memo with the one on the side of the box. There had been a crowbar leaning against the wall of the bay. He had tucked its iron teeth under the lip of the crate and pushed down. The lid had risen easily in his hands. At first he had been disappointed with the contents of the box. But then suspicion had set in. And then, something worse . . .

A sound, behind him. The square still deserted. The wind rippling the water in the fountain basins. No buses circling now, all gone to Whitehall and the Strand, up Charing Cross Road, along Pall Mall. The leaves of the plane trees danced before him as the wind slowly began to rise. Above, fast-moving clouds reflected the light of the city. He had tilted his head so far back that he almost lost his balance and tumbled to the windswept flagstones. In the distance, a dark figure scurried past the granite capstans lining the terrace, darted across the road past St. Martin-in-the-Fields, and was gone.

Still no sign of Harry. What to do? There was nowhere safe. How to get home if he failed to show? He studied his watch, a drunk attempting to decipher the hour. Buses still ran, only a little after eleven. Buses were dangerous. Anyone could be sitting next to you. He found himself at the edge of the fountain basin, stooped to splash the bitter water on his face. The shock helped him realize the irrationality of his paranoia. Five more minutes and he would go home. The square was so silent, not even the sound of traffic. A creak. A creak of—what, wood? Metal?

There it was again.

He sat hard against the basin rim, listening carefully.

And again, another metallic groan, like scaffolding in the wind, a cry of steel like a ship twisting apart in rough seas. He raised his eyes to the square before him. Nelson's column, symbol of permanence, one hundred and forty-five feet of historical rationality, and at its base, four bronze lions, the Landseer lions, each one as tall as four grown men, each twenty feet long, each as proud and as fierce as the empire herself had once been.

And as he watched, one of them turned to look at him.

His eyes widened until they began to smart. The lion was motionless, but its blank bronze eyes stared into his, waiting for him to break into a run. He held his breath, not daring to move. The groan of metal resounded once more, and before his horrified eyes the lion slowly rose from its pedestal, paused for a moment, then dropped down from its plinth onto the surrounding flagstones. The sound of screeching metal tore the air as the second lion raised its massive head and followed the steady gaze of its companion.

Brian's heart pounded within his chest, so loud that he was sure the pride could sense it. Slowly, all four lions left the base of the monument and began to cross the square in his direction, their vast bronze paws gingerly setting down on the stone, like kittens finding their first steps.

But these were no kittens. One look at their dead eyes told him that they had taken his scent and were closing for the kill. They clanged and creaked as they drew nearer, their hollow interiors reflecting the sound. Brian spun away from the fountain and ran for the east side of Trafalgar Square, toward South Africa House. The picket was still outside. Why had they not dropped their banners and run? They seemed to be oblivious to the approach of these ferrous carnivores. A new sound blasted into the sky, the broad, low pitch vibrating the air around him. One of the lions had opened its jaws and was roaring at the passing clouds as if trying to open the gates of heaven.

As he reached the railing which edged the side of the square, his shoes skidded beneath him and he fell heavily onto his chest, skinning the palms of his hands and tearing the knees from his trousers. Behind, the lions padded nearer, their great heads raised as they followed human spoor. Their leader, the first creature to rise from his pedestal, paused and sat back on groaning bronze haunches, the lights shining dully on its polished hide. It was waiting for him to rise to his feet. A soft respira-

tory wheeze, like wind through an elevator shaft, rose
from its nostrils. The others arrived behind it and stopped
at a respectful distance. They were disapproving of this
whimpering creature which lay before them. They wanted
him to die like a man. Forcing back the sobs trapped in
his throat, he rose on unsteady legs and wiped his bloodied palms on his jacket. Then he ran.

He reached the railing and ducked beneath it, rising
into the roadway beyond. He was about to head across
for the safety of the far side when he made the mistake
of looking back. The first of the lions had stepped
across the railings. Shadowed by the fanning foliage of
the plane trees, its eyes became white lights, so bright
that he could not bear to look at them. He stumbled
back, a scream bursting from his lungs into his bloodied mouth, and he knew that this was the last sound he
would ever hear.

The creature vanished from his sight as its huge front
paw fell on him, crushing his legs to pulp in a single
swipe. He felt the edge of the gutter smash into his skull,
tried to roll clear onto the tarmac and was horrified to
see the top half of his body divorce itself from the shattered lower portion. The paw descended a second time,
obliterating the night above as it exploded his head like
a detonating watermelon.

At first, the policeman took no notice of him.

Harry had reached the edge of Trafalgar Square just
twenty-five minutes after the phone call from Brian
Lack. At the side of the square nearest to South Africa
House he found a police cordon, two ambulances, several squad cars, and a large number of ghoulish spec-
tators. As soon as he saw the blankets covering—or
rather, attempting to cover—the combustion of human
debris which littered the road, he knew he was looking
at the body of Brian Lack. The shoes and the jacket
were the same ones that he was wearing when they had
met earlier in the day.

"I know the man," Harry shouted at the inattentive
young constable. "What happened to him?"

"He ran straight into the traffic," said one of the anti-apartheid students. "We saw the whole thing. The bus honked and flashed its lights but he didn't take any notice. Then the vehicles behind ran over him. They couldn't stop in time." The constable, barely a year older than the student, placed a heavy hand on his shoulder. "We'll need you to give a statement, sonny." He hated protesting students. He turned to Harry. "You say you know who this bloke is?"

Suddenly aware of the delicacy of his position, Harry took a pace back. "No, it was a mistake."

As the constable called after him, he walked back to the car as quickly and as inconspicuously as possible.

29.

A Surfeit of Information

SERGEANT LONGBRIGHT CAUGHT the telephone on its second ring. She sat up in bed and snapped on the light.

"Janice, I'm sorry to call you so late."

"That's okay. What time is it?"

"Two-thirty," said John May. "It's about our star witness, the burns boy, Mark Ashdown. I just had a call from the hospital. He's dead. They've been told not to touch anything until we get there."

"My God, I thought you said he was making a recovery?"

"He was. They think he killed himself."

"How could that be?" She tucked the receiver in the crook of her neck and slid gently out of bed, careful not to disturb the sleeping form of Ian Hargreave. "I thought the nurses were keeping him under sedation."

"They were using a graduated course of soporific drugs to minimize the possibility of serious trauma."

"Could his conscious will have overridden reactive chemical treatment?" she asked. "Is that possible? He must have been very determined."

"Or just very scared." There was a pause on the line. "Janice, I'm not sure what we're dealing with anymore. This is starting to get way out of hand."

"Have you talked to Arthur yet?"

"No. This side of the case doesn't concern him. I want to leave him free to follow his own leads and theories for the time being."

"Okay." She thought for a moment, running her free hand through stiff, unruly hair. This was a bad way to start off a Sunday. "You want me to pick you up? You're on the way to the hospital."

"Twenty minutes." The line went dead.

The staff nurse stood uneasily in the doorway, as if reluctant to let them through. Longbright's ancient standard-issue raincoat leaked pools on the tiled floor. In the half-light of the corridor she looked like the star of a forgotten noir thriller. John May ushered the way ahead and she cautiously stepped into the room.

The body was lying diagonally across the bed, legs splayed wide, one arm thrown toward the floor. His torso and chest were still swathed in bandages, his head and neck were exposed to the air. The plastic cord of his intravenous feeding tube had been pulled tight across his throat, the bottle to which it had been connected lay by its stand, shattered. As May stepped forward, glass crunched underfoot. "Can we have some more light in here?" He waved an arm at the wall. "When was the last time someone entered the room?"

"The night nurse was stationed in the corridor the whole time. She heard a crash and ran in. He was lying like that, barely moving. She raised the alarm and tried to clear his throat, but he was already dead."

He leaned close over the body. The boy's eyes had rolled to glistening white orbs.

"Presumably she couldn't undo the tube without damaging the tissue beneath it. Did you take the bandages from his face?"

"No," said the staff nurse. "He must have torn them off by himself."

"What makes you think that?" He dropped to his knees and peered beneath the bed.

"His wounds are definitely fresher than they were. The scabbing adhered to the bandages when they were removed."

"That's what would happen if you tore them off quickly? What was his level of sedation? Was he unconscious? Unrousable?"

"He would have been in a state of . . . extreme docility."

"What does that mean? Unable to tie a shoelace? Unable to stand? Do you think it possible that he could have done this to himself?"

The staff nurse sighed. She had been arguing this point with another nurse when they arrived. "In my opinion, no, he could not have exerted enough pressure on the drip."

"The stand is on wheels. Surely if he pulled it, it would have simply rolled forward and toppled over?"

"Unless the smoke damage to his throat . . ."

"Good point, Janice." He turned to the nurse. "Was his throat still forming mucus?"

"His respiratory passages were being kept clear but there was a lot of inflammation and fluid."

"So it would not have taken much pressure to close the passage up completely."

"I don't suppose so, no."

"I have to ask this," said May gently. "If the drugs you prescribed for him were not deep enough to maintain a calm conscious state, could he have awoken and become traumatized by his situation?"

The nurse beckoned to the night nurse and consulted with her. "It's possible," she said finally. "After infection, trauma is the next biggest danger to a burns patient. But this isn't the form it usually takes."

"Was he right-handed?"

"I think so, yes."

He turned to Longbright. "It looks to me as if he died by his own hand, however unlikely that may seem.

If you study the inside of his right index and forefingers, you'll find a discoloration of the flesh where the tubing was wrapped around his fingers to give him a better grip." He buttoned up his coat. "You've been very helpful, nurse. I'm afraid you'll be inconvenienced for a while further while they photograph and fingerprint."

The night nurse held out a thin white envelope. "Your colleague left this for you."

May studied it with a furrowed brow. "When was he here?"

"He left just a few minutes ago."

He unfolded the note within and read:

Dear John,

I'm sure the last thing you want is my interference in your side of things. I just thought you'd like to think about this:

The clocks on the video machines in Dell's store had been reset twenty minutes before the fire began. The boy must have unplugged something and in doing so accidentally turned off the electricity for a moment. You see my point?

Pip, pip.

Arthur

Puzzled, he passed the note to Longbright. He was damned if he did see the point.

"What was Mr. Bryant doing here so late?"

"I thought you knew," replied the staff nurse. "He'd been looking in on Mark at regular intervals, day and night. It was he who insisted that someone should be stationed in the corridor at all times."

"He knew the boy's life was in danger," said May as they crossed the rainswept car park a few minutes later. "He put someone outside the door to prove his point."

"But the night nurse saw nobody."

"Exactly. He's verified that no outside agent needs to be involved in these deaths. He knows more than he's telling us. I think perhaps it's time we changed our working methods and began to collaborate." They had always been likened to the two hemispheres of the brain, May the right side, the logical statistician who diligently collected facts, Bryant the left side, the creative theorist who strung together seemingly random details. But this time they would have to learn to pool their resources.

"You know what our problem is?" he said to Longbright, opening the car door for her. "We're suffering from a surfeit of information. There are too many elements to consider, too many facts. They're camouflaging the situation, not clarifying it. How awake are you? Could you handle a couple of hours back at headquarters?"

"I'm not tired."

"Excellent. We'll start by removing everything in the fatality file that's not directly pertinent to each death. There were leads we didn't follow up at the start because each day brought fresh developments. Let's go back and explore those."

Longbright watched May as he drove. He seemed possessed of a special energy, as if he was working against the clock to come up with answers. It made her wonder if the clock was measuring the amount of time he himself had left to run.

30.

Prayerdevils

DOROTHY ENJOYED BEING in the library early on a Monday morning. The cool peacefulness of the reading hall relaxed her. Arthur Bryant arrived just as she was unlocking the main doors to look out for him. At first it seemed to her that he had not changed a bit. The Savile Row three-piece suit, the rose boutonniere, and the battered trilby returned fond memories of their last encounter. It was not until he removed his hat that she realized how much the intervening years had aged him. He appeared to have grown smaller and grayer, as if a light had been, if not extinguished, then dimmed.

"My dear good lady. I'm sorry I couldn't come to you on Saturday. Our investigation seems to be proving rather more eventful than I anticipated." Bryant held out his hand. "How long has it been since our last little adventure?"

"Seven years to my reckoning, Arthur. Why is it that you only ever call when you want something?" Her tone was cheerfully reproachful. "You'd better come in out of the rain. We were about to undergo the ritual of morning tea and newspapers. I want to know what you've been up to all this time."

In the room behind the reception counter, Frank Drake was boiling the kettle. Dorothy raised the hinged countertop and led the way to the small back room which had been set aside for the private use of library staff. Bryant stood his dripping umbrella in a corner and lowered himself into a large faded armchair. He glanced around with an air of vague disapproval. "It's getting a bit shabby, this place," he said, sniffing the air. "Damp. Could do with some sprucing up."

"What do you expect?" said Dorothy, passing him a cup. "We're an embarrassment to the council. They don't know whether to turn the place into an aerobics center or close us down and sell the land. Last year they were planning to open a prostitutes' collective here. Now it's more likely to become another postmodern office block. They're longing for the building to fall down—and that won't take long if this blessed rain doesn't ease up soon."

"You'll fight the closure, of course," said Bryant. "There's the collection to consider."

Dorothy was not fond of discussing the arcane volumes with outsiders. In her simple role of senior librarian she was happily accepted and ignored. She had no desire to position herself in the public eye as the guardian of occult treasure. It was better that no attention was drawn to the collection. At the same time, she would have felt uncomfortable if the basement's accumulated wisdom was denied to those who could truly appreciate it.

"My mother's will stipulated that the ownership of . . . the collection . . . will only pass to the council on the condition that it is housed in the library for the span of my lifetime."

"So you reckon they're just waiting for you to shuffle off your mortal coil? What do you think will happen to the books after you die?"

"They'll be sold off to private collectors, of course, and the council will trouser the money. The books *have* to stay together. Too many of them rely on each other's texts. The collection can only be effective if it remains of a piece." She sighed and stared into her cup, as if hoping to find the answer there. "What have you been doing all this time? How's that partner of yours—what's his name?"

"John. He's fine. Angry with me because I've decided to retire."

"The last time I spoke to you, you were having a terrible time with dead bodies at the Savoy. You said then that it was going to be your last case."

"This one really is," said Bryant, setting aside his cup. "We've a series of fatalities on our hands—note that I say 'fatalities' and not murders. Engineered suicides, to be precise." Over the half hour which followed, Bryant ran over the salient points of the case. In the far corner, Frank Drake looked up from his cuttings and listened with growing interest.

"So you see the difficulty we're in," he concluded. "We've found runic symbols on three victims, four if you count the burned boy. I don't think it would be an exaggeration to say that there could be hundreds of other deaths involved over an extended period of time."

"Frank, I think you'd better tell Mr. Bryant about your own findings," said Dorothy slowly. Frank, who had been longing for an opportunity to test his theories on an outside party, needed no second bidding. He was just reaching the part about the worldwide CIA fascist conspiracy when Bryant halted him.

"These deaths are supposedly being caused by ancient runes," he said, "not the CIA. But I was told that the only way to direct the power of runes was by occult means." He withdrew one of the curses from his jacket and held it up. "Could this piece of paper actually cause someone's death?"

"I don't see how," said Dorothy. "Runic curses constantly change in appearance. They're a symbolic method of controlling natural forces. Odin, their god, is both awe-inspiring and dangerous. The members of his cult were shamans and berserks. But the language they used was a complex, subtle one. I'd be surprised if these few lines could effectively condemn someone to death. No one from today's world would believe such a thing, even if they could translate it. Besides, you've looked at the paper—why hasn't it killed you?"

Bryant tapped his teeth thoughtfully. "The victims are terrified into seeing these things as the Devil's prayers. Something is triggering their deaths, but what?"

"Let's put this into perspective for a moment, Arthur." She took the piece of paper and placed it before her. "The pagans believed that nature was magic. In just the same way that you and I understand the basic principle behind, say, a microwave oven, the pagans knew that rocks could be warmed by the breath of a goddess and that seizures were caused by the anger of a wronged deity. The mentality of modern man is so far removed from the pagan mind as to be barely related to it at all. But some things remain across the ages—subconscious reflexes, primal fears. The sight of this"—she held the paper aloft—"may have struck terror into the heart of pagan man, but there's no way that it could translate into the world of today." Dorothy adjusted her spectacles and took another look at the runes. "These look terribly familiar. Come downstairs with me, would you?"

As they descended into the basement she saw his step falter on the stairs, as if he too felt the overwhelming power of the arcane lore surrounding them. She located a bookcase filled with moldering volumes on runic mythology and withdrew a relatively new paperback from the shelf. A consultation within its index led her to another volume, then a third. Suddenly she came upon them, exact replicas of the runes Bryant had just shown her.

"I hate to tell you this, Arthur," she said, lowering her glasses to the end of her nose, "but they're not obscure curses at all." She checked the book again. "No, far from it, they're very common transcriptions, very common indeed." Bryant took the runes from her and studied the illustration in her proffered book. "You see? They're poems of protection. They ensure the safekeeping of the bearer, not his destruction. 'May the gods protect me through the darkest hours,' that sort of thing."

"But that's impossible!" exclaimed Bryant. "And if that's what they say, then the protection doesn't work."

"Perhaps it does."

"How?"

"Runes can be used to protect both people and objects. Perhaps your victims weren't the ones protected by them."

"What do you mean?"

"Suppose the runes were intended to protect whatever it was that killed them? Where did you get this piece of paper?"

"This particular one?" He thought for a moment. "We found it on the floor of Dell's video shop. It came from the sleeve of a video box," he said quietly.

"Then I have some bad news for you," said Dorothy. "Someone has found a way to adapt an ancient evil for use in modern technology."

31.

Break-in

"**T**RY TO PASS the crowbar to me casually," said Grace, kneeling before the steel trellis. "You look far too suspicious standing there with your hands in your pockets."

"I'm sure the man next door can see what we're doing." Harry slid the iron bar out of his trousers and passed it to his accomplice. In front of the next building a large black man in a tuxedo and an African headband stood guarding the entrance to a dance club. From time to time he looked over and studied them with indifference. At nearly half past one on a cold Monday morning, Greek Street was still surprisingly busy. Acid house, reggae, ska, and hopped-up soul music boomed indistinctly from club doorways. Couples passed, eating from greasy paper bags. Grace levered her weight against the crowbar and the slim chain holding the trellis shut snapped in two. She carefully rose and brushed the rust from her tight black dress.

"Give me the main door keys, and the alarm key." Grace held out her hand as Harry dug in his pocket. The box of belongings that Beth Cleveland had returned to him had included Willie's alarm code and keys to the Instant Image building. Harry just hoped that the locks had not been changed since the takeover. Slipping through the trellis and pulling it shut behind them, Grace reached up to the top of the door and inserted the key. "Let me go in first," said Harry. "I have to turn off the alarm." As she opened the door a low buzz sounded, and a red LED began to blink in the dark. Harry ran lightly across the foyer, punched out the alarm decoder number, and the buzzing stopped.

"Okay," he said. "We're free to move about. What we need is the accounts department. Don't touch the lights." The illuminated signs in the street outside furnished them with enough light to see the stairs. On the first floor they located the video duplication machines, stacked above each other on metal-framed shelves. The second floor consisted of three small administration offices with nameplates on the doors reading LACK, CLEVELAND, and BUCKINGHAM.

A partitioned space at the back of the floor proved to be the accounts department. Grace's torch picked out a bank of green filing cabinets. One of them was locked.

"Look in the desk drawers for a set of small keys," whispered Harry. "Brian took the masters home, but he must have kept duplicates somewhere."

Grace turned on a small anglepoise lamp and lowered its hood to the desk so that it threw out a low circle of light. In the bottom drawer of his desk they found a small, steel petty-cash box. Grace's size eight Doc Martens boot quickly buckled the casing until it sprang open. Inside was a slim key which fitted the cabinet.

"Make sure you twist the box lid back in shape before we go," said Harry. "Now let's find out what's been going on around here." He pulled on the top handle and the drawer silently rolled open. He shone the torch over brown cardboard files filled with order forms for video duplication services. Gently closing it, he opened the drawer below. The contents proved identical to the one above. The bottom drawer contained a large sealed envelope.

"How can you open it without anyone finding out?" asked Grace.

"Have a look around for their stationery cupboard, find another envelope like this." Harry shone his torch through the packet, but the paper within was too dense to reveal any wording. Grace returned with an envelope and held it up to check the size. Harry carefully cut through the top of the sealed packet and withdrew the contents. Inside were a number of personal documents pertaining to Brian Lack's finances. Behind these were two carefully typed pages of heavy foolscap. He spread them out on the desk and began to read.

CARMODY SHIPMENT NINE:
CALLANBERG HOLDINGS

Meeting attended by:

Daniel Carmody, managing director, ODEL, Inc.
Samuel Harwood, chairman, ODEL, Inc.
Brian Lack, director, Instant Image.
William Buckingham, director, Instant Image.
Elizabeth Cleveland, director, Instant Image.

"This document is dated over three weeks ago," said Harry, running his torch across the page. "Just around the time that the ODEL Corporation made its bid for the company." He drew Grace around the desk so that she could read with him.

On the above date Daniel Carmody and his lawyer called a meeting with the directors of Instant Image to explain the circumstances of our proposed incorporation.

After the meeting, Mr. Carmody asked me to remain in the room. He proceeded to impart some confidential material, which I herewith disclose.

On February 15 of this year, Carmody authorized, via the ODEL Corporation, the printing of five hundred (500) specially encoded three-quarter-inch Sony U-matic videocassettes for transmission use by a New York–based company called Callanberg Holdings. However, before the order could be filled, part of the shipment was stolen from his company's dispatch bay.

The theft was traced to a former ODEL employee, David Coltis, who was subsequently apprehended by the ODEL executive's own legal department. Coltis informed the company that he had sold the shipment to a number of video duplication houses in the Soho area.

The largest part of the shipment, nearly four hundred (400) tapes, was bulk-purchased by Instant Image.

Mr. Carmody insisted that one of our directors had conducted the transaction with full knowledge that the videocassettes were stolen. He was quick to stress the incalculable value of these tapes, explaining that for reasons of his own he was willing to forgo legal proceedings and would in fact make an attractive bid for Instant Image, simply to be sure of our cooperation in the full and safe recovery of the stolen shipment.

I have to confess that it was I who made the original transaction. Mr. Coltis approached me with the offer of the tape shipment and I agreed to purchase it, although I would not have done so had I known that the cassettes were, in fact, stolen property. This document, once signed, to act as a legal affidavit for the name printed below.

Brian J. Lack

"I don't get it," said Grace. "Why couldn't Carmody have just made an offer to buy his tape consignment back?"

"Because Instant Image were denying any knowledge of the deal," said Harry, elated. "Don't you see? They'd broken the law. Brian was saving the firm money, buying up used tapes, no questions asked, wiping them clean and using them again. ODEL's thief didn't divulge the name of his contact here, so Carmody was faced with a dilemma. He couldn't report the theft to the police. He was 'willing to forgo legal proceedings.' "

"You mean there was something about the shipment that he couldn't risk being made public."

"Exactly. And he couldn't get his hands on the tapes because no one at Instant Image was prepared to admit that they'd even seen them. When nobody came forward, he was faced with only one alternative—to buy up the company lock, stock, and barrel."

"Why would he go to so much trouble and expense for a bunch of videotapes?"

"The guy buys companies because he likes the color

of their stationery. I guess there's something on them that he doesn't want anyone except his original clients to see.''

"What could be so valuable? Maybe it's a drug consignment. Maybe the tape boxes are full of cocaine.''

Harry shook his head. "No, they're ordinary tapes with something extraordinary recorded on them.''

"What makes you think that?''

"Coltis didn't know he was stealing something special. Otherwise he'd have asked for more money. Brian got a bargain, remember? So the shipment must have looked like any other. The only possible difference can be on the actual tape itself.''

"Why didn't the ODEL Corporation simply scare Instant Image into handing back the tapes? They're powerful enough.''

"If Instant Image had realized the true worth of the shipment while ODEL was an enemy, they'd have had the controlling hand. Carmody chose a safer approach.''

"Coltis was the name of the lunatic who crashed your car. The letter says he was apprehended by Carmody's legal department. You think he escaped from custody?''

"Maybe they let him go because they knew he was as good as dead.''

"What do you mean?''

"Just that everyone who has been near the shipment has killed himself. Willie vetoed the buyout and died. The same thing happened to Beth. Of course, Instant Image was sold by the time Brian decided to walk into the traffic.''

"Do you think they all saw whatever's on the tapes?''

"I don't see what else could have encouraged them to act as they did.'' Harry swung the torch beam across the office. "I wonder if any of the cassettes are still left in the building.''

"They could be mixed in with a thousand others. How would we tell them apart? Listen, maybe it's some form of hypnotism. I'm not that knowledgeable about technology—could a strip of magnetic tape actually make people kill themselves?''

"What other solution is there? Carmody's got them

back in his possession, and all three directors are dead in accidents that can't be traced back to ODEL.'' He shoveled Brian Lack's affidavit into the new envelope. "We've got to locate one of the tapes. At the moment, we've no proof of anything.''

He dropped the packet back into the drawer, then screwed the damaged envelope into a ball and shoved it in his jacket pocket. "If they're still on the premises, I imagine they'd be stored in a room with lock-up facilities, like a basement. Let's take a look." He extinguished the desk lamp and they followed the thin torch beam to the stairs.

Carefully they passed between the stacks of duplication machines on the first floor. On the landing below they turned back on themselves and arrived at a darkened area near the rear of the building. The steel door before them was broad and heavy, like the entrance to a recording studio. Harry pulled at the handle, his entire body straining against it, but it felt as solid as the surrounding wall.

"There doesn't seem to be a lock, so what the hell is keeping it shut?" He stepped back, wiping the sweat from his eyes.

"This," said Grace, pointing to a narrow slot cut just above the handle. "It's electronically operated. You need a card.''

"Well, Brian must have had one," muttered Harry. A shaft of bright light pierced the window behind them, illuminating their backs.

"Jesus!" He grabbed Grace's hand. "Keep your head down.''

"I saw a key card in the petty-cash box." Grace pulled her hand free and headed for the stairs. "I'll be back in a minute.''

He grimaced as he heard her shoes clumping on the floorboards above. The torch shone back and forth across the ground floor, then moved away. A minute later, she returned brandishing the card. As she pushed it into the lock there was a soft click, and the door came open.

The cramped interior of the room was lined with videocassettes from floor to ceiling. Here were kept the

master copies of all the films Instant Image were con-
tracted to duplicate.

"How are we ever going to find one of the ODEL tapes
among all these?" asked Grace.

"I don't know. Just look around."

After a half hour of fruitless searching, the batteries
in the torch began to die. As the beam faded to a faint
ocher glow, Harry rose with a cassette box in his hand.
"I think I've found one," he said.

"How do you know?"

"The label." He held the ebbing light against the box
lid. The case was emblazoned with a runic protection
symbol, and was marked "For the attention of Bucky"
in his father's handwriting. "That's what he used to call
me when I was a kid," explained Harry.

"You mean he left this behind for you?"

There was a sudden shout in the street. A pair of shadowed figures were hunched at the glass doors beyond the
reception area, trying to see inside. A second torch beam
flashed against the wall.

"I bet that stupid bouncer called the police. We can't
go out through the main entrance."

Harry stumbled to a halt as Grace sat down in front of
him and began untying her shoelace. "Christ, this is no
time to . . ."

She pulled the heavy black boot free, placed her hand
inside it, and smashed the back window, using the toe of
the boot to snap shards from the base of the frame.

Seconds later they were running through a narrow alleyway behind Charing Cross Road, the acrid smell of
urine stinging their nostrils.

"We've left prints all over the place," panted Harry.
"Have you got a criminal record?"

"I don't know," Grace shouted back. "A policeman
took my particulars when I tried to crash the Royal Film
Performance last year, but as I used the pseudonym of
Phyllis Coates, I think I got away with it."

"Who's Phyllis Coates?"

"She played the lead in the nineteen fifty-eight film
I Was a Teenage Frankenstein; very good she was too."

"You're a very disturbed young woman." They slowed

to a walk and turned as nonchalantly as possible into the main thoroughfare ahead. Harry slipped the videocassette into his jacket.

"Harry?"

"What?" He waited for Grace to pull on her boot.

"How are we going to convince anyone that the cassette's dangerous? If it really is harmful, we can't run it without risking our own lives."

Harry gave a casual shrug. The thought had crossed his mind some minutes earlier. "There must be a scientific explanation for how it works. We'll find someone to help us take it to pieces, and analyze the tape through some kind of spectrograph."

"Harry?" Grace rose to her feet and gave an experimental stamp.

"What?"

"What does your secretary have to do with this? Her death fits the pattern of the others."

It was a point Harry had scarcely had time to consider. "I don't know. Her boyfriend was with her the night she died. I should talk to him." He placed an arm over Grace's shoulders. At Cambridge Circus a handful of hopefuls stood beneath the canopy of the Palace Theatre waiting for taxis.

"You want to stay at my place?" asked Grace.

"No, mine. I've an early start tomorrow. But you can stay with me if you want. I could do with some moral support in the morning."

"Why?"

Harry raised his hand to an approaching cab. "It's my first meeting with a brand new client. I'm being introduced to the head of the ODEL Corporation, none other than Daniel Carmody himself."

32.

Invitation

A S HIS CAR inched its way across Waterloo Bridge on Tuesday morning, Harry thought about his forthcoming meeting with the enemy. The underpass on the north side had become flooded by the torrential rain, and its closure had brought the morning rush-hour traffic to a standstill.

Harry snapped off the radio's disco drivel and the sound of steadily falling rain filled the car. Grace shifted in the seat beside him, lost in her own thoughts. Last night they had made love again, and the tenderness between them had deepened. Now the cold gray light of morning made his suspicions about Daniel Carmody seem unlikely at best; certainly the elegant philanthropist spoken of so glowingly in the columns of *Forbes* and *Fortune* seemed an outside candidate for conversion to Faustian megalomania.

"It's the logical solution, however implausible it may seem right now," said Grace, reading his thoughts. "Everyone knows that the big corporations are fighting dirty. You only have to watch the evening news. Competition is more intense than it's ever been before."

Harry was all too aware of the desperate measures that were being taken to preserve market shares. Client bribery within his own agency was increasingly subtle and sophisticated. Contracts yielded such spectacular peripheral benefits that the trade terms conveyed within them were reduced to little more than formalities. It was the art of the deal in the late twentieth century.

"Everyone does it, you know that." Grace slid forward in the seat and propped her knees against the dashboard. "X makes a movie. Y endorses it. X features Y's product in the film. Y praises X's films through its products. Imagine an R and D team from the ODEL Corporation developing some kind of advanced technology that would rid them of business rivals. They'd be killing the competition in the most literal sense. The system would be foolproof, providing you had the balls to go through with it. Their enemies meet with terrible accidents. The company gets carte blanche to carry out industrial espionage by destroying whoever stands in its way, and no one will be able to prove a damned thing."

"Unless we can convince someone that we're in possession of an 'infected' ODEL cassette," said Harry. "There must be some way of having it analyzed without going to the police."

"You can leave that to me," said Grace. "The main thing is, you musn't let your client suspect that we know anything."

"It may already be too late for that. By now I imagine that he knows who he's about to meet. The son of a man his company murdered."

Darren Sharpe folded back the boardroom doors, ushering Harry and the other account executives inside. Daniel Carmody was already seated at the far end of the table with an arc of paperwork spread before him. As the agency team entered, he pushed back the chair and rose to his full imposing height, proffering a neatly manicured hand. Introductions were made, and Harry found himself studying the young tycoon.

Carmody's manner was one of controlled charm, his movements flowing and precise as he accepted the hands of the newly appointed account team in turn. The suit he wore was tailored with a discretion that merely drew attention to its exquisite cut, his lacquered ponytail lay in a smart curl on his collar. His vitreous eye reflected the cold brilliance of the panel lighting, the movement of his head betraying the fact that it was artificial.

On one side of Carmody sat the red-haired man with watery orange eyes whom Harry knew to be Slattery, the legal adviser. On the other side sat a sharply dressed young man with hair like oiled sable, who recorded every word of the meeting, scribbling in a notebook with a gold ballpoint pen. Slattery, too, made annotations on a letterheaded pad in dense, crabbed script.

As soon as everyone had been allocated a seat, Sharpe launched into the standard opening speech he reserved for welcoming new clients. As always, it concerned commitment and creativity, learning curves and consumer awareness, a web of high-tech jargon spun around the promise of providing the client a high public profile in return for a hefty annual advertising budget.

As Sharpe reached the end of his recital, Harry prepared to take the bull by the horns. He had decided to adopt a direct, combative approach with Carmody. He knew that it would not enamor him to his colleagues, who would probably think that he was trying to upstage them, but he remembered reading somewhere that the mogul had a reputation for plain speaking in his business transactions.

"I am sure that Mr. Carmody is already aware of what our agency can offer his organization," said Harry, cutting in at the close of Sharpe's speech. "I would be interested in hearing a little more about the ODEL Corporation and what makes it tick."

"I assumed that your team would have read the corporate manuals we provided at your request," said Carmody coolly.

"We have," replied Harry, "but the manuals only provide us with statistics and PR material. I know that ODEL's main source of profit stems from the early development of fiber-optic technology. I also know that since joining ODEL you have shown a desire to shift the company from telecommunications into related leisure activities. You're buying up a number of ailing publishing concerns. You're moving into the TV networks. The dissemination of information seems to be your new chosen field. What I don't understand is why."

Harry sat back, tapping the end of his pencil against his teeth. Every face in the room was turned to him, but he was determined to take his time and choose his words carefully. "At some level a shoemaker makes shoes because that's what he enjoys doing. We're all familiar with your background, Mr. Carmody, we all know the story of how you made your first million in the newspaper business before you were twenty-one. Now you can have anything you want. And you seem to want to shift this vast new corporation of yours in a different direction to the one it has always shown expertise in. Why? Shoemakers make shoes. What is it that *you* enjoy?'' He held the slip-covered corporate manual high enough for everyone in the room to see. ''There's scant mention in here of your long-term projections, your hopes for the future of the company. You're known as a captain of industry, Mr. Carmody. Where's the ship going?''

There was an uncomfortable silence, during which Darren Sharpe took the opportunity to throw a warning glance at Harry. Finally, Carmody spoke.

''To continue your earlier analogy, Mr. Buckingham, a shoemaker will also make shoes because he perceives a gap in the shoe market. That's exactly what ODEL is doing.''

''But what gap are you filling?'' asked Harry, aware that he was pushing the limits of civility by turning the presentation into an interrogation. ''We're told that ODEL is investing heavily in 'innovative communications technology,' whatever that is. We're also told that your own satellite broadcasting system is almost ready to commence transmission. Yet there's no mention of what it's going to be used for. There are points where serious conflicts of interest could conceivably occur. Does the fact that you are currently in negotiation for a government defense contract mean that your publishing houses would be uninterested in printing an antiwar novel, for example?''

Slattery raised his orange eyes from his pad. Carmody's lips narrowed imperceptibly as he sat back and scrutinized Harry. The other executives studied their notes and examined their nails, unable and unwilling to break the silence.

''The manual you hold in your hand deals with the corporation's current business interests,'' Carmody replied in a measured tone. ''That is all which needs to concern you at the moment. Your job is to build an image for us which the general public will recognize as that of a caring, responsible organization. We wish to show that ODEL is a successful, forward-thinking British company, trusted and respected by its work force, favored by the government, friendly to the environment. You will appreciate that when a corporation such as ours expands to include so many diverse interests, it is of paramount importance that its public image is presented as clearly and as simply as possible.''

"Even if that includes lying to the public?''

Darren Sharpe stirred uneasily in his seat. "I think what Harry means is that the campaign we create for ODEL must be an honest and accurate representation of your corporation, Mr. Carmody.''

"I appreciate that,'' said the tycoon, leaning forward to study his opponent more closely. "Obviously we would not be prepared to sanction any advertising that attempted to deceive people about our true intentions.''

"That's what I'm trying to get at, Mr. Carmody. What exactly are your true intentions?'' Harry rapped the ODEL manual with his pencil, deliberately seeking to provoke his audience. "You know, I look at your company profile and I see a lot of fingers in a growing number of different pies, most of them vaguely in the area of communications. You don't seem to specialize, and that's unusual.''

Carmody remained silent, studying him, hearing him out. Unnerved, Harry quickly continued. "For example, you've made some major purchases in the last year, but there's no pattern to them. The fact that several of your takeover bids have been hostile suggests that you wanted those companies pretty badly. Last month you completed negotiations for a medium-sized TV network based in New Jersey. Just last week you forced through the purchase of a small video company in Soho. These seemingly random takeovers are . . .''

"Harry, this line of questioning has little relevance to Mr. Carmody's immediate problem.'' Harry read the anger in Sharpe's eyes and sat back, aware that he had overstepped the mark. "Perhaps we could talk about the current public perception of the ODEL Corporate image.''

''What the hell were you trying to do in there?'' hissed Sharpe as they left the meeting. ''It's taken us three months to get him to the table and you jeopardize the entire deal by virtually accusing him of being a crook. Your recent behavior has been causing everyone concern, but this is the last straw.''

Before Harry could reply, Daniel Carmody filled the doorway behind them. ''Mr. Buckingham.'' He beckoned with a long index finger. ''Perhaps you could spare me a moment.''

Harry felt a dropping sensation in the pit of his stomach as he turned back. Carmody returned to the vacated boardroom and seated himself in his former position, leaving Harry standing before him.

''Close the door behind you.''

He did as he was told, then seated himself on the opposite side of the boardroom table.

''You seem to hold some strongly critical opinions about our corporation. For an advertising man, it's an oddly ambivalent attitude.''

''Well, Mr. Carmody, advertising treads a thin line between the provision of information and mere visual pollution,'' Harry pointed out. ''Too often it falls on the wrong side. Remember the Saatchi group's Berlin Wall poster? As soon as part of the wall came down, they were pasting banner ads on the East German side. That struck many people as an offensive summation of our industry. There has to be corporate responsibility for our actions.''

Carmody smiled. ''Most issues are separated by invisibly thin lines, Harry.'' The use of his first name was a surprise. ''When the public are left to decide for themselves they fall back on sentiment. Why is it that fur coats cause offense and leather jackets don't? Why are seal cubs saved when rare insects are allowed to become extinct? Someone has to protect the public from their own taste.'' A faint smile crossed his face upon the realization that he had exposed a personal opinion. ''You seem to have done your homework about ODEL. Tell me something.

Do you believe that it's wrong for a company to wish to become more powerful?''

"Power destroys freedom if it is misused, yes.''

"Come now, we're not talking about misuse. I am concerned with the correct use of power to influence people in a positive, healthy way.''

"I'm sorry,'' said Harry, "but I maintain a healthy suspicion of philanthropic capitalists. The basic contradiction is too apparent. The idea of McDonald's promoting civic pride when the sidewalks are covered in their detritus leaves—shall we say—a bad taste in the mouth.''

"I'm not talking about tawdry PR exercises,'' said Carmody, suddenly leaning forward across the table. "Suppose a company really could make a difference in the world?''

Jackpot, thought Harry. He's going to open up. "How big a difference?'' He tried to sound casual.

"Big enough to have a global effect. Big enough to change the way we think and act.''

Harry's mouth was suddenly dry. He framed his next remark carefully. "Such a company would have to be controlled and monitored with great care, of course. Grand plans have a habit of going wrong. No one person can be allowed total control.''

"But you concede that such a concept is possible?''

"I guess I do.'' His throat was hoarse. He tried again, more forcefully. "I do.''

"Good.'' Carmody gave a glittering smile and rose to his feet. He seemed pleased with the conversation. Reaching into his jacket, he withdrew a card from his wallet. "You seem to be a man who's capable of forming his own opinions. I'm going to extend an invitation to you, Harry. ODEL's chief executives are meeting at the weekend. I'd like you to be there. I think you might find it interesting. You'll be a guest in my home. My secretary will arrange the details.''

He slid the reports into his briefcase and left the room without waiting for Harry to reply.

* * *

As soon as he had returned to his office, Sharpe called by. But before the account director had a chance to explode, Harry described the outcome of his meeting.

"Fine," said Sharpe, who was annoyed at having his anger defused. "Go along by all means, just so long as you do it on your own time. But remember that this is a team. You don't step on the backs of others to build yourself a career." He removed the dead cigar from his mouth and contemplated it.

"Come on, Darren, you know that deep down it's every man for himself." For once Harry felt that he had the upper hand. "You know what they're saying about this industry."

"What?"

"It's not enough merely to succeed. Your best friend must also fail."

He threw his coat over his shoulder and left.

He was just about to leave the building when he recognized the boy walking slowly across the chromium foyer. It was the first time Dexter had visited the agency since Eden's death, and he was clearly unhappy about it. His fashionable clothes and haircut were the same as before, but now they failed to draw attention away from his sallow features.

"Dexter?" Harry approached him cautiously, unsure of his reception.

"I came by to see you." Dexter looked around at the receptionist. "Take a walk?"

Homebound traffic was backed up along St. Martin's Lane. They turned toward the lights of Long Acre, the drizzle flecking the shoulders of their jackets with amber.

"I wanted to check with you before talking to the police," he said as they crossed the road. "I mean, they told me to call them first, but I thought . . ." He shook his head and returned his gaze to the glistening pavement, black rolls of hair falling across his eyes. Harry decided to let him speak in his own time.

"Something I remembered," he said at last. "The night she died? She had a package for you. I don't know what was in it. She tried to tell me but I wasn't listening.

You know how you don't.'' They had reached the corner of the street.

"Did she say who it was from? You realize this could have something to do with her death?''

"No, man, it was just work. I think it was delivered and you'd gone for the night, so she was looking after it for you.''

"Can you remember what the package looked like?''

"Brown paper wrapping, shaped like a book. You know.'' He indicated with his hands. "A hardback.''

"What happened to it?''

"I dunno. They didn't find it with her, so I guess she must have dropped it somewhere.''

"Was she still in possession of it when you last saw her?''

"I think so, yeah.''

"Dexter, why didn't you tell anyone about this?''

He answered slowly. "I have this picture of her, see. In my mind. The last time. Sometimes you have a picture, and it's right in front of you, and you can see all the details, and you still don't see the most obvious thing in the picture. You know what I mean? She wanted me to say 'I love you,' and I never said it. I wish I had done, 'cause I did.''

"Perhaps you can help her now.''

They stood talking in the rain for a few minutes, then Dexter walked sadly away to become one of the commuters who shuffled slowly into the entrance of Covent Garden's underground station. Harry headed off in the direction of Leicester Square. First thing in the morning, he'd call all of the messenger companies and have them check to see who'd accepted Eden's signature for the package. It was a terrible thought, but he could not shake it; suppose there had been a videocassette beneath the wrapping, and for some reason she had played it? Three-quarter-inch tapes looked like hardback books.

It would mean she had died in his place.

33.

Cracking the Ice

As JOHN MAY reached the foot of the aisle, a man and a woman moved slowly onto the stage and were bathed in a pool of soft aquamarine light, so that they had the appearance of being underwater. The couple's clothes traversed a variety of sartorial ages. The man wore a high ruff collar of starched linen, jeans, thigh boots, and a blood-stained T-shirt. As his eyes adjusted to the gloom, May could see the rumpled form of his partner slumped in the second row of the stalls. He passed to the seat behind and made his presence known.

"I'm not sure about the outfits," Bryant whispered over his shoulder. "Or the blue light. I always feel that Jacobean tragedy should be played out in crimson, very Velásquez, and formal dress. After all, it's a rigid form of theater, very stylized."

"Where the hell have you been?" hissed May. He was furious. Bryant had been out of contact all day. "Everyone's been looking for you. If you won't wear the beeper, at least have the decency to call in and tell me where you're likely to be trotting off to next."

Bryant looked genuinely surprised. "I didn't know I was that important," he said. "Anyway, I'm not a pigeon. You don't have to ring my leg. I am still allowed out by myself. And if you'd taken the trouble to check my desk calendar you would have realized where I was."

"We *did* check your calendar. You could have elaborated on the message. 'Tuesday—*Revenger's Tragedy.*' It wasn't much to go on."

"Stop complaining. You found me. They always let me sit in on the rehearsals here. Wait, this is a good bit."

He indicated the male player. "Listen to Vindice. Good advice: 'Break ice in one place, it will crack in more.' "

"Arthur, you really are testing my patience." May rose to his feet. "I need to talk to you. Outside."

"Oh, very well." May sighed and gathered his belongings: a large scarf and a number of plastic carrier bags.

"My God, you look like a tramp."

"Thank you. My landlady knitted this scarf. She'd have made it thirty feet long if I hadn't stopped her. I think she finds knitting a form of therapy. Relief for sexual tension." They had reached the freshly decorated foyer of the Phoenix Theatre. The acrid smell of fresh paint hung in the air. Bryant sniffed and looked about. "Funny place, this," he said, hanging back as May moved toward the exit doors. "Did you know, they opened up with Olivier and Gertie Lawrence in the thirties, *Private Lives*, marvelous production. Since then the place has been a bit touch-and-go. Used to be a music hall before it was a theater, the Alcazar, I think. Even that wasn't very successful. There must be a reason for it. The entrance is a bit off the beaten track, I'll admit."

May stood fuming at the door. It really did seem as if the old boy was losing his grip. "Arthur, you're behaving like an irritating child," he grumbled.

"The best way to behave, I assure you." He pulled the scarf tight and tucked the ends into his overcoat. "As you went to such trouble to find me, the least I can do is treat you to some refreshment."

They sat in a steam-filled snack bar in the Charing Cross Road, May patiently waiting as his partner dropped six cubes of sugar into his coffee and began to speak in a fast, low voice.

"Listen to me, John. I have a riddle for you. When is an accident not an accident? When it turns out to be a murder. How do you prove that an accident is murder? By linking the death to a culpable outside agent. But an accident, by its nature, has no outside agent. Anathema. So, no point in pursuing the problem. Instead, we must assume that a murder can be made to look like an accident so convincingly that even the witnesses to the crime are satisfied with the evidence of their own eyes.'' He tore a sugared doughnut into pieces and dropped a chunk into his tea.

''Next we must sort out the murder victims from the genuine suicides and from those who have suffered ordinary, everyday accidents. Well, of course, we hunt for a common link, but with so many false cards in the pack how is this possible? Better to ask ourselves *who* we are looking for. A madman? Hardly. There's far too much method in this madness. A sane man means a sane purpose, but what could that be? Revenge, perhaps? The culling of enemies, real or perceived? How could one man have so many unrelated enemies? Through some kind of social club? But the victims have no social links with each other. Through business connections then? A company man with a grudge. But how could one man perform virtual genocide? Could there be a group of them? Let's say there's a group, and they're operating to some kind of blueprint, a grand plan.''

''Business rivals have price wars, Arthur, industrial espionage. They don't get rid of the competition with runic curses.''

''If they've found a way of making the curses stick, why not?''

May ran a finger around the rim of his cup. ''Because I don't believe in supernatural forces,'' he said finally.

''Who mentioned the supernatural? Perhaps it's some kind of technological version of a curse. The microchip turns rogue. You of all people should believe in such scientific possibilities.''

''No.'' May shook his head. ''Even with the latest developments in simultaneous circuitry it still seems too way out.''

Bryant drained his coffee and hunched forward. He was anxious not to be overheard by the couple at the next table. ''I'll tell you how it's done, then,'' he said softly. ''They're using videocassettes. Three-quarter-inch U-matic tapes. I believe someone is shooting the curses with one of these video thingies . . .''

''Camcorders.''

''. . . and when the victim watches the screen he hears

or sees something so horrible that it causes him to kill himself. Perhaps there's a noise on the tape that affects his brain. It's an idea American scientists have been experimenting with for years, ever since subliminal images were inserted into movies in the early fifties. Henry Dell was a video dealer. Let's assume he saw one of the tapes and died. His shop was burned to destroy his stock. Remember I told you that several of the video machines had been reset twenty minutes before the fire started? I think the boy, Mark, also ran one of the tapes, or was forced to watch it by the arsonist. Whoever operated the machine's controls accidentally turned off the power in part of the shop and altered all the digital clocks. Mark survived the fire, but he had seen the tape, you see? It caused him to take his life as soon as he regained consciousness." He dropped the remaining lumps of the doughnut into his tea and swirled the cup. "Yesterday two of our lads found a mangled videocassette on the embankment near the tracks where the Cleveland woman kissed the 19:35 to Edinburgh. Unfortunately it appears to have been dismantled by kids, who unraveled the tape and then lost it. But at least we have the box to analyze. Finally, there's the car thief, Coltis—we've managed to track down his employment records, and they show that he held several manual jobs in companies connected with the video industry."

"Why wasn't I told this earlier?"

"I should imagine the details have gone into the case file. You know, the report gets typed on pieces of paper and inserted in a cardboard folder. Not on computer."

May narrowed his eyes at Bryant, puzzled and pleased in equal parts. So the old devil had been working after all. "These cassettes," he said, "you're sure that whoever runs the tape dies?"

"I don't know yet if it's quite that accurate. This all hinges on locating one of the tapes intact. The boxes are protected by runic charms, talismans. That's what we found in Dell's store."

"Then what were the curses we found on Dell, Meadows, and Coltis?"

"That part of it I'm still not sure about."

May sat back on his stool and thought for a moment. "Would you care to tell me how you came by this?" he asked.

"I enlisted the help of an old girlfriend."

"Not that librarian, Dorothy something-or-other."

"Huxley. The very same."

"But she's batty. I thought you said she believes in all kinds of mystical rubbish."

"You met her once, John, don't you remember?"

"How could I forget? She talked me into having acupuncture."

"It worked, didn't it?"

"Oh yes, wonderful. I couldn't sit down for a fortnight. For God's sake don't tell anyone else we're consulting paranormal experts for information. We'd get slaughtered by the tabloids. Have you anything else for me?"

"A question." Bryant consulted his pocket notepad. "We know there was no sign of a cassette in Coltis's belongings. Have you carried out similar checks with the other victims in the file?"

"Yes, and we've found nothing. I don't know, maybe the damned things self-destruct."

"It's more likely that someone simply takes them back, isn't it? I think it's time for you to go to work with your computer. We need to sift out the genuine murders."

"Janice and I are already working on that," said May. "We're due to start indexing the collected data tonight. Care to join us?"

"I couldn't think of anything worse." Bryant paid the bill at the counter. "Besides, I have other arrangements."

"Then promise me you'll stay in touch."

"I'll make a concerted effort this time. Give my regards to Janice."

"I don't suppose you want to tell me where you're going?"

"Not really." He thought for a moment, head on one side. "First I think I'll head back to the theater. I need to think Jacobean. It's just as the revenger says. We've broken the ice in one place. It will crack in more." Bryant placed his hand on May's arm. The pupils of his eyes showed broad and dark. "You see why I must retire, don't you? We live in a society fueled by two obsessions, youth and success. But imagination plays such a large part in the shaping of the world. Imagination, as ageless and unbounded as the moon." He looked out at the crowded pavement. "Nobody out there needs it anymore."

As he watched Bryant's scruffy figure retreating back to the theater through the milling afternoon shoppers, May felt a great affection for him. He only wished that he could do something to dispel his colleague's sense of disillusionment.

" 'Scuse me," called a voice behind him. He turned to find the large Italian woman behind the counter of the snack bar waving at him. "Your friend, 'e left somethin' behind." She brandished the black plastic object in her hand.

It was Bryant's beeper.

34.

The Glass Halo

I T WAS THE first time Harry had stayed at Grace's apartment, and the first uninterrupted night they had spent together. In bed, Grace's warmth and generosity had forced him to reconsider his sexual etiquette and learn anew. In the morning he attempted to display equitable prowess with a frying pan while Grace slid reluctantly from the sheets into the shower.

"I wish this rain would stop." She stood at the window wrapped in a white bath sheet and watched the water dripping from the eaves. "It's as if the world were coming to an end."

"It's not ending, just changing." Harry slipped his hands around her waist. Her skin was warm through the damp cloth. She pressed her body back into his. "We could go somewhere with a broad blue sky."

"No, I like it here. London feels comfortable. Safe." Grace cleared the condensation from the glass with a towel-wrapped palm. "But there's something new out there. Hidden by the rain." She turned to kiss him, and his strengthening embrace returned them to bed.

"I'll arrange for Frank Drake to come and collect the cassette," she said over breakfast, smearing a layer of strawberry jam across her bacon. "He knows everything there is to know about the encoding of secret messages. He's still playing heavy metal albums backward trying to discover the hidden meanings."

"Are you sure you can trust him? He won't take it to anyone else?" Grace's ancient dog sat motionless between them, hypnotized by the bacon dangling from their forks.

"He'll guard the tape with his life."

"How can you be so sure?"

"He's hopelessly in love with me. Always has been."

"Just make sure he understands the danger involved. But don't tell him everything."

"Do you think Daniel Carmody was sounding you out?"

"I think he was surprised to find me still alive. That's why I got invited to his country retreat. He figures I'm a survivor, and survivors are useful to him."

"He'll be on his home ground, he'll have all the advantages. Suppose he tries to have you killed?"

"First he'll want to find out how much I know. We'll play the game. I'm a corporate man, too." The dog stared in anguished disbelief as Harry finished his bacon.

"So how do we go about fighting a corporation?"

"There's only one way. From the inside." He wiped his mouth as the telephone rang. Grace took the call.

"I don't want to speak to you, I want to speak to *him*," said Hilary.

"Hello, Hilary, how did you get this number? How are you?"

"It's in the Yellow Pages under 'Tramps.' And you should be worrying about your own welfare, not mine; she's probably infested you with sexual parasites by now. As it happens, I'm calling on a matter of business. There's a package here with your name on. I was going to send it to your office, but that would have meant spending money on you."

His heart paced up. It had to be the package accepted by Eden. "When did it arrive?"

"A few days ago. I've been in the Midlands coordinating our regional sales meetings. It was here when I returned, and you can jolly well come and pick it up yourself."

Harry thought fast. Eden had dropped off work at Hilary's Wigmore Street apartment before. She must have delivered the tape after her concert. She couldn't have known that he and Hilary were no longer together.

"Hilary, listen to me. Whatever you do, don't open the box."

"Now look, I really don't care about your tawdry secrets, just don't tell me . . ."

"Hilary, the box could kill you, just leave it alone!"

"Too late, I already opened it. It's only a stupid videotape."

Harry's blood ran cold. "You didn't play it?"

"I did and it was very weird. I have no idea what you're getting yourself into these days with your *new* friends, but—"

"Wait, how could you run it?" He knew that the three-quarter-inch tape would not be compatible with standard home cassette recorders.

"Didn't I tell you? I got my promotion. Professional video equipment comes with the position."

"My God, don't leave the flat, just stay there until I reach you. Do you feel all okay?"

"Harold, what on earth is the matter with you? It was hardly top secret material."

"What was on the tape? What did you see?"

"You should know, it had your name all over it, and a little label with squiggles on."

"Just tell me!"

The panic edging his voice forced her to think. "There was a company logo . . ."

"Which company?"

"I'm trying to remember!" He was making her scared.

"ODEL. Was it the ODEL Corporation?"

"I think so, yes."

"Then what?"

"A color, I think it was red. Then the most extraordinary—" The line went dead.

Harry hit the street running.

Hilary stared at the receiver. Had he actually had the nerve to hang up on her? She tapped the tines but no line returned. Her panic receded. How utterly, *utterly* annoying. It would be just like him not to have replaced the receiver properly. Or perhaps there was a fault on the line. British Telecom were forever fooling around with the cables in the street. She crossed to the window and looked down, but found no evidence of roadworks.

What on earth was Harry getting so het up about? In a way she was rather glad that the affair was over. She had never really understood him. Glancing at her watch with annoyance, she walked into the hall and stopped at a mirror to tidy her hair, not that the smart blond plait needed any tidying.

How dare he expect her to remain indoors, waiting around for him when they weren't even on speaking terms! She had to be at work in half an hour. Ten minutes was all she would allow him. She winked in the mirror and removed a tiny smudge of blue mascara from her eyelid. The air between her face and the glass seemed hazy, filled with motes of dust.

Behind her in the lounge, the mantel clock chimed the half-hour. The sound was distorted, as if struck in an echo chamber. She turned, listened, then resumed the scrutiny of her makeup. Her reflection seemed to be growing slimmer. How could that be? The cheekbones were elongating, the chin extending like a face in a fun-house mirror. Suddenly she realized that it was the glass, bending out toward her. With a sharp bang the mirror cracked from corner to corner, showering her with razor-sharp slivers. Unable to cry out, she brushed them from her cheeks, leaving fine crimson cuts.

Hilary staggered into the lounge, half blind. Her tight beige skirt prohibited any quick movement. Ahead of her were a pair of delicate lead-light windows filled with stained-glass scenes of piety. Monks genuflected before ethereal saints. Earthy priests rejoiced in pastoral pleni-tude. It was the feature which had most attracted her to the apartment.

It felt as if there were tiny pieces of glass in her lungs. It certainly seemed painful to breathe. She wondered if she was having a heart attack. She tried to think, but the fog which had filled the air now seemed to have invaded her brain. There was a sound emanating from the win-dows, like ice splitting in a glass of water. Hilary's eyes widened in disbelief. The sections of brightly colored glass were divorcing themselves from their frames piece by piece, dividing and breaking, slowly moving through the heavy air toward her like a shoal of dazzling tropical fish.

She raised her bare arms to shield her face and took a step back. A pellucid yellow triangle was the first to ar-rive. On its surface a saint cast eyes to heaven, his hands clasped in eternal entreaty. For a brief moment it hovered in front of her before diving down to carve a lazy scallop of flesh from her shoulder. Several more sections of the window arrived together, all of them depicting priests, topaz, emerald, and violet mosaics, which dropped to her arms and scored long, deep slits with surgical pre-cision.

Hilary found her voice at last. Blood was spraying across the starched whiteness of her blouse. An artery had been severed at her wrist. Her scream lasted for sev-eral seconds before a lengthy blade of transparent coral plunged into her mouth, a ivory-robed angel who snapped in half at the back of her throat.

Now the vitreous shards formed a cloud about her in a scintillating, deadly rainbow of light. They dipped and wove like opalescent birds, prodding and slashing geometric scissures across her skin until she could feel nothing but the glass and the light and her flesh rising up in tribal welts stained dark with blood.

As consciousness faded she felt her body lifting, passing through the shimmering aureole of glass to the world beyond and the street below.

As Harry slowed the car to a halt he had a sickening sense of déjà vu. Onlookers strained against the orange cordons strung across the sidewalk between lampposts. An ambulance stood by, its lights and siren switched off. Uniformed men and women were bent low in a single small area, like rugby players preparing to scrum.

He slammed the car door and stepped up on the curb. Police were here, too many of them. He raised his eyes to the apartment building, saw the dark interior of her room through shattered windows, and knew that she was dead. The glass had exploded outward with the impact of her body. She lay half in the road, her legs protruding from a dark blanket. Blood and glass, dark and glittering in the rain. She had hurled herself from the room just minutes after speaking to him. How long after viewing the tape? He pulled free from the crowd and ran back to the car, nearly reaching it before he was sick.

He drove badly as he departed, his hands sliding slickly through the wet steering wheel. Part of him knew that the tape was still in her apartment, but nothing on earth could make him return for it now.

35.

The Camden Town Coven

FRANK DRAKE WAS marginally better at operating computers than he was at handling people. He often stayed late at the library, his thin features illuminated by the green screen, his fingers glancing over the keyboard with familiar agility. The files he had built up were complex and cross-referenced, but his attempts to keep a scientific overview on his project dwindled with the addition of each statistic. As the files grew, so did his confusion. So far he had successfully hacked into a handful of private patient records and the police files of minor offenders, and each new piece of data had exacerbated the problem. In computer hacking, as in his previous interests, enthusiasm outweighed talent. He had read that many of the major financial corporations could be entered by skilled amateurs, but he had no idea how to go about it himself.

He had been seriously thinking of abandoning the project when Grace Crispian had called him and suggested a drink. Five years before, they had been studying graphics together at Goldsmith's College. He wondered if she was aware that throughout the foundation course he had watched her across cafeteria tables and lecture rooms, hopelessly infatuated with the crazy girl everyone loved, the girl who was planning to change the look of the motion-picture industry single-handed. She had possessed the energy and the ideas to do it, but somehow the break had so far failed to materialize. Just as it had yet to happen for Frank. Since those days they had met for a drink no more than once a year, and always the meeting had been initiated by him.

Grace's call had come as a welcome surprise, and he

had offered to assist her as best he could. But in his enthusiasm he had come on too strong, too intense. He had sensed the distance growing between them as he explained his theories, and even though she thanked him for his help at the end of the evening, he doubted that she would ring again. The second phone call was a bigger surprise than the first. He decided that perhaps he hadn't made such a bad impression after all. Grace told him how much she'd enjoyed the other evening. She wanted to ask a favor. It was the story of his life. The kids at school had always wanted him to do their homework. Could he possibly come around to her apartment to collect a videotape?

He tapped at the keyboard, running through endless lists of letter configurations in an attempt to break the passcodes of yet another city company. Apparently you could sometimes gain access to the multinationals, the megacorporations, by going in at a grass-roots level and attacking them through their smallest, least important branches. Remembering his promise to Grace, he flicked on the battered tape machine purchased by the library in the headier days of local funding, and loaded the cassette she had given him.

Apparently she had purloined it from a company whose staff were suffering accidents of the type he was collecting. He had laughed at the coincidence: his research and her request. But as he watched the static ebbing across the screen he wondered if it was coincidence at all. There had been several articles on the phenomenon in national newspapers, particularly the day before yesterday, when a prominent MP had drowned in a storm drain. Others were probably at work on the same project: they would beat his book to the publishers. All his research would have been in vain. Grace had told him that her reasons for knowing the contents of the cassette were personal, but what if he was actually aiding a competitor?

He stopped and looked at the monitor screen. Something was flashing. The video recorder had no remote. He reached forward and thumbed the FAST FORWARD button. Grace had warned him not to watch the cassette. She had insisted that it could harm him. When she had asked him if there was any other way of discovering what was actually recorded onto the tape, he had told her something about reading off magnetic imprints. It was all bluff, of course; but she considered him an expert, had come to him for help, and he couldn't let her down by revealing his lack of knowledge on the subject.

He figured that if there really was such a thing as an image which could harm, he would be safe by watching it in a mirror reflection, just like Perseus did with Medusa. Accordingly, he set up a hand mirror at a forty-five-degree angle to the video monitor before running the tape. The library was silent but for the distant hiss of wet tires on the nearby motorway. Perhaps the rain would have stopped by the time he left. He turned his attention back to the screen. The static had cleared from the start of the tape, and the familiar blue-and-white copyright warning had appeared. He slowed the image to normal speed. It was easy to decipher the reversed lettering.

WARNING

This tape is the property of the ODEL Corporation and exists under copyright to the Protection of Information Act. Access may only be granted by current staff members of the ODEL Corporation. Unauthorized use of this information may result in prosecution, fines, and criminal proceedings.

Frank gave a shrug and continued watching the screen. He'd make a copy of it later, from the section beyond the warning, in case there was an in-built identification code. The warning cleared and a new message came up.

DANGER—PROCEDURE BEYOND THIS POINT MAY RESULT IN ACTUAL PHYSICAL HARM

This is what Grace must have seen. After hesitating for a brief moment, he continued to study the reflected image in the mirror.

* * *

If Frank had not told Dorothy that he was planning to work late at the library, she would have asked him to accompany her on a visit to the Camden Town Coven. His skepticism of such matters had, however, grown considerably since their previous jaunt into the world of the paranormal. Edna Wagstaff and her talking cats had provided him with sufficient experience of psychic phenomena to last for quite a while. Consequently, Dorothy had set off alone, stepping into the night rain with a vast white golfing umbrella over her perm and a mysterious packet of books beneath her arm.

Although it had existed for around two hundred years, the Camden Town Coven was no longer a big noise in witchcraft circles. There were only seven members left these days, six of them women. They met on Monday nights in a private flat above the World's End public house opposite Camden Town tube station. Until a few years ago the pub had been known as the Mother Red Cap, gaining its name from Camden's most infamous witch. Here they would have a sing-song and a bit of a dance, sort out correspondence and attend to outstanding business, then retire to the snug downstairs for a few gin and tonics. Occasionally they met up with the members of other covens, but most of the time they operated alone. Dorothy had occasionally allowed them access to the collection of arcane law stored in her basement. Tonight, however, they had requested her attendance at an emergency meeting.

As she knocked on the side door of the public house, she wondered how the existence of the coven had remained undetected for so long. Particularly as a scruffy steel plaque below the bell read:

COVEN OF ST. JAMES THE ELDER
NORTH LONDON DIVISION
NO HAWKERS OR CIRCULARS

"Oh, hello, so sorry to keep you waiting." The woman who opened the door was small and bright, in her early forties. She had a broad, friendly face and spoke in clear, precise tones that suggested she was either used to public speaking or was going deaf. A bandanna held her unruly crimson hair in place. Her earrings were shaped like bunches of bananas. A pair of purple plastic spectacles with diamante wings hung on a chain at her bosom. She gave a wide smile, her eyes narrowing to crescent moons. "We've only just started, so you haven't missed much."

"It's nice to see you again, Maggie," said Dorothy as she stepped inside. "I've brought some books you might find useful in your experiments."

"Thanks, but I'm afraid we've had to suspend regular operations in light of the emergency situation." She led the way up the tilting, dimly lit staircase.

"Tell me what's happened."

"Well, it's all a bit worrying," she said, opening the door ahead of them. "You see, last Tuesday Doris was supposed to do an Enchantment for us, but her pressure cooker blew up so she couldn't attend, and Betty was off with her legs, so we went through the charts instead. Anyway, we did some calculations and the long and the short of it is, we think we've got Armageddon coming." She stopped herself. "That sounds a bit grand, doesn't it? The end of the civilized world, anyway."

Dorothy was ushered into the small first-floor lounge. The rest of the coven faced out from a circle in the middle of the carpet. "Hello!" called one of them, giving a little wave. "You've just caught us in mid-carole. Neema forgot to bring her cassette recorder in, so we're having to do it without music tonight." The group shuffled around with their backs touching and their hands linked across each other. Dorothy found an old upright dining chair near the window and sat down to watch.

The room was shabby but cheerful, with newspapers, pamphlets, and manuscripts piled in the corners, and not a black candle in sight. Astrological charts and graph tables covered the walls, their statistics entered in colored pencil. A desktop computer sat in a corner, reeling its way through miles of numerical data. The group broke from its strange shuffling dance and the members found themselves places to sit. Preferential choice was given to a young Asian woman who was heavily pregnant. The solitary male, a pale insurance clerk with a face like a hamster, shyly acknowledged his presence to Dorothy, shrugging his shoulders as if he'd just been caught doing something illegal.

"Of course, Armaggedon, the last great war on earth, has always been scheduled for the end of the twentieth century," said Maggie. Her voice was serene and sensible. "As you know, our coven has traditionally been concerned with the welfare and well-being of our fair city. We monitor the signs. We're the vanguard, here to recognize the forces of evil."

She rose and pointed to one of the colored maps, like a history teacher instructing her class. "In the past two months we've had some pretty unmistakable signs. Our brothers in St. James the Elder, Hendon branch, have also noticed them. All the prophecies are coming true. It is said that the first sign will be that of the dead canceling out the living; London's death rate has recently bisected its birth rate. It is then told that harmful powers will rise from the ashes of the fallen; the city's financial institutions are merging into powerful new conglomerates following the stock exchange crashes. It is also told that one of these powers will lay waste to the earth. Take a look at this." She unfolded a copy of the *Financial Times*. The headline read:

BRITISH INDUSTRY'S GLOBAL BOOST

The Minister of Trade is preparing to relax tax constraints for British companies planning to expand into new overseas markets, it was announced today.

The news follows fresh negotiations with the USA on the lowering of trade barriers, and will provide a particularly welcome boost for new businesses.

"You don't know anything about the Four Tasks of the Devil, by any chance?" asked Dorothy, remembering what Edna Wagstaff's cat had told her.

"Ah, now that's very interesting because the Tasks fit in very well with the Prophecies, you see." Maggie gave a benign smile. She could have been speaking of last night's television programs. "They're unusual in that their application is to industry rather than individuals. For years occultists the world over have been watching for the birth of the Antichrist, always expecting the Devil to take the form of a single human being. How were we to know that we should have been reading the *Financial Times* Share Index instead of the *Psychic News*? All that time wasted scouring the births and deaths columns for six-six-sixes!"

"How do the Four Tasks apply to industry?" asked Dorothy.

"Let's see now, we made some notes." She rooted around in the stacks of paperwork behind her and dragged out a dog-eared exercise book, donning the spectacles to read.

"The Deception of Fools, that's the power of false images—so we could say it refers to modern media manipulation, advertising, public relations, things like that . . ."

"The president of America's speeches," added the insurance clerk. "They're rewritten according to the results of computer polls about what the electorate wants to hear. That's public relations, isn't it?"

"Thank you, Nigel," said Maggie in a voice that suggested she would rather not hear from him again. "Then there's the Corruption of the Innocent, well, that's happening all the time. Businesses will do anything to stay afloat these days. As I remember it, the third one is the Destruction of the Pure; now that refers to the removal of competition in business . . ."

"I thought it was destruction of the rain forests," said Neema.

"No," said Maggie firmly. "Removal of competition. We decided." She gave her colleague a look. "And finally, the Veneration of Evil is the triumph of the global conglomerate."

"All of which the business world is currently experiencing," Nigel defiantly pointed out.

"But that's not the worst of it." Maggie slammed the notebook shut with ominous finality. The women shifted uncomfortably on their chairs. "Predictions mean nothing by themselves, of course."

"Why?" asked Dorothy. "What do you need?"

"Positive proof. And luckily, we have been able to uncover it." She removed something from a Tesco carrier bag and placed it on the table with a thump. Dorothy stared at the object in disbelief. She had always tended to think of the coven as little more than a well-meaning occult social group. She had allowed them to use her private library because they were dedicated to learning more, in whatever misguided a fashion, about the spiritual power of the world. The worst that could be said about Maggie and her fellow white witches was that they were harmless. Now she began to wonder.

"It's a packet of frozen cocktail sausages," she said aloud.

"We know that," said Maggie, rolling her eyes. "Read the label."

Dorothy arranged her spectacles. " 'Thorn Brand Cocktail Sausages. The tasty treat for any occasion!' " An unimaginative serving suggestion showed the pallid tubes of meat arranged in a sunburst on a silver salver with several sprigs of parsley thrown on top.

"The back, look at the back," said Neema impatiently.

"There's nothing except the supermarket bar code."

"Tip it to the light!"

Feeling somewhat foolish, she tipped the packet. Etched in silver, a pattern on the bar code showed a triangle with two lines extended from its base. Thorn. The Wendigo. The Ice Demon. The runic symbol used to promote, among other things, accidental death.

"It's similar to a death rune, I'll agree," she said carefully. "It's just coincidence. Is this a new brand?"

"It's a whole new supermarket," said Nigel. "They're opening everywhere. There's one just behind here—twenty-five checkouts, fully computerized. Many of their products are marked with runic symbols. Much of their frozen meat carries the green Ur sign."

Dorothy knew this to be the ancient pagan symbol for the breeding and killing of domesticated cattle. She smiled to herself as she imagined members of the coven creeping through the supermarket examining the produce.

"I really wouldn't worry," she said. "Advertising people are always looking for something new and different. Somebody's simply using runic symbols for the purposes of packaging design." She was prepared to believe that runes could be built into modern technology, but *cocktail sausages*? What would Arthur Bryant make of this? "Besides," she added, "they'd hardly want to place a curse on their customers."

"That's the whole point," said Neema. "We think it's a system of slow corruption. Runes used singly in this fashion can't cause harm. They probably just help to exert subconscious pressure on the consumer to choose this brand."

"It's the last part of the Prophecies," Maggie agreed. "The curse of the ancients resurfacing in the language of the present."

"Would anyone like a cup of tea?" asked Nigel. Several hands were raised.

Maggie was displeased with the interruption. "The point is," she said loudly, "that our meager powers are useless against pagan magic. It's just too strong. They were here before us, you understand. What always bothered us about the Horned One's return to earth—apart from the obvious—was that if he followed the path of Christ he would choose to be born as a human infant. And if he made as much fuss about turning up as Our Lord did, with stars and portents and what-have-you, he'd be easy to track down and destroy. So you see, he's been very clever coming back in this manner, in the corporate camouflage of our times."

Dorothy was at a loss for words. Despite the crackpot construction of their theory, there was no faulting the coven's logic. With her hands resting on her swollen stomach, Neema gazed down at her unborn child. Her voice had a gentle lilt.

"Occultists always tell you that the darkening of the world will be a gradual process. But it is happening now, and the events are occurring ahead of schedule."

Maggie nodded vigorously, her earrings jangling. "The Devil has come back to earth," she said, "and this time he's in the express lane of the checkout."

36.

The Empty Man

FRANK DRAKE CYCLED home through the empty city streets with an uneasy feeling in the pit of his stomach. He was beginning to wish that he hadn't watched the ODEL video, even reversed. After he had passed the warning, the screen had displayed a random series of squiggles which looked like illuminated script from one of Dorothy's old books. Beyond this, the images had settled into a much more familiar mode. Although he found it hard to believe that the tape was as deadly as Grace said it was, something about the scenes he had witnessed continued to scratch away at his subconscious mind.

At this time of night, the darkened factories and warehouses standing between the roadway and the river took on the appearance of abandoned tenements. Vast poster sites stood before them, their ill-proportioned messages dominating the decaying urban landscape, their life-style–promoting images in active betrayal of the disadvantaged men and women who slept rough beneath them. As the glistening tarmac passed beneath his wheels, Frank became aware of a large vehicle approaching from behind. An articulated truck sloshed past on its way to New Covent Garden, cutting so tightly on a bend that it forced him to cycle against the curb. Slamming on his brakes and sliding to a halt, his angry shout was lost in the thunder of the truck's passing exhaust. He leaned over and checked his handlebar light. Still working. The driver hadn't seen him. Typical, he thought, German license

plates. That was the worst part of taking this route
home—the drivers of shipments heading for the Continent
acted as though they owned the road. He could have been
killed. Wheeling out into the center of the road, he
mounted the bicycle and set off once more, the rain-hazed
lights of Nine Elms marking his homeward route.

John May had been studying the file on Harry Buckingham. Now he closed the cardboard cover and returned
it to Janice. "First his father, then his secretary, then his
father's partner, and now his girlfriend," he said. "I
don't care if he's got an alibi tighter than a squirrel's ass,
I want him brought in and detained. I don't care what
the pretext is, just so long as he remains under lock and
key until we've cleared this up."

"Want me to send someone over right now?" Janice
had just received a call from May asking her to come to
his office. The investigation had doubled her work load.
Having Buckingham on her hands was the last thing she
needed tonight.

"It can wait until the morning." May checked his digital watch. Another ten minutes and it would be Thursday. The operations room was thankfully quiet. A handful
of night duty staff remained on the floors below.

"You don't honestly think he's behind this?" asked
Janice. She had been coordinating interviews with the
directors of video distribution outlets for the past five
hours, and seemed as fresh as when she started. Night
work suited her. May had forgotten about the energy of
the young. He suddenly felt very tired and, despite the
coolness of the room, in need of a shower.

"Buckingham's heavily implicated, estranged from his
father, apparently ditched by the girlfriend. But he's more
of a target than a culprit. At least while he's out there
they've got someone to aim at."

"He wasn't involved with the secretary," said Janice.
"How did the search of Hilary Mason's apartment go?"

"No fingerprints but her own. The main lounge rug
had slipped, as if someone had pushed against it. Either
she fell against the glass, which seems unlikely . . ."

"Why?"

"The original leading between the plates had been strengthened with steel strips. They wouldn't have broken easily. She must have taken a run at the window, shoving the rug back in the process."

"I don't get it," said Janice. "If you're going to throw yourself out of a building, you'd open the window first."

"Never mind. We found something far more important." May withdrew a bunch of keys and unlocked the bottom drawer of his desk. He carefully placed the plastic Ziploc bag between them. Inside, Janice could make out the black oblong of an unlabeled videotape.

"How do you know it's one of the infected tapes?"

"We don't, but it seems highly likely. It was in her video machine and it had run to the end. The forensic people are taking the whole thing to pieces tomorrow and scanning it. We'll hopefully have an answer by midday."

"Any clue to its origin? It looks to me like a standard three-quarter-inch tape." Janice lifted the bag and examined it through the plastic. She hefted the bag in one hand. "It's very light."

May pointed to some numerals printed on the left-hand edge of the tape's spine. "It's only twenty minutes long. That's not a length generally available for public use. The media and advertising industries use them to screen commercials and EPKs—Electronic Press Kits."

"At least that narrows down the search."

"Unfortunately not. There are millions of the damned things in circulation." He threw Janice a sideways glance. "God, I'd love to run it right now, wouldn't you?"

"Yes, but we're not going to." She rose to her feet. "You look bushed. Want some coffee?"

"Please." Janice strode off to the drinks machine on the landing with the grace of a samurai setting forth on a quest. May loved watching her. Detective Inspector Hargreave was a very lucky man . . .

A movement at the end of the room caught his eye. Had somebody just thrown something into the corner? He saw the glint of the window as it swung in the wind. Minutes ago it had been closed. Rain was darkening the ocher carpet tiles.

As he craned forward to see, someone grabbed him

around the neck. He tried to pull forward but the powerful arms restrained him, one of them pressing into his throat, cutting off his oxygen supply before he could cry out. He shoved his legs against the desk, forcing his chair back into his attacker. A fist descended, punching him hard in the throat. He tried to force a sound from his lips, found a man's fingers stopping his mouth, and bit down hard.

The chair tipped backward and he slammed heavily to the floor. The arms released him as he fell, and now he saw the figure, dressed in black jeans and a hooded sweatshirt, as it darted around the desk and snatched up the Ziploc bag containing the videotape. A light burning sensation formed in his chest as he tried to rise to his feet, bands of pain radiating from his breastbone to his left shoulder.

Outside the office, Janice had heard the commotion. Letting the coffees fall from her hands she burst into a sprint that would have allowed her to quickly overtake the running figure ahead, had he not turned and shoved a desk across her path. Drawers spilled out, cracking against her knees. As he watched Janice stumble on, May was sure that they had lost the tape. The thief was too close to the fire-escape stairs on the far side of the building, and there was no one to impede his exit. Then he realized that there was another way to the ground floor. Ignoring the pain in his chest, he cut into the corridor and stepped inside the open freight elevator, heaving the gate shut behind him.

He arrived on the ground floor just as the running man reached the base of the stairwell. As he opened the elevator gate, he could hear Janice approaching from the stairs above. Their intruder would have to punch the security number on the door to release himself into the street. If he knew the four-digit code, he would be able to escape into a side alley and disappear in moments. The fact that he had managed to gain entry to the building suggested that he would be able to leave it just as efficiently.

May pushed himself from the elevator and approached

the hooded figure, whose back was turned toward him as he tampered with the security-code panel.

"John!" called Longbright suddenly. "Don't do it, he could be armed!"

He saw his shaking hands reaching out before him, grabbing the thief by the shoulders, felt the searing spasms expanding across his chest, but before he could find his voice to cry out the passageway dipped and dimmed, his vision sparkling with pinpoints of pain as consciousness mercifully fled.

On the floor above, Longbright hobbled back to a telephone and called the officer on the night duty desk, her anger eclipsing the pain in her legs. Below, she could hear the outer door buzz as the correct code number was received. The duty officer did not respond until the fifth ring.

"This is Longbright," she shouted, knowing that he would take no instruction until she identified herself. "A man just left the side entrance, black hooded sweatshirt and jeans, he's got a head start, somebody stop him. He might be armed."

She ran back to the foot of the stairs, where May had fallen. His lips were turning gray. He seemed barely able to breathe. She dropped to her knees and loosened his collar, tore off her jacket, and threw it over him. She was about to return to the telephone when two officers appeared on the stairs.

"Don't just stand there, call an ambulance!" she bellowed at the startled junior. "He's having a heart attack." Then she gently cradled the detective's head in her hands and wished away the pain as the grimace on his face faded and his eyelids slowly closed.

Frank Drake had arrived home soaked to the skin.

Peeling off his clothes, he had thrown them into a laundry bag and climbed straight into bed, exhausted. And now he was unable to sleep. Despite the half-open window spattering rain onto the floor, the room felt hot. He twisted onto his side, taking the sheet with him. His arms and legs were wet with perspiration. In the distance, a police siren looped an electronic whine. His head throbbed, as if he had just awoken with a hangover. He resolved to lie as still as possible, to feel the pillow pressing softly against his face. Somewhere on the river, a barge released a low, dismal honk. His eyes closed as he let the darkness in.

The rustle of material over his body brought him fully alert. Someone had pulled the sheet from his bed!

He sat up and fumbled for the light. Just as his fingers closed around the switch, the cord was pulled from his fingers and the lamp whipped past his face to shatter against the wall.

His heart pounding, Frank jumped to his feet. There was someone in the room with him. The faint aura of sodium light that washed over the bed from the street-lamp outside revealed the contours of the interloper. Between the wall and the wardrobe he stood, legs slightly apart, arms held at waist height. Although his features were obscured in the gloom, Frank recognized him in an instant. On the balls of his feet he moved toward the door and grasped the handle.

The click of the bolt withdrawing in the lock alerted the attention of his nemesis. The head slowly turned to reveal its facelessness, the muscular pale body angled to confront his, and the creature lunged forward at him. Screaming with fright, he yanked open the door and ran onto the landing, but not before he had seen his adversary at close range.

It was the being of his childhood nightmares, the one who visited him in the coldest hours of darkness to give shape to his most savage fears. How often had he sobbed bitter tears of terror upon waking, pleading to be admitted to his parents' room?

As he stood naked on the landing, his chest heaving, it seemed to Frank that the intervening years had suddenly vanished, that he was once again a scared, sickly child. The bedroom door creaked open and the man's figure stood silhouetted in the streetlight. It was wrapped like a mummy from head to foot in the bed sheet, so that no part of its body was visible. Frank knew that it was waiting for his resolve to fail, for him to turn and run. It would let him reach the head of the stairs before twisting itself around his feet and sending him crashing headlong to the floor below.

Frank wiped his brow with the back of his hand and took a step forward. The sheeted thing balanced in the doorway, then raised its featureless head before dropping its hands to its sides. It was daring him to strike first.

Frank hurled his full weight at the creature's body. His childhood fear was confirmed as his hands ripped aside the sheets to reveal a hollow shell of material, a being made only of the sheets themselves, an empty man whose white linen limbs now thrashed across his in the intimacy of death.

And as quickly as the manifestation had been brought to life, it collapsed, a sheet and nothing more. Frank fell back against the banisters, gasping for air. Nothing but a hallucination. The tape had brought it on, he was sure of it. But the images he had witnessed had been reversed, so the nightmare had been rendered imperfect. He was safe for now. But he would have to remain on his guard. He resolved to switch on every light in the house and stay awake until the arrival of morning light.

37.

Enemy Territory

GRACE AWOKE WITH a start and jabbed Harry in the ribs. "There's someone at the door," she said. "What should I do?" The figure beside her barely stirred. She dug her fingers into an exposed shoulder and shook hard. Harry opened a crimson eye. Last night he had drowned his fury at Hilary's death in vodka. Grace had agreed to stay in his apartment, and had spent most of the night watching him sleep. The bell sounded again as she rose and hunted for something to wear.

''No, wait. I'd better go.'' He struggled to untangle himself from the sheets, crawled to the window, and parted the blinds. A second later, he slammed them shut.

''It's the police.'' He began to search for his clothes, most of which were screwed up in bundles at the foot of the bed. ''They'll want to take me in again. You're going to have to deal with it. Don't let them come up, whatever you do.''

Grace hastily donned his dressing gown. ''What shall I say? It's not my place. What if they insist on entering?''

''Say anything, just get rid of them. I've got to be free to visit Carmody's house tonight.''

Grace knew he was right. Daniel Carmody's assistant had called Harry yesterday to arrange his weekend visit. Confronting the tycoon was the only chance he had left of clearing his name.

''Leave it to me.'' The bell rang a third time. ''I'll think of something. Don't make a sound.''

A few minutes later she returned to the rear of the apartment and knocked on the bathroom door. ''It's okay,'' she called. ''You can come out now.''

''Give me a minute. What did you tell them?''

''That as far as I knew, you were going to visit friends in the countryside for the weekend.''

''You dope, that's exactly what I *am* doing.''

''The countryside—in northern Wales.''

''I take it back. How did you explain your presence here?''

''I said I was looking after the place until you returned. I gave them a typed-out address where they could find you.''

''Where did you get that from?''

''I detached it from a piece of junk mail on the hall table. I've sent them to the headquarters of the *Readers' Digest* special offer department. I suppose they'll check your office next?''

''They won't find anything. I took care of the arrangements myself. Temporary leave of absence until Monday. Sharpe knows nothing about it. I left him a memo. He knows I'm due at Carmody's house for the weekend but he won't mention it.''

"How can you be so sure?"

"He'd rather die than have the police turn up on his new client's doorstep with a search warrant."

Grace returned to the bedroom and watched the squad car as it drove away. "The sooner you get out of London the better. Can't you drive up earlier?"

"I guess so." The bathroom door opened and Harry emerged, wrapped in a towel. "He's invited me to stay until Sunday."

Grace rubbed his back dry. "The main thing to remember," she said, "is not to lose your temper with him, otherwise you'll blow it. You've only got one shot at this."

"I don't even have a plan of action yet," he confessed. "I suppose I should search his house for some kind of documentary evidence."

"If you like, I'll come with you as far as Norwich and stay in a hotel. You could always sneak out and pass me anything you find."

"It's too big a risk. You'll be safer here. Just remember, don't answer the door unless you have to, and don't accept anything from a stranger. If something goes wrong we need some kind of a call sign." He threw his traveling bag on the bed and unzipped it. "Three rings on the telephone if I'm in serious trouble. That will be your signal to call the police and get them to Carmody's house."

"Others knew what he was up to, and he still managed to place curses on them," said Grace. "What makes you think that the police will be of any help?"

Frank Drake sat upright on the kitchen chair and rubbed his back. His body ached all over. Images of demons had haunted his fitful sleep, but now the night was ended, and he felt confident that the day ahead would hold no further terrors. Daylight, gray but nevertheless comforting, filled the corners of the room. Joints creaking, he rose and boiled the kettle for tea while considering what to do.

First he called Grace to warn her of the tape and its contents, but there was no reply from her apartment.

Then he rang Dorothy, but it appeared that she had already left for the library. On his way to the bathroom he was forced to pass the tangled sheet, and wondered how much his imagination had contributed to the night's events. But whether or not the hollow man had billowed briefly into life, he found himself unable to touch the contoured linen which still draped upon the stairs in fetal form, like a lizard that had shed its skin.

Daniel Carmody resided in a creeper-clad late-Elizabethan manor built of soft orange brick, situated in acres of damp flat Norfolk countryside. Steering his car in the direction of the house, Harry peered up through the windshield in awe as the heavily budded birches lining the driveway parted to reveal a scene unchanged for centuries. Only the freshly graveled courtyard below the mullioned windows and stepped gables defined the era, for here were parked a spectacular array of Bentleys, Rolls-Royces, and Daimlers. The rich men's toys seemed incongruous against the manor house, their gleaming chromium trim jarring to life from the soft earthen colors of the brickwork backdrop.

Braking his vehicle somewhat guiltily beside a glistening vintage Osprey painted in British racing green, Harry unloaded his travel bag and headed for what he presumed to be the main hall.

The maid who opened the door had the grace and complexion of a nun. She bowed her head and stepped back to allow him entrance as if she had been scolded for failing to do so on previous occasions.

''Mr. Carmody is in conference with his colleagues at the moment, sir,'' she said in a voice that was barely above a whisper. ''Mrs. Carmody is in the study.''

Harry had not considered the presence of the tycoon's wife. As he followed the maid, he studied the gloomy paneled walls with distaste. Although the few furnishings of the hall seemed generally in keeping with the building's date of construction, the feeling of sparseness suggested that a large scale asset-stripping exercise was currently in progress. Hogarth's *Marriage à la Mode* lined one wall, but of the six engravings only the last three remained. Their depiction of a duplicitous affair, death, and a deformed syphilitic child, without the explanatory benefit of the initial three prints, lent a macabre atmosphere to the passageway.

Mrs. Carmody stood waiting to receive him in the center of the cathedral-sized study, marooned in the middle of a vast Chinese carpet. She looked quite surprised to find herself there, as if she had suddenly been transported into place, and encouraged the effect by staring about the room with eyes as large as a lemur's, apparently searching for some clue as to her whereabouts. Paler and smaller than even the maid, and greatly lacking her grace, she raised a thin, stiff arm in greeting.

Harry seized the cold hand being offered to him and introduced himself. Mrs. Carmody gave a nervous smile. "You must be the gentleman from the advertising agency," she said, prompting him to wonder whether Daniel had briefed her, or if she could tell from his clothes. "My husband will be finished with the first part of his curriculum very shortly. Perhaps you would care to become acquainted with your room." Her voice was so faint and her appearance so faded that she seemed in danger of vanishing altogether. Harry could imagine the history of the marriage. She was the aristocrat who had married the tycoon, the lady of the house whose ownership she had treasured in lonely splendor, and whose tenancy she now endured in the shadow of her husband.

"I'm afraid we've had to put you in Ivanhoe," she said, disappearing around a corner at the top of the stairs like an exorcised ghost. "It's rather drafty, but all the other rooms are taken." They reached the end of a long plank-floored corridor and turned into an ice-cold room with rattling windows.

"We're having a little trouble with the boiler, but it should be sorted out by this evening. There's an intercom that's connected to the kitchen if you should need anything." With an ethereal smile she discreetly vanished, possibly into the woodwork itself.

Left alone, Harry lowered himself onto the hard mattress and watched his breath form in the air. Here, too, the meager furnishings appeared to be all that remained unsold from some kind of fund-raising auction. Carmody was a millionaire many times over. Why would he sell off the furniture? It made no sense. From somewhere far below came the sound of a droning voice reeling off statistics with cabalistic precision. Harry could feel his confidence waning with every minute he spent in the room. His numb fingers unzipped the travel bag, and he began to unpack.

38.

Celestial Flight

"I'M SURE YOU'LL be pleased to know that it wasn't a heart attack," said May, heaving himself up against the starched pillows. "Apparently I had a severe bout of angina."

"It makes no difference." Bryant sniffed as he pulled the last grape from its stem. "They both kill you in the end. Let's face it, you're falling to bits. Have you got any seedless grapes? The pips from these are getting under my dentures."

May should have known not to expect any sympathy from his partner. "It just means that I can't handle heavy loads, and that I should avoid stress for a while, in case you're wondering."

Bryant looked around for something else to eat. "That's a laugh, considering your job. What they're saying is 'Try not to die.' Did this quack mention how long you're going to be stuck in here?"

"A few days while they run some tests."

"That means a week. Tests, eh? Sounds ominous."

"It's standard procedure, that's all."

"They always say that. What time's lunch?"

"In about ten minutes. You can't have any. It's for patients only."

"It'll be vile, anyway. Mince and jelly. Baby stuff. They always give you horrible food after a heart attack."

"It wasn't a bloody heart attack, for Christ's sake!" May shouted. Several of the other visitors in the ward turned around.

"That's better," said Bryant with a chuckle. "At least now you've got some color in your cheeks. You're either getting better or having a relapse. I've arranged to have a computer terminal brought to you. They're fixing it up now." It was sound psychology. Bryant knew only too well how impossible May became when he was ill and bored. Idleness was more likely to delay his recovery than work.

"Besides," he added nonchalantly, "there's something I need you to look into."

"What?"

"The private company files of the ODEL Corporation."

"That's like asking me to check into IBM. Why them?"

"Well, while you were busy letting thieves make off with our evidence, your computer program finally came up with something useful. A discrepancy in Henry Dell's financial records. An unregistered cash withdrawal from his company account, made shortly before his death. Now, you'll remember that his storeroom was stocked with a large number of unlabeled cassettes, all of which were destroyed in the blaze."

"So?"

"It set me thinking: what if he was planning to do some serious pirating? Why else would he stock so many blank tapes?"

"So he was a video pirate. The offense doesn't exactly carry the death penalty."

"Dell bought the tapes illegally. A big batch of them. Why else should he fail to record the deal? Assuming that this was the case, I had the forensic boys analyze the remains of his desk diary. Guess what they found?"

"Surprise me."

"He paid the money to a gentleman named David Coltis. Ring any bells?"

"Dead car thief. Continue."

"At the same time, we finished tracking down Coltis's previous employers. At the time of the deal, Coltis worked for ODEL. Then they fired him. Why would they do that? Nobody there will tell us. ODEL is in the communications business, and part of their business is . . ."

". . . manufacturing videotapes."

"Well done. Now, this ODEL Corporation didn't ring a bell with me, but it did with Janice. She's got the company cropping up over her 'accidental death' files like a rash. Never directly involved, mind, but nearly always on the edge somewhere. Can I leave you to take over from here?"

"Certainly," said May, pleased at the prospect of working from his bed. "How on earth did you manage to get hold of their private files?"

"I haven't yet," replied Bryant, "but I hope to have done so by tonight."

The door opened and an orderly wheeled in an instrument trolley bearing a large desktop computer.

"There you go," said Bryant cheerfully, rising to leave. "Try not to turn off any of the kidney machines while you're playing with it."

Frank Drake paid the cab driver and took charge of the leather satchel, slinging it over his shoulder as he walked toward the terminal entrance. What he was doing was for the best; of that much he was sure. Collecting his ticket from the British Airways counter, he checked the departure board and confirmed that the flight was on time. Boarding in twenty minutes, it said, AMSTERDAM 109 GATE 21. At another counter a girl asked him if he preferred smoking or nonsmoking. What did she mean exactly? Equally thrown by the question, the girl's toothpaste grin momentarily vanished. She assigned him a seat number, and asked to check his bag. She wasn't to touch it, he carefully explained. That's fine, said the girl, regaining her smile, you can keep it in an overhead locker or beneath your seat. After she had wished him a nice flight, he slowly made his way upstairs to the cafeteria.

His mind was muddled. The only way he seemed able to keep a thread of logic to his thoughts was by counting continually from one to one hundred. Then he tried to recall the monarchs of England, things you would find in a farmyard, names of Derby winners, cricket teams, Bible chapters, anything to keep the other thoughts—the dark, the alien, the *old* thoughts—at bay. He sat in a corner with his coffee, trying to stop his shaking hands from overturning the cup, trying to remember the day's events.

He had not called Grace again. He had not gone to the library. He had returned to the kitchen and stayed there for hours, unable to move from the chair because something, some *thing* was trying to enter his mind, forcing out the logic, the sense and the light, fighting to replace it with feelings so irrational, so insane that to receive them would cause his brittle mind to shatter like overheated glass.

As the hours slowly passed, the pain of holding off the madness increased, but his fear of admitting it became even greater. Gradually, he discovered that certain thoughts could hold it at bay, mindless lists, scraps of knowledge collected across the years that could be played back like an ephemeral litany.

It was then that he had the idea; that perhaps he could pluck the demons from his mind by removing himself from their range—presuming they radiated from a single source.

During the telephone call to the airline he nearly let them in. Reading the data on his credit card was difficult, but thankfully not impossible. He had no idea what he had packed for the trip, could not recall if he had booked a single flight or a round trip. The cab driver had talked throughout the journey, tailbacks and blocked junctions. He would not have answered if he could. Why Amsterdam he had no idea, first thought that came into his head, better than what might have come in if he had relaxed his grip for a moment; gods of the earth, pagan beasts, rising from the soil half-rotted but still alive. He had to rise above the ground gods, that was it, leave the heathens for the heavens and soar to the stars.

The PA sounded. Amsterdam flight, boarding now, go to the gate. He would be all right.

At security clearance a heavyset black woman opened his hand luggage and raised her eyebrows, holding the mouth of the bag out to him with a questioning look, so that he was forced to break his concentration and follow her gaze. He saw a facecloth and a toothbrush, loose paper money and pound coins, a crucifix and a heavy mirror in a gilt frame. Unable to reply, he shrugged and smiled as she shook her head slowly and rezipped the bag.

From the cathedral windows in the waiting area he could see the Boeing 757 steaming in the clear night, waiting to receive its human burden. The line of passengers shuffled forward as a matched pair of stewardesses began to check boarding passes. If he admitted the demons now, he would endanger the lives of everyone around him. He began to count in pairs, one to one hundred.

Why had he packed the mirror? Did he imagine that he would see some visible change in himself if he allowed his devils to take hold? Perhaps it was there to assure him that the real world, this hard exterior of lights and steel and flesh, remained unaffected by his paranoia.

A matriarchal woman, presumably a senior flight attendant, stood just inside the door of the aircraft. She smiled and checked his pass, directing him to the far side of the cabin. He attempted to follow her directions, trying not to move his lips as he reversed the flow of numbers from one hundred back to one. His seat was in a bank of three, nearest to the aisle, center of the aircraft. The travel bag fell from his shoulders, and the sharp thud which sounded as it hit the floor suggested that the looking glass within had cracked.

The mirror was his assurance of unperturbed reality. If it had shattered, he would no longer be able to tell whether the pagan creatures of his subconscious mind had been released upon an unsuspecting world. As the cabin doors were sealed and he strapped himself into his seat, Frank Drake prayed not for his own salvation, but for the safe deliverance of those around him.

The meeting had broken for refreshments. As Harry sat waiting in the empty lounge, the doors at the end of the room opened and Daniel Carmody appeared, surrounded by arguing businessmen. The entourage included two Japanese, some Americans, an African in dazzling national dress, and several Germans. At the back of the group somebody was speaking French. All were clearly enthusiastic about something.

"Harry." Carmody walked toward him with his arms thrown wide. "I'm so glad you could join us. You'll meet everyone in due course, so don't worry too much about remembering names. I'm sure you won't find this evening's curriculum too arduous. We're resuming in twenty minutes, just for an hour or so. Then there'll be time to change before dinner. Tomorrow we'll get down to serious business."

Carmody flashed his famous smile before moving on. He was wearing a black silk suit with a dark collarless shirt, an effect which made him appear unnecessarily saturnine. His ponytail was tied back with a delicate silver clip, an acknowledgment of the evening's formal atmosphere. As he led the assembly to a table where champagne cocktails had been prepared, Harry resolved to speak as little as possible and listen to everything until he could discover the status and pecking order of those around him. As he sipped from the slender, stemmed glass, he took a slow walk through the guests.

". . . Naturally, the toughest problem we have to overcome is getting people to accept editorial comment, a guiding force as it were . . ." ". . . Don't approve of force-feeding children information, but now that parental advice counts for so little, the family unit must be strengthened from external forces . . ." ". . . All very well, but when Daniel says that the system will be up and running in under two years he's only referring to a single part of it . . ." ". . . At this point, it's difficult to say whether the technology will keep pace with the concept . . ."

Behind him, a bald, bespectacled man was engaged in a fierce altercation with a fellow countryman. His conversation, conducted in guttural German, and his wildly gesticulating hands, conjured up a prewar image which had long since lost its power through cliché. Suddenly their conversation switched into English.

". . . Nineteen thirty-three, but then only the *Volkischer Beobachter* clearly saw the state of things . . ."

Harry had heard of the infamous right-wing newspaper from his father. The "People's Observer" had been regularly castigated for its anti-Semitic views. With growing unease he moved away to the side of the room and accepted another glass from a passing waitress. On his right, an elderly Englishman discoursed on the state of British television in the light of deregulation.

A few minutes later, Carmody began to herd everyone back into the room from which they had emerged. Harry was given a seat between one of the Germans and an Italian woman with a nest of dyed black hair and an alarming cleavage. The large rosewood dining table in the center of the room had been replenished with notepads, pencils, and carafes of iced water. Harry produced his Filofax and laid it open at a blank page; he had no wish to be branded as the only one not making copious notes.

"Ladies and gentlemen," began Carmody as soon as everyone had settled. "You'll notice that we have a new member attending our group for this session. Harry Buckingham is employed by our newly appointed advertising agency, although I hasten to add that he is not joining us in that capacity this evening."

Of course not, thought Harry, it was my temperamental speech that won me a place here, not my position as account executive. Presumably a tacit understanding existed between them that what he heard in the course of the weekend was for his personal rather than professional benefit.

"Perhaps Miss Mariposa would care to give us a brief summary of the proceedings so far." Carmody took his natural place at the head of the table, and Harry watched as the robust Italian woman beside him hoisted herself to her feet to speak before the group.

"Well, first we have discuss' the foundation of the ODEL Corporation three years ago," she began in a deep, pronounced accent which exaggerated the length of her words, "an' how a system was found that would act as a blueprint for the running of this corporation. I have had the privilege of working with Daniel as head of international operations since this date."

As Carmody had only reached his elevated position at ODEL three months ago, Harry figured that she was referring to her status as a CEO in one of his other companies.

"It was through Daniel that I was first introduced to the runic system. This, we have explain' to our colleagues, is an ancient craft which, when applied correctly, can have great relevance in the world of modern-day finance." She paused and consulted her notes. "Daniel has explained to our friends how this system work' for centuries. We have also discuss' the too—"

"Thule Gesellschaft," said Carmody quietly.

"Thank you. Also the Deutsches Ahnernerbe"— Carmody smiled at her pronunciation—"and how the Nazis used this occult bureau to harness the power of runes. We also examined how they abuse' that power in their attempt to control the masses."

Harry had expected something weird, but his expectations were being exceeded. What was this, some kind of techno-Nazi league? His palms were starting to sweat.

"We must never forgive or forget the evils of the Nazis," continued Miss Mariposa, "a society corrupted by its own power. The runic system was abused, destroying guilty and innocent alike. Through its links with Hitler it fell into disrepute, and for the first time in centuries into disuse. It cease' to have any application in the postwar world. In reviving the runic system we are looking purely at its technological applications for the future. But we must always remember the horrors of its past, and make sure that they cannot occur again."

Amid a light shower of applause, she seated herself. Carmody rose and waited for silence.

"What we also discussed was the rise of the modern multinational conglomerate, and how it too often grows with no aspirations of its own beyond thoughts of continual expansion. From the lowliest worker to the highest levels of management, the ODEL organization is designed to be different. A thinking company which reflects the goals of its founder, Sam Harwood, a multinational which will fulfill the dreams of its staff. This is how we came to employ a runic philosophy that would combine personal beliefs with public trading, allowing us to maintain lofty ideals while yielding high profits.''

Throughout the meeting, Harry found it hard to keep his preconceived ideas of Carmody in focus. The industrialist seemed to be switching from sinner to saint and back before his eyes, yet the image of philanthropic visionary that was being presented to him tonight rang false to the core.

"It seems inevitable," continued Carmody, "that there are many who oppose the rapid growth of such an organization as ODEL. Perhaps they consider it wrong for a system of personal harmony to be allied to one which fosters business achievements— although I think that's something our Japanese cousins have been managing to do for many years with great success.'' There was a ripple of appreciation from the oriental contingent. "We are here to discuss the next step in our expansion program, our advancement into Europe and the Americas. And especially" —he held out an open palm— "to encourage the future investment of our overseas friends.''

So, just when the meeting seemed to be adopting a quasi-religious tone, its real purpose had emerged. This was part-seminar, part-fundraiser. Perhaps the ultimate aims of ODEL and its satellite companies really were noble. Harry wondered if the others in the room realized that innocent people were being murdered to achieve those aims.

Carmody continued, "The ODEL Corporation has already gained considerable financial control in the City. In Great Britain our backers are a powerful, committed body of men and women. Now that power can be spread via satellite, through our newly acquired cable networks, through video communications, through computer systems, to the other financial centers of the world."

As Carmody outlined the investment programs that would herald ODEL's arrival in the twenty-first century, a darker image began to take shape at the back of Harry's mind. Too many fundamental questions were staying unanswered. What, for example, was the company's product? Communications technology? It didn't seem an area on which Carmody was keen to dwell. What exactly were these altruistic aims of his? How did ODEL's runic system work? His questions remained unresolved in the next part of the session. As factsheets and financial breakdowns were presented at length, Harry found his attention wandering. From the window of the makeshift boardroom he could see Mrs. Carmody outlined beside a table lamp in the nearby wing. She remained motionless behind the lead-lit window for the best part of an hour. At first she appeared to be reading. Then one of the maids switched on the overhead lights, and he could see that she was simply staring at a section of blank wall.

At eight o'clock the group broke to change for dinner, and Harry returned to his drafty room. As he sat on the edge of his deep ceramic bath listening to the gurgle of water boiling in polished copper pipes, he knew that it was time to resolve a plan of action.

The quiescent form of Carmody's wife came to mind once more. Perhaps she held the key to his perception of the tycoon. So far she had shown little interest in her husband's distinguished guests. She probably had interests of her own, and remained uninvolved in his business affairs. He watched the bath gradually fill, wondering if she had any idea that her husband was a multiple murderer.

The wheels of the Boeing lifted free of the racing tarmac and the aircraft angled into the freezing night sky. As they banked on the incline over West London, Frank saw the stars tilt to become the cadmium streetlights of the motorway below. He began to count faster, first in threes and then fives. His eyelids grew heavy. They had found a new way into his mind. They were sending him to sleep. He fought to retain his consciousness but saw the lights fade from the window as he slipped back into a world of dreams.

And such dreams. He was a Thracian gladiator, armed with his buckler and dagger-scythe, battling the *mirmillones* on the blood-caked clay of the arena. He was a Samnite, gold-helmeted and plumed in white, the defeater of devils, lord of the heavens, slashing the hellish creatures aside with a swoop of his flashing blade. He was balancing in the wind on top of the mountain, bodyguard to Spartacus himself, the icy air whipping at his bare torso, the shining saber still thrusting from his crimson fist, he was—

He was standing naked in the open doorway of the aircraft smothered in blood with the sound of the engines shrieking below him. The blasting darkness tore the air from his lungs as he whipped his head back to see the chaos and carnage of the cabin. The flight attendant lay on her side in the aisle, losing blood from a wide gash in her stomach. Passengers were screaming. Two of them—no, three—were bleeding, hands clutching bloody heads and chests. He had slashed away his clothes with the gleaming swordlike shard of mirror, had twisted open the central emergency exit and pulled the door aside to stand spread-eagled in the hatch, screaming into the night as the Boeing bucked like a roller coaster. The cabin had not yet pressurized to the muscle-numbing hurricane beyond, creating a vortex which twisted through the cylinder as the pilot fought to stabilize his aircraft.

With the glittering shard of mirror embedded in his right hand and his left gripping the lintel of the exit, Frank Drake looked out at the rolling universe, at the celestial lights so pure, so bright, so *Christian* that they burned the pagan demons from his mind. The mighty aircraft cleaved its way between a million stars, its walls of curved white steel reflecting the radiance of a neon moon.

As tortured engines howled in protest, the naked figure, a backlit X suffused in the cabin's jaundiced light, rode screaming to his final destination.

39.
White Noise

WHILE THE OTHER patients on his ward were coming down with viruses, John May was coming up with one. And now that it was there on his computer screen, he did not know what to do with it. At visiting time on Friday evening he was still pondering the problem when Sergeant Longbright arrived at his bedside. She was pleased to find the detective's condition greatly improved.

"Paste sandwiches and angel cake for tea, is it?" she asked, examining his tray. "How nice to know that some things never change." May imagined that Longbright would have made a good nurse, restoring fetishistic tones to the uniform of starched apron and black stockings. "What's this?" She tapped the computer screen with a vermilion nail.

"Something from the electronic bulletin board about the ODEL Corporation," he replied. "Apparently, they're members of the Computer Threat Research Association."

"What's that?"

"An organization aimed at controlling hackers who drop viruses into computer systems," said May, peeling open a sandwich and examining it. "It's possible to design harmful software that replicates through computer networks, damaging files. You may remember America's destructive Internet Worm, and you still get instances of the famous 'Eighteen thirteen' or 'Friday the thirteenth' virus which attaches itself to programs and wastes memory space. They can be triggered to corrupt or delete

244

certain files, and get passed from one computer to another on infected floppy disks.''

"Sounds like a human illness.''

"They operate in exactly the same way. Luckily, just as doctors have discovered antidotes to certain diseases, programmers have developed 'inoculator' software that guards disks against infection. ODEL is promising to help safeguard the industry by investing heavily in new inoculation techniques.''

"This doesn't sound like the obstructive, secretive ODEL Corporation that appears throughout our files,'' said Longbright, "unless they're planning to use the inoculation process for their own ends. We've no news on your attacker, I'm afraid, although we found his abandoned car a few streets to the north, near the main-line railway station. No sign of the cassette, unfortunately.''

"If we're to incriminate an organization the size of ODEL,'' May reasoned through his sandwich, "we have to do two things: nail some hard evidence, and get our facts absolutely right. They're not the kind of adversary you antagonize lightly.''

"What's the next step?''

"Bryant said he was going to get hold of ODEL's company files.''

"You know that's illegal unless we publicly sequester them, and we're in no position to do that yet.''

"I know. In the meantime, more people will die.''

"Did Arthur say exactly how he was going to obtain these files?''

May pushed aside the remains of his meal and fell back on the pillow. "I dread to think,'' he said.

Dinner at the Carmody mansion proved to be a discreetly stylish affair. Peppered langouste with asparagus followed bitter cherry soup and prawn mille-feuilles. Unsurprisingly, Carmody's cellar held a wine selection of great delicacy and rarity. Harry found himself seated between the lawyer, Slattery, and a sour-faced Korean man who remained silent throughout the meal. He had been hoping for a position near the tycoon himself, but the evening's meeting had suggested an order of status among

Carmody's colleagues, and those with the most to invest in ODEL's satellite holdings were privileged to join him at the head of the table.

After their earlier encounter, Harry did not expect much in the way of genial conversation from Slattery, but he was to be proven wrong. After the usual pleasantries had been exchanged, the lawyer leaned close and fixed Harry with a red-rimmed eye. "I should imagine you're wondering why Daniel's asked you here," he said. "You must have gathered by now that you are not in attendance as a representative of your agency."

"The thought had crossed my mind." Harry sliced through his asparagus. "We haven't had much of a chance to talk to each other."

"Then perhaps I can enlighten you. ODEL's advertising requirements will be extremely specific. Daniel will need to create a team that can devote all of its time to the task—a liaison group between himself and the agency. At the moment your loyalty lies, naturally enough, with your company. But I think perhaps you'll be made an offer of employment in the course of this weekend."

"I'll need to know more about your working methods first," said Harry, laying aside his fork. "There are quite a few things I don't understand."

"I am authorized by Daniel to answer any questions you may have."

"All right." Harry turned his full attention to the lawyer. "For a start, I don't get this rune business. How does it work?"

"I know it sounds strange at first, but it's a purely symbolic system, nothing more. There are some books on the subject in the library. Mrs. Carmody will be happy to provide you with them."

"Is it like the Freemasons?" Harry persisted. "Are there other companies which recognize the same symbols?"

"Not to my knowledge. The structure only exists within the ODEL group, although that encompasses many different companies."

Sensing that the lawyer was blocking his questions rather than answering them, he approached the subject from another direction. "What does ODEL want, if it's not merely a question of expansion? Daniel's a well-publicized philanthropist. Is he aiming for peace on earth? An end to the nuclear deterrent?"

"Daniel Carmody wants what any sane man wants, Mr. Buckingham. A decent world in which to raise his children. He has given many lectures on the subject. Those you will also find in the library."

After this, Harry gave up and finished his meal in silence. Slattery seemed not to notice, and continued to pick at his food as he listened to his employer discussing the corporation's forthcoming entry into New York's cable television market.

After dinner the group retired to the main study for coffee and cognac. Mrs. Carmody put in a brief appearance, politely greeting the other guests in turn before retiring to an armchair far away from her husband.

The main topic of conversation remained ODEL's expansion plans, and cliques were formed among the guests, mostly according to nationality. Harry decided that now was the right time to ingratiate himself with Carmody's wife. Rising from his chair, he crossed the room and seated himself beside her. The tycoon's eyes flickered up and he registered Harry's change of position before returning his attention to the discussion at hand.

"I've been wondering what your first name was," said Harry with a smile. "I can't very well keep calling you Mrs. Carmody all weekend."

"Oh, I'm sorry, it's Celia. So old-fashioned, I hate it." She took a final drag on her cigarette before grinding it out in the ashtray. Tension showed in her face.

"I think it has a very civilized sound."

"Civilized." She virtually spat the word. Although she had been absent during the meal the smell of alcohol hung heavily on her. "Anyway, I don't suppose you'll see me again this weekend."

"Oh, why is that?"

"Nobody ever does."

There was an uncomfortable pause while Harry racked his brains for a suitable topic. Celia's gray eyes flitted around the room with disinterest. She seemed to have no

need for conversation. "Have you lived here very long?"
he asked finally.

"All my life."

"It's a magnificent house."

"Yes, it is."

She searched about, suddenly awkward. Harry watched
her hands knotting in her lap and decided to persevere.

"Do you have any children?"

"No." She answered too sharply. Realizing her error,
she tried to make amends. "Look, Mr. Buckingham . . ."

"Please, call me Harry." As he topped up her glass,
he noticed that Carmody was watching them from across
the room. "I only asked because the house seems the
perfect place to raise kids."

"My husband is a very busy man. His business frequently takes him away from the house."

"Surely that's all the more reason to . . ."

"He doesn't like . . . we don't . . . it's not something
we can do, I'm afraid."

"I'm sorry, I didn't mean to pry."

"That's all right, I don't suppose you did."

She inclined her head once more, and in that instant
he understood just how much she hated her husband. He
had invaded her home, usurped her life, and she could
not forgive him for it.

"You two seem to be getting along very cozily,"
boomed Carmody suddenly. Harry nearly had heart failure. "Celia, darling, isn't it past your bedtime?" He
reached down a hand and she meekly accepted it. "Celia
hasn't been very well lately," he explained. "I don't want
our business talk to tire her." She exited the room without a backward glance, leaving Harry with the head of
the ODEL Corporation.

"I hope she hasn't been boring you," said Carmody,
pulling on his cigar and throwing him an alarming smile.

"Not at all." Harry tried to reply as breezily as he
could. "You command great loyalty from everyone. It's
very admirable."

"I don't command loyalty, Harry, I demand it. There's
a difference. Has Slattery talked to you yet?" He did not
wait for a reply. "If I instructed him to make you a for-

mal offer of heading up my liaison team, would you accept it?''

''That rather depends.''

''On what?''

''How much more you're prepared to tell me about the corporation. I want to know how the runic system works. You use it on business rivals, don't you? On people who get in the way.''

Carmody studied the end of his cigar. ''If you want to know about your father, Harry, I'll be happy to tell you.''

A chill prickled across his chest. He tried to sound as calm as possible. ''That would be a start,'' he said slowly.

''Then walk with me.''

The financier led the way from the smoke-filled study. At the end of a tall corridor passing through to the back of the house, he stepped into a large Victorian conservatory filled with leather-skinned tropical plants, illuminating low lights from a wall panel.

''First,'' he said, folding his arms, ''tell me what you think happened. Then I'll tell you the truth.''

Harry cleared his throat. ''I know part of it. He discovered that one of his colleagues at Instant Image had accepted some property belonging to you, not realizing that the property was stolen. So you had him killed.''

''You realize what you're saying to me.''

''Yes.''

''All right. But I have to tell you that you're wrong. Your father's company made the purchase with full knowledge of the shipment's origins. What they didn't realize, though, was that the tapes weren't blanks as they'd been led to believe. Quite the reverse. Of course, Coltis couldn't have known they were special either, otherwise he wouldn't have sold them so cheaply.''

''How come he stole my car?''

''Now *that* part of it was one of life's more interesting little coincidences. Coltis's death, however, was no accident of fate. He was punished for the havoc he caused.''

''So what was on the tapes?''

''They were part of a special consignment, to be used

only in the most extreme situations. Produced through a major technological advance.''

''Involving runes?''

''Precisely. The tapes have the power to maim, and even kill. Your father took it upon himself to run one of them, and suffered the result.'' Carmody laid a cold hand on Harry's shoulder. ''I know this has been difficult for you, but can you try to appreciate my position? Imagine what would happen if, say, a thief broke into a chemical plant and stole a batch of experimental germs. If those who purchased the stolen property died as a result, whose fault would it be?'' Carmody's voice had the soothing quality of a qualified hypnotist. Harry forced himself to remember that the man standing before him was stained with the blood of all those who had stepped in ODEL's path.

''Why do you need to develop such dangerous devices?'' he asked.

''The runes protect us from our enemies and our business rivals. There's no need to look so shocked; these days it's not unusual for large corporations to actually hire the services of hit men, did you know that? In the USA several film companies are currently being indicted for that very reason. We are merely protecting our interests.''

''Not if innocent people get hurt.''

''Harry, nobody is innocent anymore.''

He considered his father's death on a rainswept London street. He saw Hilary lying in the gutter, slashed to ribbons. Beth, torn apart on the railway tracks. Eden, imprisoned within the escalator. ''Protection of interests'' seemed a hell of a poor reason to die.

Carmody was watching him closely, trying to gauge his reaction. If he blew it now, the game was over. He forced a conciliatory smile. ''I accept your position,'' he said. ''It's an interesting concept. How does it work?''

Carmody continued to watch him for a few more seconds, then relaxed into a smile. Harry knew that he had just made his most successful presentation to a client. He had convinced the magnate of his own good faith.

''Most of the work is done for us,'' Carmody was saying. "It's all there in the runic alphabet. Runes are really an ancient way of seeing. They've been all around us for centuries, but we're no longer aware of them. These simple shapes and configurations influence our lives. Projected in the right sequence they can calm or enrage us, turn us into aggressive bullies or passive receptors. Married to new technology they can help us to dream, or cause living nightmares."

"You're in the telecommunications business now. Do you think it's right to adopt such techniques?"

"Harry, Harry . . ." Carmody threw up his hands in mock despair. "What's *right* in business anymore? Is industrial espionage right? What about the tobacco cartels who print death warnings on their products, the alcohol companies who advertise glamorous life-styles to their addicts, the insurance companies who only pay up when every get-out clause has failed them? What about the manufacturers of sugar drinks and junk food, the corporations that condone immigrant labor and support apartheid, the industries that destroy the rain forests so they can print leaflets telling you how caring they are? Where *do* you draw the line, Harry? Your agency has offices in South Africa. Where do *you* draw the line?"

They were standing so close that their faces were almost touching. Carmody's glass eye threw a dead stare to one side of him. He threw down his hands in a gesture of resignation, but the tension remained between them. For Harry, it was a shock to discover some of his own passion in his adversary.

"You know, Harry, as these purveyors of everyday *lies* bury us beneath tons of unwanted paper, polluting our society with imaginary ideals we can never hope to attain, I realize more and more the absolute rightness of our path. I know that somebody has to lead the way."

He can't see it, thought Harry. He's fallen into the same self-righteous trap. He thinks business operates in some kind of moral airlock, that he's not accountable to ordinary men and women. He judges other companies, but all he sees for his own is the bottom line. He'll still make a killing, he'll just do it his way.

Carmody pulled forward a chair and seated himself,

gesturing to Harry to do the same. "We're living in a time of white noise," he said. "Everyone's shouting their wares at once. The runes are a way of cutting through that noise." He picked up a plant and examined its delicate variegated leaves. "If you were a scientist watching our encoded runes, you'd say that the configurations trigger forgotten synaptic responses in the brain. They revive deeply buried, primitive emotions, like a mind-expanding drug, forcing you to hallucinate. They can conjure up your darkest fears, the things of which you are most terrified. A childhood bogeyman, a terror of falling, claustrophobia. The experience is real. At least, it is to the beholder. And it can be programmed to happen at any time. Five minutes after you see the runes, or five days.

"But if you were a parapsychologist you'd say that the runes were a curse, a method of rendering victims beyond the laws of chance. A way of bringing the Devil back to earth."

"First you have to get someone to watch your tape."

Carmody chuckled to himself. "Oh no, Harry, you've got it all wrong. That was merely our initial experiment. Now we can digitize runes. We can code them into radio signals, store them on compact discs, hide them in computer files. We can play them through telephone lines, print, fax, and broadcast them, scatter them within the sparkling static of the airwaves. There are thousands of different ways to communicate, and we can get runes to you via any of them. Of course, we're learning to refine the message. No more death threats to business rivals or crudely drawn symbols on bits of paper. We're in the process of setting up a satellite network which will appeal directly to the consumer. We're looking at a subtle change in spending habits, a careful alteration of personal priorities, a realignment of values . . . as you can imagine, the possibilities are infinite."

Harry became aware of his own insignificance within Carmody's plans, and the thought made him suddenly fearful for Grace's safety as well as his own.

"We're using the runes to bring about a changed world," said Carmody. "It's an awesome responsibility."

"It could also create a hell on earth. Hell is the alteration of all that is familiar. Hell is the destruction of our world."

"How gloomy of you, Harry! Nobody's talking about destroying the world, just . . . improving it."

"At the very least, it poses a moral dilemma," said Harry, unable to remove a trace of sarcasm from his voice. "Especially if someone asks you to increase the sales of a certain product. Or a government lobby wants you to convince voters of their integrity."

Carmody turned his masklike face to gaze steadily into his eyes. "If I wanted you to die," he said, "I'd have a thousand different methods at my disposal. It's the biggest stick in the playground, Harry." The mask broke and a smile emerged. "Luckily, I'm aware of your career record, and I think we're on the same side. Come. The others will be wondering where we've been."

40.

Rufus

"THIS IS RIDICULOUS," muttered Bryant. "It's half past one in the morning. I shouldn't have to be doing this at my age. I should be at home, tucked up in bed with a copy of *Bleak House*. They can get somebody younger next time."

The last of the square stone archways led him to an ill-lit tunnel running parallel to the river. As he reached the far end, he saw that it opened out into a broad underground concourse enclosed by a circular concrete rim. Underpasses ran from the concourse in every direction. Bryant stopped and leaned on his walking stick, the echo of his footsteps ticking into silence. He felt dwarfed by his surroundings. These subterranean walkways had been built to allow rush-hour commuters from nearby Water-loo Station to cross the multi-lane interchange which existed at the foot of Waterloo Bridge. At night, however, the area adopted a different demeanor. Few pedestrians hurried through the tunnels after dark. The eerie pools of half-light through which they had to pass unnerved them.

Bryant looked back, and was faced with a view of endless concrete pillars, staggered across the cavernous concourse like the interior of a Gothic cathedral. Clustered around the base of each pillar, like barnacles on sea pilings, were cardboard boxes containing bundles of rags. Closer examination revealed that there were human beings within the rags, and that Bryant had reached his destination, the area known as "Cardboard City." Tourists, leaving the warmth and comfort of the National Theatre, their programs tucked under their arms, were shocked to stumble upon this makeshift township of the disadvantaged. It was a sight which could not fail to prick the conscience, causing eyes to be lowered and footsteps quickened as the more fortunate vacated the region in search of their cars.

Armed only with the physical description May had provided for him, Bryant began to wonder how he would ever locate his man. With the help of his bedside computer, May had placed a request on the electronic bulletin board which most of the hackers read from time to time, asking for Rufus to make contact with them. So far there had been no reply.

"I couldn't be a better muggers' target if I wore a sign on my back," grumbled Bryant as he stepped gingerly between the sleeping inhabitants. He knew better than to believe what he said. These people were tired and disillusioned with a system which seemed unable to accommodate their needs: that didn't make them criminals. He peered into each box, trying to fit a face to his description. Here were kids from broken homes and happy ones, young men who looked like bank clerks, women who failed to accord with the traditional image of their status. Half of these people could be on my staff, thought Bryant sadly, moving on. Behind him came the sound of a skateboard being upended.

"You lookin' for me, ol' man." The voice was American, black and young.

Bryant slowly turned to find himself facing a nine-year-old boy wearing a baggy T-shirt and Ocean Pacific shorts that diminished him still further. His hair was shaved in neat arrows across his head.

"You the detective, man, you're too *old* to be a detective!" He dropped the skateboard and jumped back onto it, laughing.

Bryant bristled. "Physical appearance can be deceiving, you should know that."

"Story o' my life, man. You must be Bryant. May's in the hospital, right?" He tried to high-five the detective, who became confused and withdrew his hand. "The man is a party *animal*, he is one solid *dude*, know what I'm saying?"

"Well," said Bryant, exasperated, "I can hear what you're saying but I have no idea what you're talking about." The boy's name was Rufus, and in the world of computer hacking he was a legend. Two years ago he had caused a national scandal by breaching the private accounts of Lady Diana and running up a charge bill on her credit cards. Too young to be prosecuted, he was held in juvenile detention, but escaped as he had done so many times in the past.

"If you read the terms of the agreement and agree, you're to come with me," said Bryant, fishing into his jacket and producing a folded envelope. Rufus accepted it and read quietly.

"Whatever you do," May had said earlier, "don't insult his intelligence. He may only be nine years old, but he has an IQ of one hundred and seventy. And don't feel sorry for him. He lives beyond the law because he enjoys it."

Rufus slipped the letter into his pocket. "I think we have a deal," he said, smiling. "Gimme a minute to lock up." He scooted off to one of the larger cardboard boxes and rummaged around in it. Bryant wondered what May had offered the boy in return for his cooperation. He had not been shown the contents of the letter. Rufus returned wearing a fresh sweatshirt with a white hood and a black cap with the peak reversed.

"I have a car parked nearby." Bryant held out his hand, then quickly withdrew it. He had to remember not to treat Rufus like an ordinary child. "I'm to take you directly to the hospital, then you can stay at the station house as a guest, until your part in the investigation is finished."

"Hell, man, that suits me from the ground up. We bin flooded out down here for days now."

"Fine, then we'll go and see John." They climbed the litter-strewn stairs leading from the subway. "How do you know my partner?"

"The man busted me last year. But it was cool. I did him some favors, he released me."

"Why did John arrest you?"

"I was running these warehouse parties, cleaning out the acid cabbages, man, it was *easy* pickings, I tell you, the setup was on *ice*."

"How very interesting." Bryant gave him a strange look and resolved not to ask anything else until they had reached headquarters.

41.

Celia

Daily Mail   Saturday 2nd May

BRITISH AIRWAYS JET IN MIDAIR DRAMA

A British Airways flight from Heathrow to Amsterdam narrowly avoided disaster last night when one of its passengers went berserk, injuring five others before forcing open the cabin's central emergency door and hurling himself to his death.

Frank Drake, 28, a librarian and college student, was traveling on the evening flight without luggage, it was revealed today. A few minutes after take-off one of the flight attendants noticed Drake attempting to remove his clothes.

"He seemed to be in a very agitated state," says stewardess Stacy Drabble. "One of the other flight attendants approached him to see if she could offer any assistance, when he suddenly leapt from his seat and stabbed her in the stomach with a piece of broken mirror."

As attractive blond stewardess Paula Cullen fell to the floor bleeding, Drake proceeded to hold the crew at bay, slashing at any passengers who moved near him. Then he raised the bar of the exit door and threw himself from the aircraft.

NEAR MISS NARROWLY AVERTED

The sudden change in cabin pressure caused the Boeing 757 to veer from its course. As the pilot sought to regain control of the aircraft, a Balkan Air jet passed within three hundred meters of the Boeing's wing-tip. Startled BA passengers saw people from Thailand finishing their meals in preparation for landing.

Today, Frank Drake's friends are being traced by the police in an effort to understand the motive behind his rampage. Drake's body crashed through the roof of number 17, Avenell Road, Highbury, North London while a family was having dinner.

INCIDENT SPARKS SAFETY ROW

BA experts denied concerns over the safety of the aircraft's exit doors. "Once the cabin is fully pressurised it is extremely difficult for one person to open the door in flight," said one BA spokesman, adding, "witnesses in this instance observed that Drake seemed to possess almost superhuman strength while holding on to the hatchway." Upon opening the door an escape chute descended, but was torn away in the wind.

Flight attendant Paula Cullen's condition is said to be "stable." The other injured passengers will be released from hospital later this morning.

(Story cont'd page 2, column 2.)

MP calls for safety checks on BA cabin exit doors. Page 2, column 4. Houseowner to sue BA over body hitting roof. Page 2, column 3.

Harry folded the paper and finished his coffee. Now Grace's friend had killed himself. It had to have been a result of watching the tape—too late now to realize that they should never have given it to him. A few minutes ago he had tried to call Grace from the heavy Bakelite telephone on the hall table, but there had been no reply.

The other members of the group were already attending their first morning meeting—a session to which it seemed he was denied access. Breakfast had been served at eight in the conservatory. Outside, the watery sunlight slanted across variegated fields and dripping hedgerows. He was the only one left in the room. As he buttered his toast he wondered what had become of their precious tape. Would Frank Drake have had it in his possession when he jumped?

"Still eating, I see." Celia Carmody stood at the other side of his table. She was wearing a fawn sweater and a white pleated skirt that made her look younger, mid-thirties perhaps, even though an air of melancholy still hung about her. The lightness of her clothes made her seem even fainter in the daylight.

"Please, join me. I think there's some tea left." Harry motioned to the chair opposite.

"For a minute only. I must get on. I hope you slept well; the bed in that room's pretty ghastly." She seemed more relaxed than the evening before, probably because the rest of the group was no longer within earshot. Although their conversation was innocent, Harry could not shake the feeling that unseen signs were passing between them, transforming them into fellow conspirators.

"Why aren't you in the meeting?" she asked, helping herself to toast.

"Apparently Daniel's dealing with something that doesn't yet concern me," he replied. "I'm only to attend the afternoon session."

"Oh, he does that to me, too. No-go areas. Most infuriating." She seemed ready to forgo the formalities of acquaintanceship in order to confide in him. Perhaps she could tell that he was different from the others. He decided to take a chance.

"I'm sorry about last night," he said, "asking you about children. It was an impertinence."

"No," she sighed, "it wasn't. Such an obvious question, I never know how to answer it."

"I'm sure you must hate us all being here. Disrupting family life."

"No, I like it, I assure you. But of course, I have no say in the matter . . ."

"Why not?"

"In the grand scheme of things my vote counts for very little." There was a clatter of dishes behind them as a maid began to clear the tables. Celia paused, catching his eye for the briefest of moments. Her look of guilt was as conclusive as a traitor's confession. He knew now that she was desperate to confide in someone, but terrified of picking the wrong person. He imagined her sounding out likely candidates month after month, never finding the one who would break his loyalty with Daniel long enough to believe in her.

"Perhaps we can talk later," he suggested. "After lunch."

"No," she said hastily. "You have to attend your meeting or you'll get a smacked wrist. Besides, I have to go into Norwich." She rose from the table. "We're having cocktails before dinner tonight. I'll probably see you there. Cheerio." And she was gone, stepping between the tables in an exaggeration of casual attitude. He felt sure now that he could gain her confidence completely.

He spent most of the morning in his room, preparing notes and questions for the afternoon meeting. Lunch was light and smart. The elegant vegetarian dishes would not have been out of place in a fine French restaurant, and Carmody held a merry court with the Japanese, who had emerged as the most powerful potential investors attending the seminar.

The afternoon conference was long and dull. Carmody continued to outline his expansion plans, this time in greater detail. Figures and flowcharts were bandied about with projected growth and potential returns always marked in red ink. Harry noticed that the industrialist adopted an evangelical turn of phrase whenever consumers were mentioned. He presumed the others knew that Carmody was proposing a crusade rather than a campaign, but if they were aware of his plans to "realign" society, they failed to show it.

At the end of the session Carmody promised that revelations would follow on Sunday morning, when he would discuss the applications of the runic system within the structure of network television. It was the only time he had mentioned runes in the course of the day.

Harry showered and changed for dinner, but when he descended to the main study for cocktails he found no sign of Celia. After spending a few minutes in polite conversation with the Italian woman, Miss Mariposa, he noted that Carmody had once more become involved in heavy negotiations with the Japanese, and slipped away to the conservatory.

He found Celia seated in the semidarkness with a brandy by her side, awaiting his arrival.

"You quite startled me," she said softly. "I came in here for a rest before dinner."

Harry knew that she would keep up the pretense of casual conversation no matter what subject they discussed. It was a safety mechanism for Celia should her husband suddenly appear.

"I can leave if you like," he offered.

"Don't be silly. Come and sit." Harry obeyed. He wondered how much time they would have alone together before Carmody came looking for them again.

"You were wrong about me, Harry," she said finally. "When you asked about children. It's Daniel who wants them, but I won't give them to him." She reached for her glass and drank nervously. It was not her first brandy of the evening.

"Why not, Celia?"

"Because I don't want them to grow up hating their father."

"He's a very successful man. You have so much here . . ."

"This was always mine. The house has been in my family for generations. We were . . . after the war, the cash was gone. The upkeep simply became too much. Now the house is his. I'm his."

He played the game. "I'm sorry, I shouldn't have asked."

"No, I shouldn't have answered. You're just being polite to the boss's wife. Is there anything else you want to know?''

"Yes, there is." Harry pointed back to the hallway, where it was apparent that a lamp bracket had been recently removed. "Why are you getting rid of the fittings? It seems such a . . . sad thing to do.''

"Do you know, you're the first person to notice?'' Celia topped up her glass with a sigh. "I'll let you in on a secret. Promise not to tell?''

"I promise.''

"Every time I do something that annoys him, he sells another piece, something I treasure greatly. He does it to punish me. Bit by bit he's dismantling my memories.'' She stared at his chest, close to tears. "Every day brings another small indignity. All because . . .'' She stopped herself.

"Because what?'' Harry prompted gently.

She raised her eyes. "Because I *know*. I know everything, and I don't approve.''

He could sense her searching his face for understanding. He reached between the chairs and took her hand. "It's okay,'' he whispered, "I know too.''

The bond between them was sealed. He could feel her gratitude radiating in the dark. "I'll go ahead,'' he offered. "It might look odd if we both go in together.''

42.

Vision

HARRY OPENED THE bedroom door as quietly as he could, but the hinges were badly in need of oiling. He had hoped that the sound of his movements would be lost in the settling of the house, but every floorboard produced a squeak as he trod on it. Most of the weekend guests were sharing the same floor. Carmody and his wife apparently occupied a separate wing on the far side of the main lounge. With any luck he would be able to search the study without being overheard.

He peered down into the flagstoned hallway from the second-floor landing, noting the empty plinths which framed the vestibule. Presumably the busts which had once adorned them had been removed at Carmody's instruction.

At the foot of the stairs he withdrew a penlight and flicked it on, lighting his path to the study beyond. A grandfather clock chimed a quarter hour past one as he passed. The house had been quiet for little more than an hour.

Although the study door was closed, the key had been left in the lock. Even turning it as slowly as possible, Harry was alarmed at the deafening noise of the tenon as it withdrew from the mortice. He pushed the door and slipped inside, aiming the torch beam at Carmody's desk. Carefully, he brought the door to a close behind him. The heavy Chinese rug muffled his footsteps as he crossed the room. Seating himself behind the desk he tried each drawer in turn.

The first contained Carmody's personal stationery, his wife's crest, printed in blue on heavy hammered vellum. The second was filled with pending financial correspondence, and the third was locked. Wedging the penlight in the arm of his chair, he took out a penknife, unfolded the smallest blade, and twisted it in the lock. The point slipped and he scored a line across the veneer of the drawer.

"Why don't you try using a pickax?" said a voice behind him. "You'd probably do less damage." Daniel Carmody reached over and switched on the desk light. "That's better. Now you can see what you're doing."

Light fell across Carmody's features. His face shone white and hard, his ebony ponytail glistening on his shoulder like a coiled snake. "This is really very disappointing of you, Harry. You passed your test last night with flying colors. At least, you had me convinced of your loyalty. What are you looking for, by the way?"

Harry slowly set down the penknife and wiped his palms on the sides of his trousers. He could see that lying would no longer help. ''I wanted proof that you killed my father,'' he said simply.

Carmody sat back on the arm of the nearby chester-field. He made an affectation of relief. ''I thought we'd gone over that already. He killed himself. They all kill themselves. Once they've accepted the runes, there's nothing else they can do. Their perceptions are changed for good. If their fears didn't kill them, they'd go insane.''

Harry recognized the lie at once. At first he'd thought that Willie had been killed by a tape. Then he remembered that the old man had been passed a rune printed on a slip of paper. His death was no accident. It had been deliberately orchestrated by the ODEL Corporation.

''What's the longest someone has lasted?'' he asked, knowing that he now had to play for time. Perhaps he could appeal to Carmody's scientific curiosity.

''I don't know. It depends on how the runes are absorbed and what they say. In less enlightened times they were referred to as the Devil's prayers—''

''I know.''

''You've done your homework. I like that. But we're still learning. The runic tapes are our greatest success to date. We've even learned to protect the cassette boxes themselves with talismanic runes—reversed ones which safeguard objects. And we've discovered single runes that cause terminal hallucinations. We sent one to Henry Dell after finding out that he'd purchased a batch of our stolen tapes. He'd barricaded himself into his flat, so we stuck it on a milk bottle and switched it with one already in his apartment. The effect was extraordinary. He ended up in the canal at Camden Lock.

''We tried again with one of our most vociferous opponents, a chap named Meadows. *He* threw himself in the Thames. We used it once more, on David Coltis—a similar over-the-top outcome. I decided that the print runes needed further refinement. In their present form they were too . . . overt. We're building an entire spectrum of new subtleties into them. Catch.'' Carmody threw him the desk key. "You only had to ask, you know."

Harry held the brass key between thumb and forefinger, hesitating.

"Well, go on. Open it and tell me what's inside."

He slipped the key into the lock and turned it. Within the drawer was a small blue box, and a tin can. He removed the can and held it beneath the desk lamp. "It's a tin of asparagus," he said, puzzled.

"That much is obvious. What else do you see?"

"There's an ODEL logo, and a supermarket bar code."

"Take a good look at the latter."

Harry studied the black stripes carefully, then let the can slip from his fingers. A wave of nausea swept over him.

"Ah good, you spotted the rune," said Carmody, pleased. "This one has quite an interesting effect. Come over here." He rose and crossed to a pair of French windows, unlocking them top and bottom.

Harry tried to stand, but the room was suddenly dipping beneath him. He grabbed the edge of the desk and managed to propel himself as far as the couch before falling to his knees.

Framed in the moonlit chatoyance of the open windows, Carmody struck a pose, one hand in his jacket pocket, the other holding an unlit cigarette, a slim saturnine parody of Noel Coward. "You're probably wondering what's happening to you," he said. "Right now, a dormant part of your brain is trying to make sense of the commands it has received. I should imagine you feel a little sick." The flare of a match illuminated his face. He blew it out and laughed softly in the dark. "Come outside and tell me what you see."

Harry rose to his feet and lurched forward. Everything in his field of vision seemed to be moving far away, as if appearing within the ellipse forming beyond an optical lens. He reached the windows, stumbling past Carmody onto the patio, then stepped onto the soft wet grass of the lawn. Far above him it seemed that the night clouds were pushing their way across the sky with accelerating anger. A deep cold wind rose around him, and for a moment it seemed as if it would lift him from the ground.

"What is it? What can you feel?" There was an urgency, a vicarious excitement in Carmody's voice.

"The world," he gasped, "moving faster."

"What else? What do you see? Down there, near the foot of the garden."

Carmody pointed to a row of cypress trees at the end of the lawn. Harry tried to focus his eyes, but the horizon seemed to be bending beneath the force of the passing sky. Then he saw the struggling figure of the old man, his mud-spattered suit outlined against the dark boles. His hands were tied by a short rope to an iron tent spike, so that he had been forced to kneel in the grass with his arms outstretched.

"A man. I see a man."

"Describe him."

"White hair. He's crying. He thinks he's going to die." Harry tried to catch his breath. The old man was jerking at the stake like a terrified animal. Suddenly he heard a tearing, rustling sound and a pair of trees began to part, scattering pieces of broken bough into the wind.

At first he was unable to reconcile the dark image appearing behind the branches with anything in his previous experience. The creature which revealed itself was almost as tall as the house at their backs. It moved with the purposeful gait of a man, but was covered in coarse black hair. It pushed between the trees, holding them apart until it had passed through, then stood wavering in the gale, watching the sobbing man with impassive eyes as pale and radiant as the moon. Its chest heaved with the exertion of tearing a path through the thicket. The wind tore strings of spittle from its heavy jaw as a stale animal odor filled the air.

The white-haired man had fallen silent now as he waited for the creature to make its move. As if suddenly reaching a decision it reached down and pulled the stake from the earth, lifting it so that its prey was hoisted high above the ground, suspended by his wrists.

Like a child with a toy, it pulled the figure back and forth, bending it this way and that. Harry could hear the unmistakable sound of bones snapping as the arms and legs were forced against their joints. Finally, bored, it tore the head from its victim and eviscerated the body with its fingers, wiping the steaming mess against its hide before tossing the remains into the wood. Then it sighted Harry.

"Don't let it come nearer!" he shouted, throwing his hands in front of his face. His knees gave way and he fell forward onto the damp earth.

"Tell me about his eyes," whispered Carmody.

Harry concentrated on the tycoon's voice and tried to formulate a reply. It was a lifeline, the only thing that could keep him from going mad.

"Eyes. No eyelids. No . . ."

"No what, Harry?"

"No pupils. Take him away!"

"You must look at him again."

Harry raised his head. The creature had come no nearer but stood motionless, carefully watching him. As before, it suddenly decided upon a plan of action and strode forward to within a few yards of the patio, reaching out its right arm. It had the stentorian, dripping breath of a large bear. Its sexual organs hung red and heavy beneath matted fur.

Harry's nostrils filled with the bitter stench of decaying animal flesh. He screamed as the beast's broad fingers reached down and closed over his head and chest, pulling him to his feet. It moved off, barely allowing Harry's legs to keep pace beneath him as it dragged him across the garden. The rough skin of its palm was pressed over his nose and mouth, crushing his face. As he began to gag, the hand released him and he fell sprawling into a bank of freshly turned earth.

He knew now that the creature would tear him into quarters if he remained aboveground. He had to burrow away from it. There was no other way of escape. Whimpering, he forced the earth aside in great handfuls, shoving his body into the soft, wet soil.

Carmody looked at his watch. "Hmmm. That's enough," he said. "Sit up and take a look at yourself."

The horror within him faded as quickly as it had appeared, as if the source of his agony had suddenly been removed. With aching limbs, Harry attempted to right his body. His clothes were smothered in mud, his mouth and hair filled with dirt. He forced his fingers between his teeth and pulled the clumps of soil free, vomiting chunks of earth onto the grass. As his sensations returned he sat anchored to the solid ground below, hawking and spitting. The feeling was like stepping from a roller coaster. The horizon slowly steadied itself, and he realized that he had tried to bury himself alive.

"Congratulations," said Carmody dryly. "You managed to uproot my prize English roses." He gestured at the wrecked flower bed. It appeared that Harry had dug a three-foot trench through the flowers. He looked around suddenly, fear crumpling his face, but neither the beast nor its victim were to be found.

"It's all right. The effects are over. You had better come and get cleaned up."

Carmody led the way back to his study. Harry walked behind him on legs of rubber, the nerves in his limbs still firing random responses.

"How do you feel?"

"Like I've just been in a car crash."

"Yes, that's usual."

He had torn a muscle in his shoulder but he did not care. Nothing mattered except being alive. "What was it?" he croaked. "You knew about the creature I saw. You could see it too."

"No, I couldn't," admitted Carmody, "although I know what it is. It's a version of the same being that most people see. Something from a collective ancestral memory. If the rune had been a white Thorn symbol you'd have got the Ice Demon, and he would have killed you. But this one, the one on the can, was a red Poerdh. It's the most mysterious symbol in the whole runic language. A lot of people think it's sexual."

"And the man who was killed?"

"Now that's interesting. You seem to have seen something that hasn't happened yet. Something that may not even happen."

"Then how could I have seen it?"

"I'm not honestly sure. I told you it was a mysterious symbol. Sometimes I think we're only scratching the surface of what we can learn." He sniffed the air. "You probably want to go and change your clothes. I think you've had an accident. Then you had better come back down here."

Carmody turned his back, dismissing Harry as he stumbled from the room, humiliated, exhausted, and ashamed.

43.

Disinfo

RUFUS SAT ON the edge of the sergeant's stool, unable to touch the floor with his feet. His fingers rattled across the keyboard as he sought access to ODEL's file system. At his back stood Janice Longbright. The soft light of the jade-colored screen rose across her face as she watched in amazement.

"The speed of it," she whispered. "I don't see how he has time to think."

"He doesn't need to think," said May. "Operating a computer is as natural to him as breathing." He heaved himself farther forward in the bed, propping up another pillow so that he could follow the boy's movements. Several extra pieces of equipment had been moved into the cramped hospital room, much to the nurse's anger. "He's supposed to have complete rest," she had told Longbright earlier that night. "How is he supposed to recuperate? Can't somebody else take over his investigation?"

"He wouldn't let anyone else come in at this point," explained Longbright, taking her arm and leading the

nurse from the room. "He won't relax until he finds corroborative evidence." Privately, she accepted the medical viewpoint. May's spirits were in better shape than his
health. She hoped Rufus would be able to come up with
something conclusive.

"Where'd you get these files?" asked Rufus, turning
on his stool. "Sumbitch who designed this shit don't
wanna let *nobody* in."

"What is he saying?" asked Bryant, baffled.

"We put two of our men into ODEL's main offices
posing as maintenance crew," said May. "This is all
they could lay their hands on."

"They couldn't have *duped* these, man. Files got heavy
pro-tection."

"They didn't. They removed the masters from the
premises."

"When they do that?"

"Six o'clock tonight. We have until seven A.M. to
crack them open and get them back in place. My men
took Polaroids of their position in the drawers from which
they were removed."

"How'm I supposed to break into these?" Rufus took
a slug of his Pepsi and returned to the keyboard. "They
got a password string for each file, you can't get in without it, hear what I'm saying? You don't got the word, you
don't got shit."

"I think I got the gist of that," said Bryant, brightening up. "The name ODEL is a rune in itself. I have a
feeling that if he types in the names of the other runes
we'll gain access to at least one of the files."

"Well done," said May, rubbing his hands in antici-
pation. "Do you have them?"

"No, I'm afraid not."

"Well, how can we get them?"

"I have someone waiting outside who remembers them
all. Hang on a sec." Bryant stuck his head out of the
doorway. "Dr. Kirkpatrick, would you come in here,
please?" He ushered in the gaunt paleographer.

"I don't know what I'm doing here," Kirkpatrick
complained. "I should be at home."

"You're always at home," said May. "You'll have to

sit on the side table. It's starting to look like the cabin scene from that Marx Brothers film in here.''

"Hello, little boy," said Kirkpatrick, looking over Rufus's shoulder. "You're doing the typing, are you? Jolly well done.''

"Get the fuck outta my face," said Rufus, indignantly shoving him away. As he booted up a new disk, the ODEL logo scrolled across the screen.

"That's interesting," said Kirkpatrick. "The name ODEL is a rune in itself. It's generally associated with the construction of a financial dynasty. It can be used to guard wealth. Tell you what, sonny," he said, patting Rufus on the head, "I'll give you the phonetic spellings of the most commonly used runes, and you type them in for me, think you can manage that?''

"D'you wanna talk to this asshole?" asked Rufus angrily. "Or shall I?''

May beckoned the doctor over to the bed and explained the situation to him. Chastened, Kirkpatrick returned to the computer and stood a respectful distance from its operator. Together they began to run through the runic alphabet.

Carmody was sitting where Harry had left him twenty minutes earlier. Beneath the soft green light of the desk lamp he worked at his computer terminal, shifting and deleting sections of reports. When Harry appeared at the door in fresh clothes, Carmody directed him to an armchair at the side of the room.

"I confess you present a problem to me, Harry," he said. "I need someone to develop a worldwide corporate campaign for ODEL, and you seem the ideal person to do it. I wanted to trust you from the start, but Slattery warned me against you. I decided you weren't worth risking an empire for." He slotted a microdisk into one of the disk drives and watched as the screen before him transformed. "On Slattery's advice, we sent you a death rune, but it seems your secretary accidentally ran it and suffered the consequences.''

Harry was about to tell him that Eden wasn't the only

victim of the coded tape, but knew that this would give Carmody even less reason to trust him.

"But perhaps your escape was fortuitous," Carmody conceded. "You're here, and you are now in possession of great knowledge. You've had firsthand experience of the runic powers. The ODEL satellite is up and functioning. Our New York cable station receives its first test transmission in two days, on Tuesday evening. I think that your loyalty to the organization is potentially far greater than your loyalty to the memory of a father you did not love. Does that mean I still think you're the right man for the job?"

"From the way you're talking to me, I guess it does," said Harry carefully. Carmody's eyes never rose from the screen. "What we need," he said, "is a test. Come over here."

Harry rose from his seat and stood by the desk. Carmody had punched up a series of names on the screen.

"I want you to study this," he said. "It's the ODEL blacklist. Slattery keeps it updated for me. These are the names of the people who have managed to infiltrate the ODEL mainframe. The system is studded with runic mines, but occasionally somebody manages to slip through."

"Perhaps they get into the system by accident," offered Harry.

"That's quite impossible. You have to possess runic knowledge to open any one of the files. Also, there are specific virus strings protecting all ODEL information." He pointed to the screen with a manicured forefinger. "The people listed here have all connected into sealed programs by using runic symbols. How much have they found out about us? Could they be working in league with each other?"

"What has this to do with me?" asked Harry.

"With so much money riding on the success of ODEL's expansion project," said Carmody, "we can't afford to have any wild cards in the pack. There's some cleaning up to do, and I'm going to put you in charge of the operation. Now. Tonight." He studied the list of half a dozen names. "I want you to get rid of these people for us."

"Feoh," said Kirkpatrick, "F-e-o-h. Then Doerg, D-o-e-r-g. That's the last one." Everyone watched the screen. Nothing happened.

Rufus sat back in the chair. Beads of sweat glistened on his forehead. "Gotta be somethin' else, man," he said. "We need some numbers on the screen here."

"Wait a minute, every rune has its own number. Let's see, Feoh is one, Doerg is eight . . ."

"Go back to the top and gimme them in the order of the runic alphabet." Rufus punched the keys as Kirkpatrick stood at his side checking the numbers from his notebook.

"I'm in," said Rufus quietly. "It's requesting a name for access to the material. Whose name you want me to use?"

"You can't put any of us," said May. "They could trace it back. Put our missing man in. Use Buckingham. Harry Buckingham."

Rufus typed in the name and sat back. The screen changed.

"Jesus, man, we've got a heavy disinfo operation goin' down here."

"What's that?" asked Longbright.

"Disinformation, ma'am. They're spreading poisoned information through other systems. You get a bug like that and it's over. You have to scrap your whole program."

"Isn't there any way of stopping that from happening?"

"There are certain command strings you can feed in, but you have to know what you're dealin' with. They'll counteract the effects of the virus string."

"Talismans," said Kirkpatrick. "To ward off evil curses. It's an updated version of a revenge system that's been with us since civilization began."

"Tell me," asked Bryant, "how far could this 'disinformation' be spread?"

Rufus thought for a moment. "I guess you could send

it worldwide with a strong enough signal. You'd have to
timecode it onto satellite transmissions.''

"ODEL is due to start broadcasting on its first cable
station any day now," said Longbright. "It's been in all
the papers for weeks. We have to find a way to stop
them.''

"Couldn't we apply for a court injunction to shut the
system down?''

"That would take too long, Arthur. See if you can find
out exactly when they're due to go on the air.''

"Man, I have never seen a system like this before.''
They turned to look at Rufus, who sat mesmerized by
the screen. It had begun to pulse, transmitting a series
of symbols at great speed, as if electronic ghosts were
making fleeting appearances within the system.

"You've triggered some kind of protection device,"
said May. "Turn it off!" Unable to find anything remotely resembling an off switch on the keyboard, Bryant
grabbed the terminal plug and tore it from the wall. The
picture dwindled to a dot.

"I hope we got it in time. Rufus, what did you see?"
Longbright turned the boy around on his stool and
checked his dilated pupils.

"I dunno, *heavy* shit. Images, biblical stuff I think.''
He rubbed his eyes with the heels of his hands. "It's
startin' to fade. Some kinda electronic code, bypasses
straight to your subconscious. I'd like to meet the guy
who invented this.''

"It took centuries to develop it this far," said Bryant.

"An interactive electronic language," said Kirkpatrick, impressed. "I suppose it's the next logical step.
Can't epilepsy be induced with a strobe? The possibilities are . . .''

"We're aware of the possibilities, thank you, Kirkpatrick. I'm more concerned right now about finding a way
to seal them off before they reach the public.''

"And before they reach us," said Rufus.

"What do you mean?''

"We triggered their warning codes," said the boy.
"They know we've gotten inside the system.''

* * *

"It shouldn't prove difficult," said Carmody, rising from the desk and turning his back to the screen. "By tomorrow morning I want everyone on the list to have seen or heard one of ODEL's most powerful runic commands."

Harry studied the names on the screen. Half a dozen hackers who had managed to scale the electronic walls of the ODEL group were now being sentenced to death. He was about to switch his attention back to Carmody when a new name wrote itself at the bottom of the list: HARRY BUCKINGHAM.

Harry's heart missed several beats. Back in London, Rufus had just loaded his name into the system on John May's command. As Carmody turned back to his desk he quickly moved in front of the terminal, blocking the tycoon's view.

"If you manage to handle the operation with a little flair," said Carmody, "we'll set up the liaison team and employ you on a full-time basis as senior promotions consultant. How does that sound?"

"Ah, perfect." Harry tried to keep his body between Carmody and the computer screen, but his position was starting to look awkward.

"You'll need addresses on hard copy." Carmody reached past him and depressed various keys, turning on the printer. He walked to the other side of the desk and waited for the list to appear on computer paper. Harry watched as his own death warrant issued from the machine. Reaching the end of the page, the printer switched itself off.

Carmody tore the sheet of paper free and studied it. His silence seemed to last for hours. Finally he raised the telephone receiver on his desk and punched out a two-digit number. "Slattery, I wonder if you'd come down here for a minute."

Harry's mind was racing frantically. "Oh, the name," he said. "It's probably my father's."

Carmody looked up. His eyes glittered blackly. "Your father is dead." He held the sheet of paper aloft. "It says 'Harry.' And it says you gained access to the ODEL system just a few minutes ago."

"How could that be? I've been here all the time."

"You've got a search program running somewhere in your name." Carmody sat forward, moving into the light. "Where is it?"

"I don't know what you're talking about," said Harry, panic rising through his chest like slivers of ice. "I'm not running anything." Behind them, Carmody's lawyer appeared in the doorway.

"Ah, Slattery. It appears that you were right after all. I'm depressed to have to admit that we have a professional hacker in our midst. He's been smarter than he looks."

"You've got it all wrong . . ." began Harry, walking forward. Carmody was free from the desk in a fraction of a second, knocking the wind from his body with a clean, hard punch that forced him to double over and fall to the floor.

"I want this kept from the others," he said, checking his knuckles for marks. "Nothing must be allowed to jeopardize the negotiations. If the Japanese get wind of this . . ." He kicked out at Harry, catching him in the stomach. "Lock him in his room while I think. This has happened once too often. We'll have to make an example of him."

Harry tried to stand but the pain in his gut forced him back down. Carmody stood over him, watching dispassionately. "Stubbornness seems to run in your family," he said. "The organization could have used someone like you." His voice dropped to a whisper. "You lost the game, Harry. Remember the Poerdh being? Well, he was nothing. I think we'll try out our latest runes on you. By tomorrow evening you'll be begging us to let you die."

44.

Barricades

THE HEAVY OAKEN door was locked from the outside. Bolted at the top too, by the feel of it. Harry pushed his shoulder against the central panels, but nothing gave. He was back in his bedroom once more, escorted there by Slattery. By the time he had considered whether the little strength he had left would allow him to jump the lawyer and make a run for it, they had arrived back at his room. Not a word had been spoken as the door closed between them, but with the key turning in the lock, Harry was already checking the telephone line and finding it dead.

He glanced at the clock on the mantelpiece and noted that there were still three hours to pass before sunrise. The windows were barred with curlicues of wrought iron that provided decoration as well as imprisonment. He had no choice but to wait and see what morning would bring. His limbs felt leaden. He gingerly lowered himself onto the edge of the bed.

Suddenly the television set beside him flickered into life, and runic patterns glittered through a white static of electrons. The sounds which emanated from the speakers seemed to exist beyond any normal decibel range. Carmody was feeding him the curse through his in-house monitor system. He threw himself across the bed and grabbed the remote handset, punching the POWER button, but nothing happened. Behind the television, a thick white cable vanished into the baseboard. Falling to his knees, he knotted the cord between his hands and pulled as hard as he could. The wiring stayed firmly connected.

The runic signals were pulsing pools of neon across the walls of the bedroom.

He ran into the bathroom and dug a pair of scissors from the bag of toiletries on the shelf above the sink. Holding them through the rubberized nylon of the bag, he returned to the television and began hacking at the cord. The whistles and shrieks emitted by the transmission were starting to make him feel sick. There was a flash of light, and his arm felt as if it had been engulfed by flame. The sounds and images died away as the TV screen faded to black. Harry sank back onto the bed, clutching his seared elbow.

The faint creak of the opening door was enough to wake him. Celia Carmody stepped into the room. Although the sun had yet to appear on the horizon, he could see that she was fully dressed. She came to the side of the bed and knelt down, holding her finger to her lips.

"Don't say anything. He'll be coming for you soon. You have to leave here."

Harry took hold of her arm. Her skin was alabaster, cool and smooth. "Can you get me out?"

"He keeps the main doors locked at night. Even I don't have the keys. You'll have to go through the conservatory."

Harry rose and began to shove his belongings into his travel bag.

"Leave that. He'll have put something in it, probably in the linings of your clothes. Don't take anything with you. You mustn't underestimate my husband." Fear registered on her pale face. Harry wondered what would happen if Carmody discovered that she was helping him to escape.

"How did you know what had happened tonight?" he asked.

"I couldn't sleep. I heard Daniel pass my door, so I got up. You can see into the study from the west-wing landing. We must hurry." She led the way along the corridor, directing him away from the boards that creaked. On the staircase they were startled by the hall clock strik-

ing five. They ran lightly along the flagstoned passageway which led to the conservatory.

"Why are you doing this?" he whispered, glancing
across at her shadowed form as it passed between ribbons
of pale light. She seemed even more delicate and ethereal
than when they first met.

"You don't belong with the others. I think there's still
a chance for you. Besides, you can leave, and I can't."
He caught a glimpse of her face as she replied. Her eyes
were those of a woman whose life had been stripped of
illusion, the eyes of someone long without love. She took
his hand and led him through an avenue of tall potted
palms.

"I've unlocked the windows. Go quickly, but don't
take your car. They've probably tampered with it. Head
straight along the lane at the end of the garden. Don't go
into the wood. You'll reach the village in less than an
hour, and you'll find a station there. He won't be up for
a while yet. Do you need money?"

Harry felt for his wallet. "I have enough. What about
you?"

"I'll think of something to tell him. I'll be all right."

On a sudden impulse, he stepped back through the
window and took Celia's hand. "You could come with
me."

"This is still my home. I can't leave. One day things
will be better."

He reached forward and softly kissed her. Celia's cool
lips parted as if being shown tenderness for the first time.
She held the kiss for just a moment, then placed a hand
on his chest and pushed him back toward the window.
Taking his leave, Harry ran across the lawn, past the
disturbed earth where he had tried to kill himself just a
few hours before. As he climbed through the hedgerow
into the road beyond, he turned for one last glimpse of
the house and saw her framed in the window, watching
his departure.

Dorothy Huxley rose early as a rule, but when the police called on Sunday morning she still was in bed. Fighting the effects of the sleeping tablet she had taken the

night before, she peered around the bedroom curtain and looked down. Two constables waited patiently at the front step. They looked barely old enough to be in uniform. Of course, they were here to ask more questions about Frank. As she dressed, she wondered how best to stall them.

Her friend's death had been a terrible shock, but strangely it had not come as a great surprise. On Friday night she had left him working late at the library, seated at the video monitor, involved with his project. Somehow, in some way, he had seen the runes. There could be no other explanation. He may have died in circumstances more bizarre than any of those in the cases he collected, but it was in the library that the seeds of his death had been planted; she was sure of it. Upon her arrival at the building yesterday she had found a number of journalists lying in wait for her at the entrance. One of them had even followed her home, and had spent several hours shouting up at the windows offering her money for an interview.

She would quietly wait for the police to leave her step, then head down to the library to search through Frank's belongings for the rune curse before anyone else decided to do the same. She was too late to save Frank, but perhaps there was still time to prevent some grotesque fate from overtaking others.

He called Grace from the station, waking her. "Say that again," she said, her voice thick with sleep. "Where are you?"

"On my way back to London. The train's due at any minute."

"I thought you went by car."

"There's no time to explain. Listen, I can't go back to my apartment. It's the first place Carmody and his men will look."

"I take it the mission wasn't a roaring success."

"Just stay there and I'll come to you. Don't pick up the telephone again until I get there, don't go out, don't watch TV or listen to the radio, and don't open your front door to anyone except me."

"I guess you know what you're doing." The line was silent for a moment. "The police called here looking for you, Harry. I told them I hadn't seen you for days. What went wrong?"

"I'm not sure. Somebody put my name on Carmody's electronic hit list just after he'd decided to confide in me." The railway lines started to ping as a train approached. "I have to go."

"Wait, wait! I have to know what he's planning to do."

Harry gave a bitter smile as he looked up at decelerating railway carriages. "Let's just say that the Devil's prayers are about to move into the public sector. I'll see you in two hours."

As the bus approached the library, Dorothy checked her purse for the keys to the main doors. If necessary, she could keep both police and press at bay while she searched Frank's desk. She adjusted the old felt hat so that it sat lower on her head. Her best defense lay in the illusion of senility.

After a brief respite from the rain, the churning sky had once more descended around the capital's tower blocks in preparation for a storm. She buttoned her coat and rose to her feet, noting with some satisfaction that it was still only half past nine. The constables had remained on her step for mere minutes before one of them answered a call on his crackling handset. As soon as they had left to attend the fresh summons, she had slipped from the building.

The library, cold and damp and silent, awaited her. Dorothy felt a twinge of unease as she crossed the familiar parquet floor toward Frank's desk. She could see from the far side of the hall that the library's video monitor had been left on. So, the evil had arrived in the way she feared most and understood least, pulsing through an invisible system of electronic particles. She appreciated the most obscure complexities of the printed page, but this new technological world was a mystery to her. As she reached the desk she found herself frightened to look at the set.

From the corner of her eye she could tell that the image
on the monitor was stable and immobile, the network's
regular test pattern. She had read the instruction book
which accompanied the video equipment, but had failed
to fully understand it. Carefully skirting the monitor, she
searched the top of Frank's desk. An empty box lay beside the video recorder. She bent down and peered into
the slot. The cassette was still lodged inside. Presumably, Frank had run the tape but had forgotten to turn the
machine off. She located the remote handset and pressed
REWIND. As soon as the tape had spooled back to the
start, she pressed PLAY. Slowly she raised her eyes to the
screen.

ODEL INCORPORATED

There followed a paragraph warning of copyright in-
fringement. And then followed a warning of real physical
danger.

It must have been like a red rag to a bull. All of his
life Frank had been searching for proof of spectacular
conspiracy theories. How could he have resisted running
such a thing as this? He had let it play to its conclusion,
and in doing so had activated a runic curse. She pressed
the EJECT button on the handset and slipped the cassette
back into its sleeve before turning off the monitor. This
was the proof she had been waiting for.

Had Frank been murdered deliberately, or unwit-
tingly? Someone had found out about their investigation.
If his death had been deliberate, perhaps the tape had
been intended for her as well! Which meant that she
couldn't even risk going back to her apartment. How
could she tell anyone of the danger to her life? Who would
believe the crazy old library lady? She thought of the
Camden Town Coven, but knew that they could easily
end up causing more harm than good.

Panicking, Dorothy ran to the library entrance and
barred the doors. She forced herself to think for a moment. The battered staff-room refrigerator was well
stocked with food. If she really intended to barricade
herself in, what else would she need? Sink. Couch. Lav-

atory. There was even a change of clothes in one of the
storeroom cupboards. Everything she needed for her survival was right here. She fumbled through her handbag
for the number of the emergency line that Arthur Bryant
had given her. She was connected within moments of
dialing it.

"I'm afraid Mr. Bryant is out of contact at the moment," said a pleasantly deep female voice.

"It's terribly important. I'm a friend of his. Do you
think he'll be at home?"

"He was visiting the hospital and left early this morning, but he hasn't arrived home yet. Can I have him ring
you?"

Dorothy grew flustered. "Surely you must have other
ways of getting in touch with each other?" she asked.

"If you're a friend of Mr. Bryant, you'll know he refuses to wear any kind of contacting device. If he does
turn up, who shall I say called?"

"Dorothy Huxley. Who are you?"

"Longbright. Sergeant Longbright."

Dorothy left her number with the sergeant, then, still
shaking, returned to guard her evidence and await res-
cue.

As Harry watched his train pull into Liverpool Street
Station, he wondered just how far-reaching Carmody's
powers could be. When the industrialist was awoken in
the morning with news of his departure, how quickly
would he be able to mobilize some kind of retaliation?
The best thing would be to assume the worst. Celia was
right; Carmody's connections in finance and technology
made him impossible to underestimate.

He alighted from the train and hurried through the almost deserted concourse to the tube entrance. It was now
nearly nine o'clock on Sunday morning. He decided
against calling Grace again. It was better to head straight
for her apartment and figure out a way of protecting
themselves from ODEL's lines of communication.

When he rang the bell of the flat Grace leaned from
the window to check his identity, and he was reminded
of the day they had met. At this time of the morning she

wore no makeup and her hair had yet to be anointed with gelling lotion. The effect removed the hard edges from her face and added warmth to her appearance. "You'd better come up and tell me about it," she said, throwing down the keys. "You look terrible." He fumbled the catch and looked up with an apologetic smile, but she was already closing the window.

Harry described the events of the weekend in detail, starting with his arrival at the Carmody home. Unfortunately, what his story lacked was a satisfactory conclusion. The point was not wasted on Grace.

"Let me get this right," she said. "As it stands, you're wanted by the police as a multiple murder suspect, you're under sentence of death from one of the most powerful new corporations in the country, you're the instigator of some form of unstoppable supernatural vengeance, and you've returned with no proof that any of this is even happening."

"Something like that, yes," he admitted, moving to the sofa and slipping an arm around her waist. "I need to be held."

"Carmody must know you've gone by now." Grace kissed him lightly, then disentangled herself. "Apart from the TV, the telephone, and the radio, what other methods can he use to transmit runes? What do we look out for?"

"That's the trouble. I only know the ways he described to me. He'll be aware of that, and he'll be looking to use a method I'd never suspect. While I'm expecting some kind of advanced technological onslaught he could slip me a simple printed piece of paper."

"He doesn't know you're here with me."

"I don't suppose it'll take him long to find out. We have to assume that he can reach us through any mode of communication used to advertise or inform—junk mail, magazines, newspapers, product labels, free samples; it's an infinite list."

"But surely his methods of getting at you are limited, because anyone else who sees the runes will also be affected."

"Either he's found a way to personalize them, or he'll

make sure that only I see them. We've got to cover every possible avenue of attack.''

"How ironic," said Grace; "after making a career of it, you seem to have wound up with the power of advertising working against you. Nobody said that when the Devil finally returned to earth he'd be a businessman. What are we going to do?''

"The first thing is to get you to a safe place. He's after me, not you.''

"Not anymore. Frank is dead because I gave him the rune cassette. Whatever happens, we stay together.''

"Good. Carmody has others he wants removed before the ODEL satellite broadcasts begin.''

"What exactly is he beaming out?''

"In the long term he's planning to build subtle runic commands into broadcast images. The idea is that they'll slowly change the social habits of his viewing audience, probably over an undetectably lengthy period of time. But there's something else, something he was saying last night . . .''

"What?''

"I think he's going to use the first broadcast to rid himself of his rivals, although I don't know how he intends to do it without killing everyone who tunes in.''

"As you said, maybe he's found a way to personalize the curses. When are these transmissions due to start?''

"Nobody mentioned a date," said Harry. "Although I remember reading something about it in one of the recent Sunday supplements.''

"Wait, I think I still have last week's papers." Grace pulled a stack from beneath the couch. "Start going through them.''

She took the telephone from its wall hook and punched out a number. "We still have a piece of concrete evidence to take to the authorities, if they'll listen.''

"Who are you calling?''

"I've been trying the library where Frank worked since yesterday. Our cassette must still be there. That's where his video equipment was kept.'' After fifteen rings she was about to hang up when her call was answered. At first she thought there was no one on the other end of the

line, but she could hear the faint sound of someone withholding their breath.

"Hello? Is someone there? This is a friend of
Frank's."

There was a long silence, which sounded as if it was
broken only after careful deliberation. "Frank Drake is
dead," said the old lady.

"I know. My name is Grace Crispian."

"Grace." Recognition sounded in her voice. Frank had
mentioned her name on several occasions.

"Ask about his belongings," whispered Harry. "We
have to get the tape back."

"I can't."

"You have to. We've no proof otherwise."

"You must be Dorothy," said Grace at last. "Frank
told me all about you. He said you took him to a sé-
ance."

"That's right. I was helping him with a project."

"So were we. It's a shame he died before he could
publish his findings."

There was a pause on the line, and in that moment
Grace sensed that they shared a common secret knowledge. She knew she had to run with the impulse.

"You know about the runes, don't you?" she said suddenly. Behind her, Harry winced. "You know they can
kill and make it look like an accident. That's what happened to Frank."

"I know."

"Then can you help us?"

"Perhaps."

"Could we come to see you right now?"

"I don't know . . ." Dorothy sounded frightened.

"Please," urged Grace. "I already have the address."

"You said 'we.' "

"I'm with a friend. He knows about the runes. He's
met the man who's causing all this to happen."

"All right, but when you get here come around to the
back. I've sealed the main doors."

"I understand. We'll be there as soon as we can." As
she replaced the receiver, Harry pushed the magazine at
her.

"Carmody's satellite network doesn't go into full operation for several weeks yet. But the technology's in place, and New York is due to receive its first test transmission this Monday at seven P.M. A half-hour broadcast, beamed out to reach the eastern seaboard at two P.M. local time. That's our deadline."

"What are we going to do by ourselves, Harry?" asked Grace sarcastically. "Knock out a TV station? Overpower the staff and blow up the building? You're talking about a corporation with vast manpower and almost infinite resources. The way I see it, we have to go to the police, clear your name, and let them do the rest."

"No. By the time we get anyone to believe us it'll be too late. There has to be another way."

"Let me know when you figure it out," said Grace, pulling on her overcoat. "I can't wait to hear this one."

"I had to leave the car at Carmody's," explained Harry as they emerged onto the street. "Anything could have been hidden in the interior."

Crossing the road, they failed to notice the gleaming dark Mercedes which waited at the bend a few hundred yards behind them. Slattery wiped the misted windshield with the back of a leather driving glove and narrowed his sore red eyes as he watched them leave.

"I could fetch the truck from the studio. It will mean going in the wrong direction to collect it, though. If we want to save time we should catch a bus." Grace slipped her arm through his. "Poor Harry, all this traveling on public transport. It's not what you've been used to, is it?"

"That's the least of my problems," he grumbled. "I can't go home without being arrested. I can't get into the agency because the police are bound to have been there. Besides, I doubt I still have a job. I can't use my company plastic because it's bound to be marked by now. I can't even use my cashcard because it goes through the bank's computer system, and Carmody's staff could pick up the time and location of the withdrawal. I'm not even safe on the street. I have nothing except the clothes I'm standing in."

"And they're covered in mud. We've got to get you

something fresh to wear. You're starting to stand out in a crowd.''

As they reached the bus stop, heavy drops of rain began to fall. ''Great,'' said Harry, squinting up at the sky, ''maybe I'll get struck by lightning as well.''

''I don't think I've got enough money to get us there,'' said Grace, digging into her purse as the bus arrived. ''Have you anything left?''

''I don't believe this.'' Harry turned out his pockets, exasperated. ''I used up every penny getting to your place. Now what do we do?''

''Look innocent,'' said Grace. ''You're about to get your first lesson in fare dodging.''

Ahead, the doorway of the library stood hidden beneath the shadow of the overpass. Grace led the way through the downpour to the rear of the building. The elderly woman who opened the door looked tired and frightened. Introductions made, she took them along a damp corridor and out into the main hall of bookcases. ''I've kept the place locked tight since I found the tape that killed Frank,'' she explained. ''No one else has tried to enter the building, but it's only a matter of time.''

She ushered them into the staff room and closed the door behind them. ''This is the driest place. The roof leaks when it rains. I wasn't sure what to do for the best. I needed to talk to someone, you understand, someone who would believe me.''

''We've been having that trouble ourselves,'' said Harry. ''Suppose we tell you what we know.''

For the next half hour the trio discussed their situation and the options that were left open to them. Dorothy's thin voice was filled with quiet authority, making Harry wonder what drove this independent woman to keep such a lonely vigil in the library. She was less cognizant of the practicalities involved in Carmody's expansion program, but seemed to possess a great deal of arcane knowledge about the laws governing runic symbology. He, on the other hand, presented a farfetched plan of action that involved the storming of ODEL's headquar-

ters, and at least managed to bring a little color back to
the librarian's face.

"It's commonly documented that the Devil will be returned to power by unwitting acolytes," she explained.
"His disciples will restore him without realizing what
they have done. I'm sure you'd like to charge into their
offices with a loaded gun, Mr. Buckingham, but that's
not the way to win. This is an ancient conflict, one in
which the battle for good and evil recurs in a thousand
different ways down through the ages. The most one can
ever achieve is a short-term triumph. And the only way
to achieve it is on a spiritual level." A sudden blast of
rain thrashed at the window, causing her to start in her
chair.

"All right." Harry held up his hands. "I appreciate
that there's a deeper meaning to all of this. But Carmody's techniques can also be explained away as . . ."
he searched for a suitable term, ". . . aggressive marketing technology." Grace gave a snort of derision. "I
want to see this man's plans buried and his corporation
wiped out," Harry continued. "Surely the only way
we can get back at them is by using their own technology."

"There is another way. Come with me please." Dorothy rose from her seat and led them back out into the
main hall. The darkness of the storm had plunged the
vast bookcases into an eerie gloom, but she was loath to
turn on the overhead lights. She did not wish to attract
outside attention to the building. At the top of the basement steps she unclipped the heavy crimson guard rope
and set it aside.

"I don't normally take people down here with me.
Frank was never at ease in the basement." As they followed her, she indicated the moldering shelves below.
"Behold," she said with undisguised pride, holding aloft
a liver-spotted hand, "this is the real library. It contains
all that's left of the Huxley collection. One of the finest
occult collections in the world, and the last to remain in
private hands."

Grace reached the foot of the steps and walked be-

tween the shelves, lost in wonder. The first book she took
down came apart in her fingers.

"Why don't you hand it over to the state?" she asked.
"They'd be able to save these manuscripts before they're
lost forever."

"They probably would," agreed Dorothy. "But they
would also hide them from public gaze, ban their use,
deny personal access to all but the privileged. There is
incitement to insurrection here, and much condonement
of perversion. These volumes represent the outer limits
of free speech. There's too much interest in evil. What
would the government have to say about library books
that discuss divinity with equal time afforded to the
Devil?"

"They give political parties equal airtime on television," said Grace.

Dorothy smiled. "No, I prefer to keep the collection
available to those who still believe in the power of the
written word, no matter how dangerous it may be."
She took the book from Grace's hands and gently
pressed the cover onto the title page, as if trying to heal
its wound. "Upstairs I have profamily pressure groups
trying to remove novels where abortion gets a favorable
mention. Needless to say, they haven't seen down
here." She stepped between the rotting pages which
had cemented themselves to the wet floor, searching the
shelves. "I have something which will help us, if I can
just find it."

"Oh great," whispered Harry, "she's going to dig out
her book of spells."

"Obviously what you suffered was a hallucination,
Mr. Buckingham," said Dorothy sharply. She removed
a large volume bound in crumbling red leather and
studied it. "Visualization is the key to much ritual
magic. Hypnosis is about forming pictures in the mind.
Pictures help us to assimilate information." She offered the book to Harry, who found himself looking at
the engravings of medieval furniture. Subsequent pages
showed the exteriors of Tudor houses, tables, chairs,
and wall hangings.

"What is it, the very first issue of *Homes and Gardens*?"

"You could be forgiven for thinking so. These pictures mean little to the casual observer." Dorothy ran her fingers across one of the illustrations, as if trying to decipher the striations of ink that decorated the page. "It might surprise you to know that there are runes here."

"I don't understand."

"You must remember that we are dealing with a suppressed alphabet, a people's language which was considered dangerous by both church and government. A pagan language which, throughout the centuries, was repeatedly driven underground. And yet, it has always managed to resurface. How?"

Dorothy set down the book and beckoned them to the page. "It's simple," she explained. "Runes had no curves. Their shapes had been based on bundles of twigs, on trees and other natural objects. In times of suppression the runic alphabet transformed itself into a code. The letters became disguised in the common items of everyday life. They took their shape in Tudor beams, in embroidered tapestries, in the patterns on the backs of chairs. They were stitched into carpets, cut into leather saddles, painted as wall designs, carved into bedheads, woven into clothing. They became a familiar part of the world about us." She pointed to the illustration. "You see? The wooden flooring in this house had a patterned border of runes. Thus the language and the religion were perpetuated."

"Do you think it would be possible to construct a runic curse of our own and send it back to Carmody?" asked Grace.

"We'd have to examine one of his own curses to do that," replied Dorothy. "We need to see what form they take. Unfortunately, it's not possible to run one without being affected."

"What if we took turns with Frank's videotape and only studied a section each? We could each write down what we see."

"That sounds like a good way to get killed," said

Harry, shuddering at the thought of accidentally witnessing another vision. "But I don't have any better ideas."

"Then it's worth a try."

The three of them headed for the stairs.

45.

Infection

AT THE SOUTHEAST Greenwich Lending Library, a man wearing a gray plastic macintosh pushed his cable cutters into the tangle of wires protruding from the eaves of the roof, and snipped the lines to the outside world.

In the room below, Harry sat his team before the video equipment. "Okay," he said, "I'm going to start running the tape. Give me your finger." He took Grace's hand and lowered it onto the remote handset. "As soon as you see the first image, press this." He pointed to the freeze-frame button. "Running—now."

Seconds later, Grace stabbed at the FREEZE button, surprised.

"What did you see?"

"It wasn't a rune at all. A woman walking into a room, and there was a huge fireplace . . ."

"Sketch out the rough layout," suggested Dorothy, passing her a pad and pencil. "The configurations are most likely encoded in each scene. You see actors and scenery. It's your subconscious that picks up the shapes within the scenes and translates them back into runes."

Grace carefully drew what she had seen, then passed the handset to Dorothy. "Your turn."

The old lady released the FREEZE button and allowed the images to continue for a few seconds before holding the frame in place once more. Silently she took the sketch pad and drew shapes across it. Grace cocked her head on one side. "Did you hear anything?" she asked. The others stopped to listen.

"The rainwater drains from the motorway onto the roof at the back of the building," said Dorothy. She passed the handset to Harry, who continued the exercise of watching and drawing.

The tape was approximately three minutes long. By dividing the images into thirds and comparing their notes they were able to compile a rough idea of the film's overall content. Spreading out the sketches on the table before her, Dorothy proceeded to rule lines through the pencil figures and reveal the runes beneath.

"Here, for example," she said, "what looks like two people in a room is actually the runic symbol for pagan man, Manu. Here in the corner, see, there's a figure four. That's the number associated with this rune. The color of the background—purple—is the color required for use with the symbol. To the outside eye it seems that what we have on the tape is a brightly colored—if somewhat amateurish—art film. The runes are created by the configurations of the actors with the scenery."

"I don't see how we're going to trick Carmody into watching a tape," said Grace. "He'd have to be really stupid to fall for it."

There was a distant thud from the back of the library. Harry jumped from his seat. "Stay here, both of you." He ran lightly along the center aisle, to a section of the hall where the overhead lights were dim with dust. Another thud sounded. Someone was trying to slide open a window, but it was stuck in the casement. Heart thudding, Harry pressed back against the wall and waited for the intruder to climb through. He searched around for a weapon. Before him was a shelf filled with weighty volumes of encyclopedias. Pulling one free, he hefted it in his hand. *Volume 24. Metaphysics–Norway*. That would do. A leg came through, then an arm. Finally a head appeared. He recognized the young man as Slattery's assistant at the estate. Swinging the book with all the might he could muster, he smashed it down onto the boy's head before he had a chance to look up. His wet body fell heavily through the window onto the parquet flooring.

Harry threw down the book and checked that his victim was unconscious.

"Dorothy, do you have any rope?" His voice reverberated dully in the book-lined hall. "I need some quickly."

Grace arrived with a heavy roll of linen bookbinding tape, and together they managed to bind his hands and feet. "He's already starting to come around," said Grace. "Couldn't you have hit him harder?"

"I might have cracked his skull," said Harry. "A little learning is a dangerous thing."

They stretched a length of tape across his mouth and rolled him into a corner, where they would not have to look at his angry eyes. Rain was flooding through the window onto the floor, but when Harry attempted to shut it the rotten lintel came away in his hands. Together, he and Grace managed to shift a children's bookcase across the hole.

"Now what do we do?" asked Grace. "We can't just stay here all night."

"It's safer than anywhere else." Harry stood up and rubbed his forehead. "Dorothy knows the building better than anyone. Besides, if we go outside, Carmody's bound to have someone else waiting for us." He leaned back against the bookcase, trying to clear his vision. "This way we can pick them off . . ." He shook his head hard. "If they try to break . . ."

Harry's legs gave way beneath him and he fell sprawling to the floor. Grace dropped to his side and grabbed at his flexing arms. "What's the matter?" she cried. "Harry, what is it?"

He seemed to be staring far beyond her. As she watched, his pupils dilated as if fixing themselves on a distant vision. She called for Dorothy.

"He just fell down. He's seeing something."

"The rune's affecting him. He's hallucinating."

"How can that be?" asked Grace. "He only watched a very small part of it."

"But he was already susceptible after his first exposure. Look at him—the little he saw was enough to revive his nightmares."

"I can't hold him much longer." Grace jumped back as Harry staggered to his feet and pushed her aside, running off along one of the alleyways between the bookcases. "He'll hurt himself if we don't stop him," said Dorothy.

"Can he get out?"

"No, the main doors are locked from the inside and I have the only keys."

"Okay, let's see if we can corner him."

They began to move slowly through the hall, checking the aisles as they went. As they reached the start of the reference section, Grace heard a sound at the end of the stacks. "Wait here," she told the librarian, running lightly between the shelves. In the shadow of the end bookcase she stopped to listen. From far above came the sound of heavy rain on slate tiles. The creaking of damp wood in the wind. One of the unlit globes above her head was shifting slightly from side to side. She peered through a gap in the shelf to the half-dark corridor beyond.

With a sudden fearful scream, Harry ran out and grabbed her across the throat. His incoherent cries brought Dorothy running. Grace felt herself being lifted from the ground, unable to catch her breath.

"Harry, for God's sake put her down!" cried Dorothy. Grace fought against his restraining arm but the hallucination was providing him with a reserve of great strength. Her feet sought a hold on the edge of the bookshelf behind her. She pushed forward with the little strength that remained. Harry stayed as steady as a rock, his eyes as wide and dead as those of a corpse. Suddenly, recognition flickered back into them and he dropped heavily to his knees, releasing his captive.

Grace clutched at her throat and gulped air, unable to speak.

"I thought it had returned for me," he whispered, staring about himself in wonder.

"What are you feeling now?"

"Don't know. Sore. Are you okay?" He held out his hand to Grace, who accepted it after a brief moment of apprehension.

"I'll be fine," she croaked. "What about you, what if it comes back?"

"You'll have to restrain me. I had no control over myself."

"We need you too much for that," said Dorothy. "You'll have to monitor your condition and warn us if you feel it starting again. Now that we know what's on the cassette, what's the next step?"

"I don't know yet," admitted Harry. "I was hoping that something would come to me once I'd seen the tape."

"Then I suggest we hole up here until we figure out how to proceed," said Grace. She turned to Dorothy. "It's freezing. Can you turn up the heat?"

"It's controlled from the boiler outside. It doesn't come on at weekends."

"Do you have any blankets?"

"I think there are some in the storeroom left over from the Bible reading group. The kids use them to dress up."

"Then you might as well get them. It's going to be a long night."

John May had reluctantly agreed to the terms.

The others would break him out of the hospital in the early hours of Monday morning only if he consented to remaining in a wheelchair for the whole of the following day. Sergeant Longbright had warned him that she was capable of sticking a syringe full of Valium into his arm if he began to excite himself, and May was quite prepared to believe her. Consenting to the conditions, he allowed himself to be lowered into the wheelchair and pushed out into the deserted corridor.

They had agreed that the course of action was drastic, but too much time had been spent in the passive correlation of reports. Now it was a matter of taking preventive measures before the case was removed from their jurisdiction and passed to another group. Even if they could find a legitimate reason for halting the broadcast, May imagined that they would face disciplinary action for failing to follow established procedure.

At some point during the previous night, probably

around the time they had wrecked the computer terminal, Bryant had managed to absent himself without telling anyone where he was going. Now, just when they needed his help, he was nowhere to be found.

They made a strange group, Longbright, Rufus, and Kirkpatrick, but together they succeeded in smuggling May from the confinement of his room. Wheeling the elderly detective into the freight elevator, they transferred him to a waiting van and headed back to the station.

"The way I see it, we gotta infiltrate the ODEL corporate computer system with a virus of our own," said Rufus. His initial duty done, he had elected to see the case through in an advisory capacity. The brief glimpse he had been given of the runic system intrigued him, as well as giving him ideas for a few interesting schemes of his own. He settled in the operations room at the station as if he had been there all his life. "We need somethin' so damn strong it'll wipe their entire system clean."

"How do we do that?"

"By comin' up with some code runes of our own. If we could build an infection program, I reckon we'd be able to get it into the system."

"You don't sound too optimistic," said Longbright.

"I ain't. They could attack our program unless we develop an inoculator."

"What's that?" asked an increasingly mystified Kirkpatrick.

"We make their system think that our files are infected, then they'll stay away."

"But all this will take time, won't it?"

"Sure. And ya have to remember, the dudes at ODEL have unlimited resources to create this shit. Time is just one problem, man. We don't got the equipment, or the manpower."

"If you did have what you needed," suggested May, "how would you go about creating this infection?"

"I'd have to break down the runic language the computer is using into its most basic components."

"I'm familiar with most of the major configurations,"

said Kirkpatrick, "but I confess that my knowledge does not extend to their semantic construction, their, as it were, assemblage."

Rufus studied him. "At least I ain't the only asshole around here that's hard to understand," he muttered.

"So what do you need?" asked May impatiently.

"Preferably someone well-versed in the occult."

"Who did Arthur visit?" May twisted around in his chair. "He went to see an expert, a woman. It was the day after his birthday, remember?" He poked Longbright in the ribs with his pencil.

"Do that again," said Longbright, "and I'm taking the brakes off your wheelchair. Check his appointments book."

"You know very well that Arthur's office is on the floor below. Go and find the number, and hurry it up."

"How long are these curses likely to be?" asked Rufus. "I mean, what kinda program are we talkin' about?"

"Their strength and subtlety is dependent on their length, their duration," replied Kirkpatrick. "I would have thought that at least twenty or thirty configurations would be needed for our purposes. They may be required to run in a repeated cycle."

"Well, that settles it. I ain't gonna be able to construct something that long by this afternoon." Rufus spun around on his stool. His feet missed the floor by eighteen inches. "We're gonna have to think of somethin' else."

"Why bother with technology at all?" asked May suddenly. "Assuming we can write the curse out, why not hand deliver it in letter form to the ODEL directors?"

"This is madness," said Kirkpatrick, exasperated. "You're a police officer. You're here to serve and protect, not to have people eviscerated."

"Kirkpatrick, if we don't stop this chap in time there'll be far fewer people left alive in this world to impede his company's progress. Now tell me, will it work if we fight fire with fire?"

"You mean by just drawing runes and delivering them? Apart from the whole idea being unethical—a fact which doesn't seem to bother you, I might add—I don't think so, no."

"Why not?"

"Because they play with the subconscious mind. They don't work in an overt manner."

"You're saying they're subliminal?"

"In a way. Printed curses seem to have an unpredictable effect. We've seen the runes found on some of the murder victims and they haven't harmed us. That's because they probably only work in conjunction with some prior knowledge of the victim. As for the tape, well, you glimpsed the screen when Rufus triggered the protective rune. What did you see?"

"Squiggles."

"Exactly. Either they run fast, or they're hidden in specially camouflaging shapes. Video technology gives ODEL a much bigger box of tricks to play with."

Sergeant Longbright entered the room with Bryant's appointment book in her hand. "He met a woman called Dorothy Huxley," she said.

"Try her number."

"I already have. There's no reply."

"Then keep trying," said May. "I want someone back inside the ODEL building as soon as possible. We need to know how their broadcast is being set up, where it's being recorded. And I want as much information about their board of directors as you can manage to get without arousing suspicion. An operation this big could launch a PR exercise to provide an instant cover-up, so I don't want them to have the faintest idea that we're on to their game."

"There's another problem," said Longbright. "I just ran into Ian Hargreave. He heard that you're back in the building. He wants to know—and I quote verbatim—'Who the bloody hell is letting my men conduct unauthorized searches of private property?' I think he's had a phone call from someone at ODEL. I expect he'll be paying us a visit shortly."

"Thanks for the warning." May squeezed her hand. He knew how difficult it had to be for Janice to keep her personal loyalties separate from the investigation. "I suppose Ian had to find out sooner or later. I don't think we have anything to gain by trying to present our case to him. Let's continue until he summons us upstairs.''

The rainstorm which had broken on the far side of the city had finally reached the windows of the operations room, and as they returned to work, the building was consumed by a thickening caul of darkness.

46.

Tape

C ELIA CARMODY EXAMINED her face in the dressing-table mirror and wondered if makeup would be able to help this time. The livid turquoise bruising ran from the top of her left cheekbone to below her swollen jaw-line. Why Daniel had refused to believe her story was still unclear. Could someone have been watching as she unlocked the conservatory doors for Harry Buckingham? Probably the legal weasel, Slattery, she decided. He seemed to be operating as Daniel's homunculus these days. Gingerly dabbing at the cut on her throat with an antiseptic pad, she supposed she would have to wear high-collared blouses for a while.

It had not taken her long to regret her marriage. When she had first met Daniel at a charity dinner, she had become entranced by him. He was everything that she and her family were not. Brash and outspoken, aggressive, *new*. The past held no memories for him, bitter or plea-surable. Daniel exultantly faced the future, awaiting his own time. She had been raised by parents of a more retiring nature than her own, discreet landowners living in slowly reducing circumstances, discreetly fading into their own landscape. Daniel had offered her a way out. It was only later that she realized his way would involve the destruction of everything she held dear, but then she had placed so little value on her former life.

She flinched as she heard him approaching the bedroom. Just lately it was the most she could do to keep from screaming when he drew close to her. He restricted her freedom now, keeping her a virtual prisoner in the house, and yet he happily displayed a public affection for her. To the gentlemen of the press she appeared at ease in her role as the refined wife, an elegant reflection of her husband's good taste. She provided proof that the captain of industry had a private side and was at heart a lover of all things English. She maintained this appearance of ease by drinking.

Daniel hated weakness of any kind. It was his biggest weakness. She smiled at her reflection, dabbing with the powder brush. The strength she had once so admired in him was more than she could take these days. She still loved him in a distant, respectful way but his plans to change the world had outstripped her own simple ambitions of happiness. She imagined that he was suffering from a sickness, some kind of disease that only struck men in positions of power. Thinking of it as an illness allowed her to cope. She lowered the brush and stared back at her forlorn mirror image. I'm one of his belongings, she thought. The one thing Daniel had lacked in his life was a pedigree, so he had purchased one. Perhaps he would one day regret the purchase.

"You realize that you'll be on television with me tonight?" said Daniel, making her jump. His form filled the mirror, obliterating her own image. He leaned against the edge of the dressing table, preventing her from reaching her makeup kit, and the silver bottle hidden within it. The Gaultier suit he wore was beautiful, but too consciously stylish. Gelled neatly in place, his ponytail rested on the collar of his jacket, giving him the vacuous appearance of a fashion plate.

"After the broadcast there's to be a live satellite link between here and New York. You'll be expected to answer some questions." He plucked a pair of nail scissors from the table and toyed with them. "The interview will be brief. There won't be anything too demanding. Favored charities. Favorite walks. Hobbies and pastimes.'' He leaned forward and touched her chin, his glass eye staring through her. ''You'll have to make up something in that department. We can't let the great unwashed think that you have no outside interests. It will help if you don't let them see inside your handbag.''

Suddenly the cloud passed from his face and he smiled. ''The car will be here in a few minutes.'' He checked his watch. ''It's just gone four. We should be in town by six.''

''Daniel, why do we have to go in so early?''

''There has to be a technical run-through.'' He reached forward and ran his forefinger lightly over her swollen jaw. ''I don't suppose you believe me, Celia, but I hate what's happened between us. It's just that this time we can't afford to make any mistakes. As our friends at Coca-Cola would say, it's the Real Thing.'' He rose and adjusted his cufflinks in the mirror. ''Cheer up. When this is over I'll take you somewhere far away. We can go anywhere you please. By then the world will be on its way to becoming a better place.''

''That's right,'' said Celia bitterly. ''There won't be anyone around to disagree with company policy.''

''There's no such thing as altruism anymore, darling, you should know that. You're president of the Wildlife Aid Group. You know that it's nothing more than a social climbing frame. If your ladies couldn't have their fancy-dress fundraisers attended by the royal bimbo set, they'd soon be telling the animals to go and fuck themselves.'' He pinched her cheek between his fingers, causing her to wince with pain. ''It's time to wake up, Celia. We're doing something new. We're stripping away the subterfuge. It's an honest attitude for surviving the nineties.''

''Someone will stop you.''

''Oh, really? Who?'' He released his grip and she fell back. ''Newspapers lie. TV news is censored and even restaged for us. How can they do it? Why are there no watchdogs of freedom? I'll tell you why. We are the watchdogs.'' He stabbed a finger at his chest. ''*Us*. Except there's no 'us' anymore. We sold our freedom for increased profits. Our great nation will turn a blind eye to anything if the price is right.''

He left the bow tie loose around his neck. ''You'll need a lot more makeup to hide that bruise. Really darling, you look like hell.'' He watched as she powdered over the blackened parts of her cheek and neck, applying the makeup thickly until she resembled a gaily painted doll.

''Perfect.'' He gave a nod of approval as he surveyed the finished picture. ''Now let's get out there and present the world with an honest face.''

Harry was awakened from a troubled half-sleep on the floor of the central hall by a series of knocks at the main door of the library. He threw back the blanket of his makeshift bed, heaved himself into a sitting position, and checked his watch. Seven-thirty. Monday morning at last. His arms and back ached like hell. Wincing, he rose to his feet and looked around for the others. They had begun the evening by taking turns to keep watch, but had all eventually fallen asleep. On his way to the door he met Dorothy. ''Stand behind me,'' he warned. ''Whoever's out there could try to rush in.'' Bracing himself, he pulled back the bolts.

''At last! I was beginning to think there was nobody here.''

Arthur Bryant stood beneath the dripping eaves shaking his umbrella. Only his eyes were visible above his scarf. ''Can you believe this weather?'' he asked. ''Well, are you going to stand there like a tailor's dummy or can I come in?''

Harry stepped back, confused, as Bryant brushed past and kissed Dorothy's cheek. ''By the way,'' he said, ''your telephone wires are cut and there's a shifty-looking blighter watching the building. He's sitting in a black Mercedes beneath the overpass, not even attempting to appear inconspicuous. You look as if you've been up all night. I'll just use this for a moment.'' He set down a portable telephone and turned it on.

Dorothy was surprised to see Arthur embracing technology, but even more surprised by his timely arrival. Bryant, on the other hand, had planned his appearance carefully. His casual attitude masked his acute awareness of the surrounding danger. "So you're Harry Bucking-ham," he said, eyeing the rumpled executive. "You've been a real pain in the backside. The time and effort you could have saved us by coming forward is quite—Hello?" He shook the receiver, then shouted into it.

"Kindly connect me with Detective Inspector John May if you would be so . . . don't give me that, I know he's there." He placed his hand over the mouthpiece and turned to Dorothy. "I suppose a fellow has to die around here before he's offered a cup of tea?" Harry gave Grace a look of disbelief.

"Ah, JOHN! I know I'm shouting. It's a bad line. I'm on one of those portable telephones. Well, you kept on at me about the beeper, and as I didn't have it anymore . . . no, possibly at the dry cleaners . . . I thought I'd better get something to replace it. The man in the shop suggested the telephone. I charged it to expenses. Well, I'm at the library with Dorothy. My dear fellow, that's exactly what I'm about to do, I'm miles ahead of you. Please try to relax and take the pressure off your valves. You know that Daniel Carmody is due on the air in a few hours? Leave it to me. By the way, we're being watched here. You might send a man over, someone unobtrusive. No, not 'Mad Dog' Bimsley, he's a walking nightmare. I'll call you if I need you." He replaced the receiver, tutting to himself.

"Now," he said, "as nobody else seems to have come up with a solution to our problem, I'd better tell you my plan. Harry, could you give me a hand with something I've got in the car? Young lady, perhaps you'd keep an eye on the door. We don't want anyone else coming in."

As they dashed out in the rain together, Harry recognized Slattery in the Mercedes watching them. Bryant propped open the door of his Mini as he pulled out a large cardboard box. As soon as they were safely back inside, he produced a Swiss army knife and slashed the tape sealing the lid.

"You'll have to read the instructions as we go," he

said, pulling the Betacam video system from its poly-styrene packing. "We know it's impossible to develop a computer program that will play back a curse virus in the time we have left, but it occurred to me that we might be able to shoot our own runic tape. The trick, of course, will be getting it on to ODEL's monitors so that Carmody will see it. Now as I understand it, you can shoot in almost zero light and play the thing back as soon as it's been shot, is that right?" Harry nodded weakly. The run to the car had disturbed his equilibrium. He wondered if he would suffer any more side effects from the runes.

Dorothy sat Bryant on a straight-backed chair in the main hall and explained the problem of creating sublim-inal images for the tape.

"Suppose we set up simple situations like the ones on our tape, and made runic configurations by rearranging the books in the background?" Grace moved in front of the largest bookcase and demonstrated. "We could or-ganize the bindings according to width and color, so that each scene would hide part of the curse. Dorothy, could you devise the deadliest rune code possible for this?"

"That part is easy," she replied. "I can put together the symbols for violent death, accidents, whatever we have time for. The time-consuming part will be arranging the book spines."

Over the next two and a half hours Grace, Bryant, and Dorothy emptied each of nine bookcases and filled them with volumes arranged according to the diagrams set out in the runic bibles from the Huxley collection. Harry set up the equipment and ran test shots.

"We've added two more runes," said Dorothy. "One is the symbol showing that man is barred from immor-tality by the poisoned needles of the yew tree. The other is the symbol of attentiveness. Theoretically, the viewer won't be able to take his eyes from the screen once the tape has begun."

"Theoretically," said Grace. "Theoretically, this is crazy behavior."

"We have nothing else," Bryant said. "We could send

the entire force in there and disrupt the broadcast on grounds of reasonable suspicion . . .''

''Then why don't you?''

''It only covers Carmody's personal involvement in the investigation. We can't halt his entire staff on 'reasonable suspicion.' Of what?''

''Don't broadcasters need a license?'' asked Grace. ''Couldn't you find an irregularity?''

''My esteemed partner has already checked out the possibility. ODEL is covered by paperwork ten feet thick.''

''Meanwhile, time's almost out,'' said Harry. ''We'll need to position our foreground characters so that they don't obscure the runic book patterns. Everyone get in place.''

''The nerve of the man,'' fumed May. ''For years he refuses to adopt any kind of technological advance, then he suddenly discovers it and goes mad.''

''At least we know where he is,'' said Longbright. ''I've sent a man over to cover the library. And Arthur promised to call again. We'll just have to trust him.''

''That's what worries me. We'll need a full team standing by for his call.''

Rufus and Kirkpatrick had been up all night. They had managed to develop the basis of a simple rune virus but further progress was impeded by the fact that Rufus had fallen asleep, and was now lying in Longbright's office with her raincoat over him. Although he had the brain of an adult genius, he was still hampered by the physical needs of a nine-year-old.

As the sergeant left the room, May turned his wheelchair about and stared at the telephone. ''Come on, Arthur,'' he said. ''For God's sake bail me out of here.''

Harry slid the finished cassette into its case and handed it to Bryant. They had succeeded in creating a short play of flickering color and light, a bizarre series of static shots that would hopefully coax the viewer's subconscious into a hallucinogenic state. The filming had just been completed when he began to feel sick. The attack which followed was different to the previous one. This time the walls of the library had seemed as if they were closing in on him, the floor turning into a mudslide on which it was impossible to maintain a balance. He had fallen to the floor, jarring his hip, but at least the sudden pain had caused the spasm to pass.

"I'm sorry, Harry, but there's no way you can come with us." Grace placed her arm through Bryant's. "Carmody's people are watching for you. Nobody at ODEL knows me. Mr. Bryant is going to drive me there. I can find out which studio Carmody's recording in. I'll think of a way to get the tape on to their monitors."

"You haven't a hope in hell of getting beyond their reception area and you know it," said Harry. "At least if I go, I'll be able to talk to him."

"And suppose you have another relapse? You think Carmody would help you? You said yourself he wants you dead."

"But he hasn't killed me yet, has he? I'm coming with you and that's final." Harry reached out for the tape and fell forward as a fresh wave of nausea hit him.

"Look after him, Dorothy," said Grace. "And make sure that you keep the door locked after we've gone." She looked at her watch. Nearly five P.M. The production of the tape had taken all day. "We'd better hit the road."

"By the way," said Arthur Bryant, "has anyone warned you about my driving?"

47.

Gridlock

GRACE HAD NEVER seen rain like it. She peered out through the smeared windshield of the Mini and tried to decipher the road signs ahead. "It would help if you had windshield wipers,'' she said, scrubbing at the blurred glass with her sleeve.

"I've never needed them before," said Bryant testily. "I don't normally use Henrietta when it rains."

"Henrietta?" Grace patted the dashboard. "That's pretty. Did you name her after a particular lady friend?"

"You could say that," said Bryant, hunching forward over the wheel. "Henrietta Durand-Deacon was the victim in the acid bath murders of nineteen forty-nine. I identified her by her dental plate. A most interesting case."

"Oh."

Around them the traffic was at a standstill. ODEL House was situated at the foot of Kingsway in Holborn. The Mini was currently wedged across the center of the roundabout at the Elephant & Castle, on the south side of the Thames.

"Where did all these people come from so suddenly?" grumbled Bryant. "The roads are never normally like this on a Monday afternoon, even in the rush hour. The Mini's overheating. We'll never make it."

"Perhaps you should call your friend," suggested Grace. "Couldn't he get us a motorbike?"

"I can't drive a motorbike."

"I can. Ring him."

Bryant switched on the telephone and punched out the number of the station. "It's no good," he said, "the call won't go through in here. I'll have to go outside." He threw open the car door and, in doing so, hammered a sharp dent in the side of the brand-new Porsche idling beside him.

The man sitting behind the wheel looked as if he'd just witnessed the death of his firstborn. "What . . . the . . . *hell* do you think you're doing?" he screamed, starting to climb from the car. Ahead of them the traffic cleared a few feet, but Bryant's Mini was blocked by the Porsche.

"You maniac!" screamed the apoplectic driver. "I don't suppose an idiot like you has *any* idea how much this paintwork costs to repair!"

Bryant turned to his passenger and smiled apologetically. "I'm awfully sorry for what I'm about to do, Grace.

I promise it isn't like me at all.'' He reached into the shelf below the Mini's steering wheel and pulled out a .38 automatic handgun. Swinging it sharply up and bringing it into line with the Porsche driver's temple, he cocked back the hammer and spoke in reasoning tones.

"Get out of the car, sir, leave the keys in the ignition, and burn shoe leather. If you're not gone in three seconds, you'll find your spectacles staring out of your asshole." The driver's eyes widened and he leapt from the car, backing off into the jammed traffic.

"I find that American television shows can sometimes be instructive," said Bryant with a shrug of embarrassment. "The traffic's starting to move. Quick, let's switch vehicles."

They transferred themselves and the homemade tape to the vacated Porsche. "A lovely machine," said Bryant, a hint of jealousy in his voice. "I wonder why the people who drive them are always so frightful. Good, it's got a carphone. Call in for me." He handed Grace a slip of paper and gunned the engine, crashing the gears. The car accelerated with such force that he almost lost control.

"You're right," said Bryant, mounting one side of the car on the sidewalk to pass the blocked traffic, "we'll need backup to get us through this tangle. Is there a football match on somewhere? I've never seen the city in such chaos." Ahead in the center of the road were a pair of Covent Garden vegetable trucks. He judged the distance between them with his hands.

"You'll never get through there," said Grace.

"No, we should be all right." Bryant accelerated.

A terrible grinding noise indicated that he was tearing jagged strips of paint from either side of the Porsche. The car which emerged from between the trucks was considerably lower in resale value than the one which had entered.

"My fault," said Bryant apologetically, "I forgot this is wider than the Mini."

Grace stared out of the side window, the telephone receiver tucked under her chin. "I'm getting no answer." The wing mirror on Bryant's side snapped with a bang as they brushed a lamppost. The car came to a halt.

Ahead, traffic lay blocking the roadway in every direction.

"That's odd. There's a call switcher thing that should put you through on the first available line. Keep holding." He rolled down his window and leaned out. "Dear God, the whole of Waterloo Bridge is blocked. It's as if every driver in town has suddenly decided to take to the road."

"Do you think ODEL could have had something to do with it?"

"I suppose they could have tampered with the computers controlling the area's traffic signaling system, but I don't see how." Bryant nosed the car onto the curb and scraped it noisily between a storefront and a gravel bin.

"I didn't mean that. If they can kill people by affecting the statistical odds of an accident occurring, surely they could screw up the traffic."

"The laws of chance have an upper limit," said Bryant as he reluctantly left another sidewalk and dropped back into the cacophonous scrum of vehicles waiting at the foot of the bridge. "Take that business of the chimpanzees and the typewriters. They say that an unlimited number of apes, typing for centuries, would eventually produce the complete works of Shakespeare. But that's utter rubbish."

"How come?"

"Think about it. The odds of a chimp hitting a correct letter are one in twenty-six. The odds of a second correct letter being struck are twenty-six squared, the odds of a third correct letter are twenty-six to the power of three, and so on. But some letters appear more frequently than others in the English language. The letter E, for instance. The laws of chance don't make provision for this. They'll reveal that your chimps produce a random evenness in any big sample of work, bashing out the same number of vowels as consonants. Even if they type for eternity, they'll be lucky to produce a single soliloquy. They keep hitting the Chance Barrier."

Bryant turned the engine off and took the keys from the ignition. "It's no good," he said, "we'll have to start walking. Bring the phone with you."

They had just reached the midpoint of the bridge when the rain began to fall so heavily that it seemed to seal them off from their surroundings. The river below boiled with the impact of the precipitation.

"We have to find shelter," shouted Grace. "I can hardly catch my breath in this."

Bryant pointed back at the stairs leading to the walk-way beneath the bridge. "Head for there," he shouted. "Then we'll try to call John again."

Sergeant Longbright ran back into the operations room and grabbed John May's shoulder. "You were right," she said, "the entire computer traffic network is down."

"That's impossible," said one of the operators. "There's a fail-safe system that cuts in and boosts power the moment electrical reduction falls below a certain level."

"Not anymore. Could the substations be flooded out?"

"This isn't an electrical fault," said May. "They know that a police invasion of the satellite network could take them off the air. They're insuring themselves against the eventuality."

"Do you really think that's possible?"

"If we genuinely believe in Carmody's power, then we have to run all the way with the idea."

May knew that the time had come to break departmental silence, even at the risk of facing ridicule. "Janice," he said, "you'd better go upstairs and inform Ian Hargreave. We can't contain this any longer."

Detective Superintendent Ian Hargreave was no systems expert, but he had pioneered a number of revolutionary techniques that were now in regular use by the force. He could see what was happening for himself, but still he could not believe it. "The data banks are emptying out," he said, stalking back and forth in front of the chaotic computer banks. The noise level in the room was deafening. "It's as if the material in them is being offloaded into another network. But it's not. Its access is merely being sealed off from us. Someone is stripping a virus across segments of our system."

Longbright decided to stand well clear of the heavily built senior detective, who had a habit of slinging his arms out in wild gestures when he paced. She had informed him of the traffic disruption's likely source, but at the moment he was more concerned with the loss of his computer network.

"They're keeping it hidden under a house program. If this has anything to do with your pals downstairs, if they've inadvertently triggered this in any way, I'll kill them." He scratched his peppery mustache in irritation. "It's a bloody unlikely coincidence that our detection system should fail just as the traffic computers go down. I've held the heat away from Bryant and May for too long."

"Any internal discipline right now will cost us time, Ian," pleaded Longbright. "Just let them have a few hours more."

Hargreave was aware that his star detectives were in serious trouble, but without their full cooperation he was unable to help them out of it. Besides, right now they were the least of his problems. London was grinding to a complete standstill, and the fault seemed to stem from the city's own traffic system. Any minute now the robbery reports would start: the first effect of a crisis was to increase the crime rate. But with both telephone and computer lines down they could only sit back and watch, powerless to intervene.

Hargreave was angry with himself more than anyone else. "If I had forced them to keep me informed from the start I might be able to do something now."

"Just meet their demands and don't ask questions until after eight o'clock tonight."

Hargreave sighed heavily. "How can I deny you anything, Janice?" he asked.

"The switchboard is out as well."

"Oh God, the call switchers," groaned May. "Is there any way to bypass them?"

"They're working on it right now."

He thought for a moment, then reached a decision. "Have a surveillance unit head over to the ODEL building. Your nearest one will be Bow Street. Keep them on a combined foot/auto and don't allow anyone onto the premises unless they get the word from me.''

''They'll need bikes to get through the traffic.''

''What the hell is happening?'' May furiously slammed the arms of his wheelchair. ''Even *he* can't control the rain.'' He turned to one of the juniors. ''See if you can get through to Bryant and discover what he's up to. We sent a man to the library—find out what's happened to him.''

''The switchboard, Sergeant Longbright said it was out of—''

''Use a callbox, for God's sake!''

''Yes, sir.'' The young man hurried from the room.

''Sit down, John.'' The sergeant pushed him back into his wheelchair. ''You're getting too excited. You should take two of your tablets.''

''Perhaps you're right. Fetch me a glass of water, would you Janice?''

The moment he was sure that Longbright was beyond range he slipped from the chair, pulled on his raincoat, and headed for the building's rear exit.

Huddled behind a silver curtain of rain at the base of the bridge, Grace squatted by the portable telephone punching out numbers. She tried the station house on a direct line to the operations room, then called John May on his unlisted number, only to hear the same flat electronic tone buzz in her ear.

''It's no good. Electrically, the place is completely isolated.'' She grabbed a length of soaked sleeve and attempted to wring it out. ''I can't get through to Harry and Dorothy. Even if we managed to reach the ODEL studios in time, no one in their right mind would let us in with no credentials and no appointment, looking the way we do. It's hopeless.''

''There's a force at work here,'' said Bryant solemnly. ''It's keeping us all at bay. I'm beginning to think that we wouldn't be able to stop it even if we could get there. Perhaps we aren't meant to.'' He checked his watch, then looked out at the effervescent river. ''Carmody com-

pletes his international link in a little under one hour and
ten minutes. He's used the city itself to hold us back.''
He looked down at the rune tape which lay uselessly
between them. ''We've failed,'' he said sadly. ''Worse
still, we've failed London.''

48.

Beat the Devil

SLATTERY WAS TIRED of doing Carmody's dirty work
for him. It was bad enough that he had been sent out
to follow Harry Buckingham like a common errand boy,
but the capper was being told to stay in the car and allow
his assistant to enter the library alone. After the boy had
failed to return from his reconnaissance, Slattery had ra-
dioed the ODEL chief executive for help. Carmody had
not been pleased by what he saw as Slattery's incompe-
tent handling of the situation. As a penance he had instructed the lawyer to spend the night in the Mercedes,
watching for signs of life within the library. Now he found
himself awaiting further instructions, unable to leave even
though the quarry had driven off on the back of a police
motorcycle.

Carmody's voice suddenly broke through on the radio,
making him start. He picked up the handset.

''Daniel, I don't see what I'm supposed to be doing
here,'' he complained. ''You know Buckingham's gone.
Don't you want me to try and find him?''

''He's on his way here,'' replied Carmody. ''Surely
that's obvious.'' A loudspeaker broadcast echoed somewhere behind his voice. It sounded as if he was calling
from the new studio at the top of the ODEL building.
''He'll try to stop the broadcast. I'm not worried about
that, of course, I'm more concerned with clearing away

the loose ends this evening. The girl and the old man, we'll wait until they've separated to remove them, that's no problem. But you'll have to shut the librarian up. She's still in the building?''

''If she'd come out I'd have seen her.''

''Good. I need everyone else here. Can I leave you to handle it?''

''Daniel, you know I don't do this kind of 'hands-on' work anymore.''

''I know, but we all have to make sacrifices if we want tonight to run smoothly. Obviously, you'll be well recompensed for your trouble. You'd better have a good check around for incriminating evidence after you've finished. Then come back to ODEL as quickly as you can.''

Slattery signed off with a sigh and clipped the radio mike back in its holster. He reached behind the seat and fished out his favorite pair of leather driving gloves. The crimson *craquelure* surrounding the pupils of his sore eyes seemed to glow in the shadows as he turned his attention toward the library. God, he thought, the things I do for the company.

Dorothy walked back through the darkened aisles of the library's main hall and checked the bookcase which had been wedged in front of the broken window. A large puddle of rainwater was gathering at its base, building its surface tension on the waxed parquet blocks, then bursting forward in fresh rivulets which flooded away between the stacks. Keeping evil at bay is impossible, she thought. You might just as well try to keep out the rain. It's a natural force that ebbs and builds, and we can only hope to dam it, or coax it aside.

Through the gap between the window and the bookcase she watched as Carmody's lawyer left the Mercedes and started walking toward the rear of the building. Panic began to rise in her breast as she searched for something with which to protect herself. There was nothing here. A blunt knife, perhaps, in the kitchen drawer of the staff room. The most dangerous objects in the entire building were the books in the basement . . .

She ran for the steps, reaching them just as Slattery

threw his weight against the bookcase. When the wood in the window refused to give, he began to hammer on it. She knew that it would not hold long beneath his blows. Reaching the bottom of the steps she kicked aside piles of rotting volumes and pulled the basement door from its place against the wall. She had not used the door for a number of years because sealing the cellar meant shutting the books in with the damp, fetid air, encouraging decay. Now, as she scraped it wide and shoved it into place, a gray nest of spiders broke at her feet, covering her shoes with a brown web of interlocking legs. She stepped back with a grimace, sliding on spiders, and pulled the bolt into position across the door. The screws were loose in the wet stone wall. She hoped they would last long enough to serve her purpose.

There were four particular books she would need. Moving to the dampest shelf in the farthest corner of the basement, she located two of the volumes and tore them from the mildewy morass which held them in place against the wood.

Above her head she heard a smash of glass, followed by a thud. The intruder paced back and forth, searching the aisles. She wondered how long it would be before he thought to look down here. The third and fourth books were kept at the opposite end of the basement. It was important to keep these particular rune volumes separate. Dorothy had long been aware of their lethal properties. Men had died to complete the volumes, which were quite harmless until placed in a square, whereupon the incomplete pictures drawn within them were united to form one single seamless incantation to the Devil's forces, a Möbius strip of evil that would protect the invoker and damn all attackers. Until now, she had never had cause to put the myth to the test. She had witnessed the secret properties of other tomes held within the basement. Her mother had raised her as a true believer. Why should the apparition not appear for her? There was danger, of course. Once summoned, the being could not then be sent away empty-handed.

She carefully lit a pair of candles and stood them in pools of melted red wax on the stone floor. On aching knees she opened each book at its appropriate page, then arranged them in the required formation. One volume was badly damaged. Mold had eaten the glutinous bindings, discoloring the pages. She propped it as best she could against the others.

The footsteps above her turned, then stopped. He had noticed the door to the basement. The mildewed temple of books which stood before her seemed to be having no effect. Something else was needed to attract the powers of darkness. Climbing to her feet, she took a paper knife from the work table and jabbed the tip into her arm, allowing the blood to drip freely onto the pile.

Behind her, the door handle rattled. He could smell the burning candles. Dorothy knelt before the book temple and began to softly recite. The flames wavered on either side, yellow pears of flame bobbing and flickering with the cadence of her voice. She moved her arm from one volume to the next, allowing droplets of blood to fall and soak the absorbent pages.

With a sudden bang the door bowed inward, causing the bolt screws to burst from the wall in a shower of rotting plaster. Slattery shoved the door open, saw Dorothy kneeling between the candles a few feet from him, and stopped. Before he could speak, Dorothy realized that something was beginning to form in the chilled, heavy air of the basement.

The figure which she could now see crouched before her seemed to have stepped from within the bookcases themselves. It was shorter and of slighter build than a normal man, but far more disturbing than anything human. Three sharply pointed antlers thrust from the tip of its skull above the hairline. Beneath the nose, a catlike cleft led to a tongue which seemed too large for its mouth. On its chest and knees, and at its groin, were the pale features of the dead, small corpse faces which creased and puckered with each movement of its body. Dorothy had once seen something like it in a fifteenth-century manuscript held in the Bibliothèque Nationale in Paris. It was a creature which appeared in the illustrations scattered throughout the four volumes grouped below it, a typical medieval conception of a devil. It stood watching the old woman who knelt before the books mumbling to herself, then turned its attention to the man at the door.

Dorothy turned her head away as the creature quickly scuttled around the edges of the room, nails scraping on stone, to pinch the surprised Slattery by the throat. Lifting him from the ground with one hand, it lowered the soft underside of his chin onto its antlers, piercing his flesh. As Slattery screamed and his limbs began to thrash about, it continued to push its victim's head down toward its own skull, until the one was firmly impaled upon the other. Then, with a guttural wheeze emanating from its thin throat, it approached the old woman.

She looked up as the creature's hands reached above its head and twisted the intruder's skull back and forth, wrenching it from its grisly skewer. It threw the body aside with a single careless gesture, and thus satiated, stepped back into the melanic confines of the bookcase just as Dorothy began to cry.

49.

Empire

Evening Standard   Monday 4th May

GRIDLOCKED LONDON!

City seizes up as traffic system fails

The experts said it could never happen, but this afternoon the capital came to a standstill as its main thoroughfares became blocked solid with traffic—and all because a so-called ''infallible'' computerized traffic system ceased to function. The system, originally purchased by the Ministry of Transport from French manufacturers, succumbed to a virus similar to the one which recently reinfected America's Internet system.

TODDLERS DIE IN BLAZE AS 999 CALLS FAIL

Ambulances answering emergency calls found themselves trapped in streets filled with stalled vehicles. In Tufnell Park two small children died in a blazing flat when fire engines were unable to pass through the congested streets. As radiators boiled and tempers flared, traffic wardens vainly attempted to redirect the flow of cars and trucks.

FREAK CIRCUMSTANCES PARTLY TO BLAME

In addition to the malfunctioning traffic computer system, police blamed the freak statistical circumstances which brought such a large proportion of the populace onto the city's streets at the same time. Driving rain hampered the efforts of police, who appealed to drivers not to leave their vehicles. The Automobile Association registered a record number of call-outs throughout the day.

Congestion on the London Underground forced many stations to close their platforms, and just to prove that it was "business as usual" in some quarters, staff walkouts brought the Northern Line to a standstill.

Tonight the traffic was slowly starting to move once more, but it will be several days before the capital's transport system will be fully cleared of the deadly new bug, which has yet to be traced to its source of origin.

The Minister of Transport is cutting short his holiday in the Seychelles to conduct an inquiry into the breakdown of the system.

Tragedy of blaze toddlers. See page 2.
MP calls for British computer-system subsidies. See page 3.

Harry Buckingham alighted from the pillion of the motorbike and looked up at the vast steel building rising before him. The mirrored towers of the ODEL Corporation, as cool and uncompromising as the man who inspired their construction, were lost far above in rolling dark clouds. He drew a deep breath. Carmody was due to green-light the transmission of his premiere broadcast in less than thirty minutes. He checked the reassuring weight of the duplicate videocassette beneath his macintosh, and took the steps to the entrance two at a time.

Harry had hated the thought of leaving Dorothy alone, but when the motorcycle cop had arrived at the library with an offer of help, an idea had presented itself.

His main worry was that Grace and Bryant would fail

to be admitted to ODEL. Carmody was far more likely to permit his entrance than theirs. On his initial search through the library he had noticed another dustcover-clad video recorder, property of the library's Family Bible Group. It had been a simple matter to wire the machines together and run off a copy of the tape. On the journey across the river he had prayed that he would reach his destination without suffering another relapse. Now, as he approached the uniformed security guards patrolling the foyer, this fear was quickly replaced by the problem of gaining entrance to the building.

On the far side of a circular marble hall an extravagantly decorated commissionaire sat with his eyes glued to a small television, presumably waiting for his company's first broadcast to appear. On the counter beside him, stacks of glossy brochures proclaimed a great future with Hemisphere Television. Sensing the presence of the figure before him, the guard tore his attention from the screen and gave Harry the once-over.

"Yes?" There was insolence in that single word. Harry was still in the same clothes he'd been wearing when he had fled the Carmody estate. Luckily, he had thought to cover them with the policeman's borrowed macintosh.

"I have an appointment with Daniel Carmody."

The security officer gave him a look of frank incredulity. "I don't think so," he said slowly. "Mr. Carmody is attending to important business right now. He can't be interrupted."

Harry had prepared himself for this. Summoning up memories of his former incarnation as an arrogant adman, he rested his knuckles on the desk and leaned forward, towering over the security officer. "Your job description doesn't involve making decisions," he said, his crisp intonation crackling with menace. "Pick up the phone and tell Daniel Carmody that Harry Buckingham is here to see him."

The guard appeared momentarily disconcerted, then regained his former composure. "Mr. Carmody is doing a television broadcast," he said finally. "He left strict instructions not to be disturbed."

Harry glanced up at the clock behind the commission-aire's desk. Twenty minutes to go. He returned his attention to the guard. Slowly baring his teeth, he picked up a pencil and drew a curve on the blotting pad which lay between them. The guard watched, puzzled.

"This," announced Harry, "is the trajectory of your career." He tapped the top of the curve. "You are currently here." Drawing a line down to the bottom of the sheet he pressed so hard that he shattered the pencil and tore the blotter in half. "This," he shouted, hurling the pieces into the alarmed officer's wastebin, "is where your job will be if you don't pick up that phone in the next two seconds."

It occurred to the commissionaire that the man standing before him was crazy enough to be someone important. His arrogant attitude seemed a familiar trait of the guard's superiors. Reluctantly, he began to dial.

On the top floor of the ODEL building the studio was hectic, but under control. Tonight's transmission consisted of a "turning on" ceremony attended by the press—there was nothing to actually turn on, so a popular television soap queen was preparing to pull a beribboned dummy switch—and the loading of a prerecorded half-hour cassette which would play as an extended commercial for the company's upcoming product. Following this, a further tape would run. The duration of the second video was a mere three minutes, but its effect would be long felt. As he relit his cigar, the tycoon afforded himself a smile of self-congratulation. The new station would close down following tonight's broadcast until it was geared for full transmission in a month's time. For the rest of the evening, Daniel Carmody and his wife would be available for television and press interviews over cocktails and canapes.

Carmody accepted the call from his secretary with an even bigger smile. Tonight he could afford to be generous. "Actually, I've been expecting Mr. Buckingham," he said. "Please show him up." He sent his assistants and technicians from the room, and sat back to wait.

* * *

As the elevator doors closed silently behind him, Harry found himself standing in a black marble hallway lined with video monitors. At the end of the corridor was a circular reception area similar to the foyer thirty floors beneath it. A single huge room led from the circle, its broad doors ajar. Harry pushed against one side and entered.

As usual, Carmody had his long legs tucked behind a desk. This one was carved from a single slab of green-veined marble, and gave the financier the appearance of a priest attending a sacrificial ceremony.

"Harry," he cried, half rising from his seat, "this is an unexpected pleasure." He gave a dark chuckle. "Somehow I didn't think you'd be able to stay away from our little opening ceremony."

Harry walked forward and held out his hand. He was conspicuously scruffy in the immaculate surroundings. Carmody declined the offer. "I'd prefer it if you would stay in the middle of the room, where I can keep an eye on you." A tight smile returned to his face. "I've always wanted to say this—I'm afraid I can't let you leave this building alive. It's a marvelous cliché, but how often does one get the chance to say such a thing nowadays? The language of the modern businessman is couched in euphemism." He carefully blew cigar ash across the marble into the palm of his hand, then emptied it into a wastebin. Harry's fingers curled around the cassette held within his raincoat.

"To be honest though, you're really not much of a danger to us," said Carmody. "There's no one to believe your story—but that's another cliché, isn't it?" He rose from his seat and came around from behind the desk. "At this point in the proceedings we seem to be veering into the world of pulp fiction. But you know, Harry, even now you still interest me." He tilted his head and jetted cigar smoke. "Why are you so determined to go against the grain of things? Why are you fighting so hard against a new idea? Surely it's better to wait and see what happens? I think that in the long run you'd have been favorably surprised by our plans. Most of our prospective partners are—and we're talking about reasonable, moral men and women.''

"A lot of people thought the Nazi movement was a good idea.''

"That's a typical knee-jerk attitude, Harry, and you know it. Of course Nazism was a bad idea, anyone who can tell right from wrong can see that. Why is it that when someone with foresight comes up with a new view of society he's instantly compared to Hitler? What I want is just a hair's breadth from what you want. I'm merely less sentimental than you.'' He checked his watch. "Now if you'll excuse me, I must go and watch this ghastly woman flick the cardboard switch that—if she did but know it—heralds the dawning of a new era in confrontational business techniques.'' He gave an impish grin and turned to leave.

"Wait,'' called Harry. "Don't you want to see what I have for you?''

"Not really. If you'd have been carrying a weapon it would have been picked up by the security sensors in the lobby.''

A harassed-looking secretary click-clacked across the floor and spoke quietly with Carmody. The smile fell from his face as she left the room.

"It looks like you have a few more minutes of my company,'' he said with half-hearted geniality.

"Why?'' asked Harry. "Aren't you going to make the broadcast?''

"We have a short delay on our hands. Just a small technical problem. Adverse weather conditions. Don't worry, they'll be ready for me in a few minutes.''

Well, Harry decided, it's now or never. As he removed the videocassette from his pocket and held it out, he could sense a side of Carmody that admired his tenacity. The magnate was loath to lose a potentially resourceful CEO. Part of Daniel still wanted to trust him.

"Play this. I think what it has to say will surprise even you.'' He dropped the tape onto the desk, allowing the challenge to lie between them.

Carmody studied his face, then slapped the intercom.

"Call me as soon as you're ready to transmit. I'll be upstairs until then."

Harry followed behind the director as he walked to the elevator bank and waited for the doors to part. Once inside, Carmody produced a small, steel key and plugged it into a socket at the top of the button panel. The elevator rose a single floor and opened on to a private suite, immaculately decorated in the cold corporate colors of the building—black, green, and silver. One entire wall consisted of angled glass overlooking the rainswept city. The financier removed the tape from its sleeve and slotted it into a polished black wall of video equipment.

Harry could not believe his luck. Daniel was actually going to run it! He would avert his eyes as the images appeared . . .

Carmody picked up one of several remote control units and thumbed the PLAY button. Harry caught a glimpse of Grace and Dorothy posing in front of the library stacks before he looked away. A minute passed as the tape ran on from one grainy tableau to the next.

Harry continued to study the view from the glass wall until he heard an amused snigger. He looked around at a chastened Carmody.

"I'm sorry, Harry." The director shamefacedly rubbed the side of his nose, trying not to laugh. "But is this it? Is this all you've come armed with? I was expecting you to try and palm back the tape you stole from Instant Image, but I knew as soon as I saw the cassette it wasn't one of ours."

He watched for a moment more, then pressed the EJECT button. "Honestly, I really was hoping for something a little more ambitious." He shook his head as he rose to the bar and poured himself a drink. "We left you alone all day, and this is the best you could come up with. It's very sweet, of course. I think I'll keep it as a souvenir." He cracked ice from a silver bucket and dropped it into the drinks.

"I don't understand," said Harry.

"You're so naive. Runic tapes are our forté. I can't believe that you'd pick on our main strength and try to use it as an Achilles' heel. Bad strategy. Maybe it's just as well you're dropping out of the ad industry." He handed Harry a tall, frosted glass and sat down beside him, too close for comfort.

Harry looked suspiciously into his drink.

"It's a gin and tonic," said Carmody, amusement playing in one of his eyes. "The only way it will hurt you is if you drink a lot of them for many years."

Harry took a sip. "Why doesn't my tape work?" he asked, trying to show detached professional interest.

"Harry . . ." Carmody shook his head in mock disappointment. "It's not something you just throw together. It's nowhere near as simple as that. Each one of our tapes is a densely encoded microform peppered with subliminal symbols. Do you have any idea of the production charge on each cassette? Each one costs approximately one and a half million pounds to manufacture! Why else do you think we went to such lengths to get our shipment back? We'll reduce the cost when we begin assembly-line production, naturally, but these were prototypes. Take a look at this."

He picked up another of the remote-control units and punched out a six-digit code number. As he finished doing so, the black video wall opposite them slowly rolled back to reveal banks of glittering amber microcircuitry that rose into the ceiling. Within these geometric whorls a million efflorescent pulses rose and fell between their connections in chemical duplication of the neural process.

"This is what I brought to ODEL," said Carmody, pride coloring his voice. "This is what they paid through the nose for."

Harry started in his seat, amazed at the beauty and complexity of the system.

"Don't worry," said Carmody, "it's not the main operations center. Nothing will happen if you throw a spanner into it; this isn't a Bond film. The runic creation process has simply become so sophisticated that it can no longer be housed on a single floor. It took ten years to develop, and just three months to manufacture. Pretty, isn't it?"

He looked at his watch, then at the rain dropping in

sheets across the sweeping wall of glass. "Anyway, you've failed your last test. I'm reluctant to do it, but I'll have to find another man for the job. Never mind, I'm sure we can still find somewhere for you to be useful within the ODEL group, albeit in a less responsible capacity. Freshen the drinks, would you?"

Harry accepted Carmody's glass and rose to his feet. He was being dismissed, reduced to the status of a servant. He knew now that there would have to be violence. The ice pick was still in the bucket where Carmody had left it. As he dropped a chunk of ice into his drink, he slid the sleeve of his jacket over the freezing spike and carefully removed it.

Beyond the penthouse thunder broke, shaking the windows with a reverberative boom. As he walked back to the sofa he could feel his heart pacing up, thumping beneath his shirt. It would have to be as he handed the drink across. As if reading his mind Carmody reached forward, his hand outstretched to accept the glass, a thin smile curving his lips.

Harry let the wet ice pick drop from his sleeve and slide forward until the point rested in his palm. Releasing the glass from his other hand he suddenly lunged at Carmody, aiming for his throat. It took several seconds after the muffled thud which followed for Harry to realize that he had been shot. A searing heat flooded through the right shoulder of his jacket as his shirt began to blossom with crimson petals.

"Good, Harry, you went for the ice pick. I'm impressed. You see, it doesn't take much to bring your natural instincts to the fore. Regrettably though, the job offer is now closed. I don't think I'd ever be able to completely trust you." Carmody slipped the revolver back into his jacket. Then he removed the ice pick from where it had lodged in the wall of the sofa and sent it skittering across the green marble floor.

Although the pain in his shoulder had begun to ebb slightly, Harry felt his knees folding beneath him. As he fell, he wondered if he was going into shock.

"Don't worry," said a distant voice. "You won't be left with too much of a scar. I aimed wide of your heart.

It's just damaged bones and nerves.'' Hands reached down and tore open his shirt, checking the entry wound. The sudden burst of pain brought Harry back to full consciousness. Somewhere behind them an intercom buzzed. Carmody answered the call as Harry attempted to pull himself up into a sitting position.

''Apparently they're ready to start the transmission,'' Carmody said. ''I'll be right down.'' He started to lower the receiver, then raised it again. ''What? Tell her that playing a bitch on-screen doesn't entitle her to live out the role. No, on second thoughts, have Celia calm her down.'' He turned back to Harry. ''The soap-opera woman is giving them merry hell about starting late. Are you going to come and join us?'' He checked Harry's bloody shirt and drained, pale face. ''No, I have a better idea.'' He punched out another number and addressed his producer. ''I'll watch the broadcast from up here, Jim. There's nothing for me to do in the studio; I only get in the way. Well, of course I have faith in you. Patch it through to the main monitor, the ED17. No, I know how to do it myself. But be there when I call you. That's right.''

Returning to Harry's side, he slipped his arms beneath the bloodied jacket and hauled him onto a long seat facing the video screen. ''You'll find this interesting,'' he said, flicking to the appropriate channel on the unit. ''Our follow-up tape is the most advanced thing we've developed so far. It's specifically tailored to the brain patterns of a handful of people. Apart from developing the technology, the hardest part of the operation was obtaining medical data on ODEL's political opponents.''

The sparkling static which filled the screen was quickly replaced with views of the small studio and editing suite on the floor below. ''It can't influence you or me, of course. But you can probably figure out the effect it will have on seven corporate executives watching on the other side of the Atlantic.''

The soap queen appeared in frame, a makeup girl darting on to give her handiwork a last minute touch-up.

''She's looking old,'' Carmody commented. ''We

should have gotten someone younger. How are you feeling, Harry?''

''Bad. Losing blood.''

''You know, you're right; that's exactly what's happening. The bullets are tipped with an anticoagulating enzyme. It's only a small wound but you'll need to have it stitched fast if you want to live. The more you move around, the more heavily you'll bleed.

Cheering rose from the monitor's speakers as the actress cut the ribbon and pulled her cardboard switch. ODEL's Hemisphere TV logo superimposed itself over the scene in black, green, and silver. The tycoon sat forward, entranced by the scene. Harry looked down, and what he saw made him slip from the seat where he had been propped. Dark blood had soaked his shirt through, and was now pooling on the seat around his thighs. The wound wasn't healing. As he looked back at the screen he could feel his ability to concentrate ebbing. The wall of iridescent circuitry behind the screen glittered as the particles within its metal veins tacked through their electronic maze, fulfilling commands that changed with every passing millisecond.

Harry knew that he was dying. It was no longer a question of whether he would live, but how long he had left to live. He had behaved with total predictability, walking back into the financier's chill embrace, only to screw up his final interview for the position of liaison officer to the new world. The game was over. He had failed to influence anyone or anything. Grace and Bryant were stranded somewhere on the other side of the city. Dorothy was alone and unarmed in her dark library. Nothing was where it should be. He slowly slid to the floor in his own blood as the crowd cheered on through the speakers.

Suddenly the picture on the monitor fuzzed and faded, to be replaced by a new image. For a moment Carmody appeared confused, and checked the remote unit. As Harry raised his head to watch the screen he felt the now-familiar warning tingle in his forehead. It was an incoming runic signal, very hostile. He snapped his head away to the side, praying that he had ceased to watch before the subliminal message reactivated his recent subjection to the tapes. Carmody was still studying the monitor, his mouth slowly widening in alarm.

Just then, the elevator doors opened at the far end of the lounge and Celia Carmody emerged.

"Am I in time for the broadcast?" she asked, walking over to the couch. She was immaculately coiffed and dressed for her interview session, doll-like in her movements. She looked psychotic. Her delicate features had been so accentuated with makeup that she appeared to have been carved from flesh-toned plastic. She hovered nervously at Harry's side, ignoring his plight, her eyes fixed on her husband's face. The rushing sound of static filled the room. Beneath this sound was something else, something which resembled human speech, the chattering of imps. Something strange was happening. Carmody continued to stare at the screen as it threw bomb blasts of solarized color against the walls. He appeared to be in the grip of a powerful narcosis.

Harry desperately wanted to stand, to run away from the funnel of sound and light which was filtering in electronic matrices from the monitor, but found himself denied the power to move. Celia's lips touched his ear. "Don't look at the screen," she warned. "We have to leave. He can't hurt me now. He'll never hurt me again." As she reached down to take his hand, she saw the extent of his blood loss.

"He has a gun," said Harry stupidly, slurring his words. Carmody released a sudden shout of fear. He had turned in his seat, and now rose to face the vast wall of circuitry before him. Obviously he could see something within it, some terrible vision that no one else in the world could share . . . but as a wave of nausea began to crawl over him, Harry realized that he could see it too.

He squeezed his eyes tight and raised his palms to his pounding temples. The brief glimpse he had caught of the transmission had been enough to trigger his already susceptible subconscious. Hearing the squeak and rattle of steel on marble, he prepared to open his eyes and meet the demons of his mind once more.

But this time there was no unimaginable pagan deity with which to contend. Instead, the sparkling circuits which conducted ODEL's runic pulses appeared to have come alive, the printed boards and transformers shifting toward the tycoon as if they were part of a living object. The razor-fine silver veins of circuitry whipped at him with mercurial speed, slashing the exposed surfaces of his flesh, the cheeks of his face, the palms of his raised hands. Tearing at his jacket, Carmody pulled his revolver free and aimed wildly.

"There's nothing there," said Celia. "What can he see?"

The first shot exploded within the maze of turbulent wiring, releasing showers of sparks which cascaded and bounced on the polished stone floor. The next bullet ricocheted from a panel to punch a hole in the glass on the other side of the room, suddenly altering the tension of the angled wall. With the pinging of lake ice, it split in vitreous arcs and fell down in an explosion of rain and glass. Beyond, somber storm clouds coursed through an angry sky.

Harry turned his attention back to Daniel Carmody. The sparkling circuitry had now engulfed him, the wires curling back like attacking snakes to bury their connectors deep in the flesh of his face and arms. It seemed as if he was becoming part of the system itself, the ferrous lifelines of the computer driving themselves into his veins until it was impossible to see where the man ended and the machine began.

Harry felt a hand on his sleeve. Realizing that he was suffering the same hallucination, Celia was trying to pull him toward the elevator doors. Behind them the runic images vanished from the monitor, transmission suddenly ceasing as plugs were pulled in the editing suite below.

"Harry, we've got to get downstairs before they find the correct broadcast tape and run it." Harry pushed himself away from the floor and together they stumbled toward the steel doors. As Celia slapped the elevator button, Harry looked back. In an aureole of thrashing silver wires Carmody had twisted his pierced, tumorous body around to fire at them, the bullet smashing a hole in the elevator door inches from Harry's face. Celia screamed and hammered at the elevator button, to no avail. Harry dug his fingers into the rubber seals at the center of the doors and tried to prize them apart, but as he did so he felt the wound in his shoulder open afresh. A spurt of hot blood cascaded down his chest and he fell back, dizzied.

He looked up in time to see Carmody running toward them, his arms flailing the air as the circuits connecting him were wrenched from his skin. Before Harry could realize what was happening, Carmody had seized his wife's hand and was dragging her back with him as the wiring tightened around its prey once more.

Celia cried out in bewilderment as he threw her to the rainsoaked floor between himself and the shattered glass wall. She tried to raise herself up, but he kicked out with his remaining free limb and sent her sprawling among the glinting shards.

The elevator doors opened at Harry's back. Celia had risen to her feet once more and now cried out in horror as she saw her husband wedging his lacerated body into the circuit panels of the computer, still in the grip of his runic psychosis. She was about to run toward Harry when Carmody threw out his hand and grabbed her wrist. In the next instant he seized her around the waist and hurled her with all his might at the shattered glass wall.

Harry ran at Celia, throwing his body the last few feet to snatch at her free arm. For a moment she seemed suspended by the gale itself as she balanced on the narrow sill. Blood and water mixed together on the marble floor as Harry's feet began sliding under him. A second later he fell. Celia's arm slithered from his grasp, and the eleutherian force catapulted her into the violent sky. She hung in the night air momentarily, a rag doll borne on the tide of the storm wind, then her body was lost from sight as the clouds closed over her.

Harry climbed to his feet, blood flooding hotly across his chest. Carmody was now within the machinery itself, the razor points of the connectors shoved deep into his eyes, his gums, his ears, his skull. He thrashed as the silver circuits tightened over his throat, sawing open the skin in a single broad incision. As blood sprayed from the gash, he called out to Harry in a voice which bubbled through viscous liquid.

"This isn't the end!" he cried as the cables surrounding him turned molten with electric current. "Wait and see! Better the Devil you know . . . than the one you don't!"

High above the rainswept city, in the penthouse apartment of ODEL's corporate headquarters, blood spattered the walls as the overloaded circuits of Daniel Carmody's runic computer system grew white hot, and the sudden force expanding within it separated the industrialist's organs in an extravagant, gory display of electrical combustion.

Daniel Carmody had become one with his creation.

50.

Remembrance

W HEN HARRY REGAINED consciousness, he found himself lying on a couch in the tiny hospitality suite of the ODEL studio. He raised his hand to his chest and gingerly touched his wound. Someone had washed and stitched it, sealing the skin with a thick plastic strip. He tried to sit up but his head throbbed so much that he was forced to lie back against the pillow. From the corner of his eye he could make out the editing-suite monitors at the end of the hall. None of them appeared to be operational.

"Oh good, you're awake." Arthur Bryant's face filled his vision. The old man poked him in the arm, not very gently. "You're probably a bit tender."

When Harry found his voice, his throat was dry and hoarse. "Where's Grace?"

"Downstairs, waiting for you. We didn't want too many people up here until we'd made sure that everything was shut down. You'll be relieved to know that the broadcast wasn't completed."

"Why—what happened? Who stopped it?"

"John May," said Bryant, with a touch of pride in his voice. "You fell out of the elevator covered in blood and collapsed into the studio, much to the surprise of some horrible loudmouthed television woman who kept saying she was a star. May got here just as Carmody's wife hit the sidewalk."

"Daniel climbed inside the computer."

"I don't know about that, but there was a fire on the floor above which seriously damaged the transmission. The technicians couldn't get hold of their boss, and were still trying to sort out the mess when May arrived and took control. The building is under police guard now, and will remain so until everything can be sorted out. What happened upstairs? Threw your weight about, did you?"

"No." Harry eased himself painfully into a sitting position. "Celia Carmody switched tapes on her husband. But I don't understand why he owned a tape that could cause him personal harm. He would never have let his technicians develop such a thing. And Celia couldn't have constructed one by herself."

"If you wish to discuss technical matters you'll have to speak to my partner," said Bryant with a sigh. "Unfortunately, that won't be easy."

"Why not?"

"Because the exertion has put him back in the hospital. It's just as well he took it upon himself to come here. All you managed to do was smash the place up, get yourself shot, and let our key defendant kill himself."

Harry decided not to argue with the elderly detective. He knew that Celia Carmody had acted because of what had passed between them at her house the previous weekend. Bryant vanished for a few minutes and returned with a steaming mug of tea.

"What's going to happen now?" asked Harry, accepting the mug.

"Well, I dare say you'll be given a ride downstairs on a comfortable stretcher while I, an elderly frail person, will be forced to travel in the elevator you so generously redecorated with your blood."

Harry watched as the elderly detective headed off along the corridor, irritably thumping his stick against the walls and grumbling under his breath.

The observatory garden at Greenwich Park is an oddly overlooked place. Its steeply banked lawns give way to a rise of rockeries entwined with overgrown paths. Although small, it is designed in such a way that while the trees are in leaf it is overlooked only by the green copper ball of the observatory itself. Between the angled flower beds at the rear of the garden is a shelter with a wooden bench. From her earliest years when she had come here with her mother, this had been Dorothy's favorite place to sit. Today, she sat back and breathed the cool, loamy air as the shadows lengthened before the setting sun, and squirrels darted through the lavender bushes.

The aftermath of Slattery's death in the library basement would have been a nightmare to endure if it had not been for the kindness of Arthur and his partner. When Dorothy had finally managed to summon the aid of a passing constable, the frightened boy had carefully reported the condition of the deceased. Slattery's body had been found pierced through the neck with the spiked head of an iron candelabra. He had apparently slipped and skewered himself while trying to force open the door to the book repository. Dorothy spoke to no one about the events of that day. Not even to Arthur. She checked her watch once more. Looking down at the black crenellated railings of the park, she wondered what on earth could have happened to her guests.

"There you are! We've been searching everywhere for you." Bryant pushed the rhododendron bush apart and climbed out, brushing the petals from his lapels. "I couldn't find the main gate so we climbed over the railings. Took me back to my youth. John, she's up here! Couldn't you have found an easier place to meet?''

May appeared on the pathway beside them. ''When Arthur told me you were taking us to dinner over your end of town, I didn't realize we'd be going on a picnic,'' he said. ''Turned out nice though, hasn't it?''

''Did you drive?'' asked Dorothy.

''Yes, in Arthur's car, I'm sorry to say. We're parked by the statue of General Wolfe.''

As the trio climbed through the wet grass toward the observatory, the sinking sun suffused the few clouds hanging in the sky with a tint of pale rose.

''I love London when it's like this,'' said Dorothy. ''The air is so clear after it rains.'' She turned to look back at the colonnaded walkways of the Maritime Museum, the quadrangles of the Royal Naval College, and the misted river beyond. ''This scene will soon be gone. Look at all the cranes. They're building more sky-scrapers—banks, as if we need more of those—on the north side of the Thames. It's an ancient view, unspoiled for countless generations. Some of us raised objections. The bank people were terribly nice, and very patronizing. They obviously thought us mad. Scenery? you could see them thinking, that's all very well, but it's no *use* to anyone.''

''What will you do about the library?'' asked Bryant.

''What *can* I do? I'll stay on, fighting off the council and the developers. The collection must remain protected. It can't be allowed to fall into the wrong hands.''

They reached the statue which stood at the top of the incline. ''What's happened to ODEL?'' Dorothy asked, pausing to regain her breath.

May gave a cynical smile. ''Haven't you heard?'' he said. ''Their broadcasting arm has been temporarily suspended while we investigate their financial records. There's nothing else for us to hold them on except a handful of fiscal technicalities. It seems that the moment the police moved into the ODEL building all of the incriminating disks, tapes, and other infected products disappeared. Everything was wiped clean. Nobody seems to know where it all went.''

"You must have your suspicions."

"John and I have more than suspicions," said Bryant. "Thanks to you we did have a videocassette."

"You're using the past tense . . ."

"That's because I removed it from one of the station's evidence lockers to find that someone had magnetically erased the whole thing. And that's only part of the story. Hargreave has been told that the case is now beyond the jurisdiction of his staff, pending an official internal enquiry."

"Sounds to me like one of Frank's conspiracies."

"Before the investigation was closed down I did some checking on ODEL's share ownership. Directly and indirectly, the largest single shareholder is Her Majesty's Government. Senior ministers are tied to ODEL in a variety of ways, mainly through a parcel of defense contracts, the details of which presumably remain under lock and key in some gloomy Whitehall office."

"We should have realized that the whole business was politically sanctioned from the start," said May, "but we behaved like detectives. We couldn't see beyond the dead bodies. Then, when Carmody killed himself . . ."

". . . it became obvious," said Bryant, opening the car door and ushering Dorothy in. "In his own perverse way, Daniel Carmody was a man of vision. Even so, he would never have allowed the production of a tape that could cause his own death. Someone had to have control over him. I assume the Ministry of Defense arranged for the tape to be manufactured, probably by Carmody's own technicians. It was a fail-safe, in case their prodigy ever decided to bite the hand that fed him."

"And his wife found out about it."

"Perhaps she was even told of its existence. One thing we'll never know is what finally persuaded her to use it. Do you think ODEL will go back into business?"

"They can try." Bryant gave a laugh as he crunched the car into gear.

"What's so funny?" asked Dorothy.

"We've encouraged a friend of ours to take up a new hobby," said May. Even as he spoke, Rufus was working with Kirkpatrick on the other side of town, surreptitiously using the station computer's downtime to develop a runic virus string that would infect the entire ODEL network when it came back on-line. Perhaps because they were both intellectually gifted outcasts, they thoroughly enjoyed working with one another.

"They will be back, of course," said Bryant, departing from the park by riding one side of the car over a flower bed, "but next time we'll be ready for them."

"I thought you were retiring," said May. "I thought modern crime was too dirty for you. You said you were going to see out your twilight years in your allotment, digging up carrots."

"How dare you, I haven't got an allotment," said Bryant indignantly. "Carrots, indeed. If you care to cast your enfeebled mind back, you'll remember that Instant Image didn't take the whole of Coltis's stolen tape shipment. There are still about a hundred rogue videocassettes floating about out there. Someone has to remain vigilant. Besides, you've been hospitalized twice. The next time there's a decent drama you could peg out. It's no good me leaving you on your own."

May gave Dorothy a look. "So you'll stay on."

Bryant gave a careless sniff and studied the road ahead. "I suppose I'll have to." The little car circled the Blackheath roundabout twice before locating the correct exit and turning off toward the city.

"We'd better try to reach a restaurant before the sun's gone," said Bryant. "I don't seem to have any headlights."

The Independent   15th June

ODEL CHAIRMAN MYSTERIOUSLY DIES

A body discovered by children playing in a South London sewage outlet two days ago has been identified as that of Samuel Harwood, 71, the recently indicted chairman of ODEL Incorporated, the communications multinational which is currently the subject of an ongoing police investigation. Forensic experts are puzzled by the circumstances of Harwood's death, which suggest that he had somehow blundered into the outlet at night, and was drowned by a sudden deluge of rain.

In the weeks prior to his disappearance, Sam Harwood had become a vociferous critic of the corporation he had helped to create, and had launched a number of increasingly bitter public attacks on his fellow directors. Colleagues had ventured to suggest that the former chairman was suffering from a form of mental aphasia.

Earlier this year, the reigning managing director of the ODEL group died along with his wife in a blaze that destroyed the top floor of the company's headquarters. Full story, page 6.

Why Danger Drains Must Be Closed—MP. See page 8.

"That's him," said Harry, pointing to the chairman's photograph in the newspaper. "That's the man I saw being torn to pieces in my hallucination."

"How strange. I wonder if Carmody knew he'd only just started to tap the real power of the runes." Grace leaned on the railing at the stern of the river bus, watching it pull away from Westminster Pier. The sky had cleared now, leaving the evening cool and clear. The severe cut of her hair had been trimmed into a softer style, although she still insisted on wearing her raincoat and boots. Harry handed her a steaming polystyrene cup.

"Why do you suppose the British drink so much tea?" she asked, swirling the plastic spoon.

"It helps us to think."

"Are you going to miss your flat?"

Harry thought for a moment. "Only the view," he replied. He had put the apartment up for sale after returning home to find it ransacked for the third time. He assumed that the new regime at ODEL were keeping tabs on him, although he had no proof of their involvement.

"By the way," he said, "I've got another interview."

"Who with?"

"The Consumer Research Board. They're an industry watchdog. God knows I've got the experience for the job." As the river bus passed into the shadows beneath Blackfriars Bridge, Harry slipped his arm around Grace's waist. "I've been thinking about the Devil," he said.

"What about him?"

"I believe he really did come back to earth. And I

think he was stopped by a handful of people who were brought together by little more than a trick of fate.''

"I thought you were cold and rational about such things.''

"I used to be. But work it out; you knew Frank Drake. He worked with Dorothy Huxley. She knew Bryant, and May knew that kid he's got designing the antirune virus. If any link in the chain had been missing, ODEL couldn't have been stopped.''

"You missed out the most important link. If you hadn't shown Carmody's wife some kindness, just by talking to her, she'd never have been brave enough to use his own system against him.''

Harry remembered his final vision of Daniel Carmody, twisted within the machine, blood and circuitry. He shuddered.

"Are you ready?''

"Ready.''

Grace opened her satchel and withdrew two red roses. As the boat cleared the shadow of the bridge she threw the first one into the sluggish gray river. The wind batted her hair into her eyes. "For Frank,'' she said, brushing her hand across her face.

Harry held the rose Grace had given him for a moment, quietly thinking to himself. Then he threw it high and wide, so that for a moment it was silhouetted by the dying sun.

"For Willie Buckingham,'' he said, watching the rose turn on the surface of the water. Below, the propellers thumped and churned as the river bus continued its evening passage toward the sea.

"This is *weird* shit, man.'' Rufus sat back on his stool and studied the screen. He beckoned to Kirkpatrick. "Every time I enter the rune string, something blocks it an' sends the damn thing back.''

"How is that possible?'' Kirkpatrick tilted the anglepoise away from the computer terminal and massaged his tired eyes. "You said yourself that this part of the ODEL system was a dead end, that closing it down would be easy.''

"That's what I thought, but there's something in here. Watch, I'll do it ag'in. This is s'posed to clear the file out. Wipe it *dry*." His hands flew across the keyboard, his thumb flicking across to press ENTER.

IDENTIFY USER CURRENT EMPLOYEE ODEL INC. Y/N?

Rufus typed Y and pressed RETURN. The words erased themselves, then the screen slowly started to fill with attenuated figures, forming a fibrous diagrammatic network from corner to corner. Gradually the picture cleared, solarizing out until several sharply legible words were left.

THE DEVIL YOU DON'T KNOW

"What's that, some kind of a code?" asked Kirkpatrick.

"Beats me, man." Rufus scratched his neck, puzzled. "Looks like we got a program with an identity crisis." He reached forward and scrolled the page down. There in bright green letters was a single large word:

DANIEL

Something Harry had said about Carmody's death came back to him. Blood and circuitry.

"He's in the system," said Rufus.

About the Author

Christopher Fowler is a former advertising copywriter and drama writer for the BBC. In addition to *Roofworld*, he has written short horror fiction, which has been collected in *The Bureau of Lost Souls*.

Christopher Fowler lives in London.